SIMS

ALSO BY F. PAUL WILSON

*FORTHCOMING

SIMS

F. PAUL
WILSON

A TOM DOHERTY ASSOCIATES BOOK
NEW YORK

SIMS

Copyright © 2003 by F. Paul Wilson

This book is printed on acid-free paper.

A Forge Book
Published by Tom Doherty Associates, LLC
175 Fifth Avenue
New York, NY 10010

www.tor.com

Forge® is a registered trademark of Tom Doherty Associates, LLC.

Library of Congress Cataloging-in-Publication Data

Wilson, F. Paul (Francis Paul)
    Sims / F. Paul Wilson.—1st Forge ed.
        p. cm.
    "A Forge book"—T.p. verso.
    ISBN 0-765-30551-8
    1. Genetic engineering—Fiction. 2. Chimpanzees—Fiction. I. Title.

PS3573.I45695 S57 2003
813'.54—dc21

                                        2002035248

First Edition: April 2003

Printed in the United States of America

0 9 8 7 6 5 4 3 2 1

ACKNOWLEDGMENTS

I owe a debt of thanks to the following:

Daniel F. Murphy Jr., Esq., for his generous assistance and advice
regarding the labor relations issues and legal procedures so vital
to the plot in Parts One and Two; Coates Bateman, editor-at-large;
J. R. Peter Wilson, brother and defense attorney; Mitchell Galin
for early encouragement; David Auerbach, genetics maven and
fellow Jill Sobule fan; Barry Rosenbush for being a believer;
David Hartwell, Elizabeth Monteleone, Steven Spruill, and
Al Zuckerman for the usual editorial help.

AUTHOR'S NOTE

Sims takes place just around the corner, timewise, in your town, your country, your world. It may seem like science fiction, but it isn't. For right now, as you read these words, someone somewhere is altering a chimpanzee's genome to make it more human. *Right now*. So it won't be too long before we all come face-to-face with the same issues challenging the characters in *Sims* . . .

ONE

LA CAUSA

I

A good walk spoiled, Patrick Sullivan thought as he trudged toward the rough where his slicing golf ball had disappeared. Somebody had got that right.

Patrick didn't actually hate golf, but he suffered from a condition he'd come to call GADD—Golf Attention Deficit Disorder. Nine holes and he'd had it. Maybe that was because during his first nine holes he racked up more strokes than most golfers did in eighteen. But today he was playing with Ben Armstrong, CFO of the Jarman department store chain and a valued client, who, although even less skillful than Patrick on the links, seemed immune to GADD.

Maybe it was the clothes. Armstrong, a florid-faced fellow in his sixties, sporting a neat goatee the same steel-gray shade as his hair, had decked himself out in a blue-and-raspberry-striped shirt, raspberry pants, and white golf shoes. Patrick wasn't into sherbet shades; he wore a white shirt, navy slacks, and tan shoes.

Golf or not, he was having a good walk on a bright September day among the luxuriously verdant rolling hills of upper Westchester where the Beacon

Ridge club nestled its links. The air was redolent of fresh-mown grass and money.

Christ, he wanted into this place. Not so much for the golf, but because golf was such a great way to do business.

Like today. Armstrong, a club member, had asked Patrick out for a two-some. Wanted to get caught up on the upcoming negotiations with the sales-clerk union. Patrick's specialty was labor law, and though he worked both sides, lately he'd found himself billing more and more hours to the management end.

Beacon Ridge was packed with heavies like Armstrong. A goldmine of potential clients and billable hours. Patrick's firm loved billable hours—little else mattered at Payes & Hecht—and if he could tap into this mother lode . . .

A sudden screech from ahead and to his left drew his attention. His caddie was pointing at the ground. "Here, sir, here! I find! Here!"

"Good eye, Nabb," Patrick said as he walked over.

"Yessir," Nabb said, his head bobbing as he grinned broadly at the praise. "Good eye, good eye."

Typical of the Beacon Ridge caddies, Nabb was an average size sim, about five-three, maybe 130 pounds; he sported a little more facial hair than most sims. Armstrong's caddie, Deek, was a bit different—beefier, and seemed taller, although that might be due to better posture. They looked like homi-nids yanked from the Stone Age and wrestled into the Beacon Ridge caddie uniform of lime green shirt and white pants, but they moved with a certain grace despite their slightly bowed legs.

Beacon Ridge had introduced sim caddies a couple of years ago, the first golf club in the country to do so. Caused quite a stir at the time, but the club members seemed to enjoy the status of being pioneers in the transgenic revolution. Other clubs soon followed suit, but Beacon Ridge remained fa-mous for being the first. By now sims were practically part of the scenery around the links.

"Come on, movie star!" Armstrong called from the green. "You can do it!"

Movie star . . . on their first meeting he'd said Patrick reminded him of Axel Sommers, the latest digital heartthrob. Patrick figured Armstrong needed glasses. Sure, they both had blue eyes and slightly wavy blond hair, but Sommers looked just a little too pretty for comfort.

Patrick waved and turned to Nabb. "Let me have the five wood."

The sim's dark brown eyes shifted between the ball nestled in the rough against a broad-leafed weed, and the green a hundred yards away atop a slope.

"Seven better, sir."

"That five's especially made for rough"—Christ knows I'm in it enough—"and this is as rough as it gets."

Nabb pulled out the seven and handed it to him. "Five too far, sir."

"What makes you think you know my game?" Patrick said, trying to keep his annoyance out of his tone. He'd take golf advice from just about anyone, even a sim, but he knew his own limitations. "This is the first time you've caddied for me."

"Nabb watch Mist Sulliman before."

"Really?" He didn't get to play here all that often. How could this creature know his game?

The sim thrust the iron forward. "Seven."

Patrick snatched the club. "Okay. We'll do it your way. But if—I should say, *when*—it falls short and rolls back down that hill, I'm gonna have your hide."

Nabb said nothing, simply stepped back to give Patrick room.

Patrick took two practice swings, stepped up to the ball, and whacked it. The ball sailed high, sailed straight, and plopped out of sight somewhere atop the slope.

Armstrong started clapping. "Nice shot! Less than a dozen feet from the hole!"

Patrick turned to Nabb and had to laugh when he saw the huge grin on the sim's apelike face. "Don't say you told me so!"

"Nev say, sir. Just want Mist Sulliman win."

Wants the nonmember to win? Odd. But who could figure what went on in an animal's head.

Patrick one-putted and birdied the hole—an event rare enough to warrant a victory jig, but he resisted. Armstrong's caddie seemed as pleased as Nabb.

As they strolled toward the next tee, Patrick noticed swelling and bruising around Deek's right eye.

"What happened to you?"

"Bump door, sir."

"Deek ver clums," Nabb said. "Always bump self. Not watch where go."

"Quit jawing with the help, Patty," Armstrong said. He laughed. "Next thing you know you'll be trying to unionize them."

Nabb dropped Patrick's golf bag.

"Sorry, sir," he said as he knelt to gather up the clubs. "Sometime Nabb too ver clums."

2

Patrick won the round by a single stroke, so Armstrong would have to buy the drinks. Before heading for the bar, Patrick slipped Nabb a ten-dollar bill.

Armstrong snatched it from the sim's fingers and handed it back to Patrick. "No tipping sims. That's a no-no."

"I always tip my caddie."

"If he's human, sure. But what's a sim gonna do with money?"

"Buy candy bars, or maybe a bottle of Cuervo. Who cares?"

"Better not. Holmes'll have a fit."

Patrick knew all about Holmes Carter: club president and a notorious pain-in-the-ass stickler.

Patrick winked at Armstrong. "You ever caddie?"

"Me? Naw."

Of course not, Patrick thought. You were probably getting private golf lessons instead.

"I did. Right here, before anyone ever heard of sims."

And I don't care if he's human, sim, or some kind of robot, Patrick thought, I will *always* tip my caddie.

When Armstrong turned toward the locker room, Patrick rolled up the bill and palmed it to Nabb.

Inside, they had a corner of the bar to themselves, and while they were talking and drinking—Armstrong a Gibson up and Patrick a Rob Roy on the rocks—he had the odd feeling of being watched. But whenever he looked around he saw only the sims bustling about. The wait staff was human, but sims did all the bussing.

Patrick listened to Armstrong's idea about opening negotiations with the clerks by demanding a few choice give-backs from the full-timers' benefits package. Figured that would put them on the defensive. What an asshole. The idea sucked, truly and big time. Not because of the give-backs—nothing Patrick liked better than putting the screws to the opposition—but because the clerks' negotiator was a bitch on wheels who'd take that kind of opening salvo personally. From there on negotiations would go straight downhill.

But he said, "The idea's got merit, Ben. Let me think on how to approach it."

No sense in miffing a deep-pocketed client.

Patrick ran a hand over the polished mahogany of the bar and looked around at the well-heeled members gathering in clusters on either side or filtering into the adjacent dining room. He wanted to belong here so bad it made his gut ache. Wander in whenever he damn well felt like it, set his foot on the brass rail, and hang with the high rollers, trolling, setting his hooks, reeling them in.

But he'd already been turned down three times.

While Armstrong was ordering another round, Patrick headed for the men's room. After he washed up, the white-coated sim attendant handed him a towel.

"May sim speak, Mist Sulliman?"

Patrick glanced at him in the mirror. An older sim, touches of gray at his temples and above his large ears. Patrick had been here often enough to recognize him. His brass name tag read "Tome."

"You know my name?"

"Read you in paper, see play golf—"

"Wait-wait-wait. Read in paper? Sims can't read."

"This sim read."

That jolted Patrick. The world was still trying to get used to talking animals, but reading—sims weren't smart enough. Or at least they weren't supposed to be.

"How'd you learn to read?"

"Taught self, sir," Tome said, puffing his chest. "Not good, but can do."

Patrick stared. "This is amazing! Why haven't you told the world?"

Tome shook his head. "Other sim name Groh learn read. Tell evyone. Mans come take way. Nev more see Groh."

"Really?" Who could that have been but SimGen? But why recall a reading sim? Unless it was to see how they could replicate the ability.

"Please not tell."

"Okay. Mum's the word." But a reading sim . . . he shook his head in wonder. "So what'd you want to say?"

"Mist Sulliman lawyer, yes?"

"Yes." Patrick grinned. "This isn't going to be a lawyer joke, is it? Don't tell me you do stand-up too."

"No, sir. You lawyer for union, is true?"

"Some days, yes; some days I'm for management. Where's this going, Tome?"

"Sims been talking and . . ." His voice trailed off.

Impatience nibbled at Patrick. Out there on the bar the ice in his drink was melting.

"And what?"

"And . . ." The words rushed out: "And sims want you start sim union."

Patrick's jaw dropped—he was looking in the mirror when it swung down and he saw it hang open like a trapdoor. Slowly he turned.

"A sim union? Have you been nipping at the aftershave, Tome?"

"Have money," Tome said. "Have saved. We give you make sim union."

"Wait a minute . . . wait a minute . . ."

Patrick suddenly had a wild thought. He looked around for a video camera. When he didn't see one, he checked the stalls—all empty. Laughing, he came back to Tome.

A reading, AFL-CIO sim. Sure.

"All right, who put you up to it? Armstrong? Rogers? Come on, who?"

"No, Mist Sulliman. We know you. Want hire."

Could this cloned ape be serious?

Patrick sighed. "Tome, you have no idea what you're saying. Unions are for people. Sims aren't people. That's the law."

"Yessir, but Mist Sulliman lawyer. Lawyer change law. You—"

Just then the door swung open and Holmes Carter waddled in. About Patrick's age—mid-thirties—but he looked older and had a commanding lead in the gut department. A bulbous forehead and no lips to speak of, and where Patrick's hair lay thick and fair, Carter's was dark and thinning; his scalp gleamed through his comb-over. Soon he'd be a chrome dome.

Or maybe not. Looking at Carter's hair now, Patrick noticed that it was thicker; didn't appear to be a rug or a weave either. Must have gone and got himself a splice to replace his baldness gene. You ol' devil, you.

Too bad the genemeisters couldn't do anything to reduce his fat. Scalps were easy: a limited number of cells to splice. Fat was a whole other deal—trillions of fat cells in a body.

But fat, thin, bald, or pompadoured, Carter would always be a first-class dork. No splice for that. But he was also third-generation Beacon Ridge and first in line to inherit the family's string of car dealerships. In his teens Patrick had caddied for the two preceding generations of Carters and they'd been pretty decent. But Holmes . . . Holmes must have been fashioned from what had collected in the skimmers of their gene pool.

Although Patrick qualified for the club professionally and financially—at least on paper—he hadn't been able to squeak past the membership committee. The blackball rule was alive and well here, and he was pretty sure Holmes Carter had used it to keep him out. Probably couldn't tolerate the idea of a former caddy hobnobbing with the members.

"Talking to yourself again, Sullivan?" he said, baring his teeth in what passed for a smile.

"You might not believe this, Holmes, but Tome and I were just . . ." Patrick noticed a sudden fearful widening of the sim's eyes ". . . having a little chitchat."

Carter swung on Tome. "You know the rules! No talking to people—even if it's a nonmember. You are to be barely seen and *never* heard!"

"Yessir," Tome said. He turned away and hung his head.

Patrick spotted the ID number and bar code tattooed on the nape of the sim's neck.

"Lighten up, Holmesy," he said, then eyed the man's gut. "In more ways than one. What's he supposed to do when I talk to him? Ignore me?"

Carter bellied up to the urinal. "If it's you, yes. What's the matter? Can't get any people to listen to you?"

"I guess I like sims better than some people I know—present company included."

Carter had that shark grin again as he returned from the urinal and began rinsing his hands. "You never learn, do you, Sullivan. Why do I keep seeing you around here? When are you going to quit cadging rounds of golf from our members and bamboozling them into sponsoring you? Didn't you get the message when the committee turned you down? You're not wanted around here."

That stung. But Patrick hid the hurt and said nothing, simply stared at him.

"What's the matter?" Carter said as he dried his hands. "Cat gotcher tongue?"

"No," Patrick said. "Just wondering why you sprang for a hair splice and passed up one for a personality." Figuring he didn't have to worry about burning nonexistent bridges, he added: "Also wondering why I'm standing here listening to a used car salesman—"

"They're *not* used!"

"—who has to use a homing pigeon to get his belt around his waist."

Carter's pie face reddened toward cherry. "You think you're funny?"

"I'm no Bill Hicks, but I have my moments."

"Keep it up, Sullivan. I hear you tipped a caddie today. Just keep it up and I'll have you banned from the grounds, so no matter how many friends you have here, you'll never step on our course again."

He threw his towelette at Tome and stormed out.

Patrick waited for the door to close, then turned to Tome.

"When do you get off?"

"Club close ten," Tome said.

"I'll meet you then. You may have found yourself a lawyer."

3

Patrick buzzed around in his new Beemer 1020i, more car than he cared for, but if you wanted to snag the big clients, you had to look like you didn't need them. As he drove he pondered how to tackle this sim union thing, and wondered why he was attracted to it. He smiled, realizing the two things he most enjoyed in his professional life were making money and pissing off people he didn't like—in that order. And when he could combine the two, that was heaven. Better than sex. Well, almost.

A bid to unionize the Beacon Ridge sims would be a definite two-fer.

As he wound through the back streets of Katonah he tried to organize what he knew about sims. They weren't news anymore but they hadn't been around long enough to be taken for granted. He was old enough to remember the uproar when Mercer Sinclair introduced the first sim at an international genetics conference in Toronto.

He shook his head. He remembered how at the time it had been all anybody talked about. Religious groups, animal rights groups, and branches of the government from the FTC to the FDA had raised holy hell. You couldn't turn on a TV or radio without hearing about sims or the Sinclairs.

Everybody knew the Sinclair brothers' story. Sims hadn't been their first brush with genetic notoriety. Ellis and Mercer started gene-swapping while grad students at Yale, published some groundbreaking papers, then quit and went into business for themselves. Their first "product" had been an instant success: a dander-free feline pet for people allergic to cats. They used the enormous profits from that to start work on altering apes.

What they came up with was a creature more than chimpanzee and less than human. As Mercer Sinclair, the brother who seemed to do all the talking, had tirelessly explained on every show from Leno to Letterman to Ackenbury, and anyone else who had an audience, they'd settled on the chimpanzee because its genome was so close to a human's—a ninety-eight-point-four percent match-up in their DNA. As Sinclair liked to point out, there was far greater genetic difference between a chimp and a gorilla, or between the different species of squirrels running around the average backyard.

One-point-six percent, Patrick thought, shaking his head . . . the difference between me and a monkey. If ninety percent of DNA was useless junk, how many genes was that? Couldn't be many.

With so much shared DNA, it hadn't taken a whole lot of germ-line engineering to produce a larger skull—allowing for a larger brain, greater intelligence, and the intellectual capacity for speech—and a larger, sturdier, more humanlike skeleton. That took care of functional requirements. Smaller ears, less hirsute skin, a smaller lower jaw, and other refinements made for a creature that looked far more human than a chimp, one that might be mistaken for a *Homo erectus*, but never for a *Homo sap*.

The result was the sim: a good worker, agile, docile, with no interest in sex or money. Not an Einstein among them, but bright enough to speak a stilted form of whatever language they grew up with.

To manufacture and market the product—Mercer Sinclair insisted from the get-go on referring to sims as a product—the brothers had formed SimGen. And SimGen got the government to agree that the creatures were just that: a product.

How they accomplished that feat remained a mystery to Patrick and lots of other folks. President Bush the Second had come out against the whole idea, calling it "Godless science," and the Democratic congress, with its hands deep in the pockets of the very anti-sim Big Labor, was ready to put the kibosh on the whole thing. SimGen stock was in the toilet.

But somehow anti-sim legislation kept getting deadlocked in various committees; for some unfathomable reason, union bluster tapered off.

Instead of waiting for the ax to fall, SimGen started cranking out sims for the unskilled labor markets. Common consensus was that the Sinclair brothers had lost their minds and very soon would lose their shirts. Who'd want transgenic laborers during a global recession with millions of humans out of work.

The Bush administration, wrapped up in the seemingly endless war on terrorism, failed to pass any regulatory bills. And then came the boom of the mid-oughts, making the nineties look like a pop gun and tightening all the labor markets. Suddenly sims weren't such a godless idea after all. In fact, they made good economic sense. They even allowed the US to compete with Asia in the textile markets. The result: A lot of senators and congressmen who previously might have been expected to vote against, came out in support of pro-SimGen legislation.

Patrick remembered how animal rights activists had cried foul and said the fix was in, but nothing was ever proven, and in those days SimGen hadn't anywhere near the money to buy off so many legislators.

Now was a different story, of course. SimGen had been raking in the megabucks for years. As the darling of mutual funds and small investors alike, its market cap value was soaring.

All of which made Patrick feel like a microminiature David. Because the real heavyweight opposition to organizing the sims would come from the SimGen Goliath. The last thing they'd want was someone unionizing their property.

What he needed were allies. But who? The religious fundamentalists would be no help; Orthodox Jews, Moslems, and Christian Born Agains had found common ground in their opposition to sims, but they wanted sims abolished, not unionized. The animal rights groups like PETA and Greenpeace were a possibility, but they seemed to be in disarray; they'd tried guerrilla tactics like raiding piecework shops and "liberating" the sim workers; but the sims, unused to freedom, and lost and confused in the big wide world, wound up returning to the shops on their own.

Patrick could see that he was going to be all alone out there.

On the other hand, maybe SimGen wouldn't bother to lift a finger. Maybe they'd know what Patrick knew: that he didn't have a kitten's chance in a room full of pit bulls. But what he could do was raise a ruckus and embarrass the hell out of Beacon Ridge, then settle out of court for a nice piece of change. That was what he'd aim for.

But after that . . . what? What would the Beacon Ridge sims do with their money? Maybe Patrick could convince them to start a practice of tipping the *golfers*. He smiled. Wouldn't that be a kick.

He checked his watch: 10:14. Time to meet with his new clients.

He parked on a side street near the creek that ran through the grounds. Yellow legal pad in hand, he stepped out, found an opening in the high privet hedge, and for some reason thought of his father.

Mike Sullivan was a retired steamfitter who had been a diehard union man all his life. He'd raised his family within earshot of the Rensselaer railyards outside Albany until Patrick was twelve, then moved them to Dobbs

Ferry. Patrick remembered how proud he'd been when his son became the first member of the family to graduate college. But he hadn't been so crazy about Patrick's idea of a career in law. He couldn't afford to send him, so Patrick had paid his own way through Pace Law. If he'd gone on to become a champion of the labor movement, Dad might have bragged about his son the lawyer; but Patrick had shied away from the crusader role, opting to join the lumpen proletariat of the profession in a medium-size firm, and scratch his way up through the ranks.

Dad had been able to live with that. But would he be able to live with the idea of his son as a labor organizer—of sims?

Do I really want to do this?

Patrick knew he should give himself a little more time—maybe a lot more time—to weigh the pros and cons. He had an impulsive nature which he managed to control at the bargaining table, but it had put him in hot spots more than once. Did he want to start this fire?

Damn right he did. Hell hath no fury like an attorney scorned. Beacon Ridge didn't want him? Fine. They were going to regret that. Not only was there a buck or two to be made, but instead of seeing less of the man he'd blackballed, Holmes Carter was pretty soon going to feel like he was married to Patrick Sullivan.

Here comes the bride, Patrick thought as he stepped through the hedge onto Beacon Ridge property.

4

Beacon Ridge quartered its sims in a long barracklike building in the low corner of the club grounds, a section that flooded during a heavy rain. The lights were on, the windows open, and music filtered out into the cool night air. Patrick stopped and listened. Was that . . . ?

"Ma-gic . . . mo-ments . . ."

Perry Como?

He saw a sim silhouetted in the lighted doorway. It pointed to him and ducked back inside, crying, "Is him! Comes now! Just like said, he come!" A babble of voices arose from within.

What am I? Patrick thought. The messiah?

Tome met him at the door and motioned him inside. "So happy come you, Mist Sulliman. Welcome to sim home, sir."

Patrick stopped and looked around. The two dozen Beacon Ridge male and female sims who carried the golf bags on the links, set and cleared the tables in the dining room, washed the dishes and peeled the potatoes in the kitchen, and cut the grass and weeded the flower beds, stood gathered before him in the front room of their quarters. Overhead fluorescents shone on scattered stuffed chairs, long mess-hall style eating tables, and industrial carpeting. Two TVs, one in each far corner, were on but no one was watching; soft music crooned from the radio.

Patrick had once visited a client in a mental hospital; this reminded him of that institution's day room.

"What's behind the wall?" he said.

"We sleep."

With most of his fellow sims trooping behind like lemmings, Tome led Patrick to the dormitory section where triple-decker bunks lined the walls. A toilet and shower area lay beyond the next wall. Patrick wondered about the coed living conditions, then remembered reading that in addition to being sterile, sims' libidos were genetically suppressed.

Back in the front room, Tome led Patrick to a graying female sim seated in one of the easy chairs.

"This Gabba, sir," he said. "She oldest. Like mother here."

"Yessir." The aging female started a slow, painful rise from her chair. "So pleased meet—"

Patrick waved her back—probably take the arthritic old thing ten minutes to stand and another ten to sit down again. "Don't get up. I'm gonna sit anyway."

He looked around, found an empty chair, and lowered himself into it. The rest of the sims gathered around in a circle. He spotted Nabb but didn't see Deek. He'd never been this close to so many sims at one time and was struck by how similar they looked. You didn't notice when you saw them singly or in pairs, but crowded together like this . . .

He'd read where SimGen made minor variations in the genomes as they cloned them so sims wouldn't look like they'd all been cast in the same mold. Maybe this crowd didn't exactly have a cookie-cutter appearance, but no question they'd all been baked from the same batter.

Now, here, with their pidgin English and weird looks and odd way of moving, he felt as if he'd dropped in on a colony of simple folk of a different race and culture.

But these folk were *owned*. He could not allow himself to forget that. Anything he'd read about SimGen credited two moves for its success: First was the company's patents on nearly all the viable recombinant chimp genomes, guaranteeing the field to itself; second was the Sinclair brothers' decision not to sell their product, but to lease it instead.

A sim lease was too pricey to allow it to be a common household servant, but the creatures were a huge bargain as unskilled labor—no social security taxes, no pension plans, no compensation or unemployment insurance. And when one got hurt or too infirm to do the job, SimGen replaced it.

As a result, more and more businesses all over the industrialized world were lining up for sims.

And since the creatures were all genetically sterile, preventing black-market types from growing their own, SimGen had an absolute lock on the market. Special legislation had classified sims as neither humans nor animals; since they did not occur naturally, and since SimGen owned the patent on their genome and, in a very real sense, manufactured them, they were deemed a product, a commodity—*property*—and SimGen owned every damn one of them.

He leaned toward Gabba. "Okay, the first thing I have to ask is where the hell you came up with the idea of a union?"

"See TV," Tome said.

Patrick had expected Gabba, the apparent matriarch of the group, to respond, but obviously Tome was the spokessim.

"Read also paper," Tome added.

"Yeah, that's right. You can read." He still couldn't quite believe it. "How about the rest of you?"

"Only Tome read," the sim said.

"Okay, so you came up with this idea of starting a union. That means you want something you don't have. To tell you the truth," he said, looking around, "compared to other sims who work in sweatshops or on production lines or digging ditches, you've got it pretty cushy here."

Never failed. With humans, and now apparently even with sims: The more you have, the more you want. But maybe he should be careful here. Didn't want to change their minds.

He quickly added, "But that doesn't mean, of course, that your living conditions can't be improved. So what are our demands gonna be? More food? Better quarters?"

"Sim want family, sir," Tome said.

Patrick felt as if he'd been slapped. Talk about coming out of left field . . .

Family? Uh-uh. No way that's gonna happen.

"You don't mean like becoming wives and husbands and having children, and all that, do you? Because if—"

"No, sir," Tome said, waving his arms around at his fellow sims. "This family."

"I don't get it."

"Sims grow up large group, no mommy, no daddy, just child sims. Get know others, make friend, then take away. Come here, make friend, then take away. No want take away. Want stay together. Want family."

"I see," Patrick said slowly. "Family . . . interesting concept."

He looked around at the intent faces of the creatures encircling him. The faces were definitely simian, but far less so than any monkey in the wild. They'd been retooled from chimpanzees, a creature genetically damn near human. But pure chimps had mothers and fathers and a family structure. Sims were even closer to humans yet they were raised like cattle and leased out as soon as they were fit for work. And then they were traded in or swapped around like used cars.

Nowhere along the line did they have any semblance of a family.

Patrick felt a twinge of discomfort, almost like sympathy. He brushed it away. Never get emotionally involved. Stick to the facts.

But hey, if I feel something . . .

This was good. Oh, this was very good. He could use this. He could embellish this a little and tug like mad on all sorts of heartstrings.

He began scratching notes on his pad: Poor lost sims, raised without parents or siblings, cast out into the cold cruel world to work long hours for no pay. They weren't asking for wages, not for anything material, they just wanted a little personal continuity in their lives . . . the right to keep certain close-knit groups of sims from being broken up . . . allowed to live together and work together . . . as a makeshift family of sorts . . .

I *love* it!

Maybe he could even start up a nationwide Sim Legal Aid Fund.

This was looking better and better.

"Okay. That kind of family just might fly. So that's what we'll shoot for. Let's do it."

Tome's eyes lit. "Is yes? Mist Sulliman do?"

"That's what I said."

Tome pumped his long arms in the air and the rest of the sims began screeching and jumping about, capering in circles, leaping in the air. Only Gabba remained seated, but she was clapping and grinning.

Patrick had to smile. What a rambunctious crew. Something innocent and almost childlike about them, like early humans might have been before hundreds of generations of social conditioning turned them into the uptight species they were today.

Tome raised his fist and screeched, "La Causa!"

The rest of the sims took up the cry, turning it into a chant.

Patrick raised his hands to calm them.

"Where did you pick up 'La Causa'?" he said when he could hear himself.

"From Jorge," Tome said.

"Who's Jorge?"

"He cook kitchen. Ask him union. He give smile and do fist and say, 'La Causa.' "

Again exuberant jumping and running and chanting.

When finally they calmed down, Patrick said, "The best way to approach this may be to demand a union and then settle for all of you staying together as a group."

"Settle?" Tome said, frowning. "That mean no union?"

Don't start going Cesar Chavez on me, Tome.

"A union could be a long shot, I'm afraid," Patrick said. Like to the moon and beyond. "I'm telling you this up front so you won't be disappointed if we lose on that one." Never raise a client's expectations. Always low-ball the outcome. "But I think we could possibly walk away from this deal with a family and some cash."

"Cash?"

"Money. It's called a settlement. I figure we ought to be able to get the club to concede on the family issue plus squeeze them for a nice piece of change in return for our shutting up and leaving them alone. And then we'll split the money fifty-fifty."

"Mist Sulliman get half?" Tome said.

Aw, we're not going to haggle are we?

"Sure. When you consider how much time I'll be devoting to this, and strictly on a contingency basis, you—"

"No," Tome said.

"No?"

"No half for Mist Sulliman. Take all."

Patrick blinked, too shocked to speak. Never in his life had he expected to hear those words pass a client's lips.

"All? But what about you guys?"

"Money not want."

"Of course you do. You could use it to fix up this place, buy one of those big picture-frame TVs, better furniture . . ."

. . . start tipping the golfers . . .

Tome was shaking his head. "All money for you."

"And all you want is this family thing?"

Tome nodded. "Family . . . and one thing other."

Patrick poised his pen over the pad. "Shoot."

Tome's big brown eyes bored into him. "Respect, Mist Sulliman. Just little respect."

Patrick felt his mouth go dry. Talk about a tall order. But he recovered and wrote it down.

"Okay. Respect. Maybe we can get into the specifics of that at a later date. Right now, the first thing we do is formally petition the club to allow you to form a union. They'll refuse, of course. When that happens, we go before the NLRB."

"Enell . . . ?"

"National Labor Relations Board."

That was when the shit would really hit the fan. Patrick rubbed his hands together in a dizzying mix of anticipation, dread, and glee.

5

MANHATTAN

SEPTEMBER 28

Romy Cadman sat at her desk in the New York branch of the Office for the Protection of Research Risks, skimming through the animal welfare report on the rat-testing protocols in Rast Corporation's psychopharmaceutical lab. The lab was testing the amphetamine potentiation effect of a number of compounds with antidepressant properties. Everything seemed to be in order.

Her phone double-rang. The British-style ring-ring meant the call was incoming on her direct line; an outside call, bypassing the switchboard. She picked up immediately.

"D-A-W," she said. If callers didn't know that meant Division of Animal Welfare, they could ask.

"Good morning, Ms. Cadman."

Romy immediately recognized Zero's deep voice on the other end. No surprise. She'd figured he'd be calling soon.

"Good morning yourself."

"You've heard, I assume."

"About the sim union thing?" What else would he be calling about. "Seems it's all people here are talking about."

"We should talk about it as well. Soon. When is good for you?"

"I was about to break for lunch anyway. I can be there in twenty minutes."

"Fine."

Where was not discussed. Romy knew.

She closed the report on her computer screen and straightened her desk, repositioning a brass paperweight inscribed with *R. Cadman* in large black letters; a gift from her mother years ago. Mom had wanted the engraver to use her full name but Romy had protested. She'd always hated "Romilda" and didn't want to see it every time she stepped into her office.

She ran a brush through her close-cropped dark brown hair, slipped into the jacket of her gray pants suit—cut to show off her long slim legs and tight, firm butt—and grabbed her shoulder bag. On her way through the cubicle farm of clerks and secretaries she stopped at her boss's office and stuck her head inside.

"I'm heading out."

Milton Ware, a spry little man with bright blue eyes and a shock of white hair, looked up from his desk, then glanced at his watch.

"A little early for lunch."

"I've got some errands to do."

"When will you be back? I want to go over that Rast report with you."

"Later."

"When is 'later'?"

"After sooner. Bye."

She offered her sweetest smile and left him with the perplexed, frustrated expression that was becoming his trademark when dealing with her. Milt was one of the world's most uptight men, always worried about his performance rating. He needed to lighten up.

Really, what did either of them have to worry about? OPRR was a division of NIH. All federal money. Didn't Milt know how hard it was to lose a federal job, especially one that no sane person would want?

Romy had been ready to quit not too long ago. Sims had always offended her. Not the creatures themselves, but the very concept of a recombinant species of primates created to be slaves. She'd waited year after year for legislation to address the situation—if not outlaw them, then place sims under the aegis of OPRR's Division of Animal Welfare. The original classification of sims as somewhere between animal and human had blocked her division from having any say in how they were treated. Bills to change that had been introduced in committees in both houses of Congress over the years but not a single damn one had ever reached the floor for a vote.

She'd been typing up a scathing letter of resignation when she received a call, just like today, and first heard that deep voice on the other end of the line. It suggested that she might feel better about her job if she accepted an opportunity to moonlight in a related field. Intrigued, she'd agreed to a meeting. Turned out to be the best move she'd ever made.

Down at street level, Romy crossed Federal Plaza at a relaxed pace, enjoying the admiring stares from the other government drones. She worked hard on her body, and not simply for looks. She needed top fitness for her ballet classes. Not that she'd ever perform in public. The dancing itself was what pleased her. The resultant grace, coordination, and body tone were happy bonuses.

She glanced briefly at the graceful spire of the new World Trade Center, finally completed after so many years of squabbling over its design, and turned uptown, stretching her long legs as she strolled Broadway for a couple of blocks, then turned left onto Worth Street. She stopped before the soaped-up windows of an empty storefront; ideograms identifying the previous owner, a Taiwanese toy distributor, still graced the windows. Romy pulled out a key, unlocked the door, and entered.

The dust on the floor was tracked with footprints—her own and an indeterminate number of others.

Which ones are Zero's? she wondered. Or does he have a private entrance?

She strode to the rear and unlocked the door to the basement. This was the part she didn't like. Had to be rats down there. She'd never seen one, but that meant nothing. She'd seen plenty of their clean, docile, many-times-removed albino cousins, the lab rat. Those she didn't mind, felt sorry for most of them, actually. But she was not at all anxious to meet a Norwegian brown in its natural habitat. She'd handle the situation if it arose, but she'd rather not have to.

The basement was a dusty, dim-lit space with water dripping in one of the dark corners. A long folding table stretched across the far end. Zero sat behind it. Romy had never arrived before him, so she assumed he called her from here. Back-lit by a low-watt incandescent bulb that reduced him to a silhouette, he was dressed as usual in a bulky turtleneck sweater, a knit watch cap pulled low to his eyebrows, dark glasses, and a scarf wrapped around his lower face all the way up to and over his nose. She'd gauged his height at around six-two, and despite those broad shoulders he appeared to be thin.

She'd almost bolted on her first visit. She'd been anxious—no, make that dry-mouthed, heart-pounding, what-the-hell-have-I-got-myself-intoterrified—but his calm, soothing voice had eased her jangled nerves. And just when she'd begun to relax, he'd jarred her with how much he knew about her: her BS in Biology from Georgetown, her doctorate in Anthropology from UCLA, the intense lobbying she had done for protective legislation for the sims, the furious letters to the editor she'd written, even the fact that she was on the verge of quitting OPRR.

But then he'd really floored her by revealing what he knew about her wild youth—the arrests for DWI, the shoplifting and assault-and-battery convictions, the month she'd spent institutionalized. He also knew how the doctors had cured her . . . or thought they had.

How had he found out? Juvenile court records were supposed to be sealed, and medical records were supposed to be privileged.

But Zero didn't care about her past. He was looking to the future and he offered her a way to work for her cause, *their* cause, behind the scenes. He said he had the money, now he needed the people.

For Romy it had been a dream come true, but she'd hesitated. Zero knew all about her, but what did she know about him? And why all this melodrama with the cellar and the hidden face and the corny code name?

Necessary, he'd told her. Absolutely necessary.

Okay, she could handle that—for a while. But one thing she couldn't handle was terrorism. She told him she wasn't going to help blow up office buildings or shoot up SimGen trucks or any of that stuff.

Not that she had qualms about destroying SimGen real estate. She was simply afraid that a certain hidden part of her would enjoy it so much she wouldn't be able to stop.

Zero told her then that the whole idea behind his organization was to wage war against SimGen and its allies in the government without their ever realizing a war was on. That was why their organization would have no name, no logo, would write no letters, make no bragging phone calls. Its style would be covert; its field of battle would be the interstices—infiltrating, instigating, creating a fifth column in society, within the company itself. Whatever it did to sabotage SimGen's plans and operations would appear to be random or, ideally, accidental.

The ultimate goal? Shut down the sim pipeline by making sims unprofitable for both the lessor and the lessee. Wake up the world and turn it against anything fashioned by slave labor, even if the slaves weren't human.

Sign me up, she'd said.

Excellent.

Then Zero had asked her why.

Good question. Romy couldn't say exactly. She wasn't trying to make up for some past failings, had no hokey memories of an animal she'd mistreated as a child or a beloved pet who'd died because of her neglect or carelessness.

It was wrong, she'd said. As wrong as wrong could be. A stain on humanity that needed to be scrubbed away. How could she describe how every fiber of her being howled at the shame, the disgrace of it?

Fair enough, Zero had said.

He wanted her to stay in OPRR. Her position in the Division of Animal Welfare would explain her repeated presence in areas sensitive to the cause. She might not have a legal right to be there, but as a representative of a government organization—an overzealous representative, perhaps, but a representative nonetheless—she'd have a plausible excuse.

That had been two years ago. Gradually, as she'd proved herself, she'd been allowed to learn more and more about the organization. First off, it was bigger than she'd imagined, and well financed. She knew only a few of its income sources—one of them had surprised the hell out of her—but the source of the bulk of Zero's money remained a mystery.

So did Zero. Romy had done her damnedest to pierce his veil of secrecy. She knew from his voice—he didn't use a distorter to disguise it—and from glimpses of pale skin at his throat and between his gloves and cuffs that he was a white male. But his age was indeterminate; twenty, thirty, forty—it was a guess.

One thing she knew for certain: He was intimately connected to SimGen. He possessed information about the company only an insider could know.

As Romy slipped into the folding chair opposite Zero, she noticed a slim briefcase on the table between them.

"Two questions," she said. "First: Don't you think it's about time I saw your face?"

She was used to the mask by now, but that didn't lessen her frustration.

Her early awe had given way to admiration, and each encounter increased her need to see the face of this remarkable man.

"Not until SimGen stops producing sims."

"*Some*body in the organization must know who you are. Why not me?"

He shook his muffled head. "No one knows. It wouldn't be good for the organization."

"Why not?"

"It might prove . . . disruptive."

"Disruptive? How—?"

"Next question," he said. "Which will be the fourth, by the way."

Romy sighed. She'd have to wait. "All right. Did we instigate this sim union thing?"

"No."

"Think it's legit?"

"I fear not."

"Well, doesn't matter anyway. Legit or not, there's not a chance in the world a sim union will happen."

"I agree. But I don't want a circus, and I don't want a shyster collecting donations from sympathetic people and then disappearing with the cash. It will set a terrible precedent and very likely undermine support for a legitimate case when it arises."

"Do we *know* he's a shyster?"

"No, but I've researched him and find nothing that leads me to believe he has the sims' best interests at heart."

"Who is he?" Romy asked, liking this less and less. "And where on earth did they find him? Attorney World?"

Zero lifted the briefcase lid and removed an eight-by-ten glossy color photo. He handed it to Romy. "Patrick Sullivan."

She saw the head and shoulders of a decent-looking guy—not a hottie, but not bad—in his mid-thirties with wavy blond hair and bright blue eyes. But he was an attorney, a member of that vast slick crew using the letter of the law to circumvent its spirit.

"When was this taken?"

"Two days ago." She gave him a questioning look and he added, "Part of the backgrounding."

She repressed a chill, knowing Zero most likely had had people on her trail, photographing her before he'd made contact.

"He's a ruthless negotiator, willing and able to go for the jugular, with no sign of regret afterward."

"That's good, isn't it? I mean, as long as he brings that to the sim case."

"So one would think. But what disturbs me is his apparent lack of any guiding principles. He'll represent a union this week, management next, and be an equally passionate advocate for both. His voter registration says he's an independent. A string of women have passed through his life with no lasting relationships. No pets. He subscribes to law journals, news magazines, and *Penthouse*. He has never given a dime to charity."

"So Patrick Sullivan is a guy with no passions and no commitments. Doesn't sound like a man who takes up a cause."

"Not unless it pays well."

"Probably has the ethics of *E. coli*." Romy could see why Zero was concerned. "What do we do?"

"We don't interfere—at least not yet. Just as great literature can be created by an author writing simply to pay his rent, great good can sometimes be accomplished by people with less than exalted motivations. This Patrick Sullivan may simply be trying to turn a buck or looking to garner some cheap publicity. If that's his goal, we'll follow the progress of the case and see if we can turn things to our advantage along the way."

"And if he's an out-and-out crook?"

"We'll be keeping a close watch on him. At the first sign of any funny business, we move."

"Move how?"

"I'm not sure . . ."

The remark disturbed her. This was the first time she'd ever detected uncertainty in Zero.

"Something else I wanted to tell you," he said. "You'll be receiving notice soon that OPRR has succeeded in obtaining a court order allowing it to inspect the SimGen facility."

Stunned, Romy could only sit and stare.

"Something wrong?"

"How . . . how did you manage *that*? We've been trying for *years* to get a look in there."

"Vee haf vays," he said in a bad German accent, and she could imagine a smile behind the protective layers.

"No, seriously. How—?"

"By employing the same tactics that SimGen has used to stall the inspection: bribery, cajoling, intimidation, the whole nine yards."

Romy frowned. "Is that the way we want to be?"

"It's the way we have to be. And even then it was pure luck that the petition came before a judge who was retiring and didn't give a damn about whatever pressure SimGen and its pet politicos were bringing to bear. He said to hell with it and signed the order."

"This is wonderful." Her admiration for Zero climbed to a new high.

"It's a start. The order allows a one-time inspection of the entire research facility."

"No follow-up visits?"

Zero shook his head. "Sorry. But at least it's a foot in the door. We've pierced their armor—now we get a chance to look into the SimGen abyss." He slid the briefcase on the table closer to her. "Take this with you. It contains various miniature spycams. Use them on your inspection tour, especially in the basic research facility. Be sure to ask for a full explanation of their security procedures—because you're interested in how well the sims are protected, of course."

"Of course. And who knows? Maybe I'll get a face-to-face with the Sinclair brothers."

"Don't count on it. But even if you do, prepare to be unimpressed."

Another shock. "You've met them?"

"Yes. A number of times."

"Then they *know* you?"

"Yes . . . and no."

"I don't get it. What—?"

He raised his gloved hand, palm out: a stop sign. "We can't get into that now."

"When?"

"Maybe never." Zero rose and extended his hand across the table. "Good luck."

Romy shook his hand, peering closely at him, thinking: He knows the Sinclair brothers. Who is he? I've *got* to find out.

6

"And I tell you, my brothers and sisters, that SinGen is doing the work of the devil his own self. Yes! The devil's work! As surely as I am standing here, Satan himself sits in those corporate offices, guiding the hand of the SinGen researchers, inspiring them to fashion beings that the Creator never intended to exist, creatures that are an abomination in the sight of God. It must be stopped or we all—and I do mean all, not just the SinGen sinners, but all of us who abide that company's evildoing—will be called to account on the day of Final Judgment!"

Mercer Sinclair, a tall, lean, youthful-looking fifty-two with dark eyes and dark hair that had yet to show a trace of gray, sighed in disgust as he turned away from the plasma TV screen hanging like an Old Master on his office wall. He jabbed the OFF button on his desktop and banished the Reverend Eckert's florid face.

Stepping to the tinted window that took up most of the western wall of his top-floor office, he gazed out at the green rolling hills, mist-layered and glistening with morning dew. All SimGen's, as far as the eye could see.

Using proxies and dummy corporations, buying up little parcels here and there, Mercer had accumulated this massive chunk of northwest New Jersey for damn near a song. He could have bought more land for less in the Sunbelt, but that would have placed him too far from the action. Yes, he was in the boonies here, but these boonies were only a twenty-minute helicopter ride from Wall Street, while the isolation afforded a form of natural protection from prying eyes.

Closer in, nestled in this tight little valley, stood the gleaming glass and steel offices, the labs and natal and nurturing centers that fed the world's ever-growing need for sims. Here they were bred and housed until ready to be shipped to training centers all over the globe. Here beat the heart of SimGen's—Mercer's—far-flung empire.

He opaqued the window and turned to the three other men in his office. " '*Sin*Gen'? I wonder who thought that up for him."

His brother Ellis, two years older, taller, grayer, and almost gaunt, slouched on one of the black leather sofas to the left, far from the desk. Mercer expected no reply from Ellis, and received none.

Luca Portero, SimGen's chief of security, remained silent as well. Compact, muscular, in great shape for a man in his early forties, he stood with feet apart, arms behind his back; despite the blue blazer and tan slacks, he looked every inch a soldier.

Mercer hadn't picked Portero. He'd been *assigned* to SimGen as security chief. But he'd looked into the man's background. A self-made sort, starting off as a street urchin with an Italian first name in a mostly Mexican border town in Arizona, father unknown, mother of very dubious reputation—oh, hell, why not say it? The town whore. As soon as he was old enough he joined the Army and apparently found his métier.

And like a good soldier, he rarely spoke unless spoken to. That was the only thing Mercer liked about the man. Portero had always struck him as more snake than human. He didn't walk, he glided. On the rare occasions when he spoke, it was barely above a whisper. And those cold dark eyes . . . always watching . . . like a snake. Mercer often wondered if Portero had indulged in a trans-species splice or two before joining SimGen . . . something reptilian. The heart, perhaps?

"Don't underestimate Eckert," the third attendee said in a thick Alabama drawl.

Mercer glanced at Abel Voss, SimGen's general counsel. In his mid-fifties, with longish silver hair and twenty extra pounds packed around his waist, he filled the seat on the other side of the desk. Which didn't mean he was close— a string quartet could have set up and played on the vast gleaming ebony surface of Mercer's desktop. Only two colors here: furniture either black leather or ebony, carpet and curtains all a uniform light gray.

"You know him?"

"No, but a few years ago nobody'd even heard of that boy, and now he's a household name."

Voss liked to come on as a slow-witted, somewhat bemused good ol' boy. He used it to lull opponents until he sprang and crushed them with one of the sharpest corporate law minds in the world. Mercer liked that. The crushing part.

Mercer grunted. "And he galloped there on *my* back."

"*Your* back?" Ellis said. "How about my back as well? I wind up being painted with the same brush as you, something I do *not* care for."

Well, well, well, Mercer thought. Look who's speaking up.

He couldn't understand why his brother bothered with these meetings. He'd arrive, slump in a chair without saying a word to anyone, stare into space without participating, then leave.

Ellis had been in an emotional tailspin for years. Mercer had heard that only a complex antidepressant cocktail enabled him to get out of bed these days. Somehow he dragged himself to meetings, and managed to maintain a decent work schedule in his lab, but his productivity was zilch.

Today he'd actually offered a comment. Hallelujah. Maybe Ellis had finally found a combination of drugs that worked.

Mercer turned toward his brother. "That's what happens when you're the co-founder."

"But *I'm* the co-founder who has kids. What's said about me reflects on them. They go to school and have to hear that their father's in league with the devil!"

Ellis's kids . . . Robbie and Julie. Good kids. But Ellis didn't get to see them much since the divorce. Truth was, they seemed to prefer their Uncle Mercer to their downer dad. Mercer liked playing uncle, but he lived alone; always had, always would. Robbie and Julie were the closest he ever intended to come to parenthood.

But the divorce hadn't caused Ellis's depression—no, it had been the other way around. Who could live with someone in Ellis's state of mind?

"Don't blame me, bro. Blame Eckert."

"I know who to blame," Ellis said with a glare.

"Gentlemen," Voss said, "this can be saved for another time."

Mercer turned toward the lawyer. "I didn't call you here about the Eckert matter, but we might as well address it. It seems every time I turn on the damn TV I see his face."

"That's because the boy's syndicated. He does one show a day and it's farmed out to local stations all over the country. The local station managers plug it into a slot where they think they'll draw the most eyeballs."

"I can't believe people watch him day after day. He's got one goddamn issue and he beats it to death."

Voss shrugged. "Them Bible humpers've had it in for you two since sim one. Eckert is just more aggressive in grabbing the reins of that wagon."

"And he's been riding it for all it's worth ever since." Mercer rapped his knuckles on his desktop. "Can't we get anything on him?"

"Tried that. Took a look-see into his business affairs and personal life. Lives high but not too, too high. No bimbos, or if there are, he hides 'em well. On the surface he appears clean. No obvious belly-crawlin like Swaggart or Baker. Sockin away all those contributions until he's got enough to set up his own satellite network to—as he likes to put it—'spread the word to the world about the sin of sims.' "

"So let's probe a little deeper," Mercer growled.

"Gotta be careful with that sort of thing. The Rev's got a bunch of real loyal eggs around him. You try to crack one of them, you could wind up with yolk on your face. I'm talkin a tar-and-feather overcoat in the PR department. I say give it time. These preacher boys, most of them got this sort of arc, y'see—they rise fast, then they fall back. And meantime, if he's like most other preacher boys I've seen, all that money he's pullin in will somehow find its way into his own pocket instead of being used to mess with us. You just be patient, son."

Usually Mercer didn't mind when Voss called him "son"—just one of the man's Alabamisms—but today it irritated him. With his mother dead since his Yale days, and his father DOA with a cardiac arrest two years ago, he was now no one's son. His own man, answering to no one.

"Patient! Do you know he's scheduled to be on Ackenbury tomorrow night? *Ackenbury at Large*! Millions who've never even heard of the creep will see him do his anti-SimGen rant. What's Ackenbury thinking? Don't we buy enough time on his lousy show?"

"Hey, it's all show biz, you know that. That boy gets hold of the most controversial folks he can find. That's why he's rackin up better numbers than Leno and Letterman. I know we got a buncha cow flop flyin at us at once now, what with Eckert, the unionization thing, and havin to open our doors for an OPRR inspection, but I wouldn't let this rattle you."

"I'm not rattled," Mercer said.

But he wasn't particularly comfortable either. He didn't mention his growing uneasiness, a sense of malevolent convergence. If he believed in fate or astrology, he might have said he felt the stars aligning against him.

Utter nonsense, of course. You made your own destiny. You grabbed what you could and then did your damnedest to keep it. And if you lost it, that was because someone else outsmarted you. Flaming gasballs floating millions of light-years away had nothing to do with it.

But if the stars weren't aligning against him, then who?

"Good," Voss said. "Glad to hear it. 'Cause there's nothin here to get rattled about. Take this damn fool unionization thing, for instance. You have to be human to be in a damn union, so *res ipso loquitur*, the suit can't succeed. It's a sham, a PR stunt for this nobody shyster who—"

"PR," Mercer said. "*That's* what I'm worried about. PR that's good for him and bad for us. We can't have people thinking of sims as anything more than brighter-than-average animals. Nobody talks about unionizing race horses or seeing-eye dogs. But start connecting the word 'union' to sims and you open a Pandora's box. I can just see this shyster—what's his name?"

"Sullivan," Voss said. "Patrick Sullivan."

"I can see this Sullivan character portraying sims as some poor mistreated underclass, when it's just the opposite. We've never sold a sim, we lease them. Why? So we can limit how they're used and oversee how they're treated."

"And, coincidentally, maximize profits," Ellis said acidly.

"Nothing wrong with profits," Mercer replied through his teeth without looking at his brother.

"You're preachin to the choir, son."

"No, I'm telling you the message we need to get out: We are a humane corporation that looks out for these creatures. We created them and we feel responsible for them."

"Humane," Ellis said in that same tone. "Now there's a concept."

Mercer wheeled on his brother. "Are you going to contribute something or just sit there and snipe?"

"That *was* a contribution, Merce," Ellis said, leveling a soulful gaze at him. "A very relevant one."

Mercer turned back to Voss. He couldn't stand Ellis's holier-than-thou stance. "We can't take any chances with this, Abel. I've heard of crazy things coming out of these NLRB hearings—especially where the regional office in Manhattan is involved. The wrong kind of decision and you'll be using your stock options for toilet paper."

"Don't have to worry about no labor relations shenanigans. Sullivan thinks he's got an edge because the director of NLRB's Region 2 is a maverick. Well, I've already seen to it that he never gets to the NLRB."

Mercer abruptly felt his mood lighten. "How did you manage that?"

"Had myself a talk with Beacon Ridge's attorney—bright kid named Hodges—and told him to seek a declaratory judgment in Federal court. He'll argue that since Congress has designated sims as property, they cannot be humans. And if they're not humans, then they're not employees, and therefore not protected by the statutes of the NLRB."

"*I* like the argument," Mercer said. "But what if the judge doesn't?"

Voss puffed out his chest. "He will. I've seen to it that the case comes up before Judge Henry Boughton."

"Is he one of ours?"

Voss shook his head. "We don't own this one. Don't have to. He's our kinda guy—least so far as this union thing goes. Conservative with a capital C. Hates unions. Probably one of Reverend Eckert's loyal listeners to boot. He'll toss this case in two seconds flat."

"Abel . . ." Mercer shook his head, grinning. "You are amazing."

"That's what you boys pay me for—to be amazin."

"That leaves the OPRR inspection."

"We've been discussing that," Luca Portero said.

The sound of the security chief's soft voice never failed to rattle Mercer. "Really. All by yourselves?"

Portero went on as if Mercer hadn't spoken. "We decided that I'll be the tour guide."

Good idea. OPRR would get nothing out of Luca the snake.

"Excellent choice."

Voss rose and straightened his suit coat. "Knew you'd like that. Matter of fact, Mr. Portero and me are gonna have us a little sit-down right now in my office. I'm gonna lay out the legalities we're up against, and how we're gonna slide around 'em."

"What about my lab?" Ellis said. He'd come out of his crouch now, sitting up with a rigid spine. "I won't allow them in my lab. And as for the sealed section—"

"Hey, ain't no one from OPRR or anywhere else gonna be anyplace we don't want 'em to be. Mr. Portero will see to that."

Portero only nodded.

"Thank God," Ellis said.

Voss and Portero headed for the door. "Talk to y'all later," Voss said.

When they were gone, Mercer turned and found his brother on his feet, a small smile playing about his lips as he approached the desk.

"Hear them?" Ellis said.

"Hear what?"

"The trumpets. They've started to blow. And the first cracks are starting to show in the walls of your Jericho. Soon this will all come tumbling down. And then where will you be?"

"Nothing's going to happen. You heard Abel—everything's under control."

"No, Merce. Everything's spinning *out* of control. Can't you feel it?"

"You're breaking with reality, Ellis." The worst of it was that he was echoing Mercer's own inchoate fears. "You need to adjust your meds."

Ellis had reached the far side of the desk where he continued that wide-eyed stare. "Knowing what you know, Merce, how do you sleep at night?"

Not this again.

"I sleep just fine. If you've got such a problem with the company, why don't you simply turn your back and walk away?"

"If it weren't for Robbie and Julie, I would—and go straight to the networks and blow the lid off."

Spicules of ice crystallized in Mercer's veins. Ellis was just unstable enough to do something like that. Probably thought he'd find some sort of redemption in self-immolation. But he couldn't burn alone. He'd drag Mercer into his auto-da-fé. And his children as well. Thank god Ellis loved Robbie and Julie too much for that.

"You wouldn't be blowing the lid off just SimGen, Ellis," he said softly. "It's not like we're in this alone."

"You think I don't know that?" Ellis cried.

"Then you should know that the walls could have ears."

Ellis blanched and leaned against the desk. "I hate this, hate this, *hate* this!"

"Well, any time you want to sell out, brother, you know my offer."

"We're both multi-billionaires. What would I want with *more* money?"

"You could go off, buy yourself an island somewhere, declare yourself king, and—"

Ellis straightened again. "And leave the company under your sole command? Not yet. Not till I've finished what I started out to do."

"Meaning what? Treading old ground we've covered too many times? You should be working on projects that will move the company forward instead of wasting your time on sims."

"It's *my* time and I'll decide how I spend it. Once I've perfected a sim—*my* sim—and we start putting them out there, then I'll sell out to you, Merce—in a heartbeat. But not a second before."

"We've *got* sims, damn it!"

Ellis glared at him. "How do you live with yourself, Merce? How?"

Mercer sighed. "How? By being a realist. By knowing what is and what isn't. By facing the hard cold fact that life is chemistry, nothing more, nothing less. When the chemicals are reacting, life goes on. When the reactions stop, so does life. That's it, and that's all it is. I am a collection of reacting chemicals; so are you; so are sims. To view existence as anything else is mysticism, romanticism, a myriad other isms, but it isn't real. Only the chemistry is real. Everything else is self-delusion."

He felt a pang as he considered his brother's flushed face and blazing eyes. It hadn't always been like this. He remembered their days in New Haven, inseparable, spending late hours in the labs, unafraid, pushing the limits, trying the impossible. Then the university had become too interested, looking for a piece of the action. Forget it: They'd dropped out, started their first venture to market no-shed house pets, and were on their way.

He could still visualize in perfect detail the day the Nakao team decoded the chimpanzee genome. He and Ellis immediately printed out a copy and unfolded it along a hallway; then they synched up a print-out of the human genome next to it, and together they walked along, comparing, pointing out the uncanny parallels and match-ups.

Mercer remembered stopping and gazing at his brother, finding Ellis staring back at him across those print-outs, realizing that Ellis was thinking what he was, seeing in his eyes the shared rapture of knowing what could be done, and that they could do it.

Heady times, those. The joy of discovery, the sense of the pulse of the world throbbing under their fingertips, the near omnipotent feeling that anything was possible.

And now, the hour-to-hour reality of managing one of the hottest new corporations in the world, of fighting day by day to catch up with the Microsofts and GEs of that world consumed him. He would not rest until SimGen was number one.

But that was his dream, not his brother's. At some point along the road of years he and Ellis had parted ways.

Mercer knew the exact moment. He'd deceived Ellis. Just once. A crucial matter, true, but only that once. He'd hoped to carry the secret to his grave, but truth will out. Ellis had never forgiven him. Or himself.

If I could go back, he wondered, would I do it all over again?

Yes. In a New York minute. Because without that one deception, SimGen would be just another also-ran in the gen-mod field.

"The genie's out of the bottle, Ellis. And now it's grown too big to fit back in. I've accepted that. It's about time you did too."

"No!" He wheeled and headed for the door, yanked it open, and strode through. "Never!"

7

Pamela's voice and her fist pounding on his back wrenched Patrick from slumber.

"Patrick!" she was shouting. "Something's burning outside!"

"Huh?"

And then a crash—breaking glass—an object smashing through the window only a few feet away, and he was awake, sitting up, his heart jackhammering in his chest as he looked around his dark bedroom. His alarm clock read 1:04. Outside he could hear a car burning rubber as it pulled away.

"What happened?"

"Look!" Pamela said, her voice hushed with fear. "Out on the lawn!"

Flickering light through broken glass . . . Patrick swung his legs toward the floor.

"No!" Pamela cried. "You'll cut your feet!"

Good thinking. He reached down, felt around till he found his loafers, then slipped them on. He hurried to the window, glass crunching under his soles, and looked out on his front yard.

His lawn was on fire.

"What the hell?"

He blinked. Well, not the whole lawn, but a circle of it along with some of the grass inside the circle blazed in the night. He was reaching for the phone to dial 911 when he heard the sirens. Apparently one of his neighbors had called the cops or fire department or both. So he reached for the lamp switch instead.

"Oh, shit, what's happening?" Pamela cried. "What's happening?"

He glanced at her. She crouched on the bed, blinking in the light like a fawn caught in the middle of the road. Pamela was his latest pseudo-live-in, meaning she owned her own place in New Bedford but had spent most of the last eight months at his place here in Katonah. Worked as a broker for Merrill Lynch; a few years younger than Patrick but her accumulated year-end bonuses put her far closer to early retirement. Dark hair, big blue eyes, and a dazzling bod that she was now shielding to the neck with the bed sheet.

Pamela . . . terrified. In spite of the flames and the sirens and the broken glass, that was what gripped him. So out of character. The ultracompetent Pamela was even more driven than he; give her a goal and she became a heat-seeking missile. She'd never shown him the little girl who lived inside her, the one who could be frightened.

"I don't know," he said, reaching across and giving her trembling shoulder a gentle squeeze. "But it's all right. We're okay."

He hoped.

Patrick was dressed only in boxer shorts, and the cool fall air flowing through the window raised goosebumps. Maybe it wasn't just the air. He straightened and did a slow turn, checking out the glass-littered floor until he spotted a bottle on its side against the far wall. He crunched over and re-trieved it. A Fruitopia bottle, empty but reeking of gasoline. And a piece of paper rolled up inside. He fished it out.

"What is it?" Pamela said.

"A note."

With trembling fingers Patrick unrolled the wet piece of blue-lined loose leaf and held it up to the light. The gasoline had acted as a solvent, running the ballpoint ink, but the words were still legible. His gut crawled as he read them aloud.

"*Forget about a sim union or next time it won't be empty.*"

"Oh, Christ!" Pamela cried. "Who'd do something like this?"

"Not signed."

A threat. He had trouble rereading the message because his hands had begun to shake. Jesus, he'd heard of things like this happening, but never dreamed . . .

He forced his racing brain to slow so he could examine the possibilities. SimGen popped into his head immediately, and just as quickly he discarded it. This was hardly their style, especially since they knew they couldn't lose in the long run. One of the anti-sim hate groups? Could be. He'd seen them on TV, mostly losers who resented animals taking human jobs—Wake up, guys: Machines have been doing that for a couple of centuries—but he hadn't heard of any in the area.

He didn't want Pamela to see how rattled he was. "One of your old boyfriends, maybe?"

"This isn't funny, Patrick! Someone just threatened your life!"

Just then a couple of Katonah's finest screeched to a halt at his front curb.

"Sorry." Couldn't she see he was just trying to break the tension? "Bad joke." He looked around for his pants. "I'm going to go out and talk to the cops."

"What am I supposed to do?"

"Get dressed and stay out of sight. You're better off not being involved in this."

He pulled on his slacks and a shirt, and hurried toward the front door.

. . . next time it won't be empty . . .

What the hell had he got himself into?

8

It was a little after nine when Patrick arrived at his office at Payes & Hecht, but he felt as if he'd already put in a full day.

The fire trucks had arrived on the heels of the first patrol car and doused his flaming lawn. It looked like the vandals had tried to burn some sort of message into the grass but whatever it said had been turned to steaming mud by the time the fire hoses finished their work. The cops took his statement, bagged the Fruitopia bottle and note, and promised to have the patrols make extra swings by his place.

All fine and good, but it had left him with a sick, sour stomach and an adrenaline hangover. At least he was in better shape than Pamela who seemed totally freaked by the incident. He'd tried to explain that the threat had been against him, not her, but still she'd been afraid to leave the house.

Finally he'd put her on a train to the city, then made it to White Plains where he was surrounded as soon as he stepped into the Payes & Hecht reception area. News of the attack had been all over the TV and radio; the firm was medium size, consisting of twenty-two attorneys, and everyone knew everyone. The associates and staff were shocked and concerned and wanted to know all the details. But before he could get into it, Alton Kraft, the managing senior partner, pulled him aside for a one-on-one in his office.

"You all right?" Kraft said.

His blue eyes looked out from under thick eyebrows that matched his salt-and-pepper hair. He had a lined face and looked grandfatherly, but he could be a buzzsaw with any associate who strayed off the beaten path. Patrick was up for partnership next year and Kraft was one of his main supporters.

"I'm fine. Really."

The two of them had hit it off from the first brief Patrick had prepared for one of Kraft's cases. He'd said it was the best he'd seen in years, and had taken Patrick under his wing.

"Good. I want to talk to you about this sim union thing. I'm not sure it's consistent with the image of the firm."

"It's pro bono," Patrick said. "Aren't we always being encouraged to take some pro bono cases? This is one of mine."

"That's all fine and good, but I don't like seeing the firm's name mentioned in connection with fire bombings."

Patrick stiffened. He was well aware that when Alton Kraft said "I" he was speaking for the senior partners.

"Alton, believe me," Patrick said, smiling in the hope of lightening things up, "I like it even less when it's my own name mentioned in connection with a fire bombing."

Kraft grinned. "I can imagine. But Patrick . . ." The grin faded. "You're an excellent attorney and you've got a big future with this firm. I admire your tenacity—when you're handed a problem, you stick with it until it's solved."

Tenacity, Patrick thought. Better than "stubborn as a mule," which was how his mother used to characterize him.

"But that same tenacity can *cause* problems too. When a situation looks like trouble for you or the firm, you have to know when to back away and cut your losses."

"I hear you, Alton. Loud and clear. But I'm sort of stuck with the sims for now."

"Not for long, fortunately."

"What do you mean?"

"Oh, I guess you haven't had time to sift through your messages yet. Judge Boughton has been assigned to decide on the declaratory judgment."

"Henry Boughton?"

"The one and only."

Patrick felt as if he'd been punched. Shit. What else could go wrong today?

"I think I'd better go talk to my clients."

9

Tome answered Patrick's knock at the barrack door. His large dark eyes widened at the sight of him. His grin was pure joy.

"Mist Sulliman! You all right? You not hurt?"

Does *everybody* know? "I'm fine, Tome. I just—"

"Look!" Tome cried, turning to the nearly empty room where half a dozen off-duty sims were either clearing the breakfast plates from the long mess tables or lounging in front of the TV. "He comes. He safe!"

The other sims jumped up and began screeching. They rushed forward and crowded around, some reaching out to touch him, as if to reassure themselves that he was real. Patrick was touched in another way—they must have been genuinely worried about him.

"We see TV," Tome said. "See burn. Say men who hate sim hate you."

"Well, we don't know that for sure."

Tome cocked his head and his dark eyes stared at Patrick from beneath his prominent brow. "Why men hate sim?"

"Just *some* men, Tome—a very small number. Dumb men. Let's not worry about them. We've got a bigger worry."

"More fire?"

"No. A judge, a very tough judge, has been assigned to our case."

"No problem for Mist Sulliman. Him best lawyer world."

Patrick had to grin at that. "You keep thinking those good thoughts, Tome. But this is very bad news for our case."

"No problem for Mist Sulliman."

"Yes, problem. Big problem."

How to explain this to a nonhuman? Patrick wasn't all that familiar with Judge Boughton's positions, opinions, and decisions outside the labor relations arena. He did know he was a crotchety old fart who thought too much court time was being wasted on trivialities at the expense of more serious legal matters; woe to the attorney who showed up in Boughton's court with a case the judge considered frivolous—which covered a lot of territory in Boughton's field of vision. He was the terror of unions, notorious for his loathing of the picket line.

And not only is this a union case, Patrick thought, but one he'll consider inherently frivolous.

The Beacon Ridge lawyers were seeking a judgment to terminate the suit and Boughton would do just that—with relish and extreme prejudice. Probably have bailiffs waiting at the courthouse door to give him the old heave-ho as soon as he set foot inside.

Patrick had been counting on extended hearings as an avenue to the public's ear and pocketbook, an opportunity to generate ongoing press coverage and daily sound bites on the evening news, all of which would—he hoped—lead to contributions to the defense fund.

At present, the sim war chest was pretty bare. He'd set up a website and a toll-free number—1-800-SIMUNION—with an answering service to accept contributions, but the phone hadn't exactly been ringing off the hook. A little money had come in during the initial flurry of publicity when he'd filed his suit, but nothing compared to what he'd hoped for. Now it looked as if the case would be over before it began.

Which would delight Pamela and please Alton Kraft. Ben Armstrong would be happy too. He'd called as Patrick was leaving the office, ostensibly to express his concern over the incident at the house, but soon got around to the real reason: Could this sim union matter be distracting Patrick, preventing him from devoting sufficient attention to the negotiations with the Jarman clerks' union, set to open next week? Patrick had assured Ben it was not.

Looked like everyone would be happy when Boughton pulled the plug. Patrick glanced at the surrounding sims. Well, not everyone.

"Let's just say that Judge Boughton will not be our friend."

Tome cocked his head. "Him hate sim, like men who burn?"

"No. He's not like them. I'm sure of that. He's just—"

Tome turned and pointed to the television playing in a corner. "Like TV man?"

"Who?"

Tome moved away, motioning Patrick to follow. He led him on a winding course through the seats clustered before the TV set.

"This man," Tome said, pointing to the sweaty, multi-chinned face that filled the screen.

"*. . . and I say to you, good people, that those cute creatures they call 'sims' are our tour guides along the road to hell. The Bible tells us, 'Thou shalt not suffer an abomination!' And that's exactly what we do when we allow the evildoers at SinGen to go on populating the world with these godless creatures. That's Satan's* *plan, you know. Yes, it is. I've had a vision and I've seen the world overrun by* *these soulless caricatures of humankind. And where will that leave man, the* *pinnacle of Creation, fashioned by the Lord himself to have dominion over the* *creatures of the earth? Gone! Supplanted by these unholy hybrids. And then* *Satan will have won. The earth will be his, populated by* his *creations instead of* *the Lord's!"*

He then launched in a plea for pledges to finance the fight against the evil spewing forth from "SinGen."

"Sim nev hurt man," Tome said, pointing at the screen. "Why man not like sim?"

"Oh, I'll bet he likes you just fine," Patrick said.

In fact, he thought, I'll bet the Rev *loves* sims. He should. Sims are his meal ticket.

"Then why say sim bad?"

"Just a way to make money."

And I'll bet he's making lots of it. Cleaning up.

Then Reverend Eckert said that he was scheduled to be on *Ackenbury at* *Large* tonight. He urged all his regular viewers to tune in and watch him "spread the truth about SinGen to the unenlightened."

And that gave Patrick a wonderful idea.

10

SUSSEX COUNTY, NJ

Ellis Sinclair sat in his office in the basic research complex and searched for calm while he waited for Harry to bring in the sim. He toyed idly with the ExecSec plant on his desktop, brushing his pen against the leaves and watching its tendrils whip around the shaft and hold it in place. Then he'd tug on the pen and the tendrils would release it. Back and forth, give and take, noting with pleasure how the plant rotated use of its tendrils to avoid fatigue.

He sighed and let the plant keep the pen as he leaned back in his chair. The ExecSec had been a modest success back in the days before SinclairGen became SimGen. He wished they'd stuck to harmless little gimmicky products like this instead of going for the killer app. They wouldn't be fractionally as wealthy, but how much money can you spend?

And there'd be no sims wandering the earth.

He rubbed his cold palms together. The artificial sunlight streaming through the frosted panes at his back did nothing to warm him. More and more lately he craved a real window. Just one. But that was out of the question. Basic research's windowless design was his own doing, for he knew as well as anyone that a window to the outside was also a portal in. So he had allowed not a pinhole through the walls of this lead-lined box of steel-reinforced concrete.

To keep the place from looking too much like the Berlin Wall, mirror-glass panes had been set into the exterior to simulate windows and, perhaps, to tempt industrial and media spies to bounce the beams of their snoop lasers off the glass in vain attempts to hear what was being said on the other side.

Ellis could not allow anyone to know the reasons behind what he was doing here. Not even his assistants knew. Only Mercer. And then there was the sealed section, with its separate staff who were ferried in and ferried out with no one ever seeing them. If the truth about either ever leaked . . .

He shuddered.

He heard the door open and looked up to see Harry step through, followed by a handler leading a young male sim by the hand. He'd asked Harry to bring in the highest scoring sim from the latest batch of the special breed.

"Here he is," Harry said. "F27-63—at your service. We call him Seymour." He turned to the handler. "I'll take him now." The handler stepped out.

Harry Carstairs, chief of sim education, had trained more of the creatures than anyone else presently with the company; a big man, six-four at least, and probably weighing in at an eighth of a ton. He towered over the sim.

Ellis glanced down at his desktop memo screen. F27-63—yes, that was Seymour's serial number. He had longer arms and looser lips than the average commercial sim. Smaller too.

"All right," he said. "Let's see what he can do."

"Sit in the red chair, Seymour," Harry said gently. He stood with his hands clasped in front of him, staring straight ahead as he spoke, allowing the sim no hints or cues from his body language.

The sim looked around, spotted the dark red leather chair against the wall, and loped over to seat himself.

"Good. Now turn on the lamp on the opposite side of the room."

The sim rose, crossed in front of Ellis's desk, and stopped before the lamp. He looked under the shade, found the switch, and turned it on.

"Very good," Harry said. "Now—"

"I'm satisfied with his comprehension," Ellis said. Comprehension had never been the problem; he was anxious to cut to the chase. "What about his speech?"

"It's getting there."

"*Getting* there?"

"He's a great signer."

"I'm sure he is."

Sims started ASL lessons in infancy because signing stimulated development of the speech cortex; this helped enormously with vocalization later on.

"Want to see him sign?"

"No," Ellis said, balling a fist in frustration. "I want to hear him speak." He turned to the sim. "What is your name?"

The creature looked at Harry who nodded encouragement.

The sim's thick pink tongue protruded between his yellow teeth as he said, "Thee . . ." in a low-pitched voice.

Ellis was about to say that "Thee" wasn't a name when the sim continued, laboriously pronouncing, "Mmmm . . . mmmm . . ." And then he seemed to run out of gas.

He glanced uncertainly at Harry who smiled and nodded. "You're doing good. Go on."

"Mmmm . . . ," said Seymour, picking up where he'd left off. But he seemed stuck on the sound.

Ellis held up a hand. "All right. He can't say his name. What *can* he say?"

Harry turned to the sim. "Did you have breakfast?"

The sim nodded. "Eth."

"Are you hungry now?"

A head shake. "Oh."

Ellis waited but gathered from the look on Harry's face that the show was over.

"That's it? He's your best and his entire vocabulary consists of two incomplete words and half his name?"

Ellis tried to keep the anger from his voice—none of this was Harry's fault—but still he heard it slip through. Because damn it, he *was* angry. When was he going to see some results? The sim sensed his emotion and shrank back a step.

Harry rested a reassuring hand on the creature's shoulder. "Seymour's doing the best that he can."

Ellis wanted to beat his fists on his desk and scream, *It's not enough! Not nearly enough!* Instead he sighed and leaned back in his swivel chair.

"You don't work them hard enough." Maybe Harry had been around sims too long. An inherently gentle man, maybe he was identifying with them too much, cutting them too much slack. And maybe Harry was thinking about another sim, a special long-ago sim who was gone. "You're too easy on them."

"What do you want me to do?" Harry said, his face darkening. "Whip them?"

"No, of course not." What an awful thought.

"Not Seymour's fault if his hyoid's not up to par with the main breed's."

The hyoid—always the damn hyoid. The little arch of bone that supported the tongue and its muscles was crucial to human speech. Ellis's new lines all lacked a fully developed hyoid bone.

That wasn't the only thing not up to par. "Ever hear of evolutionary synergy, Harry?"

The big man's brow furrowed. "I don't recall . . ."

"You wouldn't have. It's a new theory I've developed as a result of my recent work. It's the subtle, as yet unquantifiable cooperation between genes that have evolved together. It's so subtle that I can't prove it, but I know it's there, I know it's true."

"What's that got to do with Seymour?" Harry said.

"Everything."

"I don't understand."

"I know."

He saw Harry glance at the plastic pill organizer on his desk—three compartments labeled AM, AFT, and PM. Ellis always left it in plain sight, to maintain his image as a heavily medicated eccentric. But the pills were for show. He'd been off medication for quite some time now.

Harry led the sim to the door, signaled for the handler, then closed it after them.

"Mr. Sinclair," he said, approaching the desk. "I work your new breeds harder than the main breed, and—"

"I know you do, Harry." Ellis stared at his hands, bunched into fists. "It's just that it's so damn frustrating."

"*You* think it's frustrating? How about for me and my staff? We slave with these new breeds day after day and get nowhere. And we keep asking ourselves *why* . . . why does the company keep developing breeds that are inferior to the one we already have?"

Not the company, Ellis thought. Me. Just me.

"I can't go into that, Harry."

"Then can you tell me what's wrong with the main breed that you want to correct?"

Everything! Ellis wanted to shout. *Every fucking thing!*

"I'm afraid I can't go into that either."

"It has something to do with the sealed section then." A statement.

The sealed section . . . only a handful of employees in the basic research building knew it existed, and even they didn't know that most of it was underground. No access through the main areas; the only entry and exit was through an enclosed loading dock on the northwest corner of the building. Sealed staff never mixed with other employees; they ate and slept where they worked, leaving only on weekends in enclosed trucks.

This he could answer truthfully. "No, Harry. It does not."

Harry stood silent a moment. "Then what? I would think that I've proven myself loyal enough by now to be entrusted—"

"Please, Harry," Ellis said, holding up a hand. "It's not a question of trust. It's a matter of . . ." Of what? What could he say? "A matter of deciding which way the company should go in the future. We haven't agreed—haven't decided on which way that will be. But when we do, I assure you, you'll be the first to know." Ellis noted that this seemed to salve Harry's wounded pride. "But until then," he added, "bear with the frustration. I promise you, it will be well worth it in the end."

If I succeed.

Harry's smile was lopsided. "I'll trust you on that."

Harry left and Ellis was alone with the chrome-framed faces of his children staring at him across the desktop. Robbie and Julie . . . God, he missed them. Somewhere along the course of his consuming monomania he'd forgotten about them. He didn't know exactly when he'd metamorphosed from husband and father to something other, something distant . . . obsessed . . . a shadow . . . a ghost drifting through their lives, through his own life as well. But Judy and the kids hadn't been able to live with what he'd become, and so he'd lost them.

He wasn't bitter though. Just lonely. Didn't blame Judy. He'd deserved to lose them. But he was working toward getting them back—*earning* them back.

And when he deserved to have them call him father again, he knew he'd win them back.

But not until he'd fixed SimGen.

11

The green room of the *Ackenbury at Large* show was neither green nor roomy, but Patrick had it to himself. Half a dozen upholstered chairs surrounded a maple table that had seen better days; a small refrigerator against the wall sported a fruit bowl and a coffee maker. A wall-mounted monitor leaned from a corner near the ceiling; Patrick repeatedly glanced at it as he paced the beige carpet.

Reverend Eckert was running his line for the late-night network TV audience, but in a far lower key than on his own show. Instead of working himself into a red-faced, spittle-flecked frenzy, he was coming on as a calm, intelligent man with a mission: SimGen was doing evil by producing sims, and so it had to be shut down. Any products made by sims were the devil's handiwork and all God-fearing people should shun them.

Not good, Patrick thought, drying his moist palms on his slacks.

That was the role Patrick had planned to play—a calm, reasonable, compassionate counterpoint to Eckert's frenzy.

Now what?

Maybe this hadn't been such a good idea.

Upon leaving the sims this morning he'd placed a call to Ackenbury's offices. After being shuttled around for a good ten minutes, he'd finally found himself on the line with one Catherine Tresor, assistant producer. She didn't recognize his name, but when he explained that he was the attorney for the sims union, she jumped all over the idea of putting him on tonight's show. She said she'd have to run it by Alan first, but she'd get back to him right away.

She wasn't kidding. Less than five minutes later his car phone rang and he was scheduled for the show. But she told him not to trumpet the news. Alan wanted to surprise the Reverend Eckert.

As a result, Patrick had been ushered into an empty office when he'd arrived at six—the show was recorded hours before air time—and kept out of sight until the Reverend had gone on. After a quick trip to makeup, he was led to the green room and left alone.

He wished Pam were here. He'd asked her to come along but she had to work late. She was involved in some Pacific Rim deal that would tie her up till midnight. She'd promised to watch at her office, though. She sounded as though she'd recovered from this morning. Patrick was glad for that.

"Mr. Sullivan?"

Patrick looked up. In the doorway he saw a short, owlish, clipboard-toting woman with large round glasses. She extended her hand.

"I'm Cathy Tresor."

"And I'm wondering if this was such a good idea," Patrick said, shaking her hand.

She squeezed his fingers. "You're not backing out, are you?"

"It's not as if you need me," he said, wondering at the panicky look that flashed across her features. "I wasn't even on the horizon until I called this morning."

"We do need you," she said. Her blue eyes looked huge through her thick lenses. "*I* need you."

"I'm not following."

"I pitched your appearance with the Reverend as my own idea."

Patrick stared at her. "Let me get this straight: You take my suggestion, pitch it to your boss as your own brainstorm, and pocket the credit?"

She bit her upper lip. "Well . . . yeah." She looked away. "Sorry, but it can be hard to get noticed around here."

"Sorry!" He laughed. "Don't be sorry. I love it! Just remember the name: Patrick Sullivan. You owe me one."

She smiled. "I'll remember."

"You do that." Patrick liked her. Then he glanced at the monitor and sobered at the sight of Eckert's face. "And while you're at it, figure out a way for me to steal that guy's thunder."

"Best way is to get under his skin. Goad him."

"You don't mean that."

"You kidding? We'd love it. 'Let's you and him fight'—that's the Alan Ackenbury philosophy of quality TV."

Patrick jammed his hands into his pockets and did a slow circuit of the green room.

Goad him . . . how?

Patrick's gaze came to rest on the fruit bowl and an idea sparked . . . a last resort if nothing else worked.

"Almost time," Cathy said, glancing at her watch. "You go on after the next break. Let's get you in position."

He followed her down a hall and to a spot behind a curtain just off stage. Patrick's eyes fixed on the blank monitor.

"You've got one segment," she whispered as they came out of the commercial break. "Make the most of it."

"For your sake or mine?"

"For both of us, but more for you than me. Think of this as an audition of sorts. If you make sparks fly, Alan will want you back, and that will be good for your cause."

My cause? Patrick thought, then realized she was referring to the sim union. He'd never thought of it as a cause, just a case, a job.

He said nothing, though, because his gut had begun to twitch as Alan Ackenbury reappeared on the monitor screen. He opened the segment by saying that a last-minute opportunity had arisen to bring on a guest who could provide a counterpoint to the reverend's views.

Eckert muttered something to the effect that he'd understood he'd be the only guest. Ackenbury didn't seem to hear, or pretended he didn't, and introduced Patrick.

He felt Cathy's hand against his back, pushing him toward the stage.

"That's you," she said. "You're on!"

And then Patrick was out in the open, feeling the heat of the lights, hearing polite applause from the studio audience.

The first few minutes were a blur . . . Patrick had always considered *Ackenbury at Large* a punning reference to the host's Orson Welles–class girth, and in person Alan was even larger than he appeared on screen. He didn't rise, but extended his hand across the desk as Patrick arrived. Instead of the traditional desk and couch set-up, the Ackenbury show seated guests on either side of its host who could then mediate the fray when they went at it. The barrier also prevented guests from coming to blows if the discussion became too heated.

Patrick was aware of Reverend Eckert pouting and sulking on the far side of the desk as Alan asked questions about the coming court battle to unionize the Beacon Ridge sims. Patrick didn't mention that the case was as good as stillborn with Boughton on the bench, simply reeled off the canned responses he'd spouted to the press since the news first broke.

He felt as if he were on automatic pilot at first, answering the questions by rote. But as minutes passed—minutes in which he noticed Alan Ackenbury's growing dissatisfaction with his flat, tempered answers—Patrick felt himself begin to relax. He remembered to mention the toll-free number and the website, www.simunion.org, and was casting about for a way to juice up the proceedings when his fellow guest did it for him.

"Admit it," the Reverend Eckert said, pointing across the desk. "You work for SinGen."

"Absolutely not," Patrick said. "In fact, I expect SimGen to do its damnedest to stop me." He quickly added: "That's why contributions to 1-800-SIMUNION are so vital."

"You have no idea of what's really going on, do you? Or who is chairman of the board of SinGen?"

"Mercer Sinclair."

"No! It's Satan! Satan himself—his very own self! Satan calls the shots in SinGen! And Satan has defiled the exalted holy clay of man by mixing it with the life stuff of a monkey. Through SinGen, Satan has defiled the pinnacle of the Lord's creation!"

"Depends on how you look at it," Patrick said. "You're seeing the glass as half-empty. Why not look at it as half-full? Why not see sims as a lower life form that's been improved?"

"Improved? You cannot improve on God's work! You can only defile it! Especially when you take the life stuff of man, the only being in the universe to possess an immortal soul, and degrade it by injecting it into a lesser being!"

"But a being with a shared ancestor."

"Are you talking evolution? That's blasphemy! God created man *de novo*—that means completely new!"

"Then why do humans share all but one-point-six percent of their DNA with the chimps that sims are made from? If God made humans 'de novo,' as you say, and wanted us to stand out from the crowd, wanted us to be the shining star atop the Christmas tree of his creations, you'd think he'd have come up with a new and special kind of 'clay'—not stuff borrowed from primates."

"He did! He—"

"No, he didn't. Genetically we're ninety-eight-point-four percent chimp—which means we're far more ape than human."

"Speak for yourself, sir."

As the audience laughed, Patrick grinned and gave the Rev a thumbs-up. "Good one. But it doesn't alter the fact that only a few genes separate us from the trees. And even fewer separate us from sims. If chimps are our distant cousins, then sims are our nieces and nephews."

"I will not tolerate this!" He turned to Ackenbury. "Is this why you brought this man on tonight? Had I known I was to share the stage with a blasphemer who would mock my beliefs and the beliefs of my followers, mock the Lord Himself, I never would have agreed to appear."

"No insult intended, Reverend," Ackenbury said. "Just a fair airing of all sides of an issue. You have your beliefs, and Mr. Sullivan has his."

"No! My beliefs are supported by the Word of God!"

And then the Rev was off on such a tear that not even the host could get a word in edgewise. Patrick's mind raced, at a loss as to how to salvage the situation; then he remembered the bananas he'd snagged from the fruit bowl in the green room.

His original idea had been to offer one to Eckert in an ostensibly friendly gesture, assuming no one would miss the reference to their shared simian ancestry. But subtlety wouldn't fly here; he'd have to fire all barrels at once to break the Rev's filibuster. And he had an idea of how to do that. Question was, did he dare? This could backfire and leave him looking like a grade-A jerk.

What the hell, he thought. Go for it.

Slowly, Patrick raised his legs until his feet were on the chair cushion. Squatting on the seat, he pulled out one of the bananas and, with exaggerated care, began to peel it.

Neither Ackenbury nor the Rev noticed at first, but the audience did. As laughter began to filter in from the darkness beyond the stage lights, Ackenbury turned to him; his eyebrows shot up in surprise, then he grinned. The Reverend Eckert followed the host's stare. His tirade faltered, then stopped cold as his jaw dropped open. The audience roared.

It had worked—the Rev finally had shut up. But Patrick couldn't jump into the gap because his mouth was crammed full of banana. He did the only thing he could think of. Returning to Plan A, he pulled the second banana from his coat pocket and handed it to Ackenbury.

"For me?" the big man said as he took it.

Patrick shook his head and pointed to Eckert.

"Of course," Ackenbury said, winking at Patrick, and handed the banana to the Rev.

Eckert shot to his feet and batted the banana away, sending it skittering across the desk.

"This is an outrage! I did not come here to be mocked! I refuse to stand for another minute of this!"

So saying, he wheeled and stormed from the stage.

"Reverend?" Ackenbury said, calling after him but with little conviction.

"That's okay," Patrick said after swallowing the last of his mouthful of banana. "I'm sure he's just hurrying off to phone in his donation to 1-800-SIMUNION before the lines get jammed."

Ackenbury was laughing as he turned to face the camera. "I'm afraid that's about all we have time for tonight," he said as if nothing the slightest out of the ordinary happened. "As usual, I hope you were entertained, and I hope you learned something as well. Until tomorrow night then."

As the outro music began, Ackenbury picked up the spurned banana, peeled it, and took a bite. The studio audience went wild. He leaned toward Patrick and extended his hand.

"You, sir," he said, grinning, "have a standing invitation to return anytime you wish."

Patrick didn't know how true that was, but he pretended to take it at face value. "I may be taking you up on that."

"Do. Just call Cathy Tresor."

As a stagehand came over and helped the host haul his huge frame out of the seat, Patrick felt a hand on his shoulder. He turned and saw Cathy beaming at him.

"You did *great!*"

"I hope so," he said. "I'm sort of new at this."

She fairly bounced along as she led him backstage and seated him in the green room, which he again had all to himself. She told him she'd find someone from makeup to stop by and clean him up—better that than run into the Reverend in the hallway. *Ackenbury at Large* liked to confine its conflicts to the onstage area.

As he sat alone, wondering if any of this would have a beneficial effect on the sim defense fund, he sensed movement in the doorway. He turned and found the Reverend Eckert, backed up by a steroidal slab of beef with 'bodyguard' written all over him.

Oh, shit, Patrick thought. He's come to mess me up.

"You've got cojones, Mr. Sullivan," Eckert said, hands on hips. "I'll have to give you credit for that."

"Hey, now listen," Patrick said, backing up a step. "None of that was personal. I didn't—"

But the Rev surprised him by grinning and thrusting out his hand.

"Course you didn't. It's all show biz. I understand that. Quite a scene stealer you pulled at the end there. Yessir, stole my fire good. But I'm not mad. I had my say. In fact, the reason I stopped by is I'd like to thank you for what you did."

"Thank me?"

"Yes! Just got a call from church headquarters. Our prayer lines have been ringing off the hook! Praise the Lord, never have we had such an outpouring of support. The money is all but flying through the window. And all because of you."

Hope my line is doing the same, Patrick thought. But was Eckert crazy?

"Why thank me?"

" 'Cause caller after caller's been saying they want me to keep spreading the word that they ain't monkeys." He shook his head, beaming. "The Lord works in mysterious ways, don't he. I thank Him every day, but tonight I want to thank you too. God bless you, Mr. Sullivan."

"No hard feelings then?"

"Not a bit. Hard to be mad at someone who reminds you so much of yourself. You get tired of this lawyering and unionizing business, you come to me. I promise to have a place for you."

He gave Patrick's hand another squeeze and then he was gone. Patrick stood dumbstruck. Probably looked like Eckert had when he'd spotted him with the banana.

What a strange man. Patrick had expected a punch in the nose; instead he'd received a handshake and hearty thanks and a job offer. To do what? Take their act on the road and charge admission?

Hard to be mad at someone who reminds you so much of yourself . . .

The words echoed jarringly in Patrick's head.

Like you? he thought. Not a chance. I'm nothing like you.

But was he so sure? The possibility made him queasy.

12

Romy lay in bed in her apartment in the Cobble Hill section of Brooklyn. The *Ackenbury at Large* closing credits had just begun to roll when her PCA chimed.

"Are you alone?" said Zero's voice.

"Aren't I always?"

"You really need to get more of a life, Romy."

"Maybe I'm waiting for you to take off that mask."

"It's off."

"And if I were there, would I like what I saw?"

"I doubt it very much."

She laughed. "Come on—"

"Romy . . ." He sighed. "You don't seem to be enjoying life."

"You sound like my mother."

She and her mother still spoke three or four times a week. Her parents divorced when she was a teen—her fault, she knew—and her mother had never remarried. But she had a job, men friends, women friends, a bridge club. In other words, a life.

So do I, Romy thought. Sort of.

She had her job at OPRR. She had her ballet—she'd spent two hours working out on the bar tonight and had the sore hips to prove it—and she had Zero and the organization. But beyond that . . .

Friends were a problem. Always had been. She'd had no girlfriends growing up—her wild mood swings saw to that—and still had trouble being one of the girls. As for men, she had plenty of offers, and she'd had her flings, but most of them seemed tissue thin. Nobody with a fraction of Zero's substance.

She *had* a life, damn it. Getting justice for the sims—wasn't that enough?

But it was so frustrating. She'd read up on the civil rights movements of the fifties and sixties, looking for inspiration. But that had been different.

Those seeking justice then had been human, and could march in the streets to demand it. Sims weren't human, and the idea of joining a movement or even a single protest march was completely beyond them.

So people like her and Zero had to work behind the scenes.

"Were you watching?" Zero said.

"Of course."

Usually she did the early-to-bed/early-to-rise thing, but tonight she'd stayed up to see how Reverend Eckert came across; like everyone else, she had been stunned by Patrick Sullivan's sudden appearance.

"What did you think?" Zero said.

"First tell me if you knew Sullivan was going to appear."

"Not a clue. But I'm glad he did."

"So am I . . . I think."

"He said things that needed saying. And anyone who pushes sims closer to humans in the public consciousness does us a service. SimGen is always pushing the other way."

"But squatting on the chair and eating that banana . . . do you think he went too far?"

"You mean, how did he play in the bleachers?"

"Exactly."

"Well, only time will tell. But I have to admit that Patrick Sullivan has risen in my estimation."

"Why? He's still a quick-buck artist. Did you hear how many times he managed to mention his 800 number?"

"But he projects a good image, plus he's audacious and thinks well on his feet. I like that."

Romy had to admit that Zero had a point. Sullivan had come across well—more like a crusading attorney with a wild sense of humor than a zealot or opportunist.

"I still think he'll cut and run as soon as the opposition stiffens," she said. "And if what we hear about this judge assigned to the case is true, he's going to run into a brick wall next week. And then it's sayonara sims."

Zero sighed. "You're probably right. But I've learned, sometimes to my delight, sometimes to my chagrin, that people aren't always as predictable as they seem. Patterns of behavior can be misinterpreted. And tonight I thought I caught a glimpse of something in our Mr. Sullivan, a spark of stubbornness that may work to our advantage. We'll simply keep a careful eye on him and watch for developments."

"I guess we don't have much of a choice, do we."

"Unfortunately not." Zero paused, then, "Are you ready for tomorrow?"

She'd scheduled the first leg of OPRR's inspection tour of SimGen's main facility to begin at 1:00 P.M.

"I suppose so. I just hope it accomplishes something. After all, you've had people in SimGen itself for years, and they haven't been able to learn much."

"That's because they're low- or mid-level employees, and because SimGen's cellular corporate structure reduces crossovers between divisions. They see only a tiny piece of the picture. That's been our problem all along. Everything about that company has been designed for maximum security. Look at where it's located: The hills protect it from ground surveillance, and a fly-over offers only a momentary glimpse. If we had access to a spy satellite we might learn something, but we don't."

"How about a hot-air balloon?"

"A couple of reporters tried that, remember? SimGen's copters buzzed them so much they damn near crashed."

"I was only kidding." Romy took a deep breath to ease the growing tension in her chest. "So it's all on me."

"You'll do fine. Even if you uncover one tidbit over the next few days, one little thing that OPRR can use to call the company's practices into question, it could lead to slowing or even stopping their assembly-line cloning of sims. If nothing else, this inspection has to shake them up a little. So far they've managed to insulate themselves from regulatory oversight. This is a first for them. They'll be nervous."

"And I've planned something that just might add a little extra rattle to their cages."

"Good. Maybe they'll slip up."

"We can only hope."

"I'll call again tomorrow night—on the secure PCA I'll have delivered to your apartment in the morning."

"Why? Are you worried about a tap?"

"Not yet, but after you begin sticking your nose into SimGen's sanctum tomorrow, I'll bet they'll want to learn everything they can about you."

Romy shook off a chill creeping over her shoulders. "Thanks. That's a pleasant thought."

"Sleep well, Romy."

"Sure."

She hung up, told the TV to turn itself off, and lay in the darkness. But sleep wouldn't come. Instead of throttling back, her mind raced along, veering in all directions.

She wondered at the turn her life had taken and if she might be courting futility. It didn't seem possible that Zero and the organization had much of a chance of denting SimGen, let alone toppling it, and yet he persisted. And so did she. But sometimes she felt like one of many Sancho Panzas helping this enigmatic Quixote tilt at windmills.

She'd have to be on her toes at SimGen tomorrow, staying alert not simply to what was going on around her, but to what was happening within her. She might encounter something that upset her and she didn't want it to set her off. She had to be the picture of professionalism.

The doctors had said her bipolar disorder was cured, but she knew better. She'd had no violent outbursts since her treatment, but that didn't mean she hadn't come close.

There'd been two Romys in the bad old days—the studious, compliant, Reasonable Romy, and the fierce, wild, Raging Romy. Raging Romy was supposedly gone, but Romy still heard echoes of her footsteps down the corridors of her mind.

She closed her eyes and fell into a dream dredged from an incident in her childhood. Romy had been an Air Force brat with an American pilot father and a German mother. They moved around a lot and it always seemed as soon as Romy just started getting used to a new place, her father would be transferred to another base in another state.

The dream involved the time when she was nine or ten and came upon a couple of the local boys throwing rocks at a lame old dog who'd dared to bark at them from its yard. But it wasn't a dog in the dream—it was a sim. Her dream rage was as fresh and hot and sudden as it had been all those years ago when she'd charged into those boys with flailing fists. That had been Raging Romy's debut. And in the dream, just as in real life, she sent one of the terrified boys running home with a bloody nose, and had the other on the ground, bashing him with a rock and screaming at him, *How do you like it? How do you like it?* and not stopping until someone pulled her off.

In real life he'd told his parents, who threatened Romy's folks with a lawsuit if they didn't "do something about that girl." The first of many such threats during the years to come.

And in real life the owner had come out of the house to thank her. But here in the dream, the owner came out, but it wasn't old Mrs. Moore, it was Patrick Sullivan. And there, right in front of her, he sold that old sim to a man from the university to be used in medical experiments . . .

Romy awoke sobbing.

13

"I understand what you're saying, miss, but I can't find your name on the list."

The young guard at the gate, so young his face still sported a few pimples, looked flustered as he stood outside his kiosk, staring at his hand-held computer; he pushed buttons and stared again, shaking his head.

Romy felt sorry for him but couldn't let that show. She'd shoved the court papers in his face, demanding entrance, and now she glared at him from the driver's seat of her car.

"Then call someone who *can* find my name," she said through clenched teeth, "or I'll shut this whole damn place down and you'll be lucky if you find a job pumping gas in downtown Paterson!"

He ducked inside his kiosk and made a hurried phone call. A moment later he stepped out and pointed to a small parking area to her right.

"Pull over there, please. Someone's coming down."

Muttering unintelligibly under her breath, Romy complied. Then she turned off her engine, leaned back, and smiled. This was working out just as she'd planned.

Minutes later a small four-seater helicopter lifted over the wooded rise dead ahead and buzzed toward her. It set down in the field on the far side of the road. A man stepped out of the front passenger seat and strode toward her. He didn't duck as most people do while under the whirling blades, didn't have to clutch a hat to his head because he was bareheaded, didn't have to worry about the vortex mussing his hair because it was cut too short to matter. He walked erect, purposefully, but with no sense of urgency, as if he knew within a centimeter the locations of the blades slicing the air above his scalp.

The word *military* flashed in Romy's brain like a neon sign as she took in his broad shoulders, measured step, straight spine. Or at least ex-military. She put him in his early forties. And judging from his skin tones, black hair and eyes, Romy bet on a heavy Latino ancestry. Not a bad-looking man. Attractive in an animal sort of way.

"Ms. Cadman," he said as he reached her car. He didn't smile, didn't offer his hand. "We weren't expecting you so early."

"According to your gate man you weren't expecting me at all."

"He only has the morning list. Your arrival is scheduled for one o'clock."

"One o'clock?" she said. "Ridiculous! Why would I waste half a day?"

He pulled open her car door. "Step out, please."

He said it like a cop. Romy saw no reason why not, so she swiveled in her seat—giving him a good shot of her legs before she adjusted her skirt—and stood before him.

Maybe that had been a mistake. A shiver ran over her skin as his eyes raked her blazer, blouse, and skirt. She'd seen eyes like that before. On a crocodile. She felt naked.

"You'll want this next, I suppose," she said, fumbling for her OPRR ID card and handing it to him.

"You read my mind," he said as he took the card. A smile tugged at the corners of his mouth but didn't quite make it to his eyes. "That could mean trouble." He handed it back. "Welcome to SimGen, Ms. Cadman. I'm Luca Portero, Chief of Security here."

"The head man? Should I be flattered?"

She'd read up on a number of the key people in SimGen, and Luca Portero was one of them. She'd never seen him, but knew his folder: Army Special Forces, decorated in Afghanistan, honorable discharge with the rank of sergeant after twenty years in; hired by SimGen within weeks of his discharge.

"A visit from OPRR is an occasion."

"Get used to it," she said. "If I have my way, we'll be here every week."

His smile froze, then faded. "We'll use the copter to take us to the center of the campus. It's faster."

"I'm here today as vanguard for the full inspection team; to do that I must see the facilities firsthand—from ground level."

"Of course. We'll pick up a car at center campus and continue from there."

Once inside the helicopter, conversation was impossible, especially with Romy in the rear and Portero up front next to the pilot. The security chief spent the time talking into his headset, and did not look happy.

So Romy took in the scenery. The trees were showing off their vivid fall colors but she could not let that distract her. She was looking for concealed roads, hidden installations, anything not visible in the aerial photos that might escape OPRR inspection. But she saw nothing.

Romy caught her breath as the copter cleared a hill and the center of the SimGen campus flashed into view. The glass sides of the buildings, none taller than six stories, picked up the hues of the neighboring hillsides and made them their own, integrating the manmade structures into their surroundings. As much as she hated the company, she had to admit it appeared to be a beautiful place to work.

She knew the layout of the campus by heart and immediately identified the taller executive and administration buildings. She wasn't interested in those; her inspection team would be focusing on the natal center, the sim dormitories and training centers, and the two research buildings—general and basic.

Zero had told her he was particularly interested in the basic research facility. He'd mentioned mysterious shipments in and out of an enclosed loading dock near its northwest corner, and that only a select few were allowed anywhere near the place. But was that all he knew? Was the basic research facility so secret even his high-up contacts didn't know what went on inside . . . or wouldn't tell him? Or did Zero already know and want OPRR to expose it?

What could they be doing in there that was so sensitive? Her mind flashed lurid images of experiments on human subjects, or Doctor Moreau–type vivisections, or hideous failed splices, locked in cages with their claws or tentacles reaching through the bars. She doubted it was anything that exciting. And she'd find out soon enough, wouldn't she.

Squinting against the glare of the morning sun, she located the building and spotted a medium-size delivery truck backing into a shedlike structure jutting from its flank. She reached for the binoculars in her shoulder bag— the set with a spycam concealed within—but changed her mind. She might find a better use for them later—no sense in letting Portero know now that she'd brought them along.

As she watched, a corrugated steel door rolled down, sealing the truck in the shed.

Romy could understand the need for an enclosed loading dock on a windy winter day, but the weather was positively balmy this morning. The only other purpose would be to conceal what was being loaded or unloaded.

When the copter landed, Portero led her to a blue Jeep Geronimo, one of many wheeling through the campus.

"Do you buy these by the dozen?" she asked.

"Four-wheel drive is not a luxury here, especially in the winter. When it snows in these hills, it *snows*."

Once they were seated within he gave her another penetrating up-and-down look. "Are all the OPRR investigators so beautiful?"

Puh-*leese*! Romy thought. She wanted to tell him to save his imagined wit and charm but decided it might be best not to acknowledge the compliment.

"I'm considered OPRR's plain Jane," she said brusquely. "I'd like to begin with the research facilities."

Portero started the engine. "They're not ready for you yet. We'll start with the natal center."

"I prefer research first, then natal. It's a more natural progression."

"If it was up to me, I'd take you anywhere you want to go," he said.

Why don't I believe that?

He went on: "And if you'd arrived at your scheduled time, I'd be wheeling us there right now. But the powers that be say that if you insist on starting with research, you can wait in one of our empty offices until one o'clock and start then. But if you wish to get to work immediately, natal is available."

Score one for you, Romy thought, hiding her frustration. After all, she was a professional.

"Very well. Natal it is."

But don't look so smug, she thought as she watched Portero put the Jeep in gear. The game has just begun.

14

The Natal Center—intellectually she'd been prepared for it, but emotionally . . .

Anne Twerlinger, associate director of the center, was a reed-thin middle-aged redhead who stank of cigarettes, wore retro pointy-framed glasses, and spoke with what Romy could only describe as a sniff in her tone, as if convinced that at any moment her nostrils might be assailed by a noxious odor.

Portero had stayed behind in Twerlinger's office, making phone calls, while she started the tour by leading Romy down a narrow corridor. The right wall was glass from waist to ceiling, and looked in on the natal center's cloning lab.

"I'm sure I don't have to tell you about the sim genome," Twerlinger said, then proceeded to do just that. "As everyone knows, it consists of twenty-two chromosome pairs—one fewer than humans, two fewer than chimps; much of the junk and non-functioning genetic material has been removed, leaving it one of the cleanest mammalian genomes in existence. Sims don't mate, mainly because we've genetically reduced their sex drives to nil; but even if they did, no offspring would be produced because their ova cannot be fertilized."

"Why not have just one sex?" Romy said.

"Because we're all conditioned to view work as gender specific: We're comfortable with females cleaning houses, males loading trucks. And SimGen is nothing if not sensitive to the marketplace."

"Why should the females have ovaries at all?"

"We'd rather they didn't, of course, but we've found that a regular hormone cycle is necessary to their accelerated maturation process." She waved tobacco-stained fingers at the masked and gowned workers on the far side of the glass. "New sims are cloned by nuclear transfer from a bank of identical cells, and implanted in a special class of females we call breeders. Breeder sims are as sterile as their sisters, but exist for one purpose: to incubate new sims."

They came to the end of the corridor. Twerlinger pushed through into a much larger space: wide, long, its low ceiling studded with recessed fluorescents. The place was huge—the size of a football field at least, and filled with beds. It might have been the world's largest homeless shelter except that it was filled with sims instead of humans.

Pregnant sims.

"My God," Romy said. "And you have three floors like this?"

"And two more identical buildings with a fourth under construction. We can't keep up with the demand. We've begun building natal centers abroad now. The one in Poznan is almost complete."

They ambled among the beds, arranged in clusters around common areas with sinks and toilets. Twerlinger pointed to partitioning walls rising not quite to the ceiling throughout the space.

"We divide our breeders up by how far along they are. Early, middle, late gestation: eight months overall." She spread her arms. "OPRR will find nothing to complain about here, Ms. Cadman. Breeders lead lives of pampered ease. They do not do a lick of work their entire lives."

"But they engage in labor of another sort."

A sniff. "I suppose you might put it that way."

Most of the mothers-to-be Romy passed were either napping or lounging together on sofas, watching TV.

"They look bored out of their minds."

"Breeders are provided excellent nutrition and get adequate exercise," the assistant director said as if she hadn't heard.

"And what of labor and delivery?"

"Would you like to see a delivery? I can guarantee that a number are in progress as we speak."

"I'll leave that to the team. But how does labor go?"

Twerlinger shrugged. "The breeders rarely need sedation, but if they do, they get it. Our breeder sims receive better obstetrical care than a lot of humans, Ms. Cadman."

"And after delivery?"

"It's usually single offspring, but we're beginning to have some success with increasing the incidence of twins. Once we perfect that we can double output."

"I'm surprised you don't simply clone them and incubate them ex-utero."

"We tried that. Believe me, we tried that every which way imaginable, but the resultant offspring were much less tractable and far less emotionally stable than the ones gestated in utero. That's the one thing we guarantee our lessees: stable and dependable workers. So . . ." She smiled here, a fleeting flash of yellowed teeth. ". . . we do it the old-fashioned way."

"And you still allow a mother to stay with her child?"

Twerlinger nodded. "For a year; we find the offspring adapt faster in that year when the breeders are around to help train them. And we encourage all breeders to nurse because that seems to make for healthier and more emotionally stable offspring."

"And then what?"

"We immunize them against the usual diseases. Chimps get polio and hepatitis and HIV, though they don't develop AIDS. Sims are even more susceptible. Then the offspring are PRC'd and moved on into the dormitories to start their training."

"Pee-are . . . ?"

Twerlinger touched the nape of Romy's neck. Her fingers were ice cold. "Tattooed with their serial number bar code. You've seen them, of course."

"Of course." She'd just never thought of babies being tattooed.

"It's the only way we can accurately monitor inventory."

"And the mothers?"

"Breeders, please. It's tempting to anthropomorphize them, but we discourage it. Counterproductive, you know. Certain segments of the public get all caught up in their superficial human characteristics—"

"Well, they aren't exactly white rats."

"True, but when you come down to it, sims are *livestock*, nothing more."

Romy looked around at the bored, hopeless expressions on the . . . breeders. "Nothing more."

"As for the breeders, after a year with their offspring, they're rotated back to be impregnated again."

Romy ground her teeth, biting back a tirade. She wanted to shout that they were too close to human to be treated as walking, talking incubators, to have their children—not offspring, *children!*—torn from them and then be impregnated again . . . and again . . . and again . . .

But she couldn't let on how she felt. Zero had warned her about that: Never let them know, or your status in OPRR could be compromised.

She let out the breath she'd been holding. "That means every twenty months or so—"

"Yes, that's the cycle. A hearty breeder can go through ten to twelve cycles before she's retired."

"Or just plain tired."

What an existence, Romy thought as she looked around at the lethargic breeders. Most sims in her experience tended to be full of life and energy. These seemed barely able to move. And suddenly she knew why.

"They're depressed," Romy said.

Twerlinger arched her thin eyebrows. "I wasn't aware you had training in sim psychology."

No, but I know depression, lady—firsthand and big time.

"Don't need any to realize it's an unavoidable emotional fallout from being repeatedly separated from their children."

"Ridiculous."

"Chimps, orangutans, gorillas—all mourn the loss of a child. Why should sims be any different? In fact they'd be *more* likely to mourn."

Twerlinger sniffed. "Do animal emotional states fall under OPRR's aegis?"

They didn't. They both knew that.

Disappointed, Romy followed Twerlinger back to her office. She hadn't found a thing. Maybe the full-team inspection would come up with something, but she'd struck out.

She found Portero waiting for her.

"Finished here?" he said.

"For now. Research next."

His smile tried to look sympathetic as he shook his head. "As I told you, research is scheduled for this afternoon. The dormitories and training centers are next on the list." He gave a helpless shrug.

Somehow, helpless didn't fit with Luca Portero.

As she followed the security chief back to the Jeep she wondered if the judge had lowered the boom on the sim union yet.

15

WESTCHESTER COUNTY, NY

Patrick felt no tension, no sense of suspense as Judge Boughton prepared to make his judgment. He'd been in a blue-black mood since he and Maggie Fischer, his secretary, had entered the federal courthouse in White Plains. As far as anyone was concerned, it was a done deal. Tony Hodges, the attorney for Beacon Ridge, had submitted well-researched motions that would have swayed a neutral judge; for a union hater like Boughton, they were like tossing gasoline on a bonfire. Add to that the amicus brief filed by SimGen on the club's behalf, and the opposition had a slam dunk. The company's legal howitzer, Abel Voss himself, looking like a cat about to be served a plateful of canaries, was seated two rows behind the defense table.

Maggie gave him a reassuring smile. A matronly forty-five, with curly brown hair and a hawklike nose, she sat straight-spined with her pen poised over her yellow pad. She was a *great* legal secretary and he hoped her two boys stayed in college forever so she'd never be able to quit.

"It will all be over soon," she said, sounding like a dental assistant before an extraction.

That was what the firm wanted, and so that was what Maggie thought he wanted. And as much as Patrick loathed the idea of defeat, a traitorous part of him was looking forward to Judge Boughton's inevitable ruling. It didn't know why he'd got himself into this, and now it wanted out.

But losing didn't sit right. Never would.

The donation hotline already seemed to have called it quits. It had experienced a nice twenty-four-hour spike after his Ackenbury appearance, but then dropped to barely a trickle.

Then he'd had a call from his father after the Ackenbury show—a long message on his answering machine he hadn't returned yet—that could be summed up as: *My son wants to unionize monkeys!?!?!?*

And the cherry on the soured whipped cream of this unwieldy concoction was the precarious state of his relationship with Pamela. She hadn't found his stunt on *Ackenbury at Large* the least bit amusing—"You made an ass out of yourself, Patrick!" She wanted him out of the sim case too. She'd decided to sleep at her own place last night. He hoped to coax her back tonight. After all, the window was fixed, and the cops were keeping an eye on the house.

He tried to imagine how things could get much worse.

He looked up as he heard the judge clear his throat. Boughton's wrinkled hatchet face reminded Patrick of an aged Edward Everett Horton stripped of any trace of humor.

"I'll make this short and sweet, gentlemen, since we all have busy schedules."

Here it comes, Patrick thought.

"I have read the arguments, such as they are, that have been presented to the court, and although my personal beliefs lean the opposite way, I have not been sufficiently persuaded to grant Beacon Ridge a declaratory judgment."

Patrick was reaching for his briefcase, preparing to gather up his papers and slink away when the key word sunk in.

Not? Did Boughton say, *not*?

He saw Maggie's stunned expression, glanced over at the defense table and saw Hodges on his feet, protesting to the judge, and Abel Voss seated behind him, pale with shock.

He did! Boughton denied the judgment!

Fighting the urge to pump his fist in the air and cheer, Patrick focused on Boughton's response to Hodges.

"No sense in getting your blood pressure up, Mr. Hodges," Boughton was saying. "I sympathize with your position, and concur on many of your points, but I believe larger issues are at stake here. At the very heart of this matter lies the question of the legal status of sims. We accord animals certain rights in this society—protection against cruelty and neglect, for instance—and if sims were mere chimpanzees, they would be covered by those laws. But sims are something more than chimps; sims did not exist when the laws protecting animals were framed; sims are not a product of normal evolution or natural selection. So how do we classify them?"

"I believe the United States Congress directly addressed that when it passed legislation—"

"I'm well aware of that legislation, Mr. Hodges. But I believe areas exist within current law that remain open to interpretation. And I believe there might even be questions as to whether congress overstepped its bounds when it passed that law. That sims are something more than animals is, I believe, beyond question; and yet because they are decidedly less than human, they cannot automatically be accorded those inalienable rights guaranteed by the Constitution. So where do they fit? What rights *do* they have?"

"If it please the court," said Abel Voss, standing now. "Sims are a commercial product, owned by SimGen Corporation. They are private property, your honor."

"As were slaves in the Old South," Boughton said, gazing askance at Voss over the top of his reading gasses. "But that changed, didn't it."

"Sims are not human, your honor, so how can they form a union?"

"If you did your homework, Mr. Voss, you'd know that the NLRB statutes—written long before the first sim was created—refer to 'persons.' The word 'human' is never mentioned. Of course sims are not human, but does that automatically mean they are not persons? An interesting question, don't you think? One that will have to be decided by the NLRB and, eventually I have no doubt, by the Supreme Court. Sit down, Mr. Voss."

Boughton looked at Hodges, then shifted his gaze to Patrick. He shook his head and smiled.

"Look at those confounded expressions. What a shame. If you'd read my rulings a little more carefully, you'd have seen this coming. You will find I am nothing if not consistent."

He rapped his gavel and began reeling off a list of dates that Patrick couldn't follow. Good thing Maggie was here. At the moment he was too stunned to hold a pen. He glanced over and saw Hodges and Voss with their heads together, undoubtedly planning an appeal.

This was going to be a protracted fight, but amazingly he'd won the first round.

Later, on the way out of the courthouse, Maggie said, "What are we going to do?"

Good question. A defeat would have solved so many problems, and yet . . . he felt exhilarated, downright jubilant.

"Do? As long as we're still alive, we're going to run with it, as hard and fast as we can."

"Really? But the partners—"

"I'll handle them."

He already had an angle worked out. He'd explain to Kraft that as much as he wanted out of the case, it would look bad for Pecht & Hayes if they dropped the sims on the heels of a favorable ruling.

But the truth was, this morning's victory had energized him. He wanted to see how far he could take this. Not just for the settlement—which had just moved a few steps closer to a real possibility—but for the *doing* itself.

"I'm glad," Maggie said, touching his arm. "Those poor things have no one to speak for them. This is a good thing you're doing."

"Yeah," he said, warmed by the motherly approval in her eyes, "I guess it is." He looked around for a reporter—from a newspaper, radio, TV, anything—but found none. That would change. "When you get back to the office, send out a press release: The unionization of the Beacon Ridge sims is going forward . . . and don't forget to mention the donation hotline."

"You're not going back?"

"I'll be in after lunch. I'm going to stop off at the golf club and tell my clients the good news."

But when Patrick arrived at the barrack he found the sims already celebrating.

"You've heard about the ruling already?" he said when he found Tome.

"No," the old sim said, his eyes bright.

"Then why the party?"

"Gabba go D."

"Is she hurt? What happened?"

Tome laughed, a wheezy sound. "No, she fine. Go D: no can wash dish now. Hands too hurt. Move old sim home."

"Oh," Patrick said. "You mean she's being retired."

"Yes-yes. Retired. Retired. Go D."

D . . . Patrick had read somewhere that the expression to "go D" had come from the clause in the SimGen lease agreement that allowed lessees to return any sim that became defective, disabled, diseased, or decrepit for a fresh replacement.

Defective, disabled, diseased, decrepit . . . which one was Gabba? One look at her gnarled fingers and hunched back told the story. Arthritis was having a field day in her joints.

And then a thought struck Patrick like a blow—obviously the club hadn't thought of it yet, but what if they decided to declare all their sims "D" and turn them in? How would that impact the case?

Or what if SimGen issued a recall that just happened to include the Beacon Ridge sims, and removed them all?

As he approached Gabba where she sat on one of the sofas, Patrick made a mental note to prepare preemptive injunctions to head off any such maneuvers. Had to be on his toes. He was playing with the big boys now.

"So, Gabba," he said, dropping into the chair opposite her. "Looking forward to retirement?"

The old sim shook her head. Her brown eyes were moist. "No. Gabba want stay."

"But winter's coming," he told her. "Those old joints will be much more comfortable in Arizona."

Years ago SimGen had pulled a public relations coup by transforming a tract of Arizona desert into a retirement community for sims who were "D." The company did it to reassure the public that sims no longer useful in the workforce were not destroyed. Instead they lived out their years in warmth and comfort. Reporters from all the media were toured regularly through the community, returning with videos and photos of disabled sims lounging in sunny tranquillity.

"No friend there. Friend here."

"A nice old girl like you? You'll make friends in no time."

"No want new friend. Want here friend."

Good lord, was that a tear slipping down her cheek? Did sims cry?

Wanting to change the subject, he looked up at the other sims crowding around. Time for an announcement.

"One thing you will miss, Gabba," he said, letting his voice rise, "is all the excitement that will be going on here during the next few months because"—he shot his fist into the air—"the judge has decided to hear the case!"

The sims began capering about and yelling.

"Is true?" Tome said, grabbing his hand.

"Sure is. I just came from there."

He let out a screech. "Mist Sulliman best!"

And then the sims took up a chant: "Sulli-MAN! Sulli-MAN! Sulli-MAN!" Stamping their feet, clapping their hands, pounding on the tables until the barrack shook with the chant. "Sulli-MAN! Sulli-MAN! Sulli-MAN!"

They love me, Patrick thought. No bitching about bills or unreturned calls. They think I'm the greatest.

He realized that these were the best damn clients he'd ever had—and most likely ever would.

16

"It's the greatest job in the world," said the bear of a man guiding her through the dorms.

Romy liked Harry Carstairs. She felt herself respond instantly to his gentle eyes, his soft manner, and the warm shake from his huge hand. As for the young sims—gangly, three-foot-tall versions of the adults, dressed in overalls color-coded for age—well, they obviously adored him, crowding around, murmuring his name, touching him as he passed as if he were a god. He cradled a yellow-overalled two-year-old female on his hip now as he showed Romy around.

"How so?" she said.

"Look at them." He gestured to the crowded dorm as they walked among the seemingly endless rows of bunk beds. "So full of life and energy. It's almost contagious. I get a buzz just walking through here."

Romy had to admit the young sims were fun to be around—a positive tonic after the breeders in the natal center. She signed "hello" to a few of the older ones and they shyly signed back.

She wondered how Carstairs could reconcile the obvious affection he had for them with the fact that they were all destined to be slaves.

"How do you channel all that energy?" she asked as they edged toward a quieter corner. "How do you get them to sit still long enough for training?"

"We've developed a whole system of operant conditioning, routines of Skinnerian techniques but with no punishment—only positive reinforcement."

"I'm glad to hear that."

Romy had heard that SimGen treated its "product" well, but she'd wanted to see for herself. It seemed true. Not, she was sure, because the company was particularly humane; it simply had learned that a benign atmosphere during development resulted in the best workers.

"We start off with the social basics," Carstairs said. "Toilet training is numero uno."

Romy smiled. "I can imagine."

"Next it's how to dress and care for themselves, then the manual skills necessary for the kind of work they'll be leased out for, and of course we stress all along the most important skill of all; language. We start with signing and move to vocalization as quickly as possible. They're not all that intelligible when they leave here, but they can comprehend what they're told and take instruction."

She noted that he failed to mention the idea that was drummed incessantly into young sims' brains throughout their upbringing: that they existed to work.

"How long does all this take?" she asked—she already knew the answer.

Carstairs' gaze drifted away. "About five years, depending on the sim."

Romy mimicked shock. "You're sending *five-year-olds* out to work?"

"The ones that are ready, sure. Don't forget, they've been genetically altered for accelerated growth and development."

"Which shortens their life spans and leaves them old before their time."

"We're working on that. We had to crank out sims fast in the early days; now we're getting to the point where we have the facilities to allow us a longer view. Longer lives are obviously better for the sims and, coincidentally, better for SimGen."

"So you won't have to send five-year-olds off to work."

"Only chronologically five. With the hormonally enhanced diets they receive here they're physically into their late teens when we let them go."

"But up here . . ." She tapped a finger against her head. ". . . they're children. How do you feel about sending children into that cold, cruel world out there?"

"Am I on trial or something here?" Carstairs said.

"Of course not." Be professional, Romy reminded herself. Cool and professional.

"SimGen does its damnedest to see that a sim's world is neither cold nor cruel. That's why we don't sell them. They always belong to SimGen—that way we can protect them."

"They're still just kids," Romy said, fighting to keep the bitterness out of her voice. "Just kids."

The rest of the dorm tour was a little tense.

"I think it's time for lunch," Luca Portero said with a grin as they once again seated themselves in the Jeep. "There's this sweet little restaurant just a few miles from here where they have the greatest . . ."

Not gonna happen, she thought as she closed out his voice. I'll eat in the employee caf.

As they passed the two buildings that made up the research complex, she interrupted him. "When we get into the research centers, I think I'll start with the basic facility, and then move on to general research."

Portero shook his head and heaved a dramatic sigh. "I'm sorry."

"What now?"

"You will not be inspecting the basic research facility."

"Of course I will. That's what it says in the order—'all research facilities.' What part of 'all' is causing confusion here?"

Another helpless shrug. "If it was up to me—"

"Cut it. We'll have SimGen back in court first thing tomorrow morning."

"That will be up to you. But the powers that be consider the basic research experiments too sensitive and proprietary to allow inspection. They're worried about industrial espionage."

"Nonsense! Every member of my team—"

"We will allow you to inspect every other facility on the campus," he said, his voice taking on an edge. "But under no circumstances do we allow outsiders in that building. We will go to the Supreme Court to protect our basic research."

Romy did not miss the sparks in his crocodile eyes. So now it's "we," is it?

She knew damned well that SimGen could barrage the courts with motions ad infinitum.

She was wearing two spycams and had been saving them for the basic research facility. Now, damn it, she wouldn't get a chance to use them.

With frustration burning like a hot poker against the back of her neck, she turned toward the window. Don't lose it . . . don't lose it . . .

As she glared through the glass she noticed a truck pulling out of the basic research building's enclosed loading dock. She couldn't tell if it was the same one she'd seen earlier, but so what?—she wanted a closer look at it. But by the time it reached the road they'd be well past it.

Finding the window button she jabbed it with one hand while she rummaged through her shoulder bag with the other. She pulled her notebook free, then let it flutter from her fingers and out the window.

"Stop!" she cried. "My notes!"

Portero hit the brakes. As soon as the car stopped—and before he could shift into reverse—Romy hopped out and ran back. She retrieved the notebook, then stood and studied the truck as it reached the road.

It looked brand-new, dark green, about the size of a UPS delivery van, but with no lettering on the side panels, no indication anywhere that it belonged to SimGen or anyone else. As it turned and roared away, she used a spycam hidden in one of her suit jacket buttons to photograph its Idaho plates.

Idaho?

And then the Jeep was backing past and skidding to a halt in front of her—directly between Romy and the retreating truck.

"Find it?" Portero said, bounding out from behind the wheel.

"Yes," she said.

"Good." He trotted around and opened the passenger door for her. He seemed anxious to get her back in the car. "Now, about lunch . . ."

Romy stepped to her right so she could see the truck again, and pointed to it. "What's in the truck?" she said so innocently, as if asking what octane gas he used in the Jeep.

"Truck?" He looked around with equal innocence as if just noticing it. "Oh. Just delivering supplies."

"Where's it going? The gate's the other way."

"I don't know. I don't keep track of delivery schedules."

A bend in the road swallowed the truck. Romy saw no point in standing out here any longer, so she stepped past Portero and slid back into her seat.

"You're SimGen's chief of security and you have no idea why an unmarked truck is rolling from the basic research building toward the company's private airport?"

Portero's eyes narrowed. "How do you know that's the road to the airport?"

Romy smiled. "Lucky guess?"

His expression hardened as he slammed her door closed.

"And just when we were starting to really hit it off," she muttered.

17

Patrick Sullivan lay in bed on his right side, face to the wall, Pamela spooned warmly against his back.

Ah, peace.

Judge Boughton's decision had started to thaw the ice between them. After all, if a federal judge thought the case warranted a hearing, then maybe Patrick hadn't gone off his head with "this sim thing," as she liked to call it. A little champagne before dinner and a Graves Bordeaux with perfectly done steaks had finished the melt, leading to a hefty serving of aerobic sex for dessert.

And now for some much-needed sleep. But his slow slide toward dreamland was cut short by the crash of shattering glass. He levered up in the bed. Not again! The sound had come from the living room this time. Anger bloomed with the crash, but the *whoomp!* that followed it shot a bolt of terror through his heart, even before he saw the flicker of flames along the hallway.

"Pam!" he shouted, shaking her. "Pam, wake up!"

She was slow coming to. Not used to all that wine. But when she saw the flames and smelled the smoke—

"My God!"

Neither of them was wearing a stitch but they still had a few seconds. Patrick found Pam's slacks and blouse on the floor and tossed them to her. As she slipped into them—God knew where their underwear might be—he dialed 911. He found his jeans as he was reporting the fire.

Less than a minute later, cold and barefoot, they stood on the curb and watched the flames fan out from the living room. The howling fire trucks arrived shortly and brought the blaze quickly under control, but not before it had gutted Patrick's house. Somewhere along the way a neighbor had draped a blanket over their shoulders; another had brought them some old sneakers, ill-fitting but a hell of a lot more comfortable than the cold wet asphalt of the street.

When it was over and the firemen were rolling up their hoses, Patrick stood mute, numb with shock, unable to move a muscle as he stared at the smoking ruin of his home. But Pamela began to lose it. She started with a few deep sobs that quickly graduated to wails. Patrick tried to comfort her but she shoved him back.

"Don't come near me!" she screamed. "This is all your fault! I told you to forget this crazy sim thing but you wouldn't listen! You had to keep pushing and pushing until you almost got us killed!"

Patrick saw the terror slithering in her eyes. He took a step toward her. "Pam—"

"No!" She held out a hand and backed away. She looked wild with her hair in disarray and her tears reflecting red and blue flashes from the police and fire vehicles. "No, you stay away! I've had it! I can't take this anymore! Everyone I work with thinks you're either a nut or an opportunist! I'm tired of defending you and I don't want to be burned alive! We're *through*, Patrick! I can't take any more . . . I just can't!"

She's hysterical, he thought. She doesn't know what she's saying. "Pam, please . . ."

"No!" She raised her hand higher and turned away, moving toward her car. Through a sob she said, "I'm going home alone, Patrick. Good-bye."

She left Patrick standing alone outside the smoking timbers of what had been his home, wondering how a day that had started out so well could go so hideously wrong.

18

"All I can say," Mercer Sinclair shouted, "is that there'd better not be any connection to SimGen! If I find out anyone here had anything to do with this, heads will roll, and I don't care whose body is attached!"

Luca Portero watched Sinclair-1—his pet name for SimGen's CEO—pace back and forth in his two-toned CEO office before his panoramic CEO window. If this display was being staged to intimidate Luca or the two other men who made up the rest of the CEO's captive audience, it was failing. Miserably.

Luca glanced around. Abel Voss had his wide butt crammed into an armchair and looked as if he was listening to a weather report, and not a terribly bad one. Sinclair-2, Ellis, the useless Sinclair, was slumped on the sofa and staring out at the clear morning sky. As for Luca himself, he stood. He preferred to stay on his feet during these gatherings.

Sinclair-1 paused, so Luca used the break to offer something useful.

"I spoke to the Westchester County Sheriff this morning. They caught the guys—two of them. Didn't take much: They were drunk and had wrapped themselves around a utility pole getting away. Had an unused Molotov and a can of gas in their back seat."

Sinclair-1 pointed at Luca. "Who hired them? You?"

Luca only stared at him.

"I asked you a question," Sinclair-1 said. "And I'd better like the answer. Because if I don't . . ."

He let it hang, but Luca didn't believe in letting things hang. "You'll . . . what?"

Sinclair-1 might be CEO, but Luca wasn't going to allow anyone he didn't take orders from to threaten him. And he took orders from no one in this room.

Voss jumped into the tense silence. "I think we can be sure our friend Luca here had nothing to do with any attack on Mr. Sullivan."

"Can we?" Sinclair-1 said, glaring at Luca. "I've witnessed your problem-solving methods in the past, Portero, and this incident, I might say, fits right in with your M.O."

"We've all seen how he solves problems," Voss said. "And that's just my point. If we consider one salient fact here, I think we can be certain Mr. Portero did not try to incinerate Mr. Sullivan."

"And what would that fact be?"

"Mr. Sullivan is still alive."

Luca fought a smile as Voss winked at him. He disliked the legal profession as a whole and found fat people repulsive, but this lard-bellied shyster was all right.

Sinclair-1 considered Voss's words, then turned back to Luca and nodded. "I apologize."

Luca went on as if nothing had happened. "The men were a couple of Teamsters who as much as confessed, making statements to the effect that no way were they calling 'a bunch of fucking monkeys our union brothers.' As far as anyone can tell, they were acting on their own."

"Thank God they failed!" Voss cried.

Sinclair-1 nodded. "Damn right. Bad enough Boughton denies the declaratory judgment. All we need now is some asshole making a martyr out of Patrick Sullivan." He turned to Voss. "Which brings me to another point: Didn't you sit in that very same chair and tell me Boughton would be on our side? 'Our kinda guy,' was the way you described him. Someone who'd 'toss this case in two seconds flat.' Wasn't that how you put it?"

"I believe I did," Voss replied, looking uncomfortable. "But you see—"

"What I see is that he did just the opposite. What the hell happened? Did he have some kind of mini-stroke? What is he *thinking*?"

"If you ask me, and you just did, I believe that ol boy's hearin the magic word that rings a bell in every judicial head: *precedent*."

Sinclair-1 stopped pacing and did a slow turn toward Voss. "Precedent? You don't mean—?"

"I do," Voss said. "Oh yes I surely do. Every judge dreams of having his name attached to a precedent-setting decision. This could be a big one. Might upgrade the legal status of sims to 'persons.' To that end any judge might be inclined to allow Mr. Sullivan more latitude than he'd ever normally tolerate."

Sinclair-1 lowered himself into the high-backed chair behind his shiny black desk. "Upgrade to . . . persons," he said, sounding as if he was running out of air.

Luca suddenly felt a little tense himself. He was about to speak when another voice interrupted him.

"Yes, Merce. *Upgrade*—as in closer to human."

The sound of Ellis Sinclair's voice startled Luca. Sinclair-2 rarely opened his mouth at these meetings. He turned to see the older brother's eyes blazing as he straightened from his perpetual slump, rising from dazed and listless to tight and focused. Luca couldn't remember the last time he had seen him like this, if ever.

Sinclair-1 glared at his brother. "If you can't add anything constructive, Ellis—"

"Upgraded close enough to human so that they can no longer be classed as *product*, as *property*. Think about that, Merce."

Luca was doing some thinking, and he knew that could mean the end not just of SimGen, but of so much more. A catastrophe. Yet Sinclair-2 seemed to relish the possibility.

"Now, now," Voss said. "I wouldn't worry about it too much. Nothin like that'll ever get past our appeal."

Sinclair-1 wheeled on him. "You said it would never get past Boughton!" he shouted. "What if the appellate court has visions of precedents dancing in its head too?"

"Feeling a little tense, Merce?" said the older brother. "Sims in court . . . an OPRR inspection team ranging across the campus." He waggled his finger in the air. "*Mene mene tekel upharsin.*"

Luca stared at Sinclair-2. First he acts like he wants his own company ruined, now he's talking gibberish. What a loser.

But a glance at the CEO's enraged expression told Luca that maybe it wasn't gibberish. Voss too looked uncomfortable. Must have meant *something*. What language? Luca wanted like crazy to know what the hell Sinclair-2's jabber meant but couldn't reveal his ignorance. The words had a familiar ring, like echoes from somewhere in his childhood, but they remained tantalizingly out of reach.

Nobody was moving. Reminded Luca of one of those freeze-frame endings in a movie. Then Voss glanced at him. He must have sensed Luca's confusion.

"It's a Biblical prophecy, Mr. Portero. The legendary handwritin on the wall. Means you've been counted and weighed and found wantin, and so

God's gonna divide up your kingdom and hand over the pieces to your enemies."

"I knew that," Luca said, feeling his face redden. He remembered it now, from the Catholic school his mother had forced him to go to.

"Forget that nonsense," Sinclair-1 snapped. "We've got to take Sullivan out of the picture."

Now you're talking, Luca thought. "I'll talk to my people," he said. "If they clear it . . ."

Sinclair-1 shot him a hard look. "I'm not talking about your methods. We'll take him out without laying a finger on him." To Voss: "He's an attorney. Find out who his clients are. He works both sides of the labor fence, so let's see what unions and companies use him."

Voss was nodding and grinning. "I see which way this breeze is blowin'."

"But let's not stop there. What's the name of his firm?"

"Payes and Hecht."

"Good. Make a list of their biggest clients. When you've put all that together, we'll sit down and see what arms we can twist, what favors we can call in."

"Right. We'll have his firm give that boy a choice: Drop the sims or we drop you."

Sinclair-1's smile was tight. "When we're finished with Mr. Patrick Sullivan, he'll wish to God he'd never laid eyes on a sim." He turned back to Luca. "That leaves OPRR. What's the status there?"

"Under control." Luca glanced at his watch. "I should be checking back with my office now."

Actually, his security force didn't need him. The OPRR team was being expertly corralled, and would see only what they were supposed to see. But he'd had enough of this meeting. And the knowledge that the luscious Cadman woman was somewhere on the campus burned like a flame inside him. Something about her had reached a deep, usually well-insulated part of him. He wanted another look at her, wanted to be in the same room, breathe the same air, catch her scent, brush against her . . .

"Maybe you should be checking a little closer," Sinclair-1 said. "I understand there was an incident yesterday."

Luca tensed. "What incident?"

"The OPRR point scout saw something she shouldn't have."

Damn! How had he learned that?

"She saw an unmarked truck, nothing more."

"She shouldn't have seen that truck *at all*."

"And she wouldn't have if she'd stuck to her schedule. She was supposed to arrive at one. The truck was scheduled to be long gone before noon. But there she was making a stink at the gate five hours early."

"What did she see?" Voss said.

"An unmarked truck pull out of Basic's secure loading dock and head up the road. No reason for her to think it was anything more than a supply truck making routine deliveries."

He didn't mention her question about it heading for the airport.

"Lucky for us," the CEO said. "But what if something untoward had happened, say, an improperly latched rear door swinging open while she was standing there staring at it? What then?"

"I don't waste time worrying about things that never happened."

The CEO stared at him a moment. "Let's just hope that little incident does not come back to haunt us."

Luca said nothing. He also didn't want to mention the fact that the truck hadn't been completely unmarked. It had had a license plate. He wondered if Romy Cadman had noticed that. And if so, had she cared. He hadn't seen her write anything down, but that didn't mean she hadn't memorized it. But why would she bother? OPRR wasn't interested in trucks.

But they'd sure as hell have been interested in what that one was carrying.

Nothing to worry about as far as Luca could see. The truck had been driven aboard the cargo plane and whisked away to Idaho. The OPRR inspection was going by the numbers—his numbers. Everything under control. No sweat.

Although he wouldn't mind getting sweaty with their chief inspector.

He yanked his thoughts away from that warm little fantasy to the matters at hand. As he saw it, this Sullivan guy and the sim unionization thing were powder kegs. Let Sinclair-1 and Voss try to put Sullivan on the ropes their way. If that worked, fine. If not, his people would step in and settle the matter his own way. For good.

Either way, the future was not going to be a happy place for a certain shyster named Patrick Sullivan.

TWO

THE PORTERO METHOD

I

"Well, it's been two weeks since the inspection," Romy said, "and we're still in court trying to get SimGen to open its basic research facilities. So, net gain thus far from all this effort is zip. Or maybe I should say *zero*—if you'll pardon the expression."

"Any time," Zero said.

They had assumed their usual positions in the dank basement under the abandoned storefront on Worth Street: Zero backlit behind the rickety table, swathed in a turtleneck, dark glasses, and a ski mask this time; Romy sitting across from him. She'd walked twice around the block today to assure she hadn't been followed.

Romy knew she'd been in a foul mood lately; she'd spent the past couple of weeks snapping at everyone in the office. And with good reason. The organization was getting nowhere with SimGen. Lots of movement but no forward progress. Like jogging on a treadmill.

And she resented Zero too, with his corny disguise and his secrets and his damned elliptical manner. She could sense him smiling at her behind the layers of cloth hiding his face. She wanted to kick over his crummy folding table, snap his dark glasses, rip off his ski mask, and say, Let's just cut this melodramatic bullshit and talk face-to-face.

Usually she didn't like herself when she fell into this state, but today she relished it. She wanted someone to push her buttons so she could tap dance on a head or two.

"But 'zero' isn't quite accurate," he said. "Your inspections confirmed that SimGen is treating its sims as humanely as advertised."

Romy nodded. That had been the plus side. Though the young sims led a barracks-style life of multilevel bunks and regimented hours, their environment was clean and they were well nourished.

"Humanely," she said. "After spending all that time with so many of them, the word has garnered new meaning in respect to sims."

"How so?"

"Well, so many typical chimp behaviors are missing. The mothers don't carry their young on their backs like chimps, but on their hips like humans. And I saw only a rare sim grooming another. Chimps are always grooming each other. I'd think if SimGen wanted to keep the public thinking of sims as animals they would have allowed *some* chimp behavior to carry over."

"First off," Zero said, "it could be learned behavior. If they've never seen or experienced grooming, they might not do it. Plus, sims don't have anywhere near the amount of hair as chimps, so it's not necessary. And if it's genetically linked behavior, it might have disappeared when SimGen 'cleaned up' the sim genome by removing most of the so-called junk DNA. Or the company might have engineered it out of them because it would interfere with their work efficiency."

"That last sounds typical. Too bad, because it seems to give chimps comfort." Romy shook her head. "No grooming, no sex, no joy, no aggression, no love, no hate . . . it's like they're half alive—*less* than half. It's unconscionable. Chimps laugh, they cry, they exhibit loyalty and treachery, they can be loving and murderous, they can be born ambitious, they can fight wars, they can commit infanticide. A mix of the good and the bad, the best and the worst, just like humans. But sims . . . sims have been stripped of the extremes, pared down to a bland mean to make them workforce fodder."

She closed her eyes a moment to hold back a hot surge of anger. No use getting herself worked up now.

"How do sims feel about it?" Zero asked. "Ever wonder?"

"All the time. I signed to a lot of the young ones during the inspection tours, asking them just that: *How do you feel?* and *Are you happy?*"

"How did they answer?"

"They answered 'Okay' to the first, but they didn't seem to know what 'happy' meant."

"Tough concept."

Romy shot to her feet and walked around in a tight circle, grinding a fist against her palm.

"Maybe I should quit this."

"Romy—"

"No, I'm serious. My life is one tangled mass of dissatisfaction. I should quit the organization, put in my time at OPRR, settle down, marry a fellow bureaucrat, buy a house, have kids, and forget all this crap! Life would be so much simpler and I'd be so much happier!"

"Would you?"

"At least I wouldn't be so damn frustrated!" *You're losing it,* she thought. *Keep a lid on it.* But she couldn't. She needed to spew. "Everywhere I turn, someone's hiding something from me: couldn't find anything useful at SimGen, you won't show me your face or let me in on who else is in the organization. Hell, for all I know, OPRR's got a secret agenda they're keeping from me too! I'm sick of it! Sick to death!"

Zero said nothing, merely sat and waited for her to cool. *Good move.*

With a little more circle walking and fist grinding, the heat seeped away and she dropped back into the chair.

"Okay," she said. "I'm back."

"What can I do to make this better?"

"Nothing. It's not you, it's me. I always seem at odds with a world that I should be so thankful for. Look what the genome revolution has done. We'll all live longer because so many genetic diseases have already been wiped out, and days are numbered for the rest of them. Heart disease, diabetes, high blood pressure, certain cancers—if they ran in your family you pretty much had to resign yourself to dealing with them at some point in your life. Not these days. Germline therapy has seen to that. Cystic fibrosis, sickle cell anemia, MS—hell, *nobody* has those anymore."

"Jerry Lewis finally stopped those telethons."

Romy had to smile. "There you go—something else to be thankful for. And then there's . . . me. You know about my splice, I assume."

Zero nodded. "Changed your life, didn't it."

Oh, yes, she thought. *You might even say it saved my life.*

She remembered adolescence as a time of chaos. Under the influence of the new hormones surging through her maturing body, her childhood fits of violence segued into other modes of acting out. When she was Reasonable

Romy she was an A student, but then somewhere in her system a switch would be thrown and Raging Romy would emerge. If Reasonable Romy had a fault, it was that she felt too much, cared too much. Raging Romy cared for no one, least of all herself, and needed to go to extremes to feel anything.

She stifled a groan as she remembered the reckless sex—she cut a sexual swath through the willing males and females in each of the three high schools she attended, then jumped into drinking, drugs, shoplifting, the whole gamut. When she was caught dancing naked on the roof of the gym she qualified for emergency institutionalization.

During her time in the locked ward of the hospital, the doctors explained that Reasonable Romy was the real Romy, the only Romy, but at times her neurohormones would undergo wild fluctuations, causing her to act out of character. They said it was a form of what they called bipolar disorder and they had medications that would keep her neurohormones—and thus her behavior—on an even keel.

Wrong.

Oh, the drugs worked for a while. She survived high school and her parents' divorce—Raging Romy's behavior playing a major part in the break-up—and got through college without too many incidents. During grad school she started noticing increasingly wide mood swings. She managed to earn her Ph.D. in Anthropology, but shortly after that she was out of control.

A parade of doctors tried a wide array of chemical cocktails to regulate her behavior. No luck. Finally someone suggested a radical new treatment—gene therapy. A defective gene in her brain cells had been identified as the cause of her disorder. Using a viral vector, they could replace the aberrant base sequence in the gene and get it back to normal functioning.

But no success was guaranteed. The therapy was still experimental in those days. The virus would target only areas of the brain that controlled her serotonin and dopamine levels; if it got to enough cells, the levels would stabilize, normalize. If not . . . well, there'd been all sorts of releases to sign.

Apparently the vector virus reached a sufficient number of cells: Raging Romy never showed her face again.

But she wasn't gone. She remained in the unspliced cells, whispering, rattling her chains . . . a ghost in Romy's machine. And when Reasonable Romy was angry or stressed, she could feel Raging Romy pushing her way to the surface, trying to break through to be reborn.

And the scary part was, sometimes Romy found herself cheering her on, almost hoping she'd make it. Because she'd felt so damn *good* when Raging Romy had the wheel.

"Yes, it did," Romy told Zero. "I had a genetic defect spliced out of me and I've never regretted it. I'm more my own boss because of it. So why aren't I overjoyed with our brave new world?"

Zero said nothing.

The perfect response, Romy thought. If I don't know, he sure as hell doesn't.

She sighed. "Anyway, our inspections were satisfactory—as far as they got. But they could be performing vivisection in that basic research building for all we know."

She'd had two ongoing problems to contend with during the inspection tour. Lack of access to basic research had been the major issue. The other had been the relentless come-ons from Luca Portero; the man somehow had developed the notion that he was irresistible to women, and that Romy's repeated refusals of his invitations to lunch, dinner, and even breakfast were simply her way of playing hard to get.

She didn't mention that to Zero. What was the point? OPRR would be locked in court with SimGen for the foreseeable future and she probably wouldn't see Luca Portero again for a long time, if ever.

But just thinking about that man only added to her edginess.

Zero said, "We'll let the courts deal with the basic research issue for now. The good news is that after many man-hours of effort by a number a people, we've finally hit pay dirt on that license plate number you so wisely recorded—a number we wouldn't know had you not thrown them a curve by showing up early. A lucky day for us when you joined the organization."

She could feel his praise mellowing her—a little. Always nice to be appreciated, but how sincere was he? Was it that he had sensed her mood and was simply trying to placate her? So damn hard to read him without a glimpse of his face or his eyes. Almost as bad as email. Worse—even email had those annoying little smilies.

But she remembered his excitement when she'd told him about the plate. He hadn't been faking that.

"About time something paid off," she said.

"Not a big payday, I'm afraid, but who knows where it will lead. The truck was leased from a firm in Gooding, Idaho, by a private individual named Harold Golden."

"Really." She drew out the word. "What's a private individual from Idaho doing on SimGen's campus?"

"It gets better: Harold Golden's MasterCard is sound, so the leasing company never checked him out. But we did, and guess what? Harold Golden doesn't exist. He's just a name on a credit card account."

"How can you be sure?"

"Can't be one hundred percent sure unless we find something like his Social Security number belonging to a soldier who died in Afghanistan or Iraq. That's not the case here. The provenance of his Social Security number appears sound, but can you imagine a man who's doing some sort of business with SimGen who has never taken out a loan of any kind? Who has one credit card on which he charges only one thing: the lease of three trucks?"

"Unlikely . . . but that doesn't mean he doesn't exist."

"I can tell you that he doesn't live at the Boise address he gave the leasing company. And that his MasterCard bill goes to an entirely different address: a mail drop in Hicksville."

"Long Island?"

"At the risk of sounding like an infomercial: But wait—there's more. The investigator I sent to Idaho turned up something else: Harold Golden began leasing these trucks four years ago. The man who runs the company remembers him because Golden wanted the exact same trucks that had been returned that very day from another lessee. Guess who that lessee was?"

Romy shrugged. "Mercer Sinclair?"

"Close. Manassas Ventures."

"Doesn't mean a thing to me."

"Manassas Ventures was the source of the start-up capital that allowed the brothers Sinclair to get SimGen rolling. Consequently it controls a huge block of SimGen stock."

"And the connection to Harold Golden?"

"At this point, nothing beyond the trucks. But guess where Manassas Ventures has its office."

"Hicksville?"

"Exactly. And it has a strange way of doing business. The company rents space in a small out-of-the-way office building but doesn't seem to have any employees. Manassas Ventures is on the door, but it's a door that remains locked all day, every day, week after week. Makes you wonder, doesn't it."

"A man who doesn't exist and a business that doesn't do any business." Romy felt a tingle along the nape of her neck. "Am I detecting a pattern here?"

"I think so. Ironically, we've been aware of Manassas Ventures all along but never paid any attention to it. I'd assumed it was simply another of the countless venture capital groups that have popped up since the early nineties—one that happened to get lucky and strike it very rich. But I should have known never to assume anything where SimGen is concerned."

"If Manassas owns a lot of company stock, then it's logical for it to be involved in SimGen doings."

"But logic seems to be taking a breather here. For instance, if you were an investment group with SimGen on your list and flush with capital, what would you be doing?"

"I'd be crowing. I'd have impressive offices to attract new ventures to underwrite."

"Exactly. Yet Manassas Ventures's only address is a deserted space in a nowhere building."

"Almost as if they're hiding."

"They are. Behind Harold Golden. I believe Manassas invented him as a layer of insulation between itself and the truck rentals. And it almost worked. We were just lucky that our investigator asked the right questions on a day when someone at the leasing company was in a talkative mood. Otherwise, we'd never know the Manassas connection."

"But why insulate itself?"

The tingle in Romy's neck moved across her shoulders and down her spine. She sensed the situation moving beyond simply wrong . . . something sinister at work here.

Zero said, "Because I'm betting that Manassas Ventures has ongoing involvement with SimGen's day-to-day workings that it doesn't want anyone to know about. And the most likely reason for keeping an activity secret is that it's illegal."

"But SimGen is one of the richest corporations in the world, with a lock on a unique product"—she hated when sims were referred to as "product," but this time it fit—"in high demand. They're practically *minting* money. They've got it all. Why risk a connection to something illegal? It doesn't make sense."

"It does if whoever is behind Manassas Ventures is pulling strings inside SimGen. Pulling strings that lead to the basic research facility, perhaps?"

That struck a nerve . . . might explain the company's adamant refusal to let OPRR near the building, even with a court order.

Zero went on and Romy could sense him fairly vibrating with anticipation. "If something illegal or even quasi-legal is going on, we may have found the lever to crack open SimGen's wall of secrecy. All because you showed up earlier than expected."

"And caught a worm."

"Maybe a snake. I'd say Manassas Ventures is long overdue for an in-depth probe of its workings and personnel, wouldn't you."

"Anything I can do?"

"In regard to Manassas, no. But as for our friend, Patrick Sullivan—"

"Oh? So he's 'our friend' now, is he?"

Romy sensed a smile behind Zero's ski mask. "Not a close friend, not a bosom buddy, but . . ." His voice trailed off.

"But what?"

"I don't know . . . there's something about him. Maybe I'm feeling a little sorry for him because he's going through the worst time of his life."

"Really?"

"His girlfriend dumped him, his house is a charred ruin, he's been living in a motel room for weeks, and SimGen is putting the screws to his career."

Romy felt her interest growing. "How so?"

"They're pressuring Sullivan's clients to drop him."

She shook her head in amazement. "How do you *know* all this?"

"I have my sources."

"You're a SimGen insider. You've got to be."

"Back to Mr. Sullivan?"

Romy tore her mind away from the tantalizing possibilities of Zero's identity. Sullivan . . . his predicament did sound pretty awful, but the shyster deserved it.

"Don't expect me to shed tears for any lawyer, especially one of the headline hunting variety who's been taking those sims for a ride."

"You're assessment of him might be accurate, but I've got to hand it to him: He's lost a number of big clients and he's still hanging tough."

"No kidding?" Romy was surprised. "I'd have thought he'd have folded like an old suitcase by now."

"Well, I don't expect him to hold up forever, so I believe it's time we stepped in. And speaking of suitcases . . ." Zero lifted a large metal attaché case onto the table. "I'm hoping the contents of this will bolster his fortitude."

He slid it toward Romy who released the catches and lifted the top. She repressed a gasp at sight of the stacks of currency.

"How much is in here?"

"Two hundred and fifty thousand."

"What's wrong with a check?"

"I feel a man like Mr. Sullivan—I am not blind to his failings—will require more concrete proof of the seriousness of our interest."

Here was concrete, all right—a whole sidewalk. "How do I approach him?"

"Directly, I would think. I'll leave the details up to you."

Zero rose. A sign the meeting was over.

"But where do I say the money's from?"

"Again, I leave that to your inventive mind. But since I know how lying bothers you, I'm going to make things easier. I'm giving the money to you, no strings attached."

"You're *what?*"

"That's right. To do with as you wish. Buy a house or a fleet of sports cars if you want. It's all yours."

As the shock wore off, she began to understand. "I see what you're up to."

Zero said, "But should you decide to approach Mr. Sullivan with it, I suggest being nice to him. You might find yourself spending a good deal of time with Mr. Patrick Sullivan."

"I can hardly wait." She snapped the lid shut on the money. "That's it? You're letting me walk out of here with a quarter of a million in cash?"

"*Your* quarter of a million. Remember?"

Romy smiled. This was turning out to be not such a bad day after all.

2

THE BRONX

Needle Lady and Needle Man take Meerm upstair. Show room. Nice room.

"This is your new home, Meerm," Needle Lady say.

"Why Meerm new room?"

"Because you're a special sim." Needle Lady smile Needle Man. "Very special."

Meerm say, "All for self? Not share other sim?"

"All yours," Needle Man say. "The rest of the sims will stay downstairs in the dorm room, just like always. But you'll be here."

Meerm walk and look. Nice bed, own bathroom, all for Meerm. Not need share. But Meerm little room still have metal bar window like sim big room downstair.

Meerm sit bed, hold out arm.

"What are you doing, Meerm?" Needle Lady say.

"Stick?"

Needle Lady smile. "No, Meerm, we won't be taking any blood from you. Except for a tiny little bit now and then, you get to keep your globulins."

No stick? This ver strange. Always Needle Lady and Needle Man stick-stick-stick. Take Meerm blood ev few day. Take-take-take. Now no stick?

"Meerm blood bad?"

Needle Man laugh, say, "Not at all! In fact, we're very happy with what we found in it. *Very* happy."

Own room. No stick. Meerm happy sim.

3

WESTCHESTER COUNTY, NY

OCTOBER 22

"Mr. Kraft wants to see you in his office," Maggie said as Patrick passed her desk. The strained look on his secretary's face told him the managing senior partner wasn't requesting a social visit.

Patrick's stomach roiled. Great. He was living out of a suitcase, Pamela wouldn't return his calls, his clients were either bailing out—like Ben Armstrong who'd taken Jarman's business to another firm with no explanation—or giving him ultimatums: Say good-bye to the sims or say good-bye to us. And now Alton Kraft was waiting for him. Just what he needed.

Well, at least things couldn't get much worse. Or could they?

Patrick laid his briefcase on his desk and glanced around. His office was small, as was his window with its limited view of downtown White Plains. But that left extra wall space for his law books. He liked his office. Cozy. He wondered how long he'd be rating a window if his clients kept heading for the hills.

He walked down the hall to Alton's office, took a deep breath, then stepped inside. A bigger office than Patrick's. Much bigger. Thicker carpet, bigger desk. Lots of window glass, and still plenty of space for books.

"Hi, Alton."

"Patrick," Kraft replied.

No "good morning" or even a "hello." Just his name, spoken in a flat tone from the man seated behind the mahogany desk. And no handshake. Kraft was something of a compulsive hand shaker, but apparently not today. His blue eyes were ice, glinting within a cave of wrinkles.

Patrick's gut tightened. This did not look good.

He dropped into a chair, trying to look relaxed. "Maggie said you wanted to see me."

"A serious matter has come up," Kraft said, bridging his hands. "One that needs to be addressed immediately. We all know about the recent exodus of your clients—"

"Just a temporary thing, Alton. I—"

Kraft held up his hand. When the senior managing partner held up his hand, you stopped talking and listened.

"We've been aware of the losses you've been suffering and we've sympathized. We were confident you'd recover. But now things have taken an ugly turn. It was bad enough when it was just your client base that was eroding, but now the dissatisfaction is spreading to the partners' clients."

"Oh, hell," Patrick said. He could barely hear his own voice.

" 'Oh, hell' doesn't even begin to say it, Patrick. Two of the firm's oldest and biggest clients called yesterday to say they're having second thoughts about staying with us. They said they'd always thought of Payes & Hecht as a firm that represented people, a firm above such *stunts*—their word, not mine, Patrick—as representing animals. Who do we prefer as clients, they want to know: people or animals? Because it's time to choose."

"The sons of bitches," Patrick muttered.

"They may well be, but they're sons of bitches who pay a major part of the freight around here."

And account for a lot of the senior partners' billable hours, Patrick thought.

The partners had sat back and watched with clucks of the tongue and sympathetic shakes of the head as his client base headed south. No need for immediate concern: The firm adjusted salaries and bonuses according to each member's billing, so Patrick's bottom line would take the hit, not theirs. But when they saw their own paychecks threatened . . . ah, now that was a different story.

Not that Patrick blamed them. He'd do exactly the same.

"I don't think I have to tell you what needs to be done," Kraft said.

Patrick knew. Shit, yes, he knew.

"And if I don't?"

"I'm already taking heat because of this, Patrick. Don't make it more difficult than it already is."

Patrick understood. Alton Kraft had been his biggest supporter for partnership. If Patrick looked bad, he looked bad. The partners had probably told him to give Sullivan a choice: Stick with the sims or stay with the firm. Mutually exclusive options.

The decision should have been a no-brainer except for the inconvenient fact that he'd become attached to the Beacon Ridge sims. He enjoyed visiting them, liked the feelings that rolled off them—probably the nearest thing to worship he'd ever experience.

But all that was going to end. Because on his next visit he'd have to tell them he was dropping their case. He'd make up something good, and they'd believe him, and they wouldn't hold it against him, because Mist Sulliman the best, Mist Sulliman never lie to sim, Mist Sulliman never let sim down.

Yeah, right.

Mist Sulliman feel like slime mold.

He fought the urge to grab Kraft by his worsted lapels and shout, Fuck you, fuck the firm, and fuck all its candy-assed clients!

Instead, he sighed and nodded. "All right."

He'd lost his house, his girlfriend, and a shitload of clients. He couldn't afford to lose his job too.

"Good man," Kraft said. He rose and thrust out his hand. "I'll tell the others."

Now the handshake. Patrick made it as perfunctory as possible and beat it the hell out of there. Or maybe crawled was more like it. Or slithered. He felt like he'd just ratted out a friend to the police. If the carpet had been shag he would have needed a machete to reach the door.

As he passed Maggie again she cocked her head toward the waiting room farther down the hall.

"New client. No appointment. Wants to know if you can squeeze her in."

"A *new* client? No kidding? What's my morning look like?"

"Empty."

Figured. "Then by all means, 'squeeze her in.' "

A few minutes later Maggie showed a statuesque brunette into his office and introduced her as Romy Cadman. Short dark hair, dark eyes, full lips, and long legs. Dressed on the casual side in a sweater and flared slacks under a long leather coat, all black.

Patrick's spirits lifted. Nothing like a new client, and a beautiful one to boot.

Maggie placed the woman's card on his desk: *Romy Cadman—Consultant.*

"I won't take up much of your time, Mr. Sullivan," she said as he rose to shake her hand.

Patrick fixed on her eyebrows, so smooth, so dark, tapering to perfect points. Penciled? No, just naturally perfect. But he couldn't find much warmth in the deep brown eyes below—at least not for him. All business. A woman with a mission. A *consultant* with a mission.

"Take as much as you need," he said, thinking, I've got *aaaaall* day. He gestured to a seat. "Please."

"That won't be necessary." Because she remained standing, so did Patrick. "I understand, Mr. Sullivan, that you've come under a lot of pressure from SimGen lately."

"SimGen?" What was she talking about? "No . . . I haven't heard a thing from SimGen."

"Indirectly, you have. They've been contacting all your clients and either cajoling or coercing them into dropping you."

Patrick decided he'd sit now. It sounded so paranoid, but only for a second or two, and then it made terrible sense.

"How do you know? How *can* you know?"

"Not important," Ms. Cadman said. "What matters is whether they're succeeding."

"What do you mean?"

She cocked her hip and released an exasperated sigh. "They want you to drop the sims. Are you going to stand up to SimGen, or cave in?"

Cave in . . . hell of a way to put it. At least he knew where Ms. Romy Cadman's sympathies lay. So no way was he going to tell her he'd decided to do just that: cave in. His eyes drifted to those long legs. They looked strong.

"May I inquire as to your interest in this?"

"I want to see the sims get a fair shake."

He glanced at her card again. *Consultant* . . . to whom?

"Are you with one of those animal rights groups?"

"My interest is personal. So what's your decision, Mr. Patrick Sullivan, attorney at law?"

The subtle little twist she put on those last three words gave Patrick the impression that somehow she'd already guessed the answer.

"I haven't come to one yet."

She stared at him a moment, her expression dubious. Then she put her briefcase on the table and released the catches.

"Very well. If you're sitting on the fence, perhaps this will tip you toward the sims."

She gave the briefcase a one-eighty swivel, lifted the top, and Patrick found himself nose to nose with more cash than he'd ever seen in one spot in his life—he'd handled bigger checks, sure, but this was *cash*.

Hoping his eyes weren't bugging, he lifted a packet and fanned it.

"All twenties, Mr. Sullivan."

"How—?" The words seemed to catch in his throat. "How many?"

"Exactly twelve hundred and fifty. To spare you from doing the math, that's a quarter of a million dollars. When I have your assurance that you will continue the fight, I will deposit all of it into the sim legal defense fund."

Patrick eyed the money. This would take him a long way into that case; and with other contributions he could stir up during the proceedings, probably all the way through, with maybe a good chunk left over at the end.

Tempting . . . Jesus, it was tempting. The added prospect of spending time with this woman because of it made the offer even more tempting. Pamela had been gone for weeks and . . .

No. Staying with the sims meant being booted from the firm . . . going solo. He didn't care for that idea. Payes & Hecht could be a cutthroat place at times, but even on the worst days he found a certain level of comfort in having a firm behind him. Like a security blanket—one trimmed with barbed wire, perhaps, but still . . .

And where would he be after the sim case, whatever the outcome? Who'd be his future clients? Sims? Hardly.

Uh-uh. Tempting as all that cash might be, he wasn't going to commit professional seppuku for it. But he couldn't say that to this beautiful woman. Painfully he pulled his gaze away from the money and looked at her.

"I'll take that into consideration, Ms. Cadman."

"Good." She snapped the cover closed on all that beautiful green. "When do you expect to finalize your decision?"

"Before the end of the day."

"Wonderful."

One word . . . but the acid she managed to lace through it seared him to the core. She was looking right through him, and her eyes, the twist of her lips, everything in her body language radiated contempt.

"My number is on the card. Call me when you decide."

She turned and walked out, leaving him mired in a pool of dismay. A woman like that, you wanted her looking at you with admiration, not like something that had just crawled out from under a rock.

But what else was he supposed to do? What else *could* he do? Sometimes you simply had to be pragmatic.

Patrick sighed. The perfect cap on the worst weeks of his life.

He heard a patter behind him and turned toward the window. It had begun to rain. Great.

With his mood darker than the weather, Patrick stepped out into the hall. Off to his right he spotted the pretty lady with the briefcase full of pretty money waiting for the elevator.

"I'm going to grab a cup of coffee," he told Maggie.

"Want me to get it for you?" she said, looking up from her computer screen.

"Thanks, but you're busier than I am at the moment."

Down the hall, laughter echoed from the open doorway of the kitchenette that housed the coffee maker and a small refrigerator. He slowed his approach when he heard his name.

A voice he recognized as belonging to Rick Berger, one of the younger associates, was saying, ". . . and so when I *still* won't give Skipper a steak instead of dog chow, he says, 'I'll get you! I'm calling Sim-Sim Sullivan!' "

More laughter. Patrick felt his face flush. Setting his jaw he turned and glanced back at the waiting area. The elevator doors were sliding open and Romy Cadman was stepping inside. He broke into a run.

"Ms. Cadman! Hold those doors!"

She turned and gave him a curious look, but put out a hand to stall the doors. He hopped into the cab beside her.

"I've made up my mind," he told her.

She blinked, shock and disbelief playing tag across her features. "You mean—"

I know I'm going to regret this, he thought, but fuck 'em. Fuck 'em all.

"Damn right. Want to meet my clients?"

Her smile lit the elevator. "I'd love to."

4

Romy's head spun as she followed Sullivan's BMW through the downpour to the golf club.

What happened back there? she wondered. There he was, standing in his office, and he's clearly out of the picture—wouldn't say so to her face, but she'd seen defeat in his eyes, his posture, *I quit* written all over him—and a couple of minutes later he's jumping into the elevator with her and not looking back.

Had he truly been on the fence and she'd misread him? She'd been so *sure* . . .

Well, no use in beating it to death. He was still on board. That was what counted. She didn't know how good Sullivan was, but at least the sims still had a lawyer.

He stopped next to a high privet hedge and she pulled in behind him. She grabbed her umbrella and stepped out of her car. The umbrella was auto open which was good because she had the briefcase in her other hand. She had no intention of leaving it in the car.

An umbrellaless Sullivan came splashing over to her.

"Let me help," he said, reaching for the briefcase.

She handed him the umbrella handle. "Help with this."

"Aaawww," he said, grinning.

Nice smile. Gave him a boyish look. Like a mischievous child.

Together they sloshed through the soggy grass toward a barrack-like building.

"Most of the caddies and gardening sims should be in. Not a golf day. You'll have to come back at night after the kitchen and dining room close to catch all of them."

Patrick knocked and they were admitted by a grinning sim he introduced as Tome. Romy was prepared for the barrack, and her tours of the SimGen dorms prepared her for the vague musty odor that attended a crowd of sims. But she was totally unprepared for the reception.

Like Jesus' return to Jerusalem: cheering, waving, jumping on furniture, and cries of "Mist Sulliman!" from a dozen sim throats. Everything short of throwing palm fronds at his feet.

Flushed and looking a little embarrassed, Sullivan turned and gave her a self-conscious shrug. "My clients."

"My God," she said, unable to hide her awe. "They . . . they love you."

A sheepish grin. "Yeah, well . . ."

"No. They truly do. How could you have ever even considered . . . ?"

His blue eyes widened, not in surprise that she'd guessed, more in fear that she'd say it out loud. But she'd never do that—not to his sims. Everyone, even sims, needed someone or something to believe in, even if their god was made of tin.

And that need in these sims further bolstered her conviction that all sims were too close to human to be treated as they were . . . as property . . . as slaves.

"It's all very complicated," he said.

Romy shook her head. "No, it's not. It's all very simple, really: You do the right thing."

"But right for whom? What's good for the right hand may not necessarily be good for the left. In case you don't know, my specialty is labor relations. It's all negotiation. The art of the possible."

His voice was smooth, his eyes intent, his smile sincere. He was good, he was persuasive, and no doubt that he was smart. She wondered if Zero looked like Patrick Sullivan. But Sullivan wasn't Zero, and Romy wasn't buying.

"You've got to draw a line somewhere."

He shook his head. "The client and the opposition draw the lines. Then I try to get them to redraw their lines in places that both sides can live with."

"But these particular clients can't draw that line," she told him. "They don't know how, they wouldn't know where. So you've got to draw it for them, making certain it's in the right place. And then you've got to stand behind that line and say, 'This far and no farther.' No matter what is thrown against you—SimGen, the Teamsters, the US Government: 'This far and no farther.' "

Now Sullivan's turn to shake his head. "It's all so clear and simple to you?"

"Crystal and absolutely."

The tumultuous greeting had run its course, but a second round of cheering followed when Sullivan introduced Romy and announced that she was contributing "lots of money" to pay for the legal battles ahead. That finally died down, and now the sim called Tome was leading a young female toward them.

"Mist Sulliman. Meet new sim. Anj."

Dressed in the bib overalls and T-shirt that seemed to be the off-duty uniform of the Beacon Ridge sims, Anj was young and slight—couldn't have weighed more than eighty pounds fully dressed—and clung shyly to Tome, not making eye contact. Romy put out her hand and Tome had to take Anj's arm and extend it for a handshake. But she needed no prompting to grasp Sullivan's. Even smiled.

The old sim grinned. "Tome tell Anj all 'bout Mist Sulliman."

The gathering's attention shifted from the two humans to the food cart that was being wheeled in by a pair of kitchen sims.

"Lunch," said Tome. "You eat?"

They both declined and watched as Tome led Anj away.

"Seems awful young, doesn't she?" Sullivan said.

Romy was seething. "SimGen can't breed sims fast enough to meet demand, so they're leasing them out at younger and younger ages."

She watched them line up, plates in hand, for servings of some sort of stew being ladled out of a big pot with SIMS hand printed in red on the side. A scuffle broke out between two of them when one tried to cut ahead in line. Tome had to leave Anj to break it up, and she stood alone, looking lost.

"It's criminal," Romy said.

Sullivan didn't seem too concerned. "Speaking of lunch, we need someplace to talk. How about—?"

"I had a big breakfast. How about right here?"

"Too crowded."

"They're busy eating," she said, gesturing to the sims seating themselves at the long tables. "Besides, I'm used to being around sims. I work for OPRR. I'm a field agent in its Division of Animal Welfare."

"Sounds government."

"Yes and no."

They found a couple of empty easy chairs angled toward each other and she explained how the Office for the Protection of Research Risks was part of the National Institutes of Health, indirectly funded by the government.

"Then that's government money?" he said, pointing to the briefcase. "I don't know if I'll be allowed to use—"

"*My* money, Mr. Sullivan," she replied, glad she could say that truthfully. "Mine. To do with as I wish, and this happens to be what I wish. But I want a commitment from you, Mr. Sullivan."

"Only judges and opposing attorneys call me Mr. Sullivan. Makes me feel like I'm in court. Call me Patrick."

And if I do, she thought, looking at him, I suppose I'm going to have to tell you to call me Romy. First names make us sound like friends. Do I want to sound like your friend, Patrick Sullivan? Can I trust you enough?

"Maybe when we know each other better . . . when I see how much of a commitment you have to this project. I'm more interested in commitment than first names, Mr. Sullivan."

"I—"

At that moment Anj appeared at his side and squeezed next to him in his chair.

"Um, uh . . . hello, Anj," he said, looking nonplused and not a little uncomfortable. "Can I help you?"

The young sim said nothing as she draped herself across his lap, then curled up and began sucking her thumb. She looked so small and fragile in those baggy overalls.

"Too young," Romy said. And through her cooking anger she could imagine Raging Romy beginning to stir. "They're sending them out too damn young."

Sullivan sat stiff as a board in his easy chair. "What's she doing?"

Romy noticed Anj's eyelids drooping. "Looks like she'd going to take a nap."

"Great. And what do I do while she's catching Z's?"

"Just sit there while we finish our discussion," Romy said, not particularly liking herself for the enjoyment she was taking in his discomfiture. "Commitment, remember?"

"You're going to make me sick of that word."

"I won't need to mention it again if I get it from you."

"Commitment how?"

"That you'll devote enough of your professional time to the sims to see that they get a fair shake."

"Time?" he said, eyebrows rising. "You want time, you got it."

"But it's more than time." How could she explain this? "There's an obscure Paul Simon song called 'Everything Put Together Falls Apart.' It doesn't get played much but—"

"I remember it. A jazzy, bluesy thing."

"That's it. I don't recall the lyrics but I've never forgotten the title, because I've always added my own coda: *unless you act.* The world does not become a better place and *stay* a better place on its own. It takes effort.

Constant effort, because entropy is the default process. And so every day is a battle against the tendency for things to devolve to a lower state—of existence, of civilization, of meaning, of everything that matters. That's why I've brought you this money. Because everything put together falls apart—unless you act."

"But I can't see sims as entropic. If anything—"

"To create a new self-aware species is a magnificent accomplishment; to use them as slaves is to drag that accomplishment through the mud; to accept that circumstance is poison for the human soul."

He sighed and nodded. "Can't argue with that. All right, I'll promise you more than time. As of today I'm quitting Payes & Hecht to devote myself full time to these guys."

Romy couldn't help but wonder if Sullivan was quitting his firm or his firm was quitting him. No matter. Either way he'd have only one client.

"Excellent, Mr. Sullivan. I'll deposit the money this afternoon."

"It's going to be a long, bumpy road," he said. He gestured around at the barrack. "I mean, let's face it: This isn't a bad life. These sims have it pretty good, don't you think?"

"Maybe, but they're a lucky minority. You can't imagine what I've seen. As a matter of fact . . ."

She stopped herself. Did she dare? Yes. Why not? Mr. Patrick Sullivan needed something to rile him up, stiffen his spine.

"Tell you what," she said. "I'll call you in the next day or two and bring you along as I wind up an investigation I've been pursuing for weeks. You game?"

He shrugged. "Sure. I'll just need—"

Anj whimpered. Her eyes remained closed in sleep.

"Misses her mother, I'll bet," Romy said.

Sullivan stared down at the young sim. "Afraid I can't help her there."

"Want me to take her?"

He raised a hand and gingerly, gently, began stroking her stiff, stringy hair. "No. That's all right."

Romy realized she was catching a glimpse of a facet of Patrick Sullivan that he hid from the world, perhaps even from himself.

"You prefer Patrick to Pat?" she said.

He glanced up with a surprised expression, then grimaced. "Pat sounds like an androgynous serving of butter, and Patty makes me sound like I should be holding up the bar at the Dublin House Pub. Just Patrick."

"All right, Patrick," she said. She hesitated, then figured, what the hell. "And you might as well call me Romy."

5

"Sullivan quit the firm rather than drop the sims!" Mercer Sinclair said.

He pushed his chair back from his desk and began to pace his office. His personal news service had picked up Sullivan's announcement that he was going into solo practice, and informed him via his computer first thing this morning. Immediately he'd called Voss and Portero. Somehow his brother had got wind and showed up as well. Not that Ellis would contribute anything. Not that Mercer cared. He was too baffled, too pissed to care.

"I can't believe it!" he went on. "Is the man crazy? Has he suddenly become a crusader? What's gotten into him?"

Abel Voss cleared his throat. "An infusion of cash, it appears."

"Really? How much?"

"Quarter mil was deposited to his sim defense fund two days ago."

Mercer was stunned. "A quarter—how do you know?"

Voss glanced at the security chief. "Mr. Portero's people have been monitoring the fund."

Portero's people . . . Mercer knew Voss didn't mean the SimGen security department Portero headed. *Portero's people*—SIRG. No one referred to them by name. They were elsewhere, far off the SimGen campus, and Mercer wasn't the least bit surprised that SIRG had devoted a small part of its vast resources to keeping an eye on Patrick Sullivan's activities.

He shivered ever so slightly at the thought of being the object of that cold scrutiny.

"Who'd give that kind of money to a small-town ambulance chaser?"

"That boy's no rube. He was ready and waitin with an injunction when Beacon Ridge tried to trade some of its sims to another club. And he had another ready in record time when we issued that recall on them. He's anticipated us at every turn. He may be an opportunist, but he's a smart one."

"Fine. He got lucky. But where did the money come from?"

"A cashier's check," Voss said. "That's all I know."

"Perfect," Mercer said, cracking his knuckles in frustration. "So we can't trace it."

"Yes, we can," Portero said, speaking for the first time. "And we did."

Mercer stared at the security chief, standing there in his dark suit with his hands tucked behind his back, straight as a board, like some parade ground tin soldier waiting to be inspected.

"Why didn't you say so in the first place?"

Mercer thought he sensed an instant of hesitation in Portero but couldn't be sure. He doubted this man had an uncertain cell in his body . . . and yet, he'd seen something flash across his face.

"We are looking into an unexpected aspect of the situation."

"Which is?"

"The purchaser of the cashier's check was a Ms. Romy Cadman. You may remember the name: She led the OPRR inspection team."

Mercer stiffened. "OPRR? You don't think—?"

Voss shook his head. "OPRR's budget just barely covers its expenses. Even if it had the surplus it wouldn't jeopardize its funding by getting involved in something like this."

"Is she independently wealthy?" Mercer said, feeling his unease growing by the second. "Where'd she get that kind of money?"

"She lives modestly on a modest income," Portero said flatly. "She purchased the check with cash. That is all we know—so far."

A quarter of a million in cash. And probably more where that came from. Someone out there wanted Sullivan to succeed.

Again that sense of malevolent convergence through which he could almost hear the gears of some giant piece of machinery starting to turn . . . an engine of destruction. But whose engine? Whose destruction?

"I don't like this," Mercer said.

"Neither do my people," Portero said. "We're going to handle matters from here."

"Meaning what?" Ellis said.

Mercer glanced at his brother. Their eyes met. On this they could agree; neither of them was comfortable with the way Portero's people handled problems.

"Meaning this situation is spinning out of control. Your attempt to stop Sullivan failed. Now it's our turn."

"Now wait a minute," Voss said, both chins jiggling as he hauled his bulk out of the chair. "Wait just one damn minute. Don't you folks say another word until I'm on the right side of that door. I don't need to hear this."

He hustled across the gray carpet and let himself out.

As soon as the door closed Ellis turned to Portero. "You're not planning to—"

"No plans have been finalized, but direct action will be taken."

"No!" Ellis said, rising. "I'm not going to sit by while you and your people pull more of your dirty tricks."

"You have no choice, I'm afraid," Portero said without changing his inflection. "The matter is out of your hands. Sullivan has proven smarter and more stubborn than anyone anticipated. Even though the chance that his suit will set a precedent is remote, the mere possibility that he might succeed is unacceptable. My people have decided to stop him now, before he uses the courtroom to plant himself in the national consciousness."

"My God!" Ellis moaned, shutting his eyes. "Why did we ever become involved with you?"

Portero didn't answer. No answer was needed. But here again, for the second time in as many minutes—a rare occurrence, to be sure—Mercer could agree with his brother. He wished at times like these that they'd found another way to finance their start-up back in the seventies. But he knew that when he settled down later and was able to regain his perspective, this feeling would pass, and once again he'd appreciate how SimGen never could have achieved its current dominance without SIRG's help.

Portero said, "We also intend to learn the source of the Cadman woman's money."

"How will you do that?"

"Not your concern." And again a flash of something in Portero's ebony eyes, almost like regret this time. "But we will know."

6

"Mr. Sullivan?"

Patrick looked up from the box he'd just folded closed. He was nearly finished packing up the books in his office. Strangely enough, he wasn't the least bit sad about leaving Payes & Hecht. And from the cool reception he'd received in the hallways, he gathered the feeling was mutual.

Only Maggie seemed genuinely sorry to see him go. She was out now, scrounging up more boxes for him, so there'd been no one to intercept his visitor.

He saw a thin, aging woman in a faded blue flowered dress and a rumpled red cardigan sweater. She wore a yellow scarf around her head, babushka style, and clutched a battered black handbag before her with both her bony hands. Her pale hazel eyes peered at him and she nodded vigorously.

"Yes, you're him," she said. "I recognize you from the TV."

"Yes, ma'am?" he said. "Can I help you, Ms. . . . ?"

"Fredericks. *Miss* Alice Fredericks." She offered a smile that might have been girlish had she possessed more teeth. "I wish to retain your services, Mr. Sullivan."

The poor woman didn't look like she had enough for her next meal. Not that it mattered. He was no longer with the firm.

"I'm afraid I—"

"I want you to sue SimGen for me. I can tell you're a brave man. You're taking on the company on behalf of those poor dear sims, so I figure you're just the man, in fact the *only* man with the guts to tackle them for me."

This was interesting.

"That's very gratifying. On what grounds would you wish me to tackle them, may I ask?"

Her face screwed up, accentuating her wrinkles, and she looked as if she was about to cry. "They took my baby!" she wailed.

Baby? Patrick stared at her. A warning bell clanged in his brain. SimGen might have some skeletons in its corporate closets, but he doubted stealing babies was one of them. And this woman was long, long past the baby-bearing years.

"When did this happen?"

She sobbed. "Years and years ago! I . . . I'm not sure how many. Things get fuzzy . . ."

"Why have you waited so long to go after them?"

"I've been to every lawyer in New York City and no one will take the case. They're all afraid!"

"I find that hard to believe, Miss Fredericks. There are literally thousands of lawyers in the city who would get in line to sue SimGen."

"Sure . . . until they hear about the space aliens."

Oh, Christ. No need for a warning bell anymore. There it was, right out on the table: a big, multicolored bull's-eye with *Looney Tunes* scrawled across it.

Patrick didn't want to ask but had to. "Aliens?"

"Yes. Space aliens abducted me, impregnated me, and then when I delivered, it was a sim. But I loved him anyway. That didn't matter, though. They took my baby boy away from me. And do you know who they handed him to? Right in front of me? Mercer Sinclair! Mercer Sinclair took my baby and I want him back!" She sobbed again.

She wasn't scamming. Patrick had a sensitive bullshit meter and it wasn't even twitching. This poor woman believed every word.

"I sympathize, Miss Fredericks, but—"

"And you know what Mercer Sinclair did with my son, don't you? He made the whole race of sims from him. And he did it for the aliens so that earth can be repopulated by a slave race that the aliens can use around the galaxy."

Patrick blinked. A living breathing talking issue of *Weekly World News* had walked into his office. It might be funny if the woman weren't so genuinely upset. And he might be tempted to sit down and listen to her—purely for entertainment—if he didn't have such a burning need to put this place behind him.

"Tell you what, Miss Fredericks. I'm leaving the firm, so I won't be able to help you. But you could try one of the firm's associates. I suggest you go down the hall and find Mr. Richard Berger's office and tell him your story. And tell him I referred you."

"Thank you, Mr. Sullivan. I'll do that right now."

That should teach Berger to call him Sim-Sim Sullivan.

7

MANHATTAN

"Perrier?" Judy said. "Are my ears playing tricks or did I just hear you order water?"

Ellis had been taking in Tavern On The Green's sunny, glass-walled Terrace Room with its hand-carved plaster ceiling and panoramic view of Central Park. The park was more impressive when in bloom, but even here in the fall he found a certain stark, Wyethesque beauty in the denuded trees. The Terrace Room's seating capacity was 150. Today it seated only four: Ellis, Judy, his daughter, Julie, and son, Robbie, the birthday boy. He'd rented out the entire space for a family luncheon.

Ellis turned to his ex-wife. Judy was looking better than ever. With her perfectly coiffed blond hair, her diamond bracelets, and her high-collared, long-sleeved, clinging pink dress made out of some sort of jersey material—Versace, he guessed, because she'd always loved Versace—she fit perfectly in this ornate setting. Judy was only two years his junior, but Ellis thought he must look like her father. She was enjoying her wealth from the divorce settlement. Far more than Ellis was enjoying his own.

"Yes," Ellis told her. "I've decided to take a vacation from alcohol."

"That's wonderful, Ellis." He knew she meant it. The divorce had been amicable: Ellis had told her she could have anything she wanted. That said, she'd taken a lot less then she could have—more than the GNP of a number of small nations, to be sure, but still, she could have grabbed for so much more. "How long has this been going on?"

"Since the summer."

"What made you . . . ?"

"Lots of developments, lots of things happening. Things I want to keep an eye on."

"And Mercer? How's he?"

"The same. Eats, sleeps, and drinks the business. Still obsessed with SimGen's profits and its image. Someday he'll look around and wonder where his life has gone." He leaned closer and lowered his voice. "Did you hold on to all that SimGen stock from the settlement?"

Her brows knitted. "Yes. Why?"

"Wait till after the earnings report at the December stockholders' meeting, take advantage of the bounce, then dump it."

"Is something wrong?"

"Things might become . . . unsettled. I want you and the kids protected. But mum's the word. Just sell quietly and stick it all in T-notes, okay?"

She set her lips and nodded.

"Good." He straightened, put on a happy face, and looked around the table. "But enough about me and Mercer and business. This is a celebration." He turned to Robbie. "How's the birthday going so far?"

His son shrugged, a typical fifteen-year-old's studied nonchalance mixing with embarrassment at being out on the town with his folks and his younger sister on his birthday. He was underdressed in denims for the occasion, but that was to be expected of a boy his age; his buzz-cut hair revealed a bumpy skull. Hardly attractive, Ellis thought, but it was the style. So was the turquoise stud in Robbie's left eyebrow. At least he showed no signs of a splice, and Ellis prayed he never would. He realized it was a teenager's duty to irk his parents, but he hoped Robbie would find his own ways rather than galloping after the herd.

"Okay, I guess."

Ellis smiled. He wasn't making any appreciable progress developing the new sim line he so desperately wanted, but he was feeling good about himself nonetheless, better than he had in years, and he wanted to share it. Only on rare state occasions did they get together as a family, but he'd used Robbie's fifteenth birthday as a reason, and it was as good an excuse as any.

"Just okay?" Ellis said. "This is your favorite restaurant, right?"

He had a big day planned. After lunch they'd head for Broadway where he had four precious front-row seats for *Wordplay!*, the hot new musical comedy everyone said was a must-see. Then dinner at Le Cirque, followed by a Knicks game in the SimGen skybox.

As Robbie shrugged, Julie chimed in. "I can't wait to see the play!"

She was thirteen and the light of Ellis's life. Judy had dressed her in a plaid wool skirt and a white blouse. Julie's pod backpack was suede, sporting the Dooney & Bourke logo. Robbie was an intelligent kid, but Julie was brilliant. She had a wonderful future ahead of her.

A memory surfaced . . . of the day SIRG had threatened Julie to assure his silence, to keep him in line. And it had worked . . . for a while . . . until he'd found another way to make things right. But God help Julie and Robbie if SIRG ever found out.

He shoved the memory back into the depths. Nothing was going to ruin today.

"You just want to see Joey Dozier," Robbie sneered.

"Who's he?" Ellis said, fully aware he was a teen heartthrob who'd moved from a hit TV sitcom to lead in a Broadway play. "Never heard of him."

Julie got a dreamy look in her eyes. "He's *gorgeous!*" she said, as if that explained it all.

Ellis started to laugh but it died in his throat as he saw the small crowd of sign-carrying protesters appear at the Terrace Room windows. Their chant of "Free sims! Free the sims!" began to echo through the glass.

The tuxedoed maitre d' hurried to Ellis's side.

"I'm so sorry, Mr. Sinclair. I've called the police. They will be here in a few minutes."

Ellis looked around the table. Judy was ignoring them, Julie was watching, fascinated, and Robbie, the birthday boy, looked ready to crawl under the table.

"How did they know I'd be here?" Ellis asked, furious. He'd booked the whole room just to avoid an incident, even used a pseudonym.

"Someone must have recognized you."

Pretty fast work, considering he left all the public appearances to Mercer. Probably someone on the Tavern staff. However it had happened, he wasn't going to let them ruin the day he had planned.

He pushed back his chair and rose. "I'll handle this."

"Ellis, no!" Judy said, placing a hand on his arm.

"Mr. Sinclair, the police—"

"Could take a while to get here. In the meantime I want to talk to these people."

He crossed to a door leading out to the lawn and stepped through. The shouting grew louder as the crowd—a three-to-one ratio of women to men—recognized him. He stood impassively for a moment or two, then raised his hands.

When they quieted enough for him to be heard he said, "Please. I'm trying to have lunch with my family."

Cries of "Aaaaaw!" and "Pity the poor man!" rose, and one woman stepped forward to snarl, "Yeah! Eating lunch grown and harvested by slave labor!"

Ellis stepped forward. He'd noticed something interesting about a number of the protesters.

"If this is supposed to accomplish something," he told them, "I assure you it won't. Perhaps a more sincere group might make a point, but not a bunch of hypocrites."

Ellis kept moving into the gasps of "What!" and "You bastard!" and "What right?" and pointed to the snarling woman's handbag.

"Balducci, right?"

Her only reply was a stunned look.

"Sim made!" Ellis pivoted and jabbed a finger at the insignia on a man's windbreaker. "Tammy Montain—sim made!" As he slipped deeper into the throng, pointing out all the popular labels that used sim labor, crying "Sim made!" over and over, he knew he should be careful. But these people angered him, and not simply because they'd interrupted his lunch.

Finally he was back where he'd started and could see by their expressions and averted eyes that he'd taken the steam out of them.

"How can you be part of the solution when you're part the problem?" he said, knowing it was a cliché but knowing too that it would hit home. "You really want to 'free the sims'? The fastest way is to boycott any company that uses them as labor. Companies understand one thing: the bottom line. If that's falling off because they use sim labor, then they're going to *stop* using sim labor. It's as simple as that. But you can't show up here wearing sim-made clothes and shoes and accessories and expect anyone with a brain to take you seriously. If you're sincere about this you're going to have to make some sacrifices, you're going to have to let the Joneses have the more prestigious sim-made car, the more fashionable sim-made sweater. Otherwise, you're just blowing smoke."

Ellis stepped back inside and closed the door behind him. He had no idea what the protesters would do next, but the question was made moot by the arrival of half a dozen cops who began herding them off.

He returned to the table to find his family staring at him.

"Dad," Robbie said, wide-eyed. "You were great!"

"Ellis?" Judy said. Ellis noticed a tremor in her voice, and were those . . . ?

Yes, she had tears in her eyes. "For a moment there you were like . . . like you used to be."

He looked into her moist blue eyes. God, he wanted her back, more than anything in the world.

"I don't know if I can ever be like I used to be, Judy," he said, knowing his soul was scarred beyond repair. "But if things go right, if a few things happen the way I hope they will, I should be able to present a reasonable facsimile."

"But Dad," Robbie was saying, "you were, like, telling them how to, like, so screw your own company."

Ellis put on a pensive expression. "You know, Robbie, now that you mention it, I believe I was. I'll have to be more careful in the future."

"Will sims ever evolve into humans?" Julie said, looking up at him with her mother's huge blue eyes.

Ellis stared at her, momentarily dumb.

"She's studying evolution in school," Judy offered.

Ellis cleared his throat and controlled the sudden urge to run from the room. He'd rather be off the subject of sims—this was Robbie's birthday after all—and especially off their evolutionary genetics, but how could he not answer the jewel of his life?

"Do *you* think they will?"

"Well," she said slowly, "we humans evolved from chimps, and sims are a mix of chimps and humans, so won't sims evolve into humans someday?"

"No," Ellis said, choosing his words carefully. "You see, humans didn't evolve from chimps; chimps and humans are primates and both evolved from a common primate ancestor, an ape that had evolved from the monkeys."

"A gorilla?"

"No. Gorillas branched off earlier. Let's just call our common ancestor the mystery primate."

Julie grinned. "Why call him '*mystery* primate'?"

"Because we haven't found his bones yet. But we don't need to. Genetics tells the story. So even though we may never identify the mystery primate's remains, we know he existed and we know that at some point millions of years ago, whether because of a flood or a continental upheaval or climactic changes in Africa, a segment of the mystery primate population became separated from the larger main body. This smaller group wound up stranded in a hotter, drier environment, probably in northeast Africa; some theories say it was an island, but whatever the specifics, the important point is they were cut off from all the other jungle-dwelling primates. And there, under pressure to adapt to their new environment, they began to evolve in their own direction."

"But didn't the mystery primates in the jungle evolve too?"

"Of course, but because they were in an environment they were used to, they had little need for change, so they evolved more slowly, and in a different direction: toward what we now call chimpanzees. Meanwhile the primates in the separated group, in a drier, savanna-like environment, were changing: They were growing taller, their skin was losing its hair and learning to sweat in the hotter temperatures; and because they were no longer in a lush jungle where food was hanging from every other tree, they had to learn to hunt to keep from starving. This added extra protein to their diet which meant they could afford to enlarge a very important organ that needs lots of protein to grow. Do you know what that organ is?"

"The brain," Julie said.

"You are *smart*," he told her. "Absolutely right. The sum of all these changes meant that they were evolving into hominids."

"Humans, right?"

"Humans are hominids, true, but it took millions of years for the first hominids to evolve into *Homo sapiens*."

"But once they got back to the jungle, couldn't the hominids get back together with the mystery primates?"

Bright as Julie was, Ellis wondered how far he could delve into the intricacies of evolutionary drift with a thirteen-year-old. He paused, looking for an analogy. He knew she played the cello in her school orchestra . . . maybe she could understand if he related evolution to music.

"Think of DNA as a magnificent symphony, amazingly complex even though it is composed with only four notes. Every gene is a movement, and every base pair is a musical note within that movement. So if one of those base pairs is out of sequence, the melody can go wrong, become discordant. If enough are out of place, it can ruin the entire symphony. But sometimes changes can work to the benefit of the symphony.

"Imagine the sheet music for a concert arriving in a city far from where it was composed. The local musicians look at it and say, 'No one around here is going to like this section, nor that movement; we'd better change them.' And they do. And then that version is shipped off to another city even farther away, and those local musicians find they must make further changes to satisfy their audience. And on it goes, until the music is radically different from what was on the original sheets.

"This is what happened to the sheet music of the hominid's DNA. It was progressively changed by different environments; but the chimp DNA never left its hometown, so it changed relatively little. And because they'd been separated, with the genes of one group never having a chance to mix with the genes of the other, each group kept evolving in its own direction, causing their genomes to drift further and further apart.

"At some point millions of years ago both groups reached the stage where neither was a mystery primate anymore. By the time the hominids started spreading into different areas of Africa, it was too late for a reunion. The hominids were playing Bach, while the chimps sounded like heavy metal. They couldn't play together. Too many changes. One of the most obvious was the fusion of two primate chromosomes in the hominids, leaving them with twenty-three pairs instead of the twenty-four their jungle cousins still carried."

"But sims have only twenty-two pairs, right?" Julie said. "What happened—?"

"That's way too long a story for now," Ellis said quickly. "Suffice it to say that the two groups had evolved so far apart that they could no longer have children together. Once that happened, their evolutionary courses were separated forever. So you see, a chimpanzee cannot evolve into a human any more than a human . . ."

His voice dried up.

Julie said, "But that doesn't mean a sim won't evolve into a human."

"Sims are different, Julie. They *can't* evolve. Ever. To evolve you must be able to have children, and sims can't. Each sim is cloned from a stock of identical cell cultures. They are all genetically equal. Evolution involves genetic changes occurring over many generations, but sims have no generations, therefore no evolution."

"This is pretty heavy luncheon chatter, don't you think?" Judy said.

Ellis was grateful for the interruption.

"Your mother's right." He chucked Julie gently under the chin. "We can continue this another time. But did I answer your question?"

"Sure," Julie said with a smile. "Sims will always be stuck being sims."

Not if I can help it, Ellis thought.

8

"You're not getting another beer, are you?" Martha called from the upstairs bedroom.

Harry Carstairs stood before his open refrigerator, marveling at the acuity of his wife's hearing.

"Just one more."

"Harry!" She drew out the second syllable. "Haven't you had enough for one night?"

No, he thought. Not yet.

"It's just a light."

"Aren't you ever coming to bed?"

"Soon, hon."

She grumbled something he didn't catch and he could visualize her rolling onto her side and pulling the covers over her head. He twisted the cap off the beer, took a quick pull, then stepped over to the bar. There he carefully lifted the Seagram's bottle and poured a good slug into his beer.

Gently swirling the mixture, he headed for his study at the other end of the house.

He was drinking too much, he knew. But it took a lot of booze to put a dent in a guy his size. Still he didn't think it was a real problem. He didn't drink during the day, didn't even think about it when he was surrounded by the hordes of young sims he oversaw. Their rambunctious energy recharged him every morning, filling his mind and senses all day.

But when he got home, when it was just Martha and he, the charge drained away, leaving him empty and flat. A dead battery. Not that there was anything wrong with Martha. Not her fault. It was all him.

He wished now they'd had kids. Life had been so fine before when it was just the two of them. And SimGen, of course. Martha worked for the company too, in the comptroller's office. SimGen became part of their household, turning their marriage into a ménage à trois. But it had been a rewarding arrangement. They'd built their dream house on this huge wooded lot, traveled extensively, and had two fat 401(k)s that would allow them comfortable early retirement if they wanted it.

But a few years ago he'd begun to feel an aching emptiness in their home, to sense the isolation of the surrounding woods. He knew the day, the hour, the moment it had begun: When Ellis Sinclair had informed him about the sudden death of a sim.

Not just any sim. A special sim, one Harry had known throughout his entire time at SimGen. He'd taught that sim chess and turned him into a damn good player. They used to play three or four times a week.

And then he was gone. Just like that. Died on a Saturday, into the crematorium on Sunday, and his quarters stripped by the time Harry returned to work on Monday morning.

The boilermakers—Martha thought they were just plain beers—numbed the ache. But the ache seemed to require more anesthetic with each passing year.

Harry settled himself at his desk and reached out to restart the computer chess match he'd paused in midgame when—

He stopped. That feeling again. A prickling along his scalp . . . as if he was being watched.

Harry abruptly swiveled his chair toward the window directly behind him and caught a glimpse of a pale blur ducking out of sight. He sat stunned, frozen with the knowledge that he hadn't been imagining it. Someone had been watching him through that goddamn window!

He leaped from his seat, lumbering toward the sliding glass doors that opened from his study onto the rear deck. He slipped, fell to one knee—damn boilermakers!—then yanked back the door and lurched onto the deck.

"I saw you, damn it!" he shouted, voice echoing through the trees, breath fogging in the cold air. "Who are you? Who the *fuck* are you!"

He stopped, listening. Where'd he go? But the woods were silent.

And then Martha's voice, frightened, crying: "Harry! Harry, come quick!"

Harry ran back inside, charging the length of the house, shouting her name. He made it up the stairs to the master bedroom where he found her standing in the dark, staring out the big window overlooking the front yard.

"What is it?"

"I saw someone out there!" Her hand fluttered before her mouth like a hummingbird over a flower. "Just a glimpse. He was moving away toward the road but I know I saw him!"

"*Now* do you believe me?"

He'd told her before about this feeling of being watched but Martha had always chalked it up to his drinking.

"Yes! Yes, I do! And I'm calling the police!"

"Good. You do that," Harry said, feeling a deep rage start to burn—damn, it was good to feel something again. He headed for the stairs. "And tell them to hurry. Because if I get to him first they'll have to scrape what's left of him into a goddamn bucket!"

"Harry, no!" Martha cried.

Harry ignored her. His blood was up, he could feel it racing through his head, his muscles. He'd been spooked, he'd been doubted, he'd even doubted himself, but now it was clear he'd been right all along and it was time for a little payback, time to kick some major donkey.

He hit the front drive running and sprinted for the street. In seconds his heart was thudding, his lungs burning.

Out of shape. And four sheets to the wind. But he was going to catch this fucker, and before he wiped up the road with him, he was going to find out why he—

Ahead . . . to the right . . . a car engine turning over, gears engaging, tires squealing on pavement.

Shit!

By the time Harry reached the street all he could see was a distant pair of taillights shrinking into the darkness.

He bent, hands on thighs, grunting and gasping for air. Maybe it was for the best. If he had caught up with the guy he might have been too winded to do much more than grab him and fall on him and hope he crushed the fucking hell out of him.

But the worst part was he still had no answers. Why was somebody watching him? Why should anyone care enough about him to come out here and sit in the cold dark woods to watch him play chess with his computer?

Get a life, man!

One thing was certain—no, make that two . . . two things were certain.

First, he was going to get a gun. Tomorrow.

Second, he was going to stop drinking. At least stop drinking so much. Also tomorrow.

Right now he was thoroughly rattled and needed a double of something. Anything. Just so long as it was a double.

9

"There it is," Romy said, pointing.

Patrick squinted down the garbage-strewn alley to where a naked bulb glowed dimly above a dented metal door. Back in the Roaring Twenties, a speakeasy might have hid behind a door like that. Here in the twenty-first century he knew nothing so innocuous awaited him.

"I don't like this."

A week had passed since Romy Cadman had barreled into his life. She'd called him this afternoon, suggesting they meet in the city for a late dinner, and then she wanted to show him a few sights.

They had an excellent meal in the Flatiron district, with perhaps a little too much wine, and Patrick found himself feeling more than a little amorous. But *amour* did not appear to be on the menu.

A real shame, because Romy Cadman was without a doubt the most exciting, most fascinating woman he had ever met. Being in her company reduced all the other women he'd known in his life to wraiths. But he couldn't get past the firewall she'd set up along her perimeter.

He came close, though. At one point during dinner the conversation had strayed from sims and legal matters to the theater; somehow the subject of ballet came up, and Patrick had seen a change in Romy as she enthused over an upcoming production of *Swan Lake*. She smiled and her eyes sparkled as she went on about her favorite dancers and performances. Patrick wished he'd known more about the subject, but ballet had always left him cold. He did a good job of looking interested, though. Hell, he'd try toe dancing himself if it would keep this woman's guard down.

But too soon the subject ran out of steam and her defenses were back in place. She wasn't playing hard to get, she *was* hard to get. At least where he was concerned.

After dessert, as he'd helped her into her long black leather coat, he said, "I'm surprised you'd wear something like this."

"Cleathre?"

"This is cleathre?" Cloned leather. He'd heard of it but had never actually seen it. He fingered the smooth, supple surface. "Feels like the real thing."

"It *is* the real thing. It's just that no animals had to die to make it."

Cleathre and furc, cloned from skin cells of cows, minks, sables, even pandas, were the hottest new thing in the fashion industry. Ethically pure, esthetically perfect, and not cheap.

From the restaurant she'd cabbed him down to this crummy ill-lit neighborhood in the West Teens, so far west he could smell the river.

He felt like a fish out of water: overdressed and under-leathered. Romy's coat matched the dominant color of the passing locals, but Patrick's white shirt, paisley tie, and herringbone overcoat made him stand out like a Klansman at an NAACP meeting.

"Nothing to worry about," she said.

"Easy for you to say. You're staying out here."

He glanced around uneasily. He was no country boy, knew Manhattan pretty well, in fact; but this was a part of the city he tended to avoid. Clubs down here were in the news too often, usually connected to stories about shootings and drug overdoses.

Romy's smile had a bitter twist. "I'd go in with you, but it's not exactly my kind of place."

"You keep saying that, but it doesn't help me. Before I walk in there I'd much rather know whose kind of place it *is* than whose kind it isn't."

"You need to find out for yourself."

"Okay then, why don't I find out in the daytime?"

"Because the action at a place like this doesn't get rolling until about now."

"This is all because I said I thought sims had a pretty cushy existence, right?"

"Stop stalling," she said, giving him a gentle punch on the shoulder. "Are you going to knock on that door or not?"

Patrick tried a grin. "I'd love to, except that it means leaving you out here alone on these mean streets."

"Oh, I can take care of myself," she said, and this time her smile had a touch of warmth in it. She pulled a finger-length vial from her pocket. "One spray of this will stop a horse."

Was this a rite of passage, a trial by fire? Was this what he had to do to win her? Or at the very least, earn the right to try? He glanced at her intent dark eyes under those perfect brows. If so . . .

"Okay," he said. "Here I go."

He walked the dozen or so paces to the door, took a deep breath of urine-tinged air, and rapped on its battered, flaking surface.

A narrow window slid open and two dark eyes peered out at him.

"Yeah?" said a harsh voice.

Feeling as if he'd stepped into a particularly corny episode of the old *Untouchables*, he said, "I'd, um, like to come in."

"Ever been here before?"

"No, um, a bartender at the Tunnel sent me."

"What's his name?"

"Tim. He told me to tell you that Tim sent me."

Actually, Patrick had never met Tim, but Romy had told him to say that.

The door opened. Fighting the urge to turn and trot back down the alley, he stepped inside. The door slammed shut behind him and Patrick found himself sharing a long narrow hallway with a two-legged slab of beef who probably held graduate degrees in bar bouncing: shaved head, earrings, crooked nose, and a steroidal body stuffed into a sleeveless black T-shirt emblazoned with MOTHER'S. An old Guns n' Roses tune vibrated from the end of the hall.

The slab held out his hand. "Twenty-five bucks."

"What for?"

"Door charge."

"Twenty-five bucks just to walk in?"

"You see busloads of gooks marchin through here? This ain't no sightseein stop. Pay up or walk."

Patrick reached into his pocket. "Tim didn't say anything about a door charge."

"He's not supposed to." The bouncer grinned and stuck out his tongue—long and forked—and waggled it in Patrick's face.

A splicer, Patrick thought, trying to hide his revulsion. What the hell has Romy got me into?

Patrick handed him the money.

"Welcome to the Jungle." The bouncer pointed toward the end of the hall. "Mona will take care of you," he said, then cupped his hands around his mouth and shouted, "Incoming! Newbie!"

Patrick hurried down the hallway, brushing the sides in his haste. The faster he went, the sooner this would be over. He hoped.

Mona—at least he assumed the obese woman in the tight red dress exposing acres of cleavage was Mona—met him at the end of the hall. Another splicer: oversized lizard scales ran up the sides of her face and across her throat and who knew where else. She and the bouncer must be a couple—both into reptiles.

Tattoos and piercings had once been considered avant garde, but eventually were mainstreamed. Then tailored genes and nonhuman splices hit the black market and the bod-mod crowd jumped on them like cats on a nip-coated mouse.

"Hi, honey," she said, showing pointed teeth in a big welcoming grin. "First time, huh?"

"Uh, yeah."

First time for *what*?

"Everybody's a little nervous the first time." She took his arm and led him around a corner. "Let me introduce you to the girls first, then you take your time and pick the one you want. The base charge is two-fifty and that allows you half an hour. We charge extra if you go over, and of course there's surcharges for any specialties you want . . ."

Patrick stopped cold when he saw them.

"Kinda gets you, don't it," Mona said. "Nobody ever imagines they could look this good."

The "girls" were female sims, but nothing like Patrick had ever seen or imagined. Someone had caked them with makeup, either styled and dyed their hair or fitted them with wigs, then dressed them in vinyl or studded leather or lingerie—satin teddies, frilly see-through nighties, the whole Frederick's of Hollywood catalog. And their legs—most of them had shaved legs. Sims as a rule were only slightly hairier than humans, and the hair was coarser, but they didn't shave their legs or underarms. Patrick had never seen a shaved female sim, or ones with such breasts—they must have had implants.

"Good Christ!" he blurted. "What have you done to them?"

He did his best to hide his revulsion as Mona gave him a sharp look, but God it wasn't easy. Sim whores . . .

She grinned again and gave him a knowing wink. "You don't like them all dolled up? That's all right. I think I know your type."

"You do?" That possibility was almost as unsettling as the sight of these sim sex slaves.

She pointed to two unshaven, unenhanced females lounging nude on a couch.

"We've got Teen and Mone over there. They work in our special jungle room for clients who like their sims just the way you'd encounter them in the wild."

"In the wild? They don't *occur* in the wild! They're . . . manufactured!"

"Hey," Mona said, her smile fading. "Are you here to have fun or nitpick my ass?"

Patrick stared, he gawked, he gaped in shock at their surreal sicko get-ups. His stupefaction that anyone could find these pathetic creatures even remotely erotic quickly faded, replaced by a deeper revulsion as he noticed the bruises on their shaved limbs, their dead dull eyes. They looked like desiccated shells as they sat and smoked and stared at him.

Smoked . . . he'd never known a sim to smoke.

He had to get out of here. Now.

"I . . . I think I've changed my mind."

"What's the matter?" She looked genuinely offended. "We got the best in town."

Patrick started backing toward the hallway. "I'm sure you do, it's just that I . . . nothing personal, but I don't think I'm ready yet."

Glaring now, Mona said, "Then why'd you come?"

"A friend told me to." God, he wanted to kill Romy. "Said I'd find it enlightening. But I don't."

He turned and headed for the door where the bouncer waited.

"Jerry!" Mona called out behind him. "Something's not right with this guy."

Jerry placed himself between Patrick and the door.

"You got a problem, pal?"

Oh, no, Patrick thought as his gut clenched. He's going to beat the shit out of me.

"Yeah," Patrick said, pressing one hand against his stomach and the other over his mouth. "I think I'm going to be sick." He retched for effect.

"Don't you even fuckin dream of it, asshole! You puke in here, you're gonna clean it up—with your tongue!"

Patrick retched again, louder this time. "Oh, God!" He doubled over.

"Motherf—"

He felt the back of his coat bunch as Jerry grabbed a fistful of fabric, heard the door swing open, and then he was propelled into the stink of the alley. He stumbled, almost lost his footing, but managed to stay upright as he skidded to a halt against the brick wall on the far side.

Patrick didn't stop to look back. He pushed off the wall and hurried from the alley at something just short of a trot. He found Romy waiting for him on the sidewalk.

"Well?" she said, raising her eyebrows.

"Damn it, Romy!"

He'd half expected some sort of ha-ha-the-joke's-on-you attitude, but she was all business.

"I take it you ran into a few sims."

"You know damn well I did!" God, he was pissed. He felt besmirched, belittled, diminished. If she'd been a guy he'd be taking a poke at her right now. "Why the hell—?"

She held up one hand to silence him and raised the other to her lips. He realized she was holding a PCA.

"My man inside confirms the sims are there. It's a go."

"What's a go?" Patrick said.

"A raid," she said. "Let's get out of the way."

She led him across the street. The first blue-and-white NYPD units were screeching to a halt in front of the alley by the time they reached the opposite curb. Patrick watched fascinated as a small horde of blue uniforms swarmed toward the dented door.

Patrick stared at Romy. "You're a cop?"

"No. And this sort of work isn't really a kosher part of my OPRR duties, but I've made it so. I snoop around. I talk to people, people talk to me. I've been watching this place for some time. Took me a while to find the rear exit. Once I had that, I brought in NYPD."

"Then what did you need me for? Why'd you send me in there?"

Her gaze was focused on the alley, her dark eyes hard and bright as she watched the cops knock open the door with a short steel battering ram.

"To make sure the sims were inside. You never know who's got a source in a precinct house. If they got wind of the raid they'd have the sims stashed out of town and I'd have egg on my face and the cops would be less cooperative next time I came to them."

If she thought that was going to mollify him, she was dead wrong.

"You could have told me, damn it! Why'd you send me in there with no idea what I'd be getting into?"

"Would you have gone in if I had?"

"Well . . ." He let the word trail off but knew the answer would have been a definite no.

"I didn't think so. But because you did, you played a meaningful part in reeling in some single-celled organisms posing as human beings, *things*"—she managed to inject so much contempt into the word—"who make pond scum look tasty." A wry smile. "Ain't that cool?"

Patrick had to admit it was, but he wasn't about to say so.

"What happens to them?"

"The humans won't see daylight for a long, long time. Those sims in there have been either abducted or leased under false pretenses. The charges will range from grand theft to fraud to pandering to cruelty to animals to operating a criminal enterprise to promoting bestiality and whatever else the prosecutors can think of. You're the lawyer. You can imagine."

Patrick nodded, mentally adding a few more charges.

Romy kept talking. "And the perps—do I sound like a cop?—are guaranteed to get slammed with max sentences. SimGen, as you've learned firsthand, is relentless when it comes to anyone messing with their product. Their contacts in the judicial system, the ones who guarantee them favorable rulings whenever necessary, also see to it that anyone who transgresses against them lands lower-lip-deep in doo-doo. And after the criminal courts are through with the bastards, SimGen chases them down in civil court and gets dibs on everything they've ever owned in their life and everything they'll earn till Resurrection Day."

"Is that admiration I hear?"

Romy shook her head. "No. But you've got to respect SimGen's efficiency. When their ends coincide with mine—as in rescuing sims from these oxygen wasters—I'm only too happy to take advantage of that efficiency. But we part on the *why*: My reasons are personal and ethical, theirs are purely business and public relations."

"What happens to the sims?" he said, remembering the tarted-up females.

"Someone from SimGen will be by to pick up the poor things and take them to the Jersey campus where they'll rehab the ones they can and retire the ones they can't."

"Doesn't exactly sound like the Evil Empire to me."

She turned and glared at him. "Oh, but they are, Patrick Sullivan. That sleazy little operation across the street couldn't have existed without SimGen, because SimGen made the sims that were mistreated in there."

"Hey, Ford makes cars and some people get drunk and kill people with them or use them to rob banks or rig them with dynamite."

She rolled her eyes. "You don't see the difference between a hunk of tin and those creatures you're representing in court?"

"Of course I do. I just—"

"SimGen created a new species and enslaved it. Sims feel pain, they feel pleasure, they laugh, they *think*, damn it! And they're slaves. A sentient slave species . . . you don't think that's evil?"

"Well, when you put it that way . . ."

"What other way is there to put it? They've got to be stopped."

Patrick laughed. "And who's going to do that? You?"

She nodded. "Yes."

He couldn't believe this. She actually seemed serious. "You don't really think—"

"Something's rotten in SimGen," she said. "They're dirty. When I was there I could smell it. And when I find out what they're hiding, I'm going to bring them down."

"You."

She set her jaw. "Me . . . with a little help from some friends."

"What friends?"

"Just . . . friends." She stepped off the curb. "I'm going in to check over those sims, catalogue any injuries or evidence of drugging before the SimGen folks arrive. Want to come along?"

Patrick hesitated. He'd already been inside once and wasn't keen on going back.

"I don't know . . . I've got an early day tomorrow . . ."

"I know. Beacon Ridge has filed some new motions on the federal appeal."

That gave him a mild jolt. "You're really staying on top of this, aren't you."

"I tend to keep a close eye on my investments. As a matter of fact, I was planning on coming up to White Plains tomorrow."

"What for?"

"To see you in action."

"Ah, yes. Your investment." He wasn't sure if he liked the idea. He wasn't some trick pony.

"If you hang around awhile you could give me a ride up there."

Now *here* was an interesting development. "Where are you staying?"

"Don't know yet. How's your motel?"

Whoa! His heart did a pole vault. "Not fancy, but decent. As a matter of fact, you could save yourself a few bucks and stay in my room."

She laughed from deep in her throat. God, what a sound. He could listen to her laugh all night. Visions of that marvelous tight body began to play in his head . . . in bed next to him, straddling him . . . Pamela had been gone for too long and right now every Y-chromosome in his body was doing a mating dance.

"I don't think so."

He raised his hands. "Nothing salacious here. The room's got two double beds. You could have the other one."

"How generous," she said with a wry twist to her smile.

"And listen, I'll be a Boy Scout. Really. You can have your bed, I'll have mine, and we'll turn the lights out and just lie there and talk."

Patrick didn't quite believe he'd just said that, but it was true. He'd settle for talk, anything to stay close to this woman.

"I appreciate the offer," Romy said, "but I'm a private sort of person. But you will drive me?"

Drive you . . . aw, lady, don't say things like that.

"Sure."

"Great. We'll have to stop at my office to pick up my overnight bag."

"No problem."

And on the way home, lady, I'm going to do my absolute damnedest to convince you that two rooms is one too many.

10

WESTCHESTER COUNTY, NY

OCTOBER 30

Romy glanced at the clock numerals glowing on the dashboard of Patrick's BMW. Hard to believe it was quarter to three already.

Time flies when you're having fun.

Well, not fun, exactly. But it had been a good night. And she felt very good about putting those sim abusers behind bars.

She watched Patrick as he maneuvered along the winding curves of the Saw Mill River Parkway, deserted at this hour except for the single pair of headlights a couple of hundred yards behind them. He'd handled himself well tonight. And she'd been heartened by how deeply the sim bordello had shaken him.

"Tired?" she said.

"A little. How about you?"

"Not a bit." She was totally wired.

"I could perk up," he said with a grin. "That is, if you decide to take up my offer on the rooming arrangements."

She laughed. "You don't give up, do you."

After those splicer slimeballs had been carted off, and the cops had returned to Manhattan South, and SimGen had picked up the sims, they'd retrieved his car from the garage, picked up her bag, and headed for the northern suburbs. Patrick had spent the early part of the trip on the make, pitching his idea of sharing a room. Finally he seemed to have run out of gas.

Romy had to admit that a bout of sweaty, energetic sex would be perfect right now. Might take the edge off this persistent adrenaline buzz. But not with Patrick Sullivan. They'd be working too closely over the next few months. That level of intimacy in their relationship would further complicate an already complicated situation.

And her track record with relationships of any sort was downright miserable. She no sooner got close to someone than she seemed to scare them away.

Like Jeff Hogan, a bright, funny computer game designer who worked for Acclaim out on Long Island. They started going out last spring, grew close, but not close enough that Romy could tell him about Zero and the organization. He must have sensed she was keeping something from him—no doubt thought she had another guy—and one night he went so far as to follow her. Fortunately she spotted him and aborted her planned meeting with Zero. But that was it for Jeff Hogan.

"Give up?" Patrick said. "I don't know the meaning of the words."

She smiled. "If you're half this tenacious on behalf of your clients, I don't think the sims can lose." The smile faded. "Still think all sims have it cushy?"

"Not those."

"Ever hear of a globulin farm?"

"Never."

Romy said, "When you get sick, when a virus or bacterium invades your body, you fight back through your immune system. It forms proteins, immune globulins known as antibodies, to kill the invaders. That's called active immunity. But let's say you jab yourself with a needle that's infected with, say, hepatitis B or C. You could ward off infection by either of those viruses through passive immunity—by being injected with antibodies or immuno-globulins from someone already immune to them."

Patrick was getting the picture. A few months ago he'd have to ask another half dozen questions to fill in the blanks, but after what he'd seen tonight, he felt up to doing some of the filling himself.

"Let me guess: Since sims are so close to humans, some slimeball gets the bright idea of kidnapping or hijacking a bunch and infecting them with viruses and selling off the immunity of whichever ones survive."

"Exactly," Romy said. "And sometimes if a sim survives one virus, they infect it with another, and then another, until they can harvest a multi-immune globulin. The more diseases covered, the higher the price per dose."

"Ain't science grand," Patrick said.

"But it's not a one-time thing. A sim will produce those antibodies for as long as it lives. All the farmers have to do is keep it alive and healthy and they've got themselves a cash cow they can literally milk for years."

"Great," he said in a sour tone.

"But even they don't have it a tenth as bad as some of the cases I've seen. Try to imagine a sim tossed into a cage with three pit bulls."

"Aw no."

"Or two sims shoved into a pit, knives duct-taped into both hands, and bullwhipped until they fight to the death."

"Stop!"

"And some are simply tied up in a basement and tortured for days, weeks."

"Christ, Romy, *please!*"

She'd seen too much, too damn much over the years. Tears welled in her eyes.

"I don't know why . . . maybe it's because they're so unassertive, or because they have no franchise, but sims seem to bring out the very worst in the worst of us. The racists who're so desperate to feel superior to something, anything, even if it's not human; others who think God gave them the animal kingdom as their playground, to do absolutely anything with that they damn well please; and the sick souls who want to vent their psychoses on something weak and defenseless. Serial killers, teenage gangs, they've found a new target: Kill a sim for kicks. Damn them." She heard her voice break. "Damn them all to hell."

"Easy," Patrick said, reaching across, finding her hand, squeezing it. "Easy."

Romy couldn't gauge the genuineness of the gesture, whether he really felt for her or was simply pressing his case to be roommates, but she didn't pull away.

The interior of the car brightened. Romy glanced in her sideview mirror and saw that the car behind them was closer now, coming up fast. Patrick noticed it too.

"Looks like someone wants to pass," he said.

She felt the BMW decelerate as Patrick eased up on the gas to allow the other car to go by. She looked out her window at the ravine beyond the guardrail and suddenly had a premonition.

"Don't slow down!" she cried.

"Wha—?"

"Hit the gas! Don't let it pass!"

Too late. The other car had gained too much momentum. It pulled alongside—Romy could see now that it was a big, heavy Chevy van—and then cut a hard right into the Beemer's flank.

She screamed as the impact sent a shock of terror through her chest. Patrick cried out and the car swerved as he was knocked away from the steering wheel. Metal screeched, sparks flew as the steel guardrail ripped along the outside of her door, just inches away. Patrick grabbed the wheel, trying to regain control, but then the van hit them again, harder, and this time the Beemer climbed the guardrail, straddled it for an endless instant, then toppled over.

Romy's window exploded inward, peppering her with safety glass as the car landed on its passenger side—she heard someone screaming and recognized the voice as her own. She hung upside down in her seatbelt as the Beemer rolled onto its roof, then over to the driver side where it slid-bounced-rattled the rest of the way down a slope of softball-size chunks of granite. She felt as if she were trapped in some wild amusement park ride that had gone horribly wrong. Finally the car hit the bottom of the ravine and bounced back onto its wheels.

Battered, shaken, her heart pounding madly, she shook off the shock and looked at Patrick. He was a shadow slumped against the wheel—the airbag hadn't deployed. She heard him groan and thought, We're alive!

But this was no accident. Someone had tried to kill them!

And then she saw forms moving into the beam of the one remaining headlight, crouching shapes in dark jumpsuits, looking like commandos.

Realization stabbed into her brain: Already down here! Waiting for us! All planned! We were targeted to be knocked off the road at that point!

She found the door lock toggle, hit it. Locks wouldn't do much good, but Patrick's window, though cracked, was still intact. She leaned close to him.

"Don't move!" she whispered in his ear.

He gave her a groggy look. "What?"

"Keep quiet and play dead!"

She pushed his head down so it was resting against the steering wheel, then slumped herself against him and watched through narrowed lids.

Three of them, moving quickly and cautiously, squinting in the light. Must have been waiting in the dark for a while. She thought she spotted a fourth figure hanging back at the edge of the glow.

She slipped her hand into her pocketbook, searching for something, anything she might use to protect herself. Her fingers closed around a metal cylinder, twice the length of a lipstick. Oh, yes. In the confusion she'd all but forgotten about that.

"Somebody kill those lights!" said the middle figure.

"Got it."

One figure veered toward Patrick's side of the car while the other two approached Romy's. A hand snaked through her window. She steeled herself as fingers probed her throat.

"Got a pulse."

"Great. Get her arm out here. I'll shoot her up. Got that recorder ready?"

The third man was rattling Patrick's door. "Hey, it's locked. Find the switch over there."

A hand fumbled along the inside of her door. Over the first man's shoulder she saw the other lift an inoculator.

No!

She felt her fear nudging Raging Romy. Come on! she thought. Wake up! Where are you when I need you?

As soon as she heard the door locks trip open, she began spraying. Not a five- or ten-percent capsicum spray, but a concentrated stream of CS tear gas. The nearer of the two caught the full brunt of it. Clawing at his eyes, he cried out and lurched backward, knocking into his partner; Romy was moving too, pushing open her door and leaping out, arm extended, giving the inoculator man a faceful. He shouted and, arms across his face, turned and tried to run blind, but tripped and fell over the first guy.

Raging Romy was back.

"What the fuck?" she heard the third man say from Patrick's side of the car. She turned and saw him start to move around toward her.

"Run, Patrick!" she screamed. "Run now!"

Before taking her own advice, she went to work on the two bastards on the ground, using her boots to hurt them where they lived, putting all the considerable strength of her legs and much of her body behind the kicks. Raging Romy wanted to give them more, take the time to do the job right so it would be a long, long while before they were able to try something like this again, but the third man had reached the front of the car and she had to run.

Patrick lay trembling against the steering wheel, trying to control his bladder, afraid he was going to be killed. The guy on his side of the car had just yanked the door open when all hell broke loose to Patrick's right—shouts, cries, moans, and then Romy telling him to run. The guy outside his door was moving away and so Patrick kicked it the rest of the way open and did just that.

He didn't pick a direction, he simply ran with everything he had. A quick glance over his shoulder showed no one in pursuit, and a slim figure, glints of light flashing from her glossy cleathre coat, fading into the night on the far side of the car. Romy. Thank God.

He ran on, still afraid for his life, but he had a chance now, and that left room enough in his panicked brain for questions: Who? Why? And room for shame. He was running instead of fighting. Even though he wasn't a fighter, he felt he should be back there kicking multiple butts to defend Romy. Instead, she'd taken the lead and sprung them both. What kind of a woman had he become involved with?

At least they were running in opposite directions. That would split the opposition.

He spotted a large dark splotch ahead to his right—a tiny grove of trees, tall bushes maybe—and headed for it. He could stop there, get his bearings, and then try to make it back up to the road.

As he entered the grove he had a vague impression of a shadow hugging one of the dark tree trunks immediately to his right, but he kept pushing into the foliage.

"Not so fast, little man," said a deep voice.

And then something rammed into his abdomen, a fist, plunging toward his spine, almost reaching it. As Patrick grunted in airless agony and doubled over, another fist slammed into the back of his neck, collapsing him to his knees. He retched.

"Got him!" the voice bellowed.

Through the red and black splotches flashing in his vision, Patrick was aware of a flashlight flicking on and off. A moment later he heard thumping footsteps approach.

"Ricker?" said the voice that belonged to the guy who'd opened his car door.

"Over here. Where's Hoop and Cruz?"

As Patrick's breathing eased and his head cleared, he glanced left and right: two pairs of identical black sneakers leading to black pants with elastic cuffs.

"Down. Bitch was playing possum. Maced them and took off. They're getting their eyes back but—"

"Damn fuck better! Got to catch her before she gets to the road and stops a car!"

"That might be up to me and you—she did some real damage to their balls before she left."

"Shit! All right, let's do this guy, dump him back in his car, and go after her."

Do? Panic clawed at Patrick's brain.

For the second time tonight, he felt himself grabbed by the back of his coat. This time he was hauled to his feet.

"Steady him," the big one, the one called Ricker, said as a pair of massive arms twined around Patrick's head and neck like anacondas.

"Wh-what're you doing?" he cried, although he sensed with a sick terrifying certainty what was coming.

"What the accident didn't, buddy boy," said Ricker's voice close to his ear.

Patrick writhed in their grasp and cried out his fear as he felt those arms tighten, but he was trapped and pinned and helpless as a moth about to have its wings plucked . . .

. . . and then a jarring impact, an agonized "Uhnh!" from Ricker, a startled "What the—?" from the other, and the murderous grip loosened, the arms fell away, and something slammed against Patrick's back, knocking him face first onto the ground. He heard scuffling feet, grunted as someone's heel kicked him in the ribs, then winced as he heard a loud, wet, crunching *smack!* followed by a brief light rain of warm heavy droplets against his head and the back of his neck. After that, a heartbeat of silence, followed by the impacts of two heavy objects thudding to the ground, one on his left, another on his right. Then . . .

. . . silence.

He waited in panicked confusion, holding his breath, playing dead, praying he'd survive the night. Silence persisted. Warily he raised his head, inching it upward, spitting the dirt from his lips. To his left he saw a pair of black-clad legs and sneakered feet, only this time they were horizontal. With growing alarm he slowly rotated his head left—

—and scrambled to his feet with a startled cry when he found a blood-stained face and dead staring eyes only inches from his own.

Heart hammering, he backed away from the two still forms, the one who'd been struggling with his car door, and the bigger one, the one called Ricker, the one who'd been about to snap his neck when—

When what? What had just happened here?

He did a full, stumbling turn as he edged out of the grove, searching the shadows for something, anything that might account for the two dead men, but found only more shadows. When he reached the edge of the foliage he ran, blindly at first, but then a passing splash of light from above told him where the roadway was. He veered right and began to claw his way up the steep slope, stumbling, slipping, the rough granite tearing his pants, cutting his skin. Finally he reached the battered steel guardrail and pulled himself over.

No one else in sight. Where was Romy? God, he hoped she was okay.

Aching and bleeding, he slumped against the cold metal and tried to catch his breath.

Not in shape, he thought as he searched his pockets for his PCA. And even if he were, he wasn't in shape for a carjacking and dead bodies. He was a talker, not a fighter. He—

Shit! He'd plugged the PCA into the recharger in the car!

All right. As soon as he claimed a second wind, he was going to start running, and keep on running until a car showed up. And then he was going to stop it and have them call 911.

Lights glowed beyond the curve to his left. As a car careened into view, he rose and staggered across the shoulder toward the roadway, waving his arms. Only when he was completely exposed and vulnerable did it occur to him to wonder whether it might be friend or foe.

Moot question. The car hurtled past without even slowing.

Patrick looked down at his wrinkled, torn, bloodstained suit. I wouldn't stop for me either.

Maybe he'd be lucky and the driver would call in about a disheveled crazy looking man wandering the Saw Mill. But the way his luck was running . . .

He ducked and turned as he heard a noise on the slope below . . . moving closer. Someone climbing his way. He peeked over the guardrail and sighed with relief when he recognized her.

"Romy!" he said, rising and extending his hand. "Thank God you're safe!"

And please don't say, No thanks to you, my hero.

He helped her over the rail and noticed she wasn't even breathing hard.

"Are you all right?" she said, giving him the once-over as she straightened her coat. "Where are you bleeding from?" Was that real concern in her eyes?

"What? Oh . . . only a little of that's mine."

He recounted what had happened in the grove.

She glanced between him and the dark pool of the ravine. "And you didn't see who it was who saved you?"

"Not a hair, not a trace."

She nodded, looking around. "Typical."

"What's that mean?" And then he realized she didn't look the least bit shocked or worried.

"It means the organization is looking out for you."

"What organization? Those 'friends' you mentioned earlier? Who—?"

She pivoted and held up a hand to shush him. "Hear that?"

He heard a car engine gunning in the ravine. No way that could be his. They both leaned over the rail, squinting into the dark.

"When I was hiding in the brush down there I spotted another van just like the one that drove us off the road. On my way back up here I noticed that the two guys I gassed were gone."

"You think they took the bodies with them?"

"I'll bet on it. This wasn't a couple of beered-up Teamsters. These people had a plan and they were following it by the numbers, military style."

Patrick noticed her stiffen, as if a bell had just rung. "What?"

She shook her head. "Nothing."

As the sound of the van's engine faded, Patrick stared again into the dark ravine, trying to locate his BMW, and was struck by how perfectly their "accident" had been planned. If he had trouble locating his car in the shadows below—and he had a fair idea where it should be—a passing car wouldn't have a clue.

A shudder cut through his body. He began to tremble inside.

"Don't tell me 'nothing,' " he said. "Somebody tried to kill us and—"

"They were going to shoot me up with something first . . . to ask me questions."

"Oh, Christ! What are we into here? Who *were* they?"

"SimGen, I suspect."

"No way! With their clout in court and Congress, they don't need to hire killers."

"Who's got more to lose?"

"No, Romy, I don't buy it—I won't buy it. They're—"

She leaned close. Intensity radiated from her like heat from a reactor core. "They're hiding something, Patrick. And whatever it is, the two of us—you, me—we've touched a nerve. We've somehow threatened that secret."

"Just great," he said. "One of the largest corporations in the world has painted a bull's-eye on my back." He held up his hands and watched them shake. "Look at me—I'm a wreck."

"The shakes are normal," Romy said, holding out her own trembling hands. "Just excess adrenaline. It'll pass. How do you feel otherwise?"

"How does terrified sound?" He wasn't ashamed to admit it: He was shaken to his core. "It's not every day someone tries to kill me."

"The all-important question is: Have they scared you off?"

"Oh, they've scared me, but not off," he said, hoping he sounded a lot braver than he felt. "You see, they made a big mistake when they ruined my practice: It left me with only one client. I *can't* quit."

Romy smiled at him, and he sensed genuine regard in her eyes. Somehow that made the terrors of the past few minutes almost worthwhile. Almost.

"And I'll tell you something else," he said, feeling a growing anger blunt the edge of his fear. "I'm still not convinced SimGen was behind what happened here, but just in case it was, I'm putting them on notice."

Her eyes never left his face. "How?"

"I'm sure I saw the word 'SimGen' on the side of the van that sideswiped us. How about you?"

"Come to think of it," she said, touching an index finger to her temple, "I believe I did too."

"Of course you did. We'll make sure it's in the police report, and I'm going to mention it in every interview over the next week or so. SimGen will deny it of course, but a suspicion will be implanted in the public mind. SimGen will be *praying* nothing happens to us."

"I love it," she said. "Turns the tables in a wonderfully underhanded way."

"I aced Underhanded 101 and 102 in law school."

"I'll bet you did." She pulled a PCA from her coat pocket. "Time to call the cops."

11

"I understand," Luca Portero said for what seemed like the hundredth or thousandth time, trying to calm the voice on the other end of the hard-encrypted line.

Truth was, he didn't understand. Not one damn bit.

He rubbed his burning eyes. Somewhere outside this sealed office in the subbasement of SimGen's Basic Research building, the sun was preparing to rise. Luca hadn't slept in twenty-three hours, but he wasn't the least bit physically tired. The fatigue weighing on him like a lead-lined shroud was mental, from hammering his brain for an explanation as to how such a simple op could go so fatally wrong.

"*Do* you understand, Portero?" said the voice.

It belonged to Darryl Lister, Luca's old CO, the man who'd brought him into SIRG. Just like back in the service, Lister was his direct superior, and the next stop up the ladder from Luca. Lister was understandably upset about being awakened ahead of his alarm clock with the news that two of their men were dead. He'd hung up on Luca, then called him back half an hour later—after checking with the SIRG higher-ups, no doubt.

"Then maybe," Lister continued, "just maybe you can help *me* understand how six pros go out to process a couple of soft-shelled yuppies, and two come back in body bags, while the yups are still walking around. You were running the op. Explain, please."

Lister's tone surprised Luca. He sounded nothing like the Captain he'd known back in their Special Forces days. Hell, they'd stalked through Kabul and Baghdad together; he was one of the few men in the world Luca respected. Why was he coming on so managerial?

Couldn't worry about that now. Had to give him answers.

Luca once more reviewed the set-up, groping for a flaw. He'd handpicked the men, all seasoned SIRG operatives. Using a bogus identity he'd personally rented the vans from two different companies—could have used unmarked SimGen vehicles but didn't want to chance a trace. Then last night, after weeks of surveillance on Sullivan and Cadman, a golden opportunity: the two of them together driving through Westchester in the dead hours of the morning. A couple of quick calls and everyone was in position, waiting for it to go down.

So far, so good. Not a hint that it was going to go down the toilet.

He reran his mental tape of what he'd learned from debriefing the survivors. According to Snyder and Lowery—the wheel man and his back-up in the first van—the hit on Sullivan's car had been perfect: over the rail and down the slope. As planned, they'd driven away and left their rented van at a body shop that knows how to keep a secret.

After that the story murked up. The two survivors of the wet team, Cruz and Hooper, had spent too much time recovering from their doses of Mace to see anything. And they were still limping from the tap dance the Cadman woman had done on them.

Luca shook his head, torn between rage and admiration. Some kind of broad, that Romy. He couldn't help but admire the way she'd engineered the raid on that sim whorehouse. And then she'd made asses of two of his best men. Maybe they were still alive thanks to her. He could use someone like her.

When Cruz and Hooper could finally see and walk again, they'd found Ricker and Green dead; they'd gathered up the corpses and hauled ass out of there in the second van.

"I put Ricker in charge," Luca said.

"Good choice," Lister replied. "I'd have done the same. But Ricker is dead, and that's what disturbs me, Portero. How does Ricker wind up with a cracked skull? Who do you know who could take Ricker in hand-to-hand?"

"Nobody."

"Damn right. He was a fucking animal."

No argument there. Ricker wasn't just big and tough, he was experienced and smart. No one was going to take him down without a struggle, and not without him taking one or two down with him. But according to Cruz and Hooper, they never heard a sound.

And Ricker's body . . . his throat had been crushed—that explained the silence—and his head had been smashed. Looked like he'd leaned out of a speeding subway and got clocked by a support girder. Same with Green.

In fact, if Luca wasn't so sure it was impossible, he'd think someone had grabbed Ricker and Green by their necks and smashed their heads together . . . like a bully brother breaking his sister's dolls. But who could manhandle two guys as fit and jacked as Ricker and Green like that?

An icy length of barbed wire dragged along Luca's spine.

"According to what you've told me," Lister said, "Ricker and the team didn't know where they were going until less than an hour before they hit the road. Even you didn't know. So how did whoever took them out know? Sounds to me like they were already there waiting."

"Or they were followed."

"But why follow them at all? Unless . . . shit! The Japs! I bet it's the Japs! That goddamn Kaze Group has been sticking its dirty fingers deeper and deeper into the biotech pie, and now—"

"I doubt it's the Japs," Luca said. "They've got no reason to protect Sullivan."

"Maybe they just want to keep us off balance."

Luca began to feel an unsettling suspicion. He hesitated, as if uttering the words might turn the possibility into a reality. But Lister—and SIRG—had to know.

"I think there's a new player in the game."

"Where'd you get an idea like that?"

"A gut feeling. And the fact that we've never had to deal with a countermove like this."

A pause while Lister digested that. "Who on earth . . . ?"

"I have no idea—yet. But I'm going to find out."

"You do that. But don't lose us any more men in the process. Whoever these people are, they play rough."

"Rough," Luca said, clamping his jaw. "They don't know rough. Not by half."

"And something *you* should know," Lister said. "Word from upstairs is that this was a bad idea."

"Bad?" Anger dueled with a sudden stab of cold fear. "It was approved! What the hell are they trying—?"

"Careful what you say, Portero. The wrong people might hear and you could find yourself back where you came from, living on your pension while pimping for your mother—and happy to be allowed to do so. Comprende?"

Lister's unexpected attack rocked Luca. "*What?* What did you just say?"

Rage flared through him, making him want to reach through the phone and kill. He didn't care about the swift and inevitably deadly reprisal from SIRG, he wanted to crush Lister's larynx, wanted to see his eyes bulge, his face turn purple while Luca screamed in his ear that yes, my mother was a whore, but only because she had to be and she's not anymore, and yes, she doesn't know who my father was, but . . .

"Sorry," Lister said. "That was uncalled for. I'm just . . . you wouldn't believe the pressure that's coming down."

Luca said nothing. All right, so SIRG was squeezing Lister, big time. That still didn't give him the right . . .

"Look," Lister said. "Whatever you thought they said before, they now say the lawyer is not key. If he goes, he can be replaced in minutes by another lawyer, maybe a better one, who might cause even more problems."

Lister paused, as if expecting a comment. They're right, Luca grudgingly admitted. No shortage of lawyers. But he said nothing.

Lister went on: "The sims—this *particular* group of sims—are key. No other group has come forward looking to unionize, only these. Why, we don't know. Why, we don't care. Point is, SIRG wants the focus of your efforts from now on to be the Beacon Ridge sims. Are we clear on that?"

"Completely."

Calmer now, Luca already was germinating an idea. A simple plan. A one-man job. And he knew just the man.

This time there'd be no slip-ups because he'd take care of it himself.

Because this had become personal.

Romy Cadman had made him look bad. Hurt his reputation. Now she was going to hurt.

12

WESTCHESTER COUNTY, NY

"I'm fine, really," Romy said.

She stood in an empty ladies' room speaking to Zero on the secure PCA he'd given her. It was clear after last night that she was under surveillance, so she'd picked a spot at random and wound up in a coffee shop not far from the federal district courthouse in White Plains. At this hour—10:32 A.M.— the dining area contained only a handful of late breakfasters, and the ladies' room was empty; she'd checked all the stalls before calling.

"You're sure? Absolutely sure?"

The concern in his voice touched her. "Absolutely. Those martial arts lessons you made me take came in handy."

"I never thought you'd be in physical danger, but I felt it best you be prepared for it."

"If nothing else, it's helped me keep my cool."

Relative cool, she thought. Her nerves were still jangled. She'd tried to rest at the motel—in her own room, much to Patrick's dismay—but sleep had remained steadfastly out of reach; so she'd compensated this morning by drinking too much coffee, which did nothing to settle her nerves.

She caught sight of herself in one of the mirrors. A little haggard looking, but not half bad for someone who'd ducked an attempt on her life just a few hours ago.

"But murder?" she said. "Somehow I don't see the brothers Sinclair sitting around and deciding to have us killed."

"That decision was reached elsewhere, I'm sure. By someone connected to the company but with his own best interests at heart."

"Someone also connected to Manassas Ventures, perhaps?"

"Perhaps. Our investigation into that little company keeps coming up empty. It seems to exist in a vacuum. We've avoided direct inquiries, keeping everything back door because we don't want to let them know anyone's interested. But if nothing pans out soon we may have to arrange a little accident."

"Accident?"

He went on without elaborating. "In the meantime we want to keep you and Patrick alive and well. Connecting SimGen to the vans was a brilliant stroke. Your idea?"

"No. Patrick's."

"Clever fellow. The Beacon Ridge sims could do a lot worse."

"I'm beginning to see that." After last night, despite his tough talk, she'd half expected him to wake up this morning and run off with his tail tucked between his legs. But he was in court now, arguing motions. "What I don't see is how you managed to be down in that ravine with us."

"*I* wasn't there."

"I don't mean you personally—the organization."

"We had a tail on Portero."

That startled her. "For how long?"

"Long enough to see him rent a couple of vans. After that, we kept an eye on the vans. When some mercenary types became attached to the vans, I suspected strong-arm tactics were in the works. Some of our people followed one van to that ravine and you-know-who intervened."

"I'm glad."

"So am I. I'd never forgive myself if . . ." He cleared his throat. "Anyway, the gloves are off, I'm afraid. The organization is going to mount its own surveillance on you and Patrick. The Beacon Ridge barrack as well."

Romy's stomach turned. "Oh, no. You don't think—"

"Anything is possible. And we must be prepared for it."

13

THE BRONX

NOVEMBER 6

Meerm not hungry. Get good food in Meerm room, special food, come on own plate. Meerm not have get self from pot like down in sim big room. Meerm room food better. Yum-yum. Meerm wish she feel better so she like food more.

Meerm lonely sometime in own room. But Meerm not downstair where Needle Lady and Needle Man stick sharp thing in sim, take blood. Take-take-take. And hair face man do very bad hurt thing to Meerm and other sim. But not here Meerm room. No sharp stick here. No one hurt Meerm in own room.

Meerm room top floor. Meerm like look window at sky. Dark now. See light on street down below. Sometime Meerm wish—

"Helloooo, Meerm!"

Meerm turn, see Needle Man come through door. Needle Lady come behind. They ver happy. Needle Man hold big bottle, drink yellow bubble water in glass.

"Your latest test results are in," Needle Lady say, "and we love you, Meerm!"

"Why love Meerm?"

Needle Man laugh, say, "Because you're going to make us rich!"

"Yes!" Needle Lady yell. "We're going to *own* SimGen!"

"Now, now, Eleanor," Needle Man say. "Let's not be greedy. We'll settle for half!"

They laugh-laugh-laugh.

"Who'd ever think," Needle Man say, "that two humble globulin farmers would be able to put a company like SimGen up against the wall?"

"We haven't put it there yet," Needle Lady say. "I still have to get up the nerve to make the call."

"And when we do, we've got to be careful. We'll be playing with the big boys, and they're not going to like what we have to tell them."

They stop laugh, stop smile. Drink more.

Ooh! Tummy hurt. Meerm want feel better. Why hurt?

14

WESTCHESTER COUNTY, NY

NOVEMBER 13

"I've got to tell you," Patrick said to Romy as they sat in the sim barrack. Anj was going through her now standard routine of draping herself across Patrick's lap whenever he visited. He'd found it cute before; a warm-fuzzy moment. Now . . . "After what I saw in that brothel, I'm not as comfortable with this as I used to be."

"That's understandable," she said. "You never viewed them in a sexual context before."

"I still don't . . . can't." The memory of the brothel still gave his gut a squeamish twist. "But knowing that other people do . . ."

She was out from the city again, checking on her investment, as she liked to put it. Night had fallen but she'd hung around. For the past week Patrick had entertained a faint hope that their ordeal in the ravine might forge a bond that would lead to a closer, more intimate relationship. That hope was fading. She seemed warmer toward him, but for the most part Romy remained all business.

"How's your car?"

"Totaled. Just like my house." And my love life, he mentally added. Why don't I just join a monastery and make it official? "Haven't seen any insurance money on either, but I'm making do."

"You still haven't been scared off then?" she said.

"I'm not looking to be a martyr, but no."

She smiled. "I never took you for the martyr type."

"You mean there's a martyr type? Who the hell would want to be a martyr?"

"More than you'd think. In the right setting it can be a form of celebrity."

"I guess so. Who was it who said that some people climb onto the cross merely to be seen from a greater distance?"

"Camus, I believe."

Patrick was startled—happily. "You've read Camus?"

She shrugged.

Here was a side of Romy he'd never imagined. He wanted to delve deeper but she steered him right back to business.

"Do you see any legal speed bumps ahead?" she asked.

"Not in the immediate future," he began, then noticed Tome hovering at his shoulder.

" 'Scuse, Mist Sulliman, but Anj must eat." He tugged the sleeve of the young sim's T-shirt. "Come, Anj. Dinner come." As he led her toward the tables, Tome turned and said, "You eat too?"

Patrick glanced around. Most of the sims had gone through the line and were chowing down. He eyed the rich dark stew being ladled from the big pot and wasn't even tempted.

"No, thanks, Tome. I'm, uh, cutting back."

Romy lowered her voice. "Maybe we should give it a try. Just a taste . . . to be good guests."

"It's made from dining-room leftovers," he whispered from a corner of his mouth.

"I believe I'll pass too," Romy called out, then turned to Patrick. "By the way, are you still living in that motel?"

"Still."

"Aren't you cramped?"

"Yes and no. I thought I'd go nuts in a place like that—you know, without all my things. But I've found I don't miss them as much as I thought I would. No house, no furniture, no office, no status car . . . I should be in a deep depression but oddly enough I'm not. I've got this strange, light feeling . . .

unencumbered, I guess you could say. I feel as if I've been cut free from weights I didn't even know were there. That sound weird to you?"

"No," she said softly, and he thought he detected some warmth in her smile. "Not weird at all." She seemed to catch herself and looked away in the direction of the sims. "By the way, if we're not eating here, where do you suggest?"

"How do you feel about Cajun food?"

"Love it. I'll eat anything blackened—catfish, redfish, potholders, you name it."

"Great. I know this little place in Mount Kisco . . ."

They talked about their favorite foods—one of Romy's was sushi which, despite heroic efforts, Patrick had never developed a taste for. He was beginning to believe that the evening was shaping up to be ripe with promise when a loud groan and a clatter interrupted them.

Patrick turned and saw that one of the caddie sims had knocked his plate off the table and was doubled over, clutching his abdomen. As he watched, a second sim slipped off the bench and slumped to her knees, moaning.

"What the hell's going on?" Patrick said.

But Romy was already on her feet. "Oh, God!" she cried. "Something's wrong with the food!" She rushed forward, shouting. "Don't eat the food! It's bad! *Bad!*"

Too late. Patrick watched helplessly as one sim after another doubled over and crumpled to the floor, writhing in pain.

"What is it?" he said. "Ptomaine?"

She shook her head, her face ashen. "Spoiled food doesn't act this quickly. They've been poisoned, damn it! Somebody's poisoned their food!"

Patrick pulled out his PCA and punched in 911. "I'll call an ambulance— *lots* of ambulances!"

"To take them where?"

"To the emer—" He stopped. "Shit!"

"Right. No hospital's going to take them. They're not human."

"Then how about a veterinary hospital?"

"Is there one around? And even if there is, how do we get them there? I don't know of an ambulance service in the world that'll transport animals." She pulled out her own PCA. "But I know someone . . ."

"This organization of yours?"

She glanced at him, then turned away. He thought he heard her say "Zero."

Patrick had to do something. With frustration mounting to the detonation point he looked around and saw Tome still standing.

"Tome! You didn't eat?"

The older sim shook his head. "Not chance."

"Get up to the clubhouse! Fast! Tell them you've all been poisoned!"

As Tome ran off, Patrick hurried to the dorm area and began pulling blankets and pillows from the bunks. He couldn't do anything about whatever toxin had been used to poison them, but at least he could try to make the sims more comfortable.

"Good idea," Romy said, close by. He looked up and saw her beside him with an armful of blankets. "Help is on the way."

"Who? How much?"

"I don't know."

They hurried back to the eating area where it looked like a bomb had exploded: benches on their sides, tipped tables, spilled trays, and moaning, pain-wracked casualties strewn about the floor. Patrick recognized Nabb, his caddie when he'd played golf here—the last time he'd *ever* play golf here—that fateful September day he became involved with these sims. He lay doubled over on his side, arms folded across his abdomen.

"Here you go, buddy," he said, slipping a pillow under his head.

"Hurt, Mist Sulliman," Nabb groaned. "Hurt ver bad."

He draped a blanket over him. "I know, Nabb. We're getting help."

He spotted Deek, another caddie he knew, and tried to make him comfortable.

"Why hurt, Mist Sulliman?" Deek said, looking up at him with watery brown eyes. "Why?"

"Because someone . . ." A blast of fury forced him to stop and look away. Who? Who would or could do something like this? He found it incomprehensible.

"Sweet Jesus!" someone gasped.

Patrick looked up and saw Holmes Carter and a slim, dapper man he didn't recognize standing behind Tome in the barrack doorway. The stranger moved into the room, leaving the pudgy Carter alone, looking like a possum frozen in the glare of oncoming headlights.

"Tome wasn't kidding!" the stranger said to no one in particular. "What happened here?"

"They started getting sick after eating the stew," Patrick said. "Who are you?"

"Dr. Stokes. I'm an anesthesiologist. And I already know who you are."
He didn't offer to shake hands; instead he knelt beside one of the sick sims,
a female. "This one doesn't look so hot."

Tell me something I don't already know, Patrick wanted to say, but bit
his tongue.

"None of them do. Can you help?"

"I'm not a vet."

Romy's eyes implored him. "Help them! Please! You treat humans. How
much closer to human can you get?"

Dr. Stokes nodded. "Point taken. Let's see what I can do."

As the doctor began pressing on the sim's abdomen, asking her questions,
Patrick glanced around and spotted a small, huddled form under one of the
tables. With a cold band tightening around his chest, he rushed over—Anj.
She lay curled into a tight, shuddering ball.

"Anj?" Patrick crouched beside her and touched her shoulder; her T-shirt
was soaked. "Anj, speak to me."

A whimper was her only reply. Patrick gathered her into his arms—
Christ, she was wringing wet—and carried her over to Dr. Stokes. Her face
was so pale.

"This one's just a baby," he told Stokes. "And she's real bad."

Patrick gently lay Anj on the floor between them. Romy was there immediately with a pillow and blanket.

"Diaphoretic," Stokes said, more to himself than Patrick. He held her
wrist a moment. "Pulse is thready."

"What's that mean?"

"She's going into shock." He turned back to the first sim he'd been ex-
amining. "This one too. They're going to need IVs and pressors. What in
God's name did they eat?"

Before Patrick could answer, he heard the sound of a heavy-duty engine,
slamming doors, and Carter saying, "You can't drive that up here!"

He looked up and saw two grim-faced men, one in a golf shirt, the other
in a sport coat, file through the door with some kind of cart rolling between
them. They pushed past Carter as if he were a piece of misplaced furniture.
Two more strangers, a man and a woman, both in flannel shirts and jeans,
followed them.

"You can't just walk in here!" Carter said. "This is a private club!"

Ignoring him, they pulled stethoscopes and blood pressure cuffs from the
cart and fanned out into the room. The woman came over to where Patrick,
Romy, and Stokes stood. She looked to be about fifty, her long brown hair

streaked with gray and tied back. She nodded to Romy, then without a word she knelt beside Anj and the other sim and began taking blood pressures.

"They're shocky," Stokes offered.

The woman looked up. Her face was expressionless, all business, but her eyes looked infinitely sad. "You a doc?"

"Yes, I'm an—"

"We've got saline in the cart. If you want to help, you can start drips on these two."

Stokes nodded and headed for the cart. The stranger moved on.

Patrick turned to Romy. "Who are these people?"

"Doctors."

"From SimGen?"

She shook her head and bit her upper lip. Romy's usually steely composure had slipped. She looked rattled, something Patrick never would have thought possible. Maybe it was the helplessness. Patrick felt it too—a need to do something but not knowing what.

"Your people then," he said. "Your organization. How'd they get here so fast?"

"They've been on standby."

"You mean you expected this?"

"Expected someone might try to hurt them." Her eyes were black cauldrons. "Excuse me. I need a little air."

He watched her breeze past Holmes Carter, still standing by the door, sputtering like an over-choked engine. Tome squatted against a far wall, his face buried in his arms. And all around Patrick, the strange, silent doctors, gliding from one sick sim to another.

Feeling useless, he decided he could use a breath of night air himself, but first he had something to say . . .

He stopped before Carter. "This your doing, Holmesy?"

Carter's round face reddened, his third chin wobbled. "You son of a bitch! If I was going to poison anyone it would be you, not these dumb animals. They're just pawns in your game."

The genuine outrage in Carter's eyes made Patrick regret his words. He backed off a bit. "Well . . . somebody poisoned them."

"If you're looking to place blame, Sullivan, find a mirror. This never would have happened if you hadn't started poking your nose where it doesn't belong."

Stung, Patrick turned away. The truth of Carter's words hurt and clung to him as he stepped out into the night.

Some sort of oversized commuter van was parked on the grass outside. The doctors had driven it straight across the club's rear lawn to the barrack door; Patrick could trace the deep furrows under the pitiless glow of the moon peering down from the crystal sky. Up on the rise he spotted a number of Beacon Ridge members standing outside the clubhouse, gawking at the scene. And Romy . . . where was Romy?

He walked around the barrack and spotted her down the slope by the border privet hedge. But she wasn't alone. A tall dark figure stood beside her. After a moment, Romy turned and began walking back up the slope; the tall man faded into the shadows of the hedge.

"Who was that?" he asked as she approached.

"No one."

"But—"

Her face had settled into grim lines. "You didn't see a thing. Now let's go back inside and make ourselves useful."

Patrick was about to comment on what seemed to be a lot of hush-hush, undercover nonsense but bit it back. It wasn't nonsense at all. Not when poison was part of someone's game plan.

Romy stopped dead in the doorway and he ran into her back, knocking her forward. He saw immediately why she'd stopped.

Chaos in the barrack. The formerly silent, seemingly imperturbable doctors were in frenzied motion, pumping ventilation bags and thumping sim chests.

"I've got another one crashing here!" one called out. He was on his knees next to an unconscious sim. He looked up and saw Romy and Patrick. "You two want to help?"

Patrick tried to speak but could only nod.

"Name it," Romy said.

"Each of you get an Ambu bag from that cart and bring them over here."

Romy was already moving. "What's an Am—?"

"Looks like a small football with a face mask attached," the doctor said.

Romy opened a deep drawer, removed two of the devices, handed one to Patrick. On their way back, to his right, he noticed Holmes Carter kneeling, using one of the bags to pump air into a sim's lungs.

Carter . . . ?

To their left, the woman doc waved and called out. "Romy! Over here! Quick!"

Romy peeled off and Patrick kept on course toward the first doc. He stuttered to a stop when he saw the patient.

Anj.

She lay supine on the floor, limp as a rag doll with half its stuffing gone; the front of her bib overalls had been pulled down and her T-shirt slit open, exposing her budding, pink-nippled, lightly furred breasts.

"Don't just stand there!" the doctor said. He was sweaty, flushed, and looked too young to be a doctor. He had his hands between Anj's breasts and was pumping on her chest. "Bag her!"

Patrick's frozen brain tried to make sense of the words as they filtered through air thick as cotton.

"Bag . . . ?" Was she dead?

"Give me that!" The doctor reached across Anj and snatched the Ambu bag from Patrick's numb fingers. He fitted the mask over Anj's mouth and nose and squeezed the bag. "There! Do that once for every five times I pump."

Patrick dropped to his knees and managed to get his hands to work, squeezing the bag every time the doctor shouted, "Now!" and wishing someone would cover her. Every so often the doctor would stop pumping and press his stethoscope to Anj's chest.

"Shit!" he said after the third time. "Nothing! Keep bagging." He pawed through what looked like an orange plastic tool box, muttering, "No monitor, no defibrillator, how am I supposed to . . . here!"

He pulled out a small syringe capped with a three- or four-inch needle. He popped the top, expelled air and a little fluid, then swabbed Anj's chest with alcohol.

Patrick blinked. "You're not going to stick that into—"

That was exactly what he did: right between a pair of ribs to the left of her breast bone; he drew back on the plunger until a gush of dark red swirled into the barrel, then emptied the syringe.

The doctor resumed pumping, crying, "One-two-three-four-five-*bag*!"

They kept up the routine for another minute or so, then the doctor listened to Anj's chest again.

"Nothing." He pulled a penlight from the plastic box and flashed it into her eyes. "Fixed and dilated." He leaned back and wiped his dripping face on his sleeve. "She's gone."

"No," Patrick said.

But Anj's glazed, staring eyes said it all. Still he resumed squeezing the bag, frantically, spasmodically.

"No use," the doctor said.

"Try, damn it!" Patrick shouted. "She's too young! She's too . . ." He ran out of words.

"Her brain's been deprived of oxygen too long. She's not coming back."

Patrick dropped the bag and leaned over her. An aching pressure built in his chest. He felt his eyes fill, the tears slip over the lids and drop on Anj's chest.

A hand closed gently on his shoulder and he heard the young doctor say, "I know how you feel."

Patrick shrugged off his hand. "No, you don't."

"I do, believe me. We couldn't save her, but we've got other sick sims here and maybe we can save some of *them*. Let's get to work."

"All right," Patrick said, unable to buck the doctor's logic. "Just give me a second."

As the doctor moved off, Patrick pulled the edges of Anj's torn T-shirt together. They didn't quite meet so he pulled up the bib front of her overalls. Then he pushed her eyelids closed and stared at her.

How could he feel such a sense of loss for something that wasn't even human? This wasn't like puddling up at the end of *Old Yeller*. This was *real*.

He pulled off his suit coat and draped it over the upper half of her body. He hovered by her side a moment longer; then, feeling like a terminally arthritic hundred-year-old man, he pushed himself to his feet and moved on.

The next half hour became a staggering blur, moving from one prostrate form to another, losing sim after sim, and pressing on, until . . . finally . . . it was over.

Spent, Patrick leaned against a wall, counting. He felt as if he'd been dragged behind a truck over miles of bad road. He'd cried tonight. When was the last time he'd cried? Romy sagged against him, sobbing. He counted twice, three times, but the number kept coming up the same: nineteen still, sheet-covered forms strewn about the floor.

The woman doctor they'd met earlier drifted by; he flagged her down.

"How many did you save?" he said.

She brushed a damp ringlet away from her flushed face. "Six—just barely. We've moved them into the sleep area. They'll make it, but it'll be weeks before they're back to normal. Counting the older sim who didn't eat, that leaves seven survivors."

"The bastards!" Romy gritted through her teeth. "The lousy fucking bastards!" She pushed away from him and began pounding the wall with her fist, repeating, "Bastards!" over and over through her clenched teeth.

She dented the plasterboard, punched through, then started on another spot.

Patrick grabbed her wrist. "Romy! You're going to hurt yourself!"

She turned on him with blazing eyes; she seemed like another person and for an instant he thought she was going to take a swing at him. Then she wrenched her arm free and stalked toward the door.

Though physically and emotionally drained, Patrick forced himself to start after her. But when he spotted Tome crouched in a corner, his head cradled in his arms, he changed course and squatted next to him.

"I'm sorry, Tome," he said, feeling the words catch in his throat. "I'm so sorry."

Tome looked up at him with reddened eyes; tears streaked his cheeks. "Sim family gone, Mist Sulliman. All gone."

"Not all, Tome. Deek survived, so did some others."

But Tome was shaking his head. "Too many dead sim. Family gone. All Tome fault."

"No-no-no," Patrick said, putting a hand on his shoulder. "You can't lay that on yourself. If anybody's to blame here—besides the son of a bitch who poisoned the food—it's me."

Tome kept shaking his head. "No. Tome know. Tome ask Mist Sulliman. If Tome nev ask, Mist Sulliman nev do."

"That doesn't make you responsible for . . . this. You wanted something better for your family, Tome, and we're not going to let this stop us. I swear—"

"No, Mist Sulliman." He struggled to his feet. "We stop. Family gone. No law bring back. We stop. Other sim die if no stop."

"You can't mean that!" Patrick said, stunned. "That'll mean that Anj and Nabb and all the others died for nothing!"

Tome turned and slid away. "No union, Mist Sulliman. Tome too tired. Tome too sad."

"Then they win! Is that what you want?"

"Tome want sim live," he said without looking back. "That all Tome want now."

Patrick fought the urge to grab the old sim and shake some sense into him. They couldn't quit now—public opinion would rush to their side after this atrocity. He took a step after him, but the utter defeat in the slump of those narrow shoulders stopped him.

He remembered the night they met, when Tome explained what he and the other sims wanted: *Family . . . and one thing other . . . respect, Mist Sulliman. Just little respect.*

And now your family's been murdered, Patrick thought. And the only respect you've gained is mine. And what's that worth?

Flickering light to his left caught his eye. He saw Reverend Eckert's face on the TV screen in the corner. The voice was muted but Patrick knew the bastard could only be spewing more of his anti-sim venom. With a low cry of rage he stalked across the room, picked up an overturned bench, and raised it above his head. But before he could smash the set, a hand grabbed his arm.

"Please don't do that," said a voice.

He turned and found Holmes Carter standing behind him. On any other day he would have teed off on the man, but Carter had surprised the hell out of him tonight—worked as hard as anyone to save the sims. And he looked it: His sport coat was gone and his wrinkled shirt lay partially unbuttoned, exposing a swath of his bulging belly. Right now he looked shell-shocked.

Patrick knew exactly how he felt.

"Why the hell not?"

"What will the survivors watch?"

Damn him, he was right.

Patrick lowered the bench and extended his hand. "I want to thank you, Holmes. I take back anything I've ever said to offend you."

"Sure." Carter gave the hand a listless, distracted shake and looked around. "Gone," he said dazedly. "Just like that, three-quarters of our sims . . . gone. Nabb . . . he used to be my favorite caddie, and now he's dead. Why?" He looked at Patrick with tear-filled eyes. "What kind of sick person would do this? What kind of a world have we created?"

"Wish I knew, Holmes. It gets stranger and stranger."

Carter sighed. "I realized something tonight. These sims . . . they're . . . they were . . . part of Beacon Ridge. We knew them. We liked them. I'm going to tell the board to grant collective bargaining rights, and I'm going to insist that the survivors remain together as long as they want."

Patrick opened his mouth to speak but found himself, for possibly the first time in his adult life, at a loss for words.

Carter smiled wanly. "What's the matter? Cat got your tongue?" He gave his head a single sad shake. "Wasn't that part of the exchange that set this whole mess in motion?"

Patrick nodded, remembering their little confrontation in the club men's room. "Yes . . . yes, I believe it was. This is good of you, Holmes."

"I just wish I'd done it yesterday."

Without another word Carter turned and wove his way through the dead sims toward the door.

We've won, Patrick thought—a reflex. The thought died aborning. He looked around at the sheeted forms and knew that if this was winning, he'd much rather have lost.

He heard an engine rumble to life outside. He looked around and realized that the mysterious doctors had disappeared. He hurried to the door in time to see the truck roll away across the grass toward the road.

Romy stood there, leaning against the barrack wall. He approached her cautiously. She seemed to have spent her rage, so he filled her in on the latest developments.

"Tome's decision doesn't surprise me," she said in a low, hoarse voice. "Sims aren't fighters. But after what you'd told me about the club president . . ."

"Yeah. I guess I had him wrong. People never cease to surprise me, for good or for ill. Like these phantom doctors of yours. Where did they come from, where did they go? They pop out of nowhere with no explanation, and then they're gone."

"I told you—" Romy began.

"I don't want to hear about some nameless 'organization' again. How about some specifics? Who's behind you? And who killed those two guys when we were run off the road the other night? I want answers, Romy."

Her expression was tight. "Do you? Well then maybe you're in for one more surprise tonight."

"I don't think I can handle another." He noticed a strange look in her eyes, wary yet flirting with anticipation. "But I'll bite. What?"

"Someone wants to meet you."

15

Romy drove. A mostly silent ride during which she replied to his questions with terse monosyllables. He sensed an inner struggle but hadn't a clue as to what it might be about. In his brain-fragged state, Patrick didn't have the strength or the will to probe.

She stopped at a small cabin on the edge of Rye Lake. Patrick stepped from her rented car and looked around.

The surrounding woods lay dark and silent; the cabin was an angular blotch of shadow with no sign of habitation; on its far side a dock jutted into the lake where tendrils of mist rose into the chill air from the glassy moonlit water.

"Doesn't look like anyone's home," he said.

Romy was moving toward the cabin. "Look again. And use your nose."

Patrick sniffed the air. A wood fire somewhere. And now he saw a thin stream of smoke drifting from the cabin's chimney. Okay, so someone was inside. But who? Along the way Romy had told him that he'd find out when they got there. Just what she'd told him when she'd led him to the sim whorehouse. This time would be different. He wasn't going through that door until—

But Romy wasn't waiting for him. She was already halfway to the house.

He hurried to catch up to her. "This cloak and dagger stuff is getting to me."

"Relax. You may find a cloak here, but no dagger." Without warning she leaned forward and kissed him—too briefly—on the lips. "Thanks."

"What for?"

"For hanging in there tonight. For caring."

Patrick touched his mouth where the warmth of Romy's lips lingered. He wanted more, but she'd already opened the door and pushed through. He followed her into the dark interior, lit only by the glow from the fireplace.

"Over here, Romy," said a deep voice near the fire. Patrick could make out a dark form seated in a high-backed chair, positioned so that the light came from behind him. The figure leaned forward and extended a hand. With a start Patrick realized he was masked. "Welcome, Mr. Sullivan."

Hesitantly Patrick stepped forward and shook the hand, surprised to find it was gloved. "And you are . . . ?"

"My name is Zero."

And that stands for what? Patrick thought. IQ? Personality rating? But he said, "Interesting name."

"Forgive the melodramatic trappings," Zero said, "but we take security very seriously."

Melodramatic barely touches this, Patrick thought. I'm standing in the dark talking to a masked man.

But it was right in tune with the nightmarish unreality of the past few hours.

"Just who might 'we' be?"

"A loose-knit organization I've put together."

"An organization . . . what's it called?"

"I've resisted naming it. Once a group gives itself a name, it tends to take on a life of its own; the group can become an end in itself, rather than simply a means."

"What end are we talking about here?"

"In a nutshell: to protect existing sims from exploitation and stop SimGen or anyone else from producing more."

"Tall order."

"We know."

"How many members?"

"Many."

"Like those doctors who showed up tonight?"

"Yes. Volunteers. They were on standby in case of disaster."

"Which we had—in spades."

"Yes. Mistakenly I had expected more direct violence, a bomb or the like. I had the barrack under guard." Zero's voice thickened. "I never thought to guard the kitchen."

Romy said, "So it was one of the help?" The flickering firelight accentuated her high cheekbones, glittered in her eyes. Even in the dark she was beautiful.

"I doubt it. That sample of stew you brought me was laced with a very sophisticated synthetic toxin we've been unable to identify. This was not the work of a jealous kitchen hand or a union goon. Whoever did this has considerable resources."

"SimGen," Patrick said.

"Not impossible, but out of character. SimGen has always protected its sims."

"But have its sims ever posed a threat before?"

Romy spoke. "That's a point, but we're coming to believe that SimGen is not quite the free-standing entity it presents to the public. That it's not pulling all its own strings. This may be the work of another shadow organization within SimGen or linked to it."

Uh-oh, Patrick thought, sniffing paranoia. What next? New World Order conspiracy? Trilateral commission? Illuminati?

Only Romy's presence kept him from backing away. He couldn't think of anyone more firmly grounded in reality. And he couldn't deny the reality of the poisoned Beacon Ridge sims.

"But why kill those sims?"

"Because what threatens SimGen," Zero said, "threatens the shadow group. And in this case, the sims were the logical target: Lawyers are replaceable, plaintiffs are not."

"Thanks a lot," Patrick said, but knew it was too true. "Any idea who they are?"

"No, but we've got the start of a trail, and we're following it. That's why I've asked you here tonight, Mr. Sullivan. We'd like your help."

"You want to hire me?"

"Not exactly. You'd be an unpaid consultant, a volunteer like Ms. Cadman."

"I don't work for free."

"Even for people who saved your life?" Romy said.

She had him there. "Glad you brought that up: Just who *did* save my life?"

Zero said, "Join us and you'll know . . . eventually."

"You need me in the legal field?"

"There, and wherever else your unique brand of ingenuity can be of service."

"Flattery will get you everywhere."

"And who knows?" Zero said. "We may be able to position you for another crack at SimGen's deep pockets."

"Now you're talking."

"I thought that might sell you," Romy said.

"I'm not sold yet. You've been calling the shots for Romy, I assume."

Zero inclined his head. "I merely suggest . . . she is always free to decline, just as you will be."

"But who's calling the shots for you?"

"No one."

"You could be just telling me that."

"I could. But I'm not."

"So you're funding this operation?"

He shook his head. "I raise money in various ways . . . donations from a number of sources."

"I must have missed the last annual *Free the Sims* telethon."

No one laughed. Tough crowd, Patrick thought. But then, after what had happened tonight, what did he expect?

"Your point?" Zero said.

"Money tends to come with strings."

"True. And these donations come with one string, and only one: Stop SimGen."

"What about freeing the sims?"

"That will be the fallout, but first we shut down the pipeline. Once we cut off the flow of new sims, we can deal with the problem of what to do with those who already exist."

"These donors . . . who are they—specifically? I like to know who's footing the bill."

"I will partially answer that when you join us, with the proviso that you never breathe a word of what you learn. But I must warn you not to accept my invitation lightly. The deeper you delve into this morass, the more you'll see that nothing connected with it is what it appears to be. And there's danger. You've witnessed firsthand on more than one occasion the ruthlessness of the other side. We're in a war, Mr. Sullivan, and any one of us could become a casualty."

Patrick swallowed. Where had his saliva gone? But if Romy was in this and willing to take the risks, how could he stand here next to her and back out? What kind of a man would that make him?

Perhaps a man who'd live to a ripe old age.

"What about if I decide I don't like what you're up to? If I want to walk, I want be able to do so with no strings."

"Of course. As long as you understand that you're not walking away from the confidentiality agreement."

Hoping he wouldn't regret this, he managed a shrug and a nod that conveyed a lot more bravado that he felt.

"Fair enough. I'll give it a try. Do I have to sign in blood?"

Zero shook his head. "Your word is enough."

He raised his hand and a TV flickered to life on the far side of the room. Diagonal lines danced across the screen, then the Reverend Eckert's face appeared.

"Jerk!" Patrick said.

"Give him a listen."

Eckert's face looked grave, anguished. His voice was at least an octave lower than his usual ranting tone.

"My friends . . . I have just heard that a number of sims—nineteen of them, I'm told—have been killed. Poisoned. These were the sims who were trying to unionize. This is very disturbing. More than disturbing, it's a terrible, terrible thing, and I hope, I pray to the Good Lord that no one in my flock is responsible. Because if one of you is, then I must shoulder some of the blame. It might have been my words that drove one of you to this terrible deed. If so, then I have been misunderstood. Terribly misunderstood.

"So hear me now, friends, and hear me well.

"I wish no harm to any sim. I have never, ever preached violence against

them. I have said they were created by evil, Satan-inspired science, and I know that to be true, but I have never said the sims themselves were evil. They are not. They are the innocent products of unnatural science who should be allowed to live out their lives in peace.

"Violence toward sims is not the way. If you kill sims, you only give SinGen the excuse to produce more. We want SinGen to stop producing sims. We must use the law—the law, my friends—to cut off the supply at its source by piercing the beating evil heart of the problem. And that heart is the devil corporation that subverts the Laws of Creation by fashioning creatures that are not part of God's design.

"Please. I beg of you: Do not harm sims. That is not the answer—it is, in fact, counterproductive. Spreading the word, boycotting businesses that lease sims, endlessly harassing SinGen in court until it finally surrenders. That is the way, my friends. The only way.

"And to continue fighting that battle, I need your support . . ."

The screen went blank.

"His standard request for contributions follows," Zero said.

"When did he broadcast that?" Patrick said.

"He hasn't. He rushed it into production and it's going out to replace his previously scheduled message."

"How'd you get it?"

"The Reverend Eckert is part of the organization. One of its major contributors, in fact."

For the second time tonight Patrick found himself speechless.

Romy smiled, her first in too many hours. The pearly enamel within her smile caught the light, giving her a Cheshire Cat look.

"If only you could see your face! Oh, God, I wish I had a camera!"

16

As soon as Luca stepped into the room, the usually listless Sinclair-2 rose from his seat and came toward him. He looked like he'd slept in his clothes; his face flushed as he started shouting.

"It was you, wasn't it! You killed those sims! You monster! You *monster!*"

"Calm down, Ellis," Abel Voss said, putting an arm around the man's shoulders. "You can't go makin wild accusations like that."

"I can!" Sinclair-2 cried. "I know this man's methods. And if he didn't do it himself, he sent one of his hired thugs!"

No, Luca thought. I did it myself. A one-man op. That's what you have to do sometimes if you want to be sure a job gets done right.

It had taken Luca about a week after the Saw Mill River Parkway debacle to put all the pieces in place. Two nights ago he'd made his move.

But the op developed an early hitch: a tail. If he hadn't been looking for one, he never would have spotted it. But he'd been prepared.

He'd driven into midtown Manhattan and valet-parked his car at the New York Hilton, then zipped through the lobby and out a side exit where he hailed a cab that took him to a second car that had been left for him in a lot near the theater district. He'd driven out of town immediately, directly to Westchester where he'd parked a good mile from the Beacon Ridge Country Club. He'd walked the rest of the way, ducking into the shadows whenever a car approached. When he reached the club, he'd huddled in the hedges until the sims were all in their barrack and the last human had left.

Or so he'd thought. That was when he'd almost got caught. He'd been about to step out of the bushes when he spotted two dark figures gliding between the shadows near the barrack. As he'd watched, they separated, one swiftly climbing a tree, the other disappearing into the bushes.

Someone had the sim quarters under guard. Sullivan? Cadman? No mat-

ter. That hadn't been Luca's destination. He was headed for the sprawling
structure on the crest of the hill, the club's main building.

Soon he'd reached his destination: the kitchen. Once he'd located the
cooking pot labeled *SIMS* he removed a vial of clear odorless liquid from his
breast pocket. A brand new compound sent down through Lister from SIRG;
so new it didn't have a name yet, only a number: J7683452.

He'd emptied the vial into the big pot and begun swirling the liquid
around, coating the sides and bottom. When it dried, it was invisible. The
only thing that could have gone wrong was somebody washing out the pot.
But it had been hung up clean, so that was unlikely.

Amazing stuff, J7683452. He could have stuck his head into that pot,
licked its insides clean, and he'd be fine. Perfectly harmless in that state. But
heat it to a hundred-and-sixty degrees or more and . . .

Bon appétit.

As for here and now, he didn't owe the Sinclair brothers an explanation.
And they didn't deserve one.

"Admit it, Portero! You murdered those nineteen sims!"

"Murdered?" he said with a calculatedly derisive snort—few things gave
him more pleasure than getting under these twits' skins. "They're animals.
They can be killed, they can be slaughtered, they can be sacrificed to the
gods, but they can't be murdered."

With a hoarse roar Sinclair-2 launched himself at Luca, only to be hauled
back by the heavier, stronger Voss.

"You don't want to be doin that, son," Voss said. "Trust me, you don't."

"Ellis, for God's sake control yourself!" Sinclair-1 said.

"Listen to them," Luca said softly.

He hadn't moved a muscle. He'd take no pleasure in hurting Sinclair-2—
it would be like fighting a woman—but he could not allow another man to
lay a hand on him.

Sinclair-2 struggled a moment, then pulled free and returned to his usual
spot on the sofa where he dropped his face into his hands.

What gives with that guy? Luca wondered. How can he be such a wimp?

"Did you?" Sinclair-1 said, staring at him. "Were you responsible for poisoning those sims?"

"Does it matter?" Luca said.

No one answered.

Just as I thought. They don't *want* to know.

"Just tell me one thing," Voss said. "And think very carefully on your
answer: Will the perpetrator or perpetrators ever be found?"

"My guess?" Luca shook his head. "Never. But whoever they were, they did us a favor. The Beacon Ridge club has surrendered. They're giving the sims what they want."

"Since when?" Voss said. "I ain't heard nothin about this."

"That's because they haven't made the announcement yet."

"If that's true," the attorney said, his eyes widening, "it takes the matter out of the court's hands."

"No precedent," Sinclair-1 whispered.

Luca watched cautious optimism grow in their eyes. He'd be sharing in that good feeling if not for a call he'd received this morning. Nothing more than a hoax, he hoped—*prayed*. Or maybe a wild fantasy cooked up by some drugged-out waste of protoplasm. He'd fed it to Lister who'd pass it up the SIRG ladder, but he'd keep it from the Sinclairs for now. He suspected a leak somewhere, and if he was right, the less said here, the better.

But he dearly wished he could lay it on these two. The mere mention now of what the woman on the phone had told him would snuff out the relief warming Sinclair-1 and Voss as if it had never been.

Because if this woman had been telling the truth about a sim named Meerm, it made the threat they'd just overcome seem like a pebble in a mountain gorge.

THREE

MEERM

I

Poor Meerm. Poor, poor Meerm. She ver sick sim. Meerm nev sick before. Not like be sick. Food come up sometime. And tummy hurt. Hurt-hurt-hurt. Bad tummy hurt all time.

Meerm stand window, look out through metal bar. Wish she be outside sometime. Not now. Cold out now. Still—

What that? Loud noise from downstair. Again! Loud noise again. *Crack!* Like giant plate break. Meerm go door, open just little and listen. Hear loud scare word by Needle Lady and Needle Man, hear new man voice shout more loud, hear sim voice, many voice cry *ee-ee-ee!* Ver fraid, other sim.

Meerm hear new man voice shout, "Where is she?" and hear ver fraid Needle Lady say, "Upstairs! We moved her upstairs!"

Meerm ver fraid. Make belly hurt badder. Hear many loud feet come stair. Meerm want close sick room door but no good. Across hall see ladder up wall. Ladder up to little door. Meerm sure locked—all door here locked— but Meerm try. Must try. Too fraid stay sick room.

Meerm jump cross hall, climb ladder, push little door. Move! Door move! Meerm so happy. Climb up roof. Cold-cold-cold. Close little door. Meerm listen. Hear new man voice shout. Ver, ver mad. Hear foot on ladder. Come roof! What Meerm do? Where go?

There. Metal hole. Meerm can fit? Run and crawl in. Squeeze ver hard. Sink inside just as mans come roof. Meerm close eye, not breathe as mans run all round roof. Man look in metal hole but not see Meerm.

Mans ver mad as leave roof. Meerm safe but still not move. Wait. Meerm will wait long long time. Wait until—

What smell? Smoke! Smoke and hot come up vent. Meerm get out and stand on roof. Tar hot on foot. Smoke all round. Meerm ver ver scare. Run round roof, see fire evwhere. Look down. Flame all round, come out bar on all window. Meerm not want die. But roof ver hot. Tar melt under Meerm foot. What Meerm do?

Meerm scream. No one hear. No one near.

2

MANHATTAN

DECEMBER 1

Patrick stood at his hotel window and gazed down at the top of Madison Square Garden and the giant Christmas snowman atop its entrance. The unrisen sun was just beginning to lighten the low clouds lidding the city. In a few hours the streets below would be packed with the weekly Saturday horde of Christmas shoppers.

Patrick had been awake for hours. This had become a pattern every night since the poisoning of the sims. Fall asleep easily—with the help of a couple of stiff Scotches—and then find himself wide awake at 3:00 A.M. or so with his mind sifting through the litterbox his life had become.

All because of an argument in a country club men's room. What if he hadn't chosen that moment to go to the bathroom? What if he'd waited until after that second drink? Holmes Carter would have been long gone, and without Carter's bad attitude, Patrick would have laughed off Tome's request to unionize the club sims. If he'd done that, where would he be now?

For one thing, he'd still have a law practice; he missed Maggie, even missed some of his clients. He'd also have a house instead of a fire-blackened foundation. And he might still have Pamela, although he wondered if that would be such a good thing. From his present perspective he could see that their relationship had been one more of mutual convenience than rooted in any deep regard.

He probably wouldn't have spent Thanksgiving alone, either. Ever since his folks retired to South Carolina, they'd always called and insisted he come down for Thanksgiving. Not this year. That was Dad's doing, Patrick was sure.

He'd known Dad had been upset with the whole idea of a sim union—he'd made that perfectly clear over the phone on more than one occasion—but Patrick hadn't realized just how much until Thanksgiving came and went without an invitation.

That had hurt. Even now, more than a week later, the wound still ached.

So here he was: jobless, homeless, alone, and functionally orphaned. And aligned with a masked mystery man who'd invited him to join a nameless fifth column movement to bring down one of the world's most powerful multinational corporations.

"And I said yes," he whispered, still not believing it.

This is not me, he kept telling himself. This is somebody else. All I wanted out of life was stability and a good living. That was why I went into law. I am not a risk taker. I am not an adrenaline junkie. How did I come to this? And how do I get out of it?

Easy. Just say no. Pack up and walk away.

And do what? Labor relations? After what he'd been through, could he go back to sitting at a table and listening to union and management argue over the length of coffee breaks or who qualified for daycare? Not likely.

And then there was Romy. Walking away from Zero meant walking away from her.

So for the foreseeable future he'd stick this out and see where it took him.

Hopefully it would soon take him out of this hotel. Zero had suggested he relocate himself and his practice to Manhattan. Romy had laughed off Patrick's suggestion that he move in with her while he hunted for an office and an apartment. So for the time being, home was a room in the Hotel Pennsylvania. Finding space—whether living or office—wasn't easy. The new boom had sent prices in Manhattan up to where the new space station was nearing completion.

The jangle of the phone startled him. He stepped through the dark room to the night table, found the phone, and fumbled the receiver to his ear.

Romy's voice: "Am I interrupting something?"

"Only my daily predawn reverie."

She gave him an address. "If you haven't anything better to do, meet me there ASAP. I'll wait for you."

Patrick sensed strain in her voice, but before he could ask for any details she hung up.

Dutifully he pulled on yesterday's clothes, grabbed a large container of coffee on his way through the lobby, and ventured into the early morning chill of Seventh Avenue in search of a taxi.

The driver shot him a look when he read off the address. "You're sure?"

"I'm sure," Patrick told him after double-checking.

The driver shrugged—reluctantly, Patrick thought—and gunned the cab into the traffic.

Patrick considered that look and thought, Romy, Romy, what are you getting me into now?

3

THE BRONX

All too soon Patrick understood the driver's reaction. The address was in the fabled borough of the Bronx. Not the nice Botanical Gardens Bronx, but the bad Bronx, the *Bonfire of the Vanities*/"Fort Apache" Bronx. This particular section embodied most people's worst expectations: a wasteland of scattered buildings, some occupied, some abandoned, all battered, interspersed with vacant, garbage-strewn lots.

"Christ, what happened here?" Patrick muttered as he stepped out of the cab.

As soon as he closed the door behind him, his taxi chirped its tires and zoomed away. Patrick couldn't blame him. At least there were lots of cops around. No need to ask why they were here: The charred, smoking ruin of what must have been a cousin to the neighboring derelict buildings was the obvious center of attention. No fire trucks in sight now, but a couple of red

SUVs bearing fire department logos stood out among the cluster of blue-and-white units blocking the street.

He glanced around and spotted Romy's long black cleathre coat among the gaggle of onlookers standing outside the yellow police tape.

"Not exactly my idea of a fun place to spend a Saturday morning," he said as he reached her.

"You're here," she said, but no smile lit her grim expression. "Good. We can get started."

" 'How are you, Patrick?' " he said. " 'Did you sleep well?' Why, yes, Romy. Thank you for asking. And how was your night?"

"Save it," she said, lifting the tape and ducking under. "Follow me."

Patrick complied as she approached a burly, clipboard-wielding sergeant.

"Excuse me, Sergeant," she said, holding up a leather ID folder. "Romy Cadman, OPRR. Please fill me in on what you've found."

The sergeant swiveled his head and gave her a quick up and down with his pale blue eyes.

"O-P-*what*?"

"Office for the Protection of Research Risks. We're federal. We monitor labs and test subjects, animal and human. Lieutenant Milancewich at Manhattan South notified me that this building might have housed an unlicensed lab and that sims could have been involved."

Patrick knew Romy had no authority to be here, but said nothing, just stood by and admired her moxie as she weathered the sergeant's hostile stare.

"He did, did he? Well, I ain't heard of no OPRR and no Lieutenant Milancewich, and you're one hell of a long way from Manhattan South. We can handle this just fine without no feds nosing into it."

"Of course you can," Romy said. "OPRR has no investigative authority. We're only offering help. We know labs. We can trace diagnostic equipment better and faster than anyone. We know lab animals. If sims were used as test subjects here, we can help you track them. Our interest is purely statistical: We're keeping tally of illegal labs and what biologicals they produce." She opened her cleathre coat to return her ID folder to an inner pocket, revealing in the process a tight, black, ribbed knit sweater and long legs slinking from a short black skirt. "We're a resource, sergeant. Use us."

The sergeant's eyes lingered on her coat as she tied it closed, then he stuck out his hand.

"Andy Yarger."

Romy smiled and shook his hand. "Call me Romy."

Patrick resisted an impulse to close his eyes and shake his head. If that had been him popping up in front of Sergeant Yarger with an OPRR ID, he'd have been kicked back on the far side of the yellow tape before he'd spoken word one. But Romy had just reduced this Bronx-hardened cop to a lap dog.

The weaker sex? Yeah, tell me about it.

"And who's this?" Yarger said, jutting his chin Patrick's way.

"That's my assistant, Patrick."

Patrick smiled and nodded at the sergeant, thinking, That's me, all right: faithful sidekick and gofer.

Yarger narrowed his eyes. "Ain't I seen you before?"

"About the lab equipment?" Romy prompted.

"Your lieutenant friend was right. We found bits and pieces of all sorts of lab equipment in the wreckage. Some of it's been identified as—lemme see." He consulted his clipboard. "Here we go: hematology machines, blood chemistry analyzers, immu . . . immuno . . ."

Romy was nodding. "I get the picture. Who identified the equipment?"

"Couple of M-E's boys."

"M-E?" Patrick said when he saw Romy's stricken look. "Sims were killed?"

"We should be so lucky. Nah. Just one very dead, very crisp human corpse. Male, age unknown."

Patrick stared at the burned-out ruins and couldn't help grimacing. They reminded him of what remained of his house, and how "crisp" he could have been.

"What a way to go."

"Wasn't the fire that got him. A bullet saved him from that."

"Really?" Patrick said. "You're sure?"

Yarger gave him a steely look.

"What he means," Romy added quickly, "is how can you tell if he was, as you say, 'very crisp'?"

The sergeant poked an index finger against the center of his forehead. "Ain't never seen no fire burn a little hole here and blow off the back of a skull, know what I'm saying?"

"I hear you," Romy said. "But no, er, 'crisp' sims?"

"Not yet anyways. Don't expect to find none either."

"But Lieutenant Milancewich mentioned sims."

"Right. We have a witness who saw armed men herding a bunch of sims and some humans into a couple of vans just before the place lit up." He shook his head. "I don't know what sort of incendiary devices they used, but they musta been beauts. Place went up like it was made of paper."

"But there *could* be dead sims in there," Romy persisted.

Yarger crooked a finger and started moving away. "C'mere. I'll show you why there won't be."

Patrick and Romy followed him to a taped-off area near the corner. Yarger stopped and pointed to the sidewalk.

"That's why."

Red spray-painted letters spread across the pavement.

FREE THE SIMS!

DEATH TO SIM OPPRESSORS!

SLA

"SLA?" Patrick said with a glance at Romy.

Her face was troubled when she met his eyes. "I know what you're thinking," she whispered. "But no. Impossible. He'd never."

"The Symbionese Liberation Army?" Patrick raised his voice to cover hers. "Didn't they kidnap Patty Hearst?"

"Different group," Yarger said. "These assholes are the '*Sim* Liberation Army.' Don't that beat all."

"How do you know?" Romy said.

"That's what they called themselves in the note they left."

"What else did it say?"

"Buncha sim-hugger garbage. The usual stuff. You know the rap."

"May I see it?"

Yarger gave Romy a you-gotta-be-kidding look. "Forensics got it." He turned as someone called his name. "Yeah. Be right there." Then back to Romy. "Look, you wanna leave me your card, we'll call you if we think we need help. But don't wait up for it. And for the time being, stay on the other side of the tape, okay?"

Patrick expected Romy to press him further, but she simply nodded. Patrick lifted the tape for her and she ducked under. She pulled out a compact camera and began snapping pictures.

"For your scrapbook?"

"For Zero. He'll want to see."

"Speaking of Zero," he said, leaning close and whispering. "Did you call him about this?

"You don't call Zero. You leave a message."

"Could he be behind this?"

She lowered her camera. Her look was fierce. "I told you—"

"Does he consult you on everything he does? Of course not. So how do you know?"

She started snapping pictures again. "I just do. He lets me take care of the brothels and places like this. That's *my* job."

"Well just what sort of place is it—or I guess I should say, *was* it?"

"A globulin farm."

"A what?"

"I thought I explained that when—wait. Did you see that Asian man?"

"No. Where?"

"He was in that knot of people over there. I just pointed the camera in his direction and he ducked away. Where did he go?"

She rose on tiptoe to scan the area, then quickly ducked back.

"Oh, hell!" She spun, turning her back to Patrick as she started moving toward the corner. "Don't look around, just follow me."

"Why?"

"Just do it. I don't want to—"

"Well, well!" said a man's voice behind him. "If it isn't Ms. Romy Cadman of OPRR. Fancy meeting you here."

"Shit!" Romy hissed; it sounded more like escaping steam than a word.

As she turned, so did Patrick. He saw a swarthy, broad-shouldered man in a gray overcoat swaggering toward them. Patrick took an instant dislike to his smug expression. But his cold, dark eyes were his most arresting feature. Patrick felt like a mouse being scrutinized by a rattlesnake. But then the man's gaze flicked away. Patrick had been demoted from lunch to background scenery.

"Mr. Portero," Romy said in a deep-freeze voice. "What a surprise."

"I don't see why it should be. Sims were reported on the scene, and SimGen has a vital interest in the welfare of all sims."

"Sure it does," Romy said, drawing out the first word. "But to send its chief of security?"

" 'Free the sims' is not a phrase SimGen takes lightly, especially when it involves murder. I decided to look into this myself."

"You should introduce yourself to that sergeant over there," Romy said. "His name's Yarger and he's anxious for all the help he can get."

"I'm sure he is." Portero jerked a thumb toward the smoking ruin. "What do you think? Globulin farm?"

"That's my guess."

Patrick remembered now. "That's where they infect sims with viruses and such and then drain off and sell their immune globulins, right?"

The man turned his glittering stare on Patrick. "And you are . . . ?

"This is a friend," Romy said. "Patrick Sullivan. Patrick, meet Mr. Portero, security chief at SimGen."

"Oh, yes," Portero said. "I believe I've heard of you. Some sort of lawyer, right?"

Patrick noticed that Portero had clasped his hands behind his back as he spoke. A handshake seemed out of the question.

"Some sort, yes," Patrick said. "But about this globulin farm . . . ?"

"A small operation from what I can gather," Portero said.

Patrick glanced at the blackened ruins. "Not any kind of operation now."

"Thanks to this so-called SLA," Portero said. He stared at Romy. "Ever hear of them, Romy?"

Patrick felt his insides clench at the sound of her first name on Portero's lizard lips, but said nothing.

Romy regarded him coolly. "Not till this morning."

"I don't understand their methods," Portero said, rubbing his jaw as he looked around. "I can see them making off with the sims, to free them later. But why fire the building? What if they'd missed a few sims in their raid? They'd have been cooked just like that corpse." He turned to Romy. "Did your sergeant friend mention finding any sim bodies?"

"No, thank God."

"Yes . . . Thank God." Portero's eyes became distant; he seemed to recede for a moment, then gathered himself. "But why did these terrorists make off with the humans as well?"

"Your guess is as good as mine," Romy said.

Portero smiled as he shook his head. "Oh, I doubt that, Romy. I doubt that very much."

And then he swaggered away.

"Something about this has got him worried," Romy said. "He's putting on a good show, but something's bothering him."

"Is that why he never blinks?"

"He doesn't have to; he has nictitating membranes."

"That figures. And his tiny reptile heart is set on you."

Romy's lips twisted. "Yeah, I know."

"But I'm taller."

She smiled for the first time since he'd arrived. "You know, sometimes I'm glad you're around."

"Only sometimes?"

She hooked her arm through his and started walking. "Let's go grab some breakfast and wait for Zero to get back to me."

"Excellent idea, but in a better neighborhood, if you please."

As they moved away he glanced back at Portero, intending to give him a look-what-I've-got wink, but thought better of it when he saw the fierce look in those icy dark eyes.

4

MANHATTAN

They were just finishing a leisurely breakfast at an East Seventies café when Romy's PCA went off. She checked the readout:

GARAGE 10AM Ø

She was glad for the change from the Worth Street basement. Use one place too often and eventually the wrong person was going to make the right connection. She and Patrick hopped a cab to the West Side.

"I don't see a garage," Patrick said as they stepped out onto Ninth Avenue in the Thirties.

He noticed the sidewalks were busy here, but nowhere near as crowded as the midtown madhouse a few blocks east.

"It's down the street, closer to Tenth. But let's stand here awhile. Just to be sure no one followed us."

The sun had poked through the clouds but did little to moderate the chill wind whistling off the Hudson.

"Do you ever ask yourself if you're crazy?" Patrick said, looking around as if expecting to see trench-coated men lurking in doorways.

"All the time."

"Good. That's a healthy sign. Because I think we're both crazy."

"I think I know where this is going."

"Do you? Great. Then maybe you can tell me why we're at the beck and call of this guy. Who is he? What's driving him? Why's he doing this? What's in it for him?"

"I can't answer all your questions," she told Patrick, "but I can tell you why he's doing it: to stop the slave trade of sentient beings."

"But what's in it for him?"

"Cessation of the slave trade of sentient beings."

"Bull. Idealistic crap."

The words stung Romy. "You don't believe people can be motivated by ideals?"

"Foot soldiers can be, and they often are. But not the generals, not the guys running the war. They've got something else driving them, whether it's a better place in history or a spot closer to their god or riches or fame or glory or power or revenge or guilt; there's always something in it for them."

"What about Gandhi? Schindler? Father Damien? Mother Teresa?"

He shrugged. "Everyone in the world knows their names. Maybe that's what they were after."

"I'm glad I'm not you," she said. "What an awful way to view life."

"Maybe I've seen too many so-called idealists caught with their hands in the till."

"A corrupt individual doesn't corrupt the ideal."

"No argument there, and I didn't bring this up to start one. But look at the situation. Here's a guy who has to have spent a fortune setting up this nameless organization to stop SimGen, and then he hides his identity from everyone who works for him. I can see him not trusting me, but what about you? You say you've worked with him for years. He's got to know you're in this for the long run. Why doesn't he let you see his face?"

"How do you know he hasn't?" she shot back.

Patrick's eyebrows jumped. "Has he?"

"No."

"See what I mean?"

"Maybe he's someone we'd recognize."

"Yeah, there's a thought. You know . . . he seems to be built a lot like David Letterman."

Romy wasn't going to dignify that with a response.

"Let's walk," she said, satisfied that no one was on their tail.

"Seriously, though, I'd feel a lot better about this Zero guy if I knew what makes his motor run." Patrick seemed to be in summation mode as they headed toward Tenth Avenue, walking sideways, the wind ruffling his blond hair as he gestured with his hands. "If it's because a SimGen truck ran over his mother when he was a kid, fine. Or if he's got huge short positions on SimGen stock, fine. Or even if it's because of something crazy like Mercer Sinclair stole his girlfriend in seventh grade, okay too. I just want to know so I can have a handle on how much he'll risk to get what he wants. Because so far we're the ones in the line of fire, not him. He wasn't in my car when it was run off the Saw Mill. He wasn't at Beacon Ridge when the sims offered to share their poisoned food with us."

Romy hated to admit it, but Patrick was making sense. She'd been taken with Zero from their first meeting. She'd sensed the fire burning beneath all his layers of disguise, and had been warmed by its heat. But what fueled that fire? It was a question she'd never asked. She'd assumed it burned the same as her own, an all-consuming desire to right a wrong. Was that foolish? Perhaps. But she had to go with what she felt.

"All I can tell you," she said, "is that I believe in his cause and he's never let me down. I don't intend to let him down."

He sighed. "Fair enough. I'm trusting your judgment. For now."

Down near Tenth, Romy stopped before a dirty white doorway next to an equally dirty white roll-up garage door and pressed a buzzer. She glanced up into the eye of an overhead security camera and nodded once, signaling that all was clear. The door buzzed open.

Inside, a single dusty bulb glowed in the ceiling. They found Zero, barely visible in the gloom, his tall lean figure swathed in sweater, jeans, ski mask, dark glasses, and gloves, pacing beside a beat-up Ford Econoline delivery van, once white, now soot gray.

"Have you heard any more about this SLA group?" he said without preamble.

Romy sensed the tension in his voice.

"Nothing. I called a few of the cops I know but nothing's broken yet beyond the identity of the corpse in the ashes: Craig Strickland, a twenty-four-year-old loser with a history of assaults."

"Doesn't sound like your typical globulin farmer."

"They figure he was security. He may have tried to resist. As for the SLA, an all-points has been issued but they and their captives seem to have vanished."

"Two vans filled with human and sim hostages and no one's seen a thing?"

"Not yet."

Zero slammed a gloved fist against the already dented side of the van.

"Damn! Who *are* these psychos? What do they hope to accomplish for sims by murdering humans? Not that the world is any poorer for the loss of a globulin farmer, but killing him shifts the focus. The public's attention is on the murder now, not on the sims the dead man was abusing."

"Pardon my paranoia," Patrick said, "but maybe that's the whole point. Maybe these aren't sim sympathizers. Maybe SimGen is behind them."

"I don't buy that," Zero said, "but let's assume SimGen has somehow come to the conclusion that the gains from high-profile murder will, by some stretch of the imagination, outweigh the risks. If that's true, and if they're going to spray paint 'Death to sim oppressors' at the scene, then why kill only one of the globulin farmers? Why not make a real statement and kill them all?"

"Hostages?"

Zero's expression was unreadable behind his mask and shades, but Romy could imagine a dour look as he stopped his pacing and faced Patrick.

"How many people can you see stepping forward to pay a globulin farmer's ransom?"

Patrick shrugged. "Okay. So much for the hostage idea."

" 'Death to sim oppressors!' " Zero said, slamming his fist against the van again. "Damn them! Idiots!"

Romy had never seen him show so much emotion. She found it oddly exciting.

Down, girl, she told herself as she pulled her digital camera's chip case from her pocket.

She said, "I may have another piece to add to the puzzle. I took a shot of an Asian man—Japanese, I think—at the scene. He ducked away as soon as he saw the camera. I've never seen him before, and it may mean nothing, but he was definitely camera shy."

Zero seemed to have calmed himself. He took the chip. "I'll see if he's anyone we should know about."

"But what's the plan?" she said. "What do we do about this SLA?"

"No choice but to wait and see. I doubt we'll have much of a wait. A group like that won't want to stay out of the headlines. But in the meantime, we're ready to make our move against Manassas Ventures."

Romy stiffened. "When?"

"Monday, first thing in the morning. Are you up for it?"

Monday . . . she'd have to take a personal day.

"I think so."

She wasn't looking forward to this. It involved playing a role, pretending she was a kind of person she despised. She hoped she could bring it off.

Zero's dark lenses were trained on her. "Something wrong?"

She didn't want to let him in on her apprehensions. He had enough on his plate.

"I just keep thinking about those sims." And that was no lie. "Whoever these SLA people are, I hope they're taking good care of them."

"Amen to that," Zero muttered. He shook his head. " 'Free the sims.' Don't they understand? Sims have never been allowed to learn to fend for themselves. A free sim isn't free at all. It's a lost soul."

5

THE BRONX

Poor Meerm.

Meerm feel so bad. So more bad than last night. Now Meerm still belly-sick but cold and hungry also too. Also too arm hurt where burn while climb down building side. And leg hurt from fall ground. Hurt-hurt-hurt. Meerm hurt all over.

And Meerm ver fraid. Hide in bottom old empty building. No window and many rat. Rat sniff at Meerm burn. Shoo way, throw rock. Bad place this. And so cold. Meerm miss own room and yum-yum food. Wish go back but room gone. She go look in dark. All burn, all gone.

Meerm ver lonely. Meerm ver fraid. Not know what do. Not know where go.

6

Shortly after 8:00 A.M. Romy stepped through the front door of the small two-story office building and made a show of looking at the directory. The vestibule was clean but showing some wear around the edges. Just like the building, which was typical of the boxy, clapboard style popular back in the seventies. The tenants listed—a dentist, a real estate office, an insurance agent—were typical of any suburban office building; all except the lessee of the small corner office on the second floor: a venture capital company she knew was worth billions.

Romy hurried up to the second floor and found the door to Suite 2-C. A strictly no-frills black plastic plaque spelled out MANASSAS VENTURES, INC in small white letters. She waited outside the door until she heard someone climbing the steps, then she started knocking. A woman in a colorful smock appeared, heading for the dental office, and Romy turned to her.

"When does the Manassas Ventures staff usually arrive?"

The woman looked dumbfounded. "You know, I don't think I've ever seen anybody coming or going from that office."

That's because no one does, Romy thought. Zero had had the place under observation for weeks.

"Really?" Romy said, putting her hand on the doorknob and rattling it. "I've been trying to reach them by phone but no one returns my messages, so I thought I'd come over in person and—"

The door swung inward.

"Now isn't that something," the dental assistant said as she stepped forward for a peek at the interior. "They must've forgot to lock it."

Morning sunlight streamed through the sheer curtains behind an empty receptionist's desk and flared the dust motes dancing through the air. No shortage of dust here—the desktop sported a good eighth of an inch.

"Hello?" Romy said, stepping inside. The air smelled stale, musty. No one had opened a window for a long, long time. "Anybody home?"

"Good luck," the woman told Romy and started back toward her office. "Thanks."

Romy had to act quickly. She glanced up, searching for the strand of monofilament she'd been told she'd find hanging from the central light fixture. There it was, a length of fine fishing line, barely visible.

Two of Zero's people had broken in over the weekend. They'd unlatched the door and rigged the fixture to drop when the fishing line was pulled.

The original plan had been to loosen the hinges on the door so that it would fall outward when Romy tugged on it. She would let it knock her down and claim a terrible back injury. But Patrick had vetoed the idea. An injury caused by the door might leave the landlord as the liable party rather than the tenant. And it was the tenant they were after.

The most open-and-shut scenario—he'd called it *res ipso loquitor*—was to arrange for Romy to be "injured" by a tenant-installed fixture. After some reconnoitering, the fluorescent box in the ceiling over the reception area had received the nod.

Romy was supposed to pull the string and let it crash to the floor, then stagger out and collapse in the hall, pretending it had landed on her.

Pretend . . . she'd never been good at pretending. How was she supposed to slump to the floor out there and moan and groan about being hurt and have anyone buy it? And the Manassas people, when they heard about it they'd know that what had happened here was all a sham, a set-up designed to drag them into the legal system and expose their corporate innards. They'd respond with lawyers using every possible legal ploy to keep their secrets.

They'll play hide, we'll play seek. A game.

But this was no game to her. Romy was serious. She'd show them just how serious.

Acting quickly, before the dental assistant could unlock her office across the hall, Romy stepped under the fixture and yanked on the line.

Her cry of pain was real.

7

Patrick sat in the driver seat of Zero's van, idly watching the little office building. He'd parked across the street in a church parking lot—Our Lady of Something-or-other—and left the engine idling to run the heater, but he was keeping his window open to let out the pungent odor that seemed to be ingrained into the van's metal frame. The driver seat felt like little more than a sheet of newspaper spread over a collection of rusty springs.

But the sharp jabs against his butt were inconsequential compared to the discomfort of sharing the van with the shadowy form seated behind him. Here was a perfect opportunity to probe Zero, maybe get a line on what made this bird tick, but Patrick found himself tongue-tied.

What do you say to a masked man?

Had to give it a shot: "Do you mind if I ask you a personal question?"

Zero's deep voice echoed from the dark recess at the rear of the van. "Depends."

"Why do you call yourself 'Zero'?"

"That is my name."

Ooookay. Try another tack. "How about them Mets?" That was usually a foolproof conversation opener, especially out here on the Island, even in the off-season. "What do you think of that last round of trades?"

"I don't follow sports."

Okay, strike that. Maybe if we concentrate more on the moment . . .

"You have any idea what this van was used for before you got it?"

"It was a delivery truck run by a Korean Christian group in Yonkers."

"Smells like they spilled a gallon of roast puppy stew on the way to the annual church potluck dinner."

Patrick heard a soft chuckle. "I can think of worse things to spill."

Hey, he laughs!

"You mean, be grateful for small favors, right?"

"Small and large. I'm grateful the Reverend Eckert has finally been able to purchase space on a satellite."

"That means he'll be beaming his anti-SimGen sermons direct."

"Right. No more worries about SimGen influencing the syndicate that distributes his show to local stations. Not only can he beam his shows to the syndicate, but he's now got direct access to anyone with a satellite dish."

"Nice. A big jump in audience."

"I'm grateful too," Zero said, "for how well you and Romy are working together."

"So far, so good. She's a piece of work."

"That she is. One very intense young woman. Tell me, Patrick, do you hope for a closer relationship between the two of you?"

Patrick blinked in surprise. Odd question. "Do you mean working or personal?"

"Personal."

"Is there something I don't know?" he said, turning to look at Zero. He wished he'd take off that mask. "Is there something going on between you and Romy? Because if there is—"

Zero gave a dismissive wave. "Nothing, I assure you. I am . . . unavailable."

That was a relief.

"Well, okay, but all I can say is, whether or not we go the next step is up to her. If you're worried about a romance between us interfering with our job performance, rest easy. The lady has thus far found the strength of character to resist my charms."

"Which I'm sure are considerable."

"As me grandma used to say," he said in a pretty fair Irish accent, "from yer lips to Gawd's ear."

"Speaking of God, I've been looking at this church. Are you Catholic?"

"With a name like Patrick Michael Sullivan, could I be anything else?"

"Practicing?"

"No. Pretty much the fallen-away variety. Haven't seen the inside of a church for some time."

"But you do believe in God."

"Yeah, sure." Where was this going?

"Did you know that some sims believe in God, even pray to Him?"

"No. I didn't." For some reason the idea made him uncomfortable. "Any particular faith?"

"They tend toward Catholicism. They like all the statues, although they find the crucifix disturbing. They're most comfortable with the Virgin Mary. Pick through any sim barrack and you'll usually find a few statues of her."

"I can see that. A mother figure is comforting."

"Sims pray to God, Patrick. But does God hear them?"

"What do you mean?"

"Do sims have souls?"

"This is heavy stuff."

"Most enlightened believers accept evolution. Genetics makes it impossible for an intelligent person to deny a common ancestor between chimps and humans. Some theologians posit a 'transcendental intervention' along the evolutionary tree, the moment when God imbued an early human with a soul. So I ask you, Patrick: When human genes were spliced into chimps to make sims, did a soul come along with them?"

"To tell the truth," Patrick said, "I've never given it an instant's thought until you just mentioned it."

Who had time to ponder such imponderables? Zero, obviously. And it seemed important to him.

"Think about it," Zero said. "Sims praying to a God who won't listen because they have no souls. Imagine believing in a God who doesn't believe in you. Tragic, don't you think?"

"Absolutely. But I wonder—"

The wail of a siren cut him off. He watched as an ambulance screamed into the parking lot across the street.

"You think that's for Romy?"

"I imagine so." Zero's voice now was close behind him. "I told her to give it her best performance."

They watched a pair of EMTs, a wiry male and a rather hefty woman, hurry inside. A few moments later they reemerged, pulled a stretcher from their rig, and hauled it inside.

"Wow," Patrick muttered. "She must be bucking for an Oscar."

He kept his tone light but felt a twinge of anxiety at the way those EMTs were hustling. A long ten minutes later they exited, wheeling the stretcher between them. But it wasn't empty this trip. Patrick could make out a slim figure in the blanket. Had to be Romy. He noticed that her head was swathed in gauze . . . with a crimson stain seeping through.

"Shit!" he cried, fear stabbing him as he reached for the door handle. "She's bleeding!"

"Wait!" he heard Zero say, but he was already out and moving toward the street.

No way he could sit in a van and watch Romy be wheeled into an ambulance by strangers when she was hurt and bleeding. Her gaze flicked his way as he dashed into the parking lot. When he saw her hand snake out from under the blanket and surreptitiously wave him off, he slowed his approach.

And when she gave him a quick thumbs-up sign, he veered off and headed for the office building. He waited inside until the ambulance wailed off, then crossed back to the van.

"She seems okay," he said as he climbed back into the driver seat.

"Wonderful," replied the voice from the dim rear.

"But what the hell happened in there?" He threw the shift into forward and took off after the receding ambulance. "She was supposed to stand clear and fake being hurt. How the hell did she cut her head open?"

"I should have foreseen this," Zero said. "This is so Romy."

"What do you mean?"

"Don't you understand? She had to make it real. She had to send a message to Manassas and SimGen and whoever else is involved that she's ready to bleed for her beliefs."

"Sheesh," Patrick muttered.

"Isn't she wonderful."

It wasn't a question. In that moment Patrick realized that the mysterious Zero, although "unavailable," was as smitten with Romy Cadman as he was.

"What is it about her?" Patrick said. The ambulance was still in sight, though blocks ahead. Tailing it was easy in the light traffic. "I mean, you're obviously taken by her, and I confess I'm drawn to her—"

"Drawn?"

"Like a moth to a searchlight. And then that guy Portero—"

"The SimGen security chief?"

"He's got it bad for her. Might as well have written it on his forehead in DayGlo orange. What is it about Romy Cadman?"

"Simple: her purity."

Patrick didn't have to ask. He knew Zero wasn't talking about virginity. He was talking about heart, about purpose.

"I hear you. But Portero didn't strike me as the kind who'd go for that."

"Some men approach purity like Romy's simply to protect it from harm; and some wish to draw closer in the hope that it will rub off on them or somehow cleanse them; and others want to possess it merely to defile it and extinguish it because it reminds them of what they have become, as opposed to what they could have been."

Patrick glanced Zero's way in the rearview. He'd obviously given a lot of thought to this.

"Well, I guess we know where Portero fits in that scheme."

"I think we do."

"But how about you?"

A long pause, then Zero said, "If my circumstances were different, I'd be content merely to warm myself in her glow. And if I couldn't do that I'd settle for curling up outside her door every night to keep her safe from trespassers."

Patrick swallowed, unexpectedly moved.

"You know, Zero," he said, his voice a tad hoarse, "I've got to admit I've had my doubts about you. Major, heavy-duty doubts. But now . . ."

"Now?"

Patrick didn't know quite what to say. Any man who could pinpoint Romy as Zero had, and who could not only feel about her the way he'd described, but come out and say it . . .

"You're all right."

Lame, but the best Patrick could do at the moment. At least it was sincere. Romy would appreciate that.

8

Patrick parted the curtains that separated Romy's treatment area from the rest of the bustling emergency room. She sat on the edge of a gurney, her head swathed in fresh gauze—but no seepage this time. She looked pale and tired, but even so, to Patrick she was a vision.

"How are you feeling?"

A wan smile. "I've got a killer headache but I'll survive."

He leaned close. "How'd you get hurt?"

"You've heard the expression, 'Shit happens'? Well—"

Patrick clapped his hands over his ears. "The 'S' word! Saints preserve us!" He wanted to throw his arms around her but made do with seating himself next to her on the gurney. "Seriously. What happened?"

"This lighting fixture fell from the ceiling and clocked me on the noggin; things get a little fuzzy after that. Took the ER doc hours to get to me, then after she stitched up my scalp there were x-rays and—"

"How many stitches?"

"The doctor said seventeen."

"Seventeen!" The number horrified him.

"It's not as bad as it sounds. She said she placed them close together to keep the scar thin."

Scar? "Jesus, Romy—"

She smiled. "Not like I'm going to look like the bride of Frankenstein, or anything. It cut my scalp, way up above the hairline. Once the hair grows back where they shaved it, no one will know, not even me."

Relief seeped through Patrick. The lighting fixture had been his idea. If it had left Romy disfigured . . .

"Why, Romy?"

"Relax, will you. I got a tetanus shot out of it, and a free ride in a stoplight-running ambulance. It's no biggie, Patrick. Really."

"Is to me. Zero too." Patrick had driven him to the garage, then rushed back here. "He wants me to call him as soon as—"

"I'll call him."

"How many days are they going to keep you?"

"Days? More like minutes. They're finishing up my paperwork now."

"You're kidding!" Patrick realized his knowledge of medicine was just this side of nothing, but wasn't it standard procedure to admit a head-trauma patient for observation, at least overnight? "They're letting you go?"

"Be real, will you. It's just a cut on my head. I can—"

"Excuse me," said a male voice.

Patrick looked up and saw a dark-haired man in a gray suit standing between the parted curtains.

"Are you her doctor?" Patrick said. If so he was going to warn him about the malpractice risks of releasing Romy too early.

The man flashed a collector's edition set of pearlies. "Not a chance. I'm an attorney and I'm looking for the woman who was injured in the Manassas Ventures offices this morning."

Patrick stared at him. He'd met his share of ambulance chasers, but this guy really lived up to the name.

"That would be me." Romy shook her head. "But I don't need a lawyer. I've—"

"You're absolutely right. And that's precisely why I'm here." He handed Romy a card. "Harold Rudner. I represent Manassas Ventures." He set his briefcase on the gurney and popped its latches. "The company called me the instant its landlord informed it of this unfortunate incident. I was instructed to find you and compensate you immediately for the pain and inconvenience you have suffered."

"Compensate me?"

He lifted the briefcase lid, removed a slip of paper, and extended it toward Romy.

"Exactly. Although your injury resulted from shoddy work by remodeling contractors, Manassas is taking full responsibility and offering you this to ease your distress."

Romy took the slip and stared at it. "A check? For a hundred thousand dollars?"

"Yes." He pulled a sheaf of papers from the briefcase. "And all you need do to have your name written on the pay-to-the-order-of line is sign this release absolving Manassas Ventures of all liability and refrain from any future—"

"Wow!" Patrick said, impressed. "Hit her while she's still dazed from the terrible concussive impact of her life-threatening head injury, then shove a check under her nose and tell her all those zeroes can be hers if she'll just sign away her legal rights to just compensation for an injury that might affect her quality of life for years, maybe decades, perhaps permanently. You *are* a smoothy."

Romy and Rudner were staring at him.

Finally Rudner spoke. "Are you her lawyer?"

"I am a very close personal friend who just happens to be an attorney."

Rudner turned to Romy. "I am offering you far more than you could hope to receive from any jury."

"We'll see about that," Patrick said. "One hundred thousand dollars barely scratches the surface of the amount this unfortunate woman deserves for her pain and suffering."

Romy smiled and handed back the check. Rudner took it with a sad shake of his head.

"You're making a big mistake," he told her. "One you'll regret when a jury offers you only a fraction of this—one third of which will go to your attorney. This could be all yours, every cent of it."

Romy's hands flew to her mouth as she gave Patrick a wide-eyed stare. "Oh, Patrick! Am I making a terrible mistake? You know how I depend on your wisdom. Tell me. I don't know what to do!"

Patrick had to look away. It took all his will to keep a straight face. When he had control, he turned back, took both her hands in his, and lowered his voice an octave. "Trust me, my dear. I am well versed in these matters. You deserve much, much more."

"All . . . all right," she said, her voice faltering. "If you say so."

Rudner shook his head again and closed his briefcase. As he lifted it off the gurney he turned to Patrick.

"And you called *me* a smoothy?"

As soon as he was gone they both doubled over in silent laughter.

"Life-threatening head injury?" Romy gasped, red-faced.

Patrick countered with, " 'You know how I depend on your wisdom'? I thought I was going to get a hernia!"

She pressed her hands against her temples. "Oh, I shouldn't laugh! It makes my headache worse!"

Patrick looked at her. "I know this is serious business, but I couldn't resist. That was fun."

She frowned. "Do you think he knew who we were?"

"Not a clue. He's a hired gun." Patrick shook his head, still amazed at how quickly the company had responded. "A hundred grand for a cut head offered to someone they might just as easily have charged with trespassing. If this is any indication of how badly Manassas wants to avoid the legal system, I think we're onto something."

SUSSEX COUNTY, NJ

DECEMBER 7

"So," Mercer Sinclair said, "the missing globulin farmers have surfaced." He'd chosen that word deliberately but his little pun went unappreciated by his audience. So he added, "Literally."

That at least elicited a smile from Abel Voss.

Mercer had invited the usual crew—Voss, Portero, and Ellis—to his office to discuss the matter. He had his agenda for the meeting posted in a corner of the computer monitor embedded in the ebony expanse of his desk while his custom news service scrolled items tailored to his topics of interest.

"Postmortem ain't back yet," Voss said, "but the M-E's on notice to copy us immediately with any and all results."

"I'm told the bodies appear to have been in the river about a week."

Voss nodded. "All three of them shackled together and weighted down. But the Hudson's gotta way of returning some of the gifts it gets. Looks like these SLA boys took 'em for a ride that very night, shot them in the head, then dumped them before sunup."

"But not before torturing them," Ellis said.

Mercer glanced at his brother. Ellis hadn't missed a meeting in months now. Maybe his latest anti-depressant cocktail was working. Mercer knew he should be glad about that but he wasn't. The closer Ellis was to catatonia, the easier he was to deal with.

"Yep, I heard that too," Voss said. "Cigarette burns, fingernails tore off." He grimaced. "Ugly stuff."

"They were globulin farmers, Abel," Mercer said, unable to keep the scorn from his tone. "Somebody improved the gene pool by removing them."

"Don't get me wrong, son. I ain't no fan of their sort. Riddin the world of their kind is all fine and good. But torture? Ain't no call to torture no one, son. No one. I think we're dealin with some real sick puppies here."

"Which segues very neatly into the reason for our meeting: the 'sick puppies' who call themselves the Sim Liberation Army. It's been a week since they raided that globulin farm and no one knows any more about them today than they did then. And where are the sims they supposedly wanted to free?" He turned to his chief of security who had yet to say a word. "Mr. Portero, if the NYPD is at a loss, surely your people have the resources to pick up the slack, don't you think?"

Portero shrugged. "We're looking into it."

"This needs more than mere looking into, Mr. Portero. We need to track them down. It's vitally important that SimGen be recognized as the true guardians and protectors of sims, not some group of murderous radicals."

Portero said, "The longer they go undetected, the lower the odds of finding them. And so far they seem to have pulled off a perfect disappearing act."

"Which means what?"

"That they're probably professionals—well-funded professionals. Which makes me wonder if they might not be connected to that lawyer Patrick Sullivan."

"Why on earth would you think that?" Ellis said.

"It's not a stretch. A quarter of a million dollars appeared out of the blue to keep his unionization case going just when it was ready to fall apart. And I saw him and the Cadman woman outside the globulin farm the morning after this SLA demolished it."

Cadman? Mercer thought. Didn't I just see that name? He'd been about to switch the topic to the annual stockholders' meeting less than two weeks away, but instead he reversed the scroll on his newsclips.

"On the contrary, Portero," Ellis said. "It's *quite* a stretch. People who try to use the legal system to seek a solution don't suddenly leap to murder and arson."

Portero's face remained impassive as he replied. "Perhaps Sullivan became a bit testy after his clients were put down."

Ellis stared at him. "You lousy piece of—"

"Gentlemen, gentlemen," Voss said, shifting his considerable bulk in his seat and raising his hands. "We're not the enemy here. The enemy is out *there*."

"Really?" Ellis said. "Sometimes I wonder."

Cadman . . . Mercer kept searching his screen. There. Found it. A suit against Manassas. He smiled. He'd long ago embraced his anal-completist nature because it so often paid unexpected dividends. Like now: Years ago, when he'd begun using the service, he'd entered 'Manassas Ventures' as a search string; this was the first hit he'd ever seen. He clicked on the abstract to bring up the full article; he felt a sweat break as he skimmed it.

"Listen to this," Mercer said. "Someone is suing Manassas Ventures."

He noticed a slight stiffening of Portero's parade-rest stance. "Is that so?"

"Manassas is in your people's bailiwick. Why don't you know about this?"

"We have lawyers for legal problems. What's the suit about?"

"Let's see . . . no dollar amount given, just 'unspecified compensatory and punitive damages.' "

"No, I mean the reason for the suit."

"Lots of things. Here's just a sample: 'physical injury, pain, suffering, mental anguish and trauma, unpleasant mental reactions including fright, horror, worry, disgrace, embarrassment, indignity, ridicule, grief, shame, humiliation, anger, and outrage.' "

Portero snorted. "Probably a stubbed toe. They'll put a check in front of him and he'll go away."

"I doubt it. It's not a him. It's a her named Cadman. Romilda Cadman."

Portero's smug reptile mask dropped and, just for a second, Mercer caught a flash of uncertainty. Portero . . . unsettled? The possibility turned his stomach sour, like curdled milk.

"The OPRR inspector lady?" Voss said. "The one who funded Sullivan's sim case? What the *hell*?"

"Care to guess what attorney is representing her?"

"I don't have to," Voss said. "Gotta be Sullivan."

Mercer noted that Portero's dumbfounded look had surrendered to tight-lipped anger. He glanced at Ellis, expecting some sort of comment, but his brother remained silent, his expression unreadable.

"Right," Mercer said. "Patrick Sullivan again. I don't like this."

"This makes no sense." Portero's voice was even softer than usual. "What can they possibly hope to gain? Are they that desperate for cash?"

"Oh, I doubt money's got a thing to do with this," Voss said. "It will take them years to get a decision, and even if they win, more years before they ever see a dime. No, instead of thinking about money, we should be asking why the man who harassed SimGen about unionizing sims is now harassing the venture capital company that helped put SimGen in business. I find that real disturbin."

The question disturbed Mercer as well. "You're the lawyer," he told Voss. "Have you got an answer?"

"I'm bettin he wants to use the discovery procedures of a civil action to dissect Manassas Ventures' workings—its board of directors, its assets and liabilities, the whole tamale."

Mercer's gnawing sense of malignant forces converging on him had receded after the withdrawal of the sim unionization suit, but now it returned with a gut-roiling vengeance.

"Why Manassas? Beyond owning a bundle of SimGen stock, it has no direct link to us."

"Not anymore, but it used to. Obviously he's sniffed out something and he's going after it."

"Maybe it's just a fishing expedition," Mercer said, but he didn't believe it.

"Could be, but why in that particular pond? And let's face it, Manassas is such a well-stocked pond, he just might hook something."

No one spoke then. The idea that anyone would want to lift the Manassas Ventures rock and inspect what was crawling around beneath it had never occurred to Mercer. He'd been assured that Manassas was a dead end. But what if wasn't? What if someone found a trail that led from Manassas to SIRG?

This had to be stopped. Now. Before it went any further.

He looked at Portero. "Your people can handle this, can't they?"

"Wait a minute, wait a minute," Voss said, holding up a hand before Portero could reply. "Before we start talking about stuff I don't want to hear, why don't you just buy her off?"

Portero stared at him. "Buy her off? You don't know this woman. I spent days with her during the OPRR inspection and let me tell you, she is not for sale."

Voss grinned. "Sure she is, son. I've waded through truckloads of bullshit in my day, but I've learned one thing always holds true: Everybody's got a price tag. Some hide it better'n others, but you look hard enough, you'll find it. Your folks've got pockets deep as a well to China. You have them tell her to name a price, and then you meet it. And that'll be it. You'll see."

But Portero was shaking his head. "I don't think there's enough money in the world."

Mercer was surprised by something in his tone. It sounded like admiration.

10

MANHATTAN

DECEMBER 8

Zero had called and asked Patrick to come over to the West Side garage. Romy was already there when Patrick arrived. With oversized sunglasses hiding her fading shiners, and a baseball cap covering her stitched-up scalp, she looked none the worse for wear.

Patrick asked her how she was doing, and of course she told him fine. She was always "fine." She said she'd be even better when the stitches came out tomorrow.

Patrick rubbed his hands together. The old radiator running along the cinderblock wall only partially countered the afternoon chill. Neither Romy nor Zero seemed to feel it. Of course Zero, swathed head to toe as usual, would be the last to chill.

"We heard from the Manassas attorneys," he told them. "They want a meeting. Soon. I set it up for next Thursday, my office." He glanced at Romy. "Can you make it?"

"I'll be there."

"My only regret is that I couldn't add my own charges to the suit."

"On what grounds?"

"Loss of services and consortium."

"You," she said, pointing a finger at him, "are incorrigible." She tried to look stern but he could see she was fighting a smile. She turned to Zero. "Did you have any luck with my photo?"

"Quite an interesting picture," Zero said, handing Romy an eight-by-ten color print.

The dim light made it hard to see details. Patrick craned his head over Romy's shoulder for a better look, but found himself gazing at the nape of her neck instead, focusing on the gentle wisps of fine dark hair trailing along the curve. He leaned closer, drinking her scent, barely resisting the urge to press his lips against the soft white skin . . .

"That's him, all right," Romy said. "Does he have a name?"

"Yes. It took me a while to trace him but—"

"Christ!" Patrick said. He pointed to a spot at the rear end of the ceiling. "Who's that?"

He'd glanced up and caught a flicker of movement above and beyond Zero, at the point where a ladder embedded in the rear wall of the garage ran up to a square opening in the ceiling. He could swear he'd seen a pair of eyes peering out at them from within that darkness.

Zero didn't turn to look. "Where?"

"There! In that opening! I saw someone!"

The opening was empty now, but he knew what he'd seen.

"I'm sure you did," Zero told him. "But it was no one you need concern yourself with at the moment. Now—"

"Wait a minute, wait a minute," Patrick said, walking over to the ladder. "If someone's up there listening, I want to know who it is."

"Someone's up there *guarding*," Romy said. "Please, Patrick. Let it go for now."

He didn't like letting it go, but short of climbing up there and entering that patch of night—something he had no inclination to do—Patrick didn't see that he had much choice. He'd come to trust Zero, and if he said someone was guarding them, then Patrick would buy it.

"All right," he said, turning back. "Where were we?"

Zero said, "The man in the photo looked Japanese so I scanned him into a computer and had it comb the databases of the Japanese government and major Japanese corporations." He held up a printout of a full-face photo of someone who bore a passing resemblance to the man in Romy's shot. "This came back with a sixty-three percent confidence match."

"That's him," Romy said without hesitation.

"You're sure? The computer wasn't."

"Don't care. I saw him live and that's him."

"Fine," Patrick said. "Now . . . who him?"

"Yoshi Hirai, Ph.D.," Zero said. "Top recombinant man for Arata-jinruien Corporation."

"Which is . . . ?" Patrick had never heard of them.

"A division of Kaze Group and one of SimGen's potential competitors. They want to raise their own sims but so far haven't met with any success. They even started a dummy corporation to pirate the sim genome but were caught. They'll do anything to cut into the sim market."

"What was a creep like that doing at the fire?" Romy asked.

"Exactly what I'd like to know."

Patrick said, "Could the SLA be Japanese? But why hijack sims when they can lease as many as they want? And why these globulin farm sims?"

"Never mind why," Romy said. "How about where? Where are those sims? That's my concern. I hope they don't end up like their farmers, or get spirited off to Japan. We'll never find them."

11

RIVERSIDE PARK

Meerm so very sad. Live all alone in bush. Walk night, hide day. Find clothes, dirty, smelly, but warm. Wear three shirt and two pant. Steal blanket. Carry all night while search food.

Pain wake Meerm in bush home. Dark come now. Many people walk. Meerm know must stay hid till late. Meerm so hungry. Peek out bush. Ver near big round building made stone. See lady point, say, "Granztoom."

Meerm not know what granztoom.

Meerm move along wall, stay dark spot. Climb to street. Put blanket over head and walk. Keep face down, look sidewalk. So fraid people hurt if see Meerm, but people walk fast, not look Meerm.

Meerm look for light-front place people eat. Can find food in dark behind. But see no place yet. Street dark. Hear noise behind. Meerm so scare, push against wall, turn. Building door open. Sim come out. Two sim, three sim, many sim. Meerm watch as more sim than count line up straight at curb.

Meerm see bus come and all sim go in. Meerm so cold, so hurt, so lone. Meerm drop blanket and go behind last sim. Climb step, sit empty seat. Bus dark and warm. Meerm curl up, close eye.

12

WESTCHESTER COUNTY, NY

Patrick's breath steamed in the night air as he strolled across the rear lawn of Beacon Ridge toward the sim barrack. He'd been back only once since the night of the poisoning. He wasn't sure exactly why he'd come tonight. Talking about sims with Romy and Zero this afternoon had made him think of Tome. He'd returned to Katonah to sign some papers dealing with his property—someone had made an offer on what was left of his home and he'd accepted—and gave in to an urge to see how the old sim was doing.

As he reached for the knob on the barrack door it opened and out stepped Holmes Carter. He jerked his portly frame to a halt, obviously startled.

"Sullivan?"

"Carter. Fancy meeting you here."

Carter didn't offer to shake hands, neither did Patrick. They'd reached a détente but that didn't make them friends.

"I was just about to say that myself," Carter replied. "You're trespassing, you know."

"Yeah, I know. But ease up. I'm not looking for new clients. Just visiting an old one. Promise."

"Tome?"

"Yeah." Patrick noticed Carter staring at him from under his protruding forehead, saying nothing. "Something wrong?"

"I guess you could say I'm amazed. I figured since the sims dropped the union idea and were no further use to you, we'd never see you again."

"That's usually the way it goes with client-attorney relationships, but these were special clients."

Another long stare from Carter. He was making Patrick uncomfortable.

"You're full of surprises, aren't you, Sullivan." Then he sighed. "Maybe it's a good thing you're here. Tome isn't doing too well."

Aw, no. "Is he sick?"

"I had a vet check him and she says no. He does his washroom duties, but just barely. He's listless, eating just enough to stay alive, and spending all of his free time in his bunk."

It occurred to Patrick that Holmes Carter seemed to know an awful lot about this aging sim.

"What brings you down to the barracks? Never knew you to be one to mix with the help."

He looked away. "Just checking up on him. So sue me, I'm worried."

Now it was Patrick's turn to stare. He remembered how Carter had pitched in to help the poisoned sims, and now this.

"You're no slouch in the surprise department yourself, Holmes." This had to be one of a handful of times he'd addressed the man by his first name.

"The board wants him declared D and replaced. I was giving him a pep talk but I'm not getting through. Want to take a crack at him?"

Patrick knew that if Tome were human he'd have been offered grief counseling after the killings. The poor old guy must be really hurting.

He stepped past Carter into the barrack.

"I'll give it a shot."

With Carter following, Patrick wandered through the familiar front room, past the long dining tables and battered old easy chairs clustered around the TVs in two of the corners. The gathered sims glanced at him, then returned to what they were doing. He thought of the joyous welcomes that used to greet him, but most of those sims were dead or still at work, finishing up in the club kitchen. These replacement sims didn't know him.

But wait . . . he remembered one sim, a caddie . . .

"Where's Deek?" he said.

Carter glanced around. "I don't see him. Might be sitting outside. The other survivors seemed to have bounced back, but not Tome."

That's because he was the patriarch, Patrick thought.

He proceeded into the rear area and looked around. The dorm area was dimly lit; his gaze wandered up and down the rows of bunk beds, searching for one that was occupied.

"Left rear corner," Carter said. "Lower bunk."

Patrick started forward, puzzled. He'd already looked at that bunk and had thought it was empty. But now he could see a shape under the covers, barely raising them, curled and facing the wall.

"Tome?" he said.

The shape turned and Patrick recognized Tome's face as it broke into a wide smile.

"Mist Sulliman?" The old sim slipped from under the covers and rose to his feet beside his bed. "So good to see."

Patrick's throat constricted at the sight of Tome's stooped, emaciated form. Wasn't he eating at all?

"Good to see you too, Tome."

He held out his hand and, after a second's hesitation, Tome reached his own forward.

"You come see Mist Carter?" Tome said as they shook hands.

"No, Tome. I came by to see you." Patrick saw something in Tome's eyes when he said that, something beyond gratitude. "But Mister Carter tells me you're not doing well. He says you spend all your free time in bed. Are you sick, Tome? Is there anything I can do?"

"Not sick, no," he said, shaking his head. "Tome sad. See dead sim ever time walk through eat room. Can't stay. Tired all time."

Patrick nodded, understanding. Tome had to go on living in the building where the sims he'd considered his family were murdered, had to eat in the room where they died. No wonder he was wasting away.

Then Patrick had an idea, one he knew would cause complications in his life. But the sense of having failed Tome and his makeshift family had been dogging Patrick since that terrible and ugly night, and helping him now wasn't something he merely wanted to do, it was something he needed to do.

"You know what you need?" Patrick said. "You need a change of scenery. Wait here."

He went back to Carter, pulled him into a corner and, after a ten-minute negotiation, the deal was set.

"All right, Tome," he said, returning to the bunk. "Pack up your stuff. You're going on a vacation."

Tome's brow furrowed. "Vay-kaysh . . ."

Poor old guy didn't even know what the word meant. Patrick decided not to try to explain because this wasn't going to be a real vacation anyway. Simply removing Tome from the barracks might be enough, but Patrick thought the old sim would want to feel useful.

"You're going to stay with me for a while. I've got a brand new office and I need a helper."

Tome straightened, his eyes brighter already. "Tome work for Mist Sulliman? But club own—"

"That's all taken care of."

Patrick had convinced Carter to allow him to take over Tome's lease payments for a month or so. As club president, Carter had the authority, and the board couldn't squawk too much because it wasn't costing the club a penny. The lease payments wouldn't be cheap but Patrick had all that money left in the Sim Defense Fund and figured it wouldn't be a misappropriation to use some of it to help a sim.

As for keeping Tome busy, the old sim had taught himself to read so it shouldn't be a big stretch for him to learn to file.

"Unless of course," Patrick said, "you'd rather stay here."

"No, no," Tome said, waddling over to a locker. "Tome come."

As Patrick watched him stuff his worldly belongings into a black plastic trash bag, he wondered at his own impulsiveness. He'd been planning to convert the second of the two bedrooms in his newfound apartment into a study, but he guessed that could wait. Let Tome have it for a month or so. Who knew how much of his abbreviated lifespan the old sim had left?

Not as if it's going to interfere with my love life, Patrick thought, thinking of the persistently elusive Romy.

"Tome ready, Mist Sulliman," the sim said, standing before him with straightened spine and thin shoulders thrown back.

"Let's go then," Patrick said, smiling at himself as much as at Tome. He felt like Cary Grant teaching Gunga Din to drill. Not a bad feeling; not bad at all. "Time to see the world, Mr. Tome."

13

·

"Hey, you sim."

Finger poke Meerm. Open eyes and see sim look in face.

"You new sim? You no work. Why you ride?"

"Cold. Hurt. Sick."

"Beece tell drive man."

"No!" Meerm sit up. Look out window. Bus on bridge cross water. Whisper, "No tell mans! Mans hurt Meerm!"

"Mans not hurt."

"Yes-yes! Mans hurt Meerm. Make Meerm sick. Please-please-please no tell mans!"

Other sim look round, say, "Okay. No tell mans." Sit next Meerm. "I Beece."

"I Meerm." Look window. "Where go?"

"Call Newark. Sim home there."

Ride and ride, then bus stop by big building. Meerm follow Beece and other sim out. Up stair to room of many bed, like room of many bed in burned home.

Meerm say, "Mans hurt here?"

"Mans no hurt. Mans feed. Sim sleep. Sim work morning."

Beece show Meerm empty bed. All other sim go eat. Meerm hide. Beece and other sim bring food. Meerm eat. Not yum-yum food like old burned home but not garbage food.

Meerm sleep on empty bed. Warm. Fed. If only sick pain stop, Meerm be happy sim.

14

Patrick paced his new office space, waiting for Romy. He'd asked her to show up early for their meeting with the Manassas Ventures attorneys. The prime reason was to offer her some coaching on how to respond to them. The second was to spring a little surprise.

He stopped next to an oblong table in the space that did double duty as his personal office and conference room, and looked around. The offices of Patrick Sullivan, Esq., occupied the fourth floor of an ancient, five-story Lower East Side building; gray carpet, just this side of industrial grade, white walls and ceiling—the latter still sporting its original hammered tin which he'd decided he liked. His degrees and sundry official documents peppered the walls between indifferent prints he'd picked up from the Metropolitan Museum store. And of course he had his books and journals scattered on shelves and in bookcases wherever there was room.

He heard the hall door open. Romy. He called out, "Back here!" but the woman who came through the door was not Romy.

"Mr. Sullivan?"

An older woman in an ancient tan raincoat, frayed at the sleeves and at least three sizes too big for her.

He recognized her: the space-alien-abducted-and-impregnated lady whose sim child had been stolen and given to Mercer Sinclair. He remembered everything about her except her name.

"Alice Fredericks," she said. "Remember?"

"Yes, of course. How are you, Miss Fredericks?"

"I could be better. I still haven't found a lawyer yet."

"To sue SimGen about the space aliens?"

"Yes. And for taking my sim child. I looked you up and learned you'd opened a new office, so I came straight here. Will you take my case now, Mister Sullivan?"

How to let this poor lady down easy?

He gave her an apologetic shrug. "I'm afraid my schedule's rather full now." He glanced at his watch. "And I'm expecting a client for an important conference in just a few minutes and—"

"Oh, I'm so sorry. I should have made an appointment."

"That's okay." He pushed a legal pad and a pen across the table to her. "But I'll tell you what. Leave me your number and I'll call you when my schedule opens up."

"Then you're not afraid?" she said, scribbling on the sheet.

"Of SimGen? Never."

"I meant the space aliens. You're not afraid of the space aliens?"

"Never met one I couldn't take with one hand."

"Thank you," she said, puddling up again. "You don't know what this means to me."

"I'm sure I don't."

"That's the number of the phone in the hall outside my room. Just ask for me and someone will get me."

Patrick nodded. He felt a little bad, giving her the brush like this, but it was the gentlest way he knew to get her out of his office.

Romy entered as Alice was leaving.

"Who was that?"

"A poor soul with a crazy story about SimGen." Patrick shook his head. "If she's representative of my future clientele, I'm in big trouble. But never mind her." He spread his arms. "What do you think of my new office?"

"Not bad," she said, looking around as she seated herself at the mini conference table.

She was being generous, he knew. "I know what you're thinking, and I agree: I need a decorator."

"Not really." She smiled faintly as she gazed up at the patterned ceiling. "I kind of like the anti-establishment air of the place."

"So do I. Gives me a feeling of kinship with the likes of Darrow and Kuntsler."

She smiled. "Darrow, Kuntsler and Sullivan. What a firm."

"Better than my old firm, Nasty, Brutish and Short."

He studied her across the table as she smiled. She looked good. The wicked shiners she'd developed after the Great Injury had faded from deep plum to sickly custard yellow. The sutures were gone from her scalp; she'd been able to hide the angry red seam by combing her short dark hair over it, but today she'd left it exposed for all the world to see.

"Want some coffee?" he said.

She shook her head. "I'm tense enough, thank you."

"How about decaf? I can have my legal assistant perk up a pot in no time."

"Assistant? I didn't know you'd hired anyone."

"You don't expect a high-powered attorney like me to stoop to filing my own papers, do you?" Patrick turned toward the file room and called out, "Assistant! Oh, assistant! Can you come here a minute?"

Tome, who'd been waiting quietly and patiently behind the door as instructed, said, "Yes, Mist Sulliman."

Romy's eyes fairly bulged. "That sounds like—"

And then Tome, ever so dapper in his new white shirt, clip-on tie, and baggy blue suit, stepped into the room.

"It is!" she cried. She leaped to her feet and crossed the room in three long-legged strides. She threw her arms around Tome and hugged him as she looked at Patrick with wonder-filled eyes. "But how? You couldn't . . . you didn't . . ."

"Kidnap him? Not quite."

She kept her arms around the old sim as Patrick explained Tome's posttraumatic depression and the arrangement with Beacon Ridge. Because she was taller than Tome, Romy's bear hug pressed his head between her breasts.

Hey, that's where I should be, Patrick thought as Tome grinned at him.

Nothing salacious or suggestive in that smile, just pure happiness. Being away from the barracks had worked wonders on the old sim. Within two days he was up and about, eating with gusto. And once Patrick had taught him the rudiments of filing, Tome took to the task with religious zeal.

Romy barraged Tome with questions about how he was feeling and what he'd been doing since the tragedy. Patrick had things he needed to discuss with Romy so he gave them a little time to catch up, then interrupted.

"Tome, would you mind doing some more filing before our guests arrive?"

"Yes, Mist Sulliman."

After Tome disappeared into the file room, Romy turned to him. "Does he bunk here?"

"No. We're roomies."

"Roomies?" She gave her head a slow shake. "Am I hearing and seeing things? I've heard hallucinations can be an aftereffect of head trauma."

"It's not so bad." The apartment he rented in an upgraded tenement not far from here was plenty of room for the two of them. "He keeps pretty much to himself. I got him one of those compact TV-DVD combinations for his bedroom and he spends most of his time there."

Her eyes were bright as she stared at him. "What a wonderful, wonderful thing to do."

"He's a riot," Patrick said, grinning. "I bought him that suit and he's absolutely in love with it. I had to go out and buy an iron and a board because he insists on ironing it every night." She was still staring at him. "Hey, no biggie. I figure it's only for a month or so, till he gets back on his feet."

"Still, I never would have imagined . . ."

"I'm told I'm full of surprises." He pulled a packet of folded sheets from an inside pocket of his jacket and slid them across the table to Romy. "But I'm not the only one."

"What's this?"

"A report from the Medical Examiner's office on the three floaters from the Hudson."

"The globulin farmers? How'd you get it?"

"It arrived by messenger this morning, no return address, but I can guess."

Romy nodded. "So can I." They'd decided not to mention Zero if there was any chance of a bug nearby. "He has contacts everywhere."

"I can save you the trouble of reading it," Patrick said as she unfolded the pages. "Remember how the bodies showed signs of torture? Well, toxin analysis revealed traces of a synthetic alkaloid in the tissues of all three. I won't try to tell you the chemical name—it's in there and it's a mile long—but the report says it's known in the intelligence community as *Totuus*; developed in Finland as a sort of 'truth' drug, and supposedly very effective."

"Totuus," Romy said, her face a shade paler. "I wonder if that's what they planned to use on me."

"When?"

"When they drove us off the road. Remember I said one of them had a syringe and said something about 'dosing' me up and getting a recorder ready?"

"Right." The memory twisted his insides. "You think there's a connection between the SLA and—?"

"I guess not. But listen to this: The report says the Totuus was administered *before* they were tortured."

"I don't get it," Romy said. "Why use torture when you've got a truth drug?"

Patrick wandered to the window overlooking Henry Street and watched the traffic. The same question had been bothering him.

"Maybe for fun. I don't know what's driving these SLA characters, but it's pretty clear now they're a vicious bunch."

"And if they want to 'free the sims' as they say, where are the ones they 'liberated'?"

"I was wondering the same thing. If they—"

A black Mercedes limo stopped and double parked on the street below. In this neighborhood that could mean only one thing.

"They're here," he said. "Fashionably early."

He watched as two dark-suited, briefcase-toting figures emerged, one male, one female; he noticed the woman lean back into the car and speak to someone still in the back seat.

Three arrive but only two come up. Odd . . .

"All right," he said, clapping his hands. "Places, everyone. Tome, you know what to do; Romy, you know your part. We've got only one shot at this so let's get it right."

The two Manassas attorneys soon arrived, trying unsuccessfully to hide their astonishment at being welcomed by a sim. Introductions were made, cards exchanged. The woman, a redhead, thin and pale as a saltine, was Margaret Russo; the heavy, dark-haired man, who looked like he scarfed up all his associate's leftovers, was David Redstone.

Russo glanced around. "Well, I must say, your office is . . . unique."

"And that elevator," Redstone said. "What an antique."

"It's steam powered," Patrick told them. "Can't be replaced because this is an historic building." He had no idea if any of that were true but it sounded good. "Shall we get started?"

He led them the short distance to the conference table where Romy waited. He made the introductions, then indicated chairs across the table from Romy for the Manassas people. He sat next to Romy.

"What's he doing?" Russo said, pointing to Tome who had situated himself on a chair behind and to Patrick's left with a steno pad propped on his lap.

"Taking notes," Patrick tossed off. "Now, before we—"

Russo was still staring. "But he's a sim. Sims can't write."

"It's shorthand. He'll type it up later."

He watched Russo and Redstone exchange glances. Good. Get them off balance and keep them there. They didn't need to know that Tome would be making meaningless scribbles or that Patrick was recording the meeting. He was sure they had their own recorders running.

"We'd like to get right down to business," Redstone said, pulling a legal pad from his briefcase. "The nitty gritty, as it were. To expedite matters I propose that we drop all pretense and skip the verbal jousting."

"No trenchant legal repartee?" Patrick said. "Where's the fun?"

"Look, Mr. Sullivan," Russo said, "we all know what this is about. We know Ms. Cadman was injured, but we also know the incident was set up."

Patrick glowered at her. "You'd better be able to back that up with proof, Ms. Russo."

"No jousting, remember?" she said. "Whatever it is you want, other than money, you're not going to get. So let's just end this charade here and now. We are authorized to make the following offer: Name a figure. Tell us the magic number that will make you walk away from this, and we will pay it."

Patrick had been expecting an attempt to buy them off, but nothing this blatant. But if that was the way they wanted to play . . .

"A magic number," he said, tapping his chin and pretending to ponder the possibilities. "How does an even billion sound?"

Russo and Redstone blinked in unison.

Russo recovered first. She cleared her throat. "Are we going to have a serious discussion or not? Did you call us here to waste our time or—"

"Whoa," Patrick said. "First off, you called us. Secondly—let me check with my assistant here." He turned to Tome. "Didn't they say, 'Name a figure, any figure'?"

The sim consulted his steno pad and said, "Yes, Mist Sulliman."

Tome had been instructed to say that, no matter what Patrick asked him.

"There, you see? 'Name a figure.' And I believe a billion is a figure."

"You can't possibly expect a small company like Manassas Ventures to come up with a sum like that," Russo said.

"Why not? It owns billions worth of SimGen stock. But maybe it doesn't have the stock anymore. I've learned that it's a wholly owned subsidiary of MetaVentures, based in Atlanta, so maybe the stock went there. Or perhaps it traveled further up the ladder to MacroVentures, a Bahamian corporation. But MacroVentures is owned by MetroVentures in the Caymans. Maybe that's where the stock ended up. Wherever it is, we know one of these companies has the financial wherewithal to pay Ms. Cadman's 'magic number' in a heartbeat. So don't cry poverty to me."

"This is preposterous!" Redstone sputtered.

"Not as preposterous as you two trying to keep me from having my day in court," Romy said.

Patrick had instructed her to play it sincere, and she was doing fine, because she was genuinely outraged.

"Oh, please—" Russo began but Romy cut her off.

Here it comes, Patrick thought.

"All I wanted was a little information," Romy said. "Nothing complicated. I simply wanted someone to explain why a truck leased by Manassas Ventures in Idaho was driving around the SimGen campus in New Jersey."

He scrutinized the two attorneys, watching their reactions as Romy dropped her bomb.

Patrick had gone half crazy trying to ferret out the principals in all the subsidiaries behind Manassas. Only the discovery proceedings of a lawsuit would give him a chance to pierce their multiple walls of secrecy. But it still might take him years to reach the end of their corporate shell game, and even then he might well come up empty. So he'd decided to shake things up by tossing a live snake into Manassas's corporate lap.

But neither Russo nor Redstone showed even a hint of surprise or concern. They either were clueless or had nervous systems of stone.

Damn.

"Write that down," Patrick said irritably, pointing to Redstone's legal pad. "It's important."

"What?"

"Your clients will want to know about those trucks. Trust me."

As Redstone made a note with a gold mechanical pencil, Russo said, "Can we stop playing games? A billion is out of the question."

"Out of the question?" Patrick said. "Gee. And we haven't even discussed punitive damages yet. I was thinking at least another billion—"

Russo slammed her hand on the table and shot to her feet. "That's it. I see no point in prolonging this farce. You two have an opportunity to be set for life. You've been offered the moon, but you want the stars."

"Very poetic."

She glared at him. "When you and your client come to your senses, Mr. Sullivan, call us."

"It won't be a call, it will be a subpoena. Many subpoenas. A blizzard of them. The first are already on their way."

"Send as many as you wish," Redstone said, snapping his briefcase closed. "You won't see a dime."

Patrick smiled. "Perhaps not, but we'll get what we want."

They stormed out.

After the door slammed, Romy said, "Wow. They're taking this personally."

"I've got a feeling they were offered a big bonus if they got the job done." He headed for the door. "Excuse me."

"Where are you going?" Romy said.

"Down to the street. I'll only be a minute."

He took the stairs and beat the Manassas attorneys to the lobby. He waited until they were outside, then trailed them to the limo. When they opened the door he caught up and leaned between them.

"You folks forgot to take my card, so I brought one down for each of you." He peered into the dim backseat and looked into the startled blue eyes of a balding man, easily in his seventies, sporting a dapper pencil-line mustache. "Hello," Patrick said. "Have we met? I'm—"

"Get in!" the man said to the two attorneys. He turned his head away from Patrick and spoke to the driver. "Go! We're through here!"

The doors slammed and the limo moved off.

Who's the old guy? Patrick wondered as he took the stairs back up. He'd half-expected to see Mercer Sinclair or perhaps that Portero fellow, but he'd never seen this guy before. Whoever he was he hadn't seemed at all happy that Patrick had got a look at him.

When he reached the office Romy was just finishing a call. She snapped the PCA closed and turned to him.

"That was our mutual friend. I told him about the meeting and he's a little upset that we didn't clear your idea with him first."

"I'm not used to having a nanny," Patrick replied. "Besides, we're just stirring up the bottom of the pond to see what floats to the surface."

"He's worried that mentioning the Manassas-Idaho truck connection at this point might give them time to cover their tracks. Or worse, precipitate a rash response."

"You mean like running my car off the road again? I don't think so."

Patrick didn't think whoever was behind Manassas would risk hurting him or Romy. That would raise too many questions; might even prompt a Grand Jury investigation.

"Still, he suggested that you invest in a remote starter for your car. Just in case."

Patrick stared at her, his mouth dry.

Romy smiled. "Joking."

Patrick was about to tell her where Zero could store his remote starter when her PCA chirped again. He watched her face, expecting the usual light-up he'd noticed whenever she spoke to Zero, but instead her brow furrowed as she frowned.

"Have you got a car available?" she asked as she ended the call.

"I can get to it in about five minutes. Why?"

"Road trip." Her expression remained troubled.

"Something wrong?"

"One of my NYPD contacts. He gave me the address of a house in Brooklyn. Said they'd found something there that would interest me."

"He didn't say what?"

"No. He said I had to see it to believe it."

15

NEWARK, NJ

Meerm here some day now. Little happy here.

Still tired-sick and hurt-belly-sick, sometime cold-sick and hot-sick. No more cold-hungry. Have place live, have food. Lonely in day when all sim go work. Meerm try help by clean and make bed. Must be quiet. Not let man downstair, man call Benny, know Meerm here.

Shhh! Benny come now. Benny come upstair ever day.

Meerm rush closet. Hide. Peek through door crack. See Benny walk round and open window. Come once ever morning. Always talk self.

"Damn monkeys!" Benny say. "Bad enough I gotta play nursemaid to 'em all night, but why they have to stink so bad?"

Benny open all window, then close all. Ver cold while window open, even in closet. Meerm shiver.

Benny leave and warm start come again. Meerm stay closet and wait. Better when sim come. Sim laugh, talk, bring Meerm food, not tell Benny. Meerm lonely till then. Wait Beece.

Beece friend. Try make better when Meerm hurt. Beece say Meerm need doctor. No doctor! Not for Meerm! Doctor hurt Meerm. No doctor! Beece say okay but not like. Meerm can tell.

Meerm little happy here. Meerm stay.

16

"One thing I've got to say about hanging with you," Patrick said as he drove them past peeling houses behind yards littered with old tires and charred mattresses. "I get to see all the city's ritziest neighborhoods. Say, you live in Brooklyn, don't you?"

Yes, Romy thought as she stared straight ahead through the windshield. She thought of the neat little shops and bistros along Court Street, just around the corner from her apartment in Cobble Hill. That was Brooklyn too, but a world away from this place. East New York was the far frontier of the borough. The economic boom of the nineties had run out of gas before it reached here, and the boom of the oughts had kept its distance as well. The faces were black, the cars along the trash-choked curbs old and battered, the mood grim.

"Hello?" Patrick said. "Are you still with me?"

She nodded and looked down at the map unfolded on her lap. She knew she hadn't been good company on the slow, frustrating drive across the Manhattan Bridge and through the myriad neighborhoods of the borough, but the nearer they moved to their destination, the tighter the icy clamp around her stomach.

Lieutenant Milancewich's call nagged at her. Her sim-abuse tips had helped him make a few busts over the years and in return he occasionally gave her a heads-up on investigations he thought might interest her. But he wasn't a friend, merely a contact, and she knew he considered her a little wacko. Maybe a lot wacko. He had no use for sims and thought her overzealous in her one-woman war, but a bust was a bust and he was glad to have them credited to his record.

Today, though, she'd heard something strange in his voice; she couldn't identify it, but knew she'd never heard it before. She'd pressed him about what it was he wanted her to see but he wouldn't say anything beyond, *I ain't been there myself, so I don't want to pass on any secondhand reports, but if what I hear is true, you should be there.*

Is it bad? she'd asked.

It wasn't good.

And that was what bothered her. The strange note in his voice when he'd said, *It ain't good.*

"I hope we're almost there," Patrick said. "I don't think I want to get lost out here, especially with sundown on the way."

She focused on the map. "Make a left up here onto—there!" She pointed to a pair of blue-and-white units just around the corner. "See the lights?"

"Got 'em."

Patrick pulled into the curb and they both stepped out. She let him lead the way as they headed toward the yellow crime scene tape. Once they were past that, Romy took the lead. Three of the four cops at the scene were either in their units or leaning against them as they talked on two-ways. Romy approached the fourth, a patrolman sipping a cup of coffee outside the front door of a shabby, sagging Cape Cod. He looked to be in his late twenties, fair-skinned, with a reddish-blond mustache.

After showing him her ID and going through the what-is-OPRR? and what's-OPRR-got-to-do-with-this? explanations, and making sure to smile a lot, she got him to open up.

"Got a call about a bad smell coming from the place." He cocked his head toward the house as he spoke in an accent that left no doubt he was a native. "So we investigated. Had to kick in the front door and that's when it really hit us. Ain't the first time I smelled that."

"Somebody dead?"

"That's what we figured, only we had it wrong. Not *somebody*—*many* bodies. And they ain't human."

Romy closed her eyes and took a deep breath. She was afraid to ask. "How many?"

"Looks like a dozen."

She heard Patrick's sharp intake of breath close behind her.

"How many sims were taken from the globulin farm?" he asked.

"Thirteen," she said without turning. "At least they think it housed thirteen." That was the count the police had painstakingly gleaned from one of the computer chips plucked from the ashes.

"Hey, you think these might be the missing sims from that Bronx fire a couple weeks back?" The cop shook his head. "Don't that beat all. I thought that job was pulled by a bunch of sim lovers."

"These may have no relation."

How could they? It didn't make sense that people who spray-painted "Death to sim oppressors" would kill the very sims they'd liberated.

The cop said, "Well, if they're the same, I'd guess from the stink and the condition of the bodies that they were done the same night as the fire." He shook his head in disgust. "Pisses me off."

Surprised, Romy looked at him. "Killing sims?"

"You kidding? No way. I mean, I'm not in favor of someone going around killing dumb animals, but what pisses me is that even though they ain't human I gotta hang around with my thumb up my ass—'scuse the French, okay?—while everybody figures out what to do and who should do it."

"How'd they die?" Romy asked.

"Don't need no forensics team for that." He poked his index finger against his temple and cocked his thumb. "Bam! One to the head for each of them. Must've used jacketed slugs because—"

"Thank you," Romy said, holding up a hand.

"Yeah, well, it was messy, all right. But not near as messy as what was done to them after they was shot."

Romy stiffened. "What do you mean?"

"Sliced them open from here"—his gun barrel finger became a scalpel and he dragged it from the base of his throat to his groin—"to here."

"Christ!" Patrick said.

Romy swallowed. "Why on earth . . . ?"

"Beats me. Dragged all their guts out and piled them in the middle of the cellar floor. Freaking mess down there, and if they think I'm gonna clean it up because it's 'evidence,' they can—"

"I want to see," Romy said.

"No, you don't, lady. If there's one thing I know in this life, lady, it's you do not want to go down in that cellar."

She looked around at the hollow-eyed buildings and the hollow-eyed stragglers with nothing better to do than stand at the police tape and stare.

He's so right, Romy thought. I don't.

But she had to see this for herself. Nothing made sense. If these were the sims from the globulin farm, what were they doing here? Had they been "liberated" just to be executed and mutilated?

Setting her jaw to keep her composure, Romy pulled a stick of gum—Nuclear Cinnamon—from her purse and began to chew.

The cop nodded knowingly. "I see you've been down this street before."

"What's going on?" Patrick said.

She turned and offered him a stick, saying, "Because sometimes the smell's so thick you can taste it."

"You're going in?" he said. He looked genuinely concerned. "That's way above and beyond, Romy. Leave it for the forensics people. You don't have to do this."

"Yeah, I do," she said. "Because they're sims the M-E will give them a cursory once-over, if that. Most likely the remains will be shipped back to SimGen and we'll never hear a thing. I don't expect you to come with me, Patrick. In fact, I'd prefer you didn't. But I need to see what's been done, so I can get a feel for the kind of monsters we're dealing with here."

She turned to the patrolman. "Let's go."

"Sorry," he said, shaking his head. "Might smell a little better in there now with the doors open, but I'm not going back in until I have to." He pointed toward the open front door. "Once you're inside, head straight back to the kitchen; hang a U and you'll be facing the cellar stairs." He handed her his flashlight. "There's no electricity so you'll need this. Just don't drop it. Or blow lunch on it."

"Thanks. I won't."

Knowing that if she hesitated she might lose her nerve, Romy immediately put herself in motion. She'd examined dead sims before, some of them in a ripe state of decomposition, and had learned some tricks along the way.

She'd gained the top of the two crumbling front steps and was pulling a tissue from her purse when she sensed someone behind her.

Patrick. His face looked pale, and despite the cold she thought she detected a faint sheen of sweat across his forehead.

"Wait for me out here," she told him.

"Sorry, no. I could have stayed in the yard if the cop had gone with you, but I can't let you go down there alone."

"Patrick—"

"Let's not argue about it, okay. I'm going in. Give me a stick of that gum and we'll get this over with."

She stared at him a moment. Patrick Sullivan was turning out to be a gutsy guy. She handed him a tissue along with the gum.

"When we head down to the cellar, hold this over your mouth and nose, pinching the nostrils and breathing into the tissue. That way you'll rebreathe some of your own air."

He nodded, his expression grim as he unwrapped the gum and stuck it into his mouth. "Let's go."

Romy led the way. Despite the open doors front and rear, the odor was still strong on the main floor; but when she rounded the turn and stood before the doorless opening leading down from the kitchen, it all but overpowered her. She heard Patrick groan behind her.

"Tissue time," she said. "And it could be worse. At least it's cold; that slows down decomposition. Imagine if this were August."

Patrick made no reply. Romy stared at the dark opening of the cellar doorway. She wished there were someone else she could dump this on, but couldn't think of a soul.

Steeling herself, she flicked on the flashlight and started down into the blackness. She kept the beam on the steps, moving carefully because there was no railing. The odor was indescribable. It made her eyes water. Even with her nostrils pinched, it wormed its way around the cinnamon gum in her mouth and made a rear entry to her nasal passages by seeping up past her palate.

When she reached the bottom Romy angled the beam ahead, moving it across the concrete. At first she thought someone had started painting the floor black and run out of paint three-quarters of the way through; then she realized it was blood. Old, dried blood. The cellar must have been awash in it.

She flicked the beam left and right to get her bearings and stopped when it lit up what looked like a pile of dirty rope. She remembered what the cop had said—*dragged all their guts out and piled them in the middle of the cellar floor*—and knew she wasn't looking at rope.

She swallowed back a surge of bile and forced herself forward, trying not to step in the dried blood—might be evidence there—as she moved. She stopped again when her beam reflected off staring eyes and bared teeth. She'd found the dead sims. Clad only in caked blood, their bodies ripped from stem to stern, they'd been stacked like cordwood against one of the walls. Their dead eyes and slack mouths seemed to be asking, *Why? Why?* And she wanted to scream that she didn't know.

Behind her she heard Patrick retch. She turned and saw him leaning against one of the support columns.

"You okay?" she said through her tissue.

"No." His voice was hoarse. He held up a thumb and forefinger; they appeared to be touching. "I'm just this far away from losing my lunch."

"I skipped lunch, thank God." She paused, then, "Look, I need to get closer."

"I don't. I'll stay back here and guard the steps, if you don't mind."

"I appreciate it," she told him. He'd already proved himself as far as she was concerned.

Turning, she spotted fresh, dusty prints ahead in the dried blood, leading to the cadavers; one of the cops, no doubt. To avoid further contamination of the scene she used them as stepping stones to move forward, knowing all along that it was wasted effort—no one was going to spend much time sifting this abattoir for clues. But there was a right way to do something, and then there was every other way.

Closer now she flashed her beam into the gaping incision running the length of the nearest cadaver's naked torso. A female. Her ribs had been ripped back, revealing lungs but no heart. Romy leaned forward and checked the abdominal cavity. Liver and kidneys gone. She craned her neck to see into the pelvis—uterus and ovaries missing too.

She moved onto another, a male this time, and the results were similar except that his testicles had been removed.

Romy straightened. They'd been gutted, all of them, and the males castrated. She took a quick turn around the rest of the basement but found no sign of the excised organs. The intestines had been removed and discarded in a pile because they were valueless and only got in the way. But all the rest were missing.

"Let's go," Romy said, taking Patrick's arm and pointing up the steps toward daylight and fresher air. "I've seen enough."

More than enough.

They hurried to the first floor and back out to the front yard. Romy didn't understand the missing ovaries and testicles—she knew of no use for them—but she understood the rest all too well.

Furious, she went straight to the cop and slapped the flashlight back into his palm.

"Didn't you notice anything missing down there?" she said.

He looked uncomfortable. "Like what?"

"Like their organs! They weren't just killed, they were harvested! And that"—she jabbed a finger at his chest—"is a felony!"

17

Beece work ver hard today. Many cloth to cut. Boss say, Faster, faster! Beece cut fast as can. Still boss yell.

Beece ver hot. Thirsty. Go sink for drink. Drink quick 'cause sink next boss office. Too long drink boss yell.

Boss door open. New man walk through. Red-hair man. Show boss papers. Beece hear talk.

"I'm from the city Animal Control Center, Mr. Lachter."

"Hey, I treat my sims good."

"No, Mr. Lachter, that would fall under the auspices of the ASPCA. We have a different mandate, and at the moment we're looking for a lost sim."

Beece almost leave sink, now stay. Lost sim? Could be Meerm? Listen more.

"I got all mine. I count 'em every morning. None missing, no extras."

"Good. But from past experience we know that lost sims tend to seek out other sims, so we'd greatly appreciate it if you'd keep your eye out for any sim that might wander in."

Boss laugh. "He does, I'll put him to work!"

"It's a female and if she shows up you should isolate her immediately."

"Why's that?"

"She may be sick. Nothing contagious to humans, but she might infect other sims."

Infect? Beece think. What mean infect?

"I don't need none of that. I can barely make production quotas now."

"If she shows she may look a little different than the average sim and—"

"Different? What is she, a new breed?"

"No. Same as the rest, but she might look a little heavier . . . perhaps 'bloated' is a better term. She's sick and we can take care of her, but we have to find her first."

Meerm! Man talk about Meerm! Meerm sick but fraid doctor. Beece feel sorry Meerm. City Man want help Meerm. No hurt Meerm.

Beece fraid talk Boss. Boss yell all time. But Meerm Beece friend. Must help Meerm.

Beece step in office. " 'Scuse, please, boss."

Boss face go mad. "What the hell you doing here! Get back to work, you lazy—"

"No, wait," red-hair city man say. He look Beece. "Do you know something?"

"Sick sim come home."

"Home? Where's home?"

"I crib them in Newark overnight," Boss say.

"Newark? Why so far?"

"Because it's tons cheaper to bus them back and forth than rent space for them around here. Sorry if that's out of your jurisdiction, pal, but—"

"Oh, don't you worry about that. Just give me the address of this place. I'll take it from there."

Beece happy. Red-hair city man nice. Help Meerm. Make Meerm better.

18

SUSSEX COUNTY, NJ

"This is good," Mercer Sinclair said as he skimmed the reports. "This is very good."

Just SimGen's security chief in the office with him today. Portero had personally delivered the police reports on the sim massacre in Brooklyn, an unusual courtesy. Perhaps the man was coming around, learning to be a team player.

Who am I kidding? Someone like Harry Carstairs is a team player, but not Portero. He doesn't know the meaning of the word "team." Mercer smiled to himself. *Come to think of it, neither do I.*

This visit meant one thing: Portero wanted something.

He'd never come right out and ask, Mercer knew. He'd use an oblique approach, try to sneak it in when no one was looking. Mercer was sure he'd find out what it was before the meeting ended.

"I thought you'd be upset," Portero said.

Is that why he came? To watch me blow my top? Sorry, Little Luca. Not today.

"I am. I hate the idea of losing a dozen of our sims. That's something people seem to forget—they're *our* sims. No matter what country they're shipped to, even if it's the other side of the world, they still belong to SimGen. We can barely keep up with demand as it is, so of course I hate to lose even one."

"But you seem almost . . . happy."

"I'm happy that these SLA creeps have been exposed for what they are. Yesterday's discovery shows they're not pro-sim activists, they're murderous organleggers." He glanced at the police report again. "They're sure these are the same sims that were hijacked from the globulin farm?"

Portero nodded. "Absolutely. Lucky thing NYPD was able to resuscitate that memory chip from the Bronx. And lucky too these globulin farmers were excellent record keepers: They scanned the neck bar codes of all their 'cows' into their computers."

"Then that nails the SLA. When they're caught they'll go down for murder and illegal organ trafficking. Any chance of tracing those organs?"

Portero shrugged. "Unlikely. They were probably shipped overseas while still warm. I've heard the Third World black market in transplant organs is booming, but . . ." He looked troubled.

"But what?"

"I know there's a big demand for human organs, but sim organs?"

"They're called xenografts—nonhuman organs. Human bodies used to reject them almost immediately, but with the new treatments that remove histocompatibility antigens, the rejection rate is about equal to human allografts. Those hearts, livers, and kidneys are worth a fortune on the black market."

Portero nodded and Mercer thought, You haven't a clue as to anything I just said.

"Hearts, livers, kidneys," Portero said. "What about uteruses and ovaries? Are they transplantable?"

"No value at all. Nor are the testicles they cut off—unless someone's developed a taste for a new kind of Rocky Mountain oyster."

Just the thought made Mercer ill.

"Then why go to the trouble to harvest them?"

"Maybe they were stupid organleggers."

"One other thing concerns me," Portero said. "The chip from the globulin farm shows records of thirteen sims housed there right up until the night of the fire. But only twelve were found in that Brooklyn basement."

"You're sure?"

"We know from the records that a female sim is unaccounted for. The only reason I can imagine why she wasn't butchered along with the rest is that she wasn't with them."

"You think she escaped?"

"I suspect she was never captured. I think she fled the raid and the fire, and is hiding somewhere in the city."

"Why on earth would she hide?"

"Maybe she saw the security man murdered and she's frightened. She could be anywhere, too terrified to show herself."

A witness, Mercer thought. A sim could never testify in court, but this one might be able to provide the police with a lead or two.

Mercer glanced down at the embedded monitor in his desktop. Damn near every headline scrolling up the screen this morning seemed to be about the sim slaughter in Brooklyn. The good part was that the phony "SLA" had shown its true colors; the bad part was the depiction of sims as helpless victims, easy prey for human scum. Too high a sympathy factor there. He needed to counter that, and this missing sim offered a unique opportunity.

"I want that sim found," he told Portero. "To make sure she is, SimGen is going to offer a million-dollar reward to whoever finds her."

Portero looked dubious. "Do you think that's necessary? I'm sure my people—"

"Forget your people. This is strictly a SimGen matter. We'll handle it."

Yes. The more he thought about this, the more he liked it. Here was a way to take back the headlines and reassert SimGen as the true champion and defender of sims.

"Very well," Portero said, rising. "Since there's nothing for me to do in that regard, I'll get back to my office."

After Portero was gone it occurred to Mercer that he hadn't discovered the reason for the security chief's personal visit. He'd been sure he'd wanted something. But what?

Well, whatever it was, he hadn't got it.

19

Luca Portero went directly from the CEO's office to the parking lot where he picked up one of the SimGen Jeeps. He grinned as he drove out the gate.

A million-dollar reward—and Sinclair thinks it was his idea. Doesn't have a clue that I steered him into the whole thing.

The meeting had been a thing of beauty, he had to admit. Knowing Sinclair-1's obsession with SimGen's public image, Luca had simply parceled out the information—first playing dumb about the xenografts, then mentioning an unaccounted-for sim, then hinting that she might be a witness—letting Sinclair pounce from one to the next like a mouse following a trail of cheese bits, until he'd ended up right where Luca wanted him.

A reward! Put SimGen in the news: The corporation with a heart as big as its market cap value!

Putty in my hands, Luca thought.

His grin faded as he thought about what lay ahead. Another meeting. This one with Darryl Lister. He and his old CO hadn't had a face-to-face in almost a year, which could only mean that the subject was as delicate as it was important.

That made him uneasy. Worse yet, they were meeting at Luca's house.

He pulled up the long drive to the rented two-bedroom cabin in the center of five acres of dense woods. He liked the isolation. This was his retreat from SimGen and lost sims.

Lister wasn't due for another half hour. Still plenty of time to get Maria out of the way and—

He hit the brakes when he saw the black Mercedes SUV parked in front of the house.

Lister? Shit!

He still had time to salvage this. Was Lister alone? With the late morning sun glinting off the SUV's windshield, Luca couldn't tell how many were in the car.

When he pulled up next to it he was startled to see that it was empty. He hurried through his front door and found Darryl Lister sitting on the couch, sipping a beer. Maria stood behind him, rubbing her hands together, her dark eyes wide with anxiety.

Luca stared at Lister. This plump country squire type was miles away from the hardbodied CO who'd parachuted with him onto the Shahi Kot mountains. He was a pogue now, in his late forties, and the brown corduroys and bulky white Irish wool sweater he wore couldn't hide the inches he'd been adding to his waist. And judging from the new gelled-up style of his light brown hair, it looked like he'd started going to a fag barber. The man was becoming a stranger.

"Luca." He rose and smiled as he extended his hand. "I was going to wait in the car, but then this sweet young thing surprised the hell out of me by opening the front door. I invited myself in." As they shook hands, his smile faded. "Who is she, Portero? I know you don't have any kids. A niece?"

"No one you have to worry about."

"You know the rules."

Luca held up the car keys. *"Maria, esperame en el auto."*

She scurried around the couch. Her jeans and bulky flannel shirt couldn't hide her ripe young figure as she grabbed the keys and ran out the door. Luca noticed Lister's eyes following her all the way.

"Nice," he said. "What is she? Sixteen?"

Luca felt invaded. He wanted to tell Lister it was none of his fucking business, but bit it back. To a very real extent, it *was* Lister's business.

"She's old enough," Luca said.

Maria had told him she was eighteen, but she might be even younger. He'd seen her begging on an East Village sidewalk last summer. Maybe it was her flat peasant face, or the desperation in her black eyes . . . something about her spurred an impulse from a nameless place to shove a couple of singles into her hand. He heard her soft, *"Gracias, señor,"* saw the sudden faraway look in her eyes as she clutched the bills between her breasts like a family heirloom, and he had to speak to her. Good thing he knew Spanish because she didn't know anything else.

He bought her lunch, took her to a Spanish film at the Angelika, bought her dinner, then brought her home. She'd been living here ever since. She cleaned his house, cooked his food, kept his bed warm at night, and thought she'd found heaven.

"She's an illegal who's young enough to be your daughter, right?"

True on both counts, but so what? "Don't worry. She doesn't know anything. Can't speak a word of English."

"But I *am* worried. It's against the rules. You're supposed to be a model citizen. A clean nose, no legal hassles. That's the deal when you come in. You agreed, now look at you: shacking up with a barely legal illegal."

"No one's going to know. Not way out here."

"But *our* people will know. Sooner or later you know they'll find out. And they won't like it. And since I sponsored you, that will reflect on me."

"Look—"

"They've already got questions about you. Like why you don't seem to own anything. You rent this place and . . ." He looked around with distaste. "And it looks like you furnish it from secondhand stores."

"It came with the territory. It's a furnished rental."

"I know we pay you enough to afford to buy."

Of course they did. But Luca saw no point in tying up money in real estate. He wanted no anchors. When the time came to move on, as it inevitably would, he wanted to be able to pick up and go without a second's hesitation, without a single look back.

"It's the way I've always lived."

"I know. I've tried to explain that to them. They don't care. They want you settled in. I went out on a limb to get you this cushy assignment, but if you don't put down some roots, they'll transfer you out to Idaho. And I'll have egg on my face."

Luca had spent a few months at the Idaho facility and had no desire to go back.

He held up his hands in surrender. "Message received. I'll see what I can do about buying this place."

"Luca," Lister said, smiling as he put a hand on his shoulder. He rarely called him by his first name. "You're making good money. And you'll be making better and better money. Enjoy it, for Christ's sake. That's what it's for. You can't take it with you."

Luca nodded. "I guess you're right."

But he was thinking, You *can* take it with you—if you've got it squirreled away in a secret offshore account.

Luca believed in being prepared. He'd learned that from his mother. She might have been a whore, but she was no dummy. She always kept a roll of cash hidden away for what she called "the rainy days," when the cops periodically would raid her place and roust her out. The cash had always kept her out of jail.

The same held true here. Who knew when the weather would change?

He could handle the proverbial rainy day, but SIRG played rough, and if a shitstorm struck, he believed in having a safe harbor to hole up in. His was in Hamilton, Bermuda.

He repressed a shudder. If SIRG ever found out about that account . . .

"But that's only half the reason for this face-to-face," Lister said.

"If it's about the missing sim," Lucas blurted, relieved to be moving away from his personal life, "I just enlisted Mercer Sinclair's help—a million-dollar reward."

Lister was looking at him. "So you told him?"

"Not yet. Not till I find the sim. I've got people combing the city, visiting any place that uses sim labor. This reward will flush out anyone who's seen her. Once I have her, the Sinclairs can take over."

Lister frowned. "You might have had this sewn up by now if they'd been on board from the start."

"They'd have added nothing but panic." Bad enough to have Lister calling twice a day, he didn't need the Sinclairs yammering in his ear every free minute too. "And don't forget, it took days for the fire department to sift through all the rubble. Until they reported no sim remains, we didn't know for sure she was missing."

"Still, if this million-dollar reward had been announced days ago . . ."

"You know my problem with telling SimGen too much."

"This 'leak' you suspect?"

Luca nodded.

Lister shoved his hands in his pockets and looked around. "I thought you were way off base with that at first. Now I'm not so sure."

"Why? What's happened?"

"The Manassas attorneys met with the Cadman woman and Sullivan. What a farce. She could have walked away with millions but she's asking for *billions* in damages."

Luca wanted to laugh. He'd known they couldn't buy off Romy Cadman.

Just hearing her name set off reactions within him, part anger, part lust. Sometimes when he was with Maria, moving inside her, he thought of Romy Cadman. Young stuff like Maria pushed his buttons, *all* his buttons, but that didn't mean he didn't have anything left over for a prime piece of mature tail like Cadman.

"Did you agree to pay it?"

Lister stared at him. "You're not serious."

"You should have called their bluff, just to see what they'd do. Because we all know they're not after money. But what does this have to do with a leak?"

"The Cadman woman said she'd come to the Manassas office because she wanted to know why a truck leased in Idaho by Manassas was driving around the SimGen campus."

"But . . ." Luca's heart stalled, then picked up again. "But there's no connection. Those leases are paid through Golden's credit card."

Hal Golden was dead, but no one knew that. His body lay six feet deep in a field in Thailand, but his credit record, active and pristine, lived on in the computers of the finance world. Golden had never even heard of Manassas Ventures while he lived, so how had Cadman and Sullivan linked him to the company?

"I know that. But at one time Manassas leased them directly. Somehow she made the connection. And I'm beginning to wonder if she might have been tipped."

"But that doesn't make sense. If someone's leaking her information about Manassas Ventures, wouldn't they tell her everything?"

"You'd think so, wouldn't you. But whatever her source, somehow this woman has identified Manassas as the tie between SimGen and our Idaho facility."

"So then, why not just abandon Manassas? It served its purpose."

"It's not like some dinghy you can cut loose at sea and forget. It's part of a chain of subsidiary corporate entities that this Sullivan fuck has already traced back four or five levels. This has *everyone* upset."

The way Lister emphasized "everyone" made it clear to Luca that this went far up the SIRG ladder.

"They want the woman and the lawyer stopped," Lister added, staring at him. "And since you were in charge of the Cadman woman when she saw the truck with the Idaho plates, that puts this square in your lap. They want you to take care of it."

"What? Take her out? If anything happens to her, anything *final*, Manassas Ventures will be a prime suspect."

"I'm talking about *information*, not termination. She's obviously not alone in this. They want to know who's behind her. They want her source. And if there's a leak in SimGen, they want to know who it is. Word has come down: This has equal priority with the missing sim. Understand me, Luca? This isn't me talking to you." Lister suddenly looked uncomfortable. "This comes from the Old Man himself."

The Old Man? Luca swallowed. That meant this went *all* the way up the ladder, and all eyes would be on him. Damn Romy Cadman for mentioning that truck. It almost seemed like she was doing everything in her power to screw him.

"Word is he's raising hell how if you'd done the job right the first time, when you rolled Sullivan's car off the Saw Mill, we wouldn't be facing this now."

Luca felt sick. "Jesus . . ."

"I went to bat for you, sent the Old Man your record in Operation Anaconda and the Baghdad sorties, and apparently that carried some weight. You know, soldier to soldier. He's giving you a chance to redeem yourself. That doesn't happen too often."

"I'm grateful," he said, forcing the words past stiff lips.

Luca felt a growing pressure in his head. Was someone out to get him . . . dump more on him than any one man could handle, then wait for him to buckle under the weight?

"I'll help you with the logistics and anything else I can," Lister told him. He looked fidgety now. Maybe Luca wasn't the only one being given a second chance. "We've *got* to know who she's fronting for." He glanced at his watch. "Got to run."

Luca followed him outside to the cars. He waved to Maria and jerked his thumb over his shoulder toward the open front door. She jumped out of the Jeep and ran back into the house.

Again, Lister's eyes followed her. "Remember what I said about putting down roots."

"Roger that," Luca said.

But not till he saw how all this settled out. Until then he wanted that Bermuda account as fat as possible.

"And ditch the kid. Put her back where you found her."

"Will do."

Lister smiled. "Or marry her."

"I don't think so."

He'd miss Maria, miss her a lot. She loved sex, cooked up a storm, and was crazy about him, would do *anything* for him. Maybe he'd keep her around till he found a replacement. Someone who could—

Luca's PCA chirped. He flipped it open and turned away from Lister as he spoke. "Yes."

"This is Grimes. We found her. She's been hiding out in a sim crib."

Relief flooded through him. "You have her?"

"Not yet. But we've got an address and we're on our way."

"Where's the crib?" Luca listened as Grimes read off a Newark address. "I'll meet you there."

He ended the call and turned back to Lister. "One of my men. We've located the missing sim. We're on our way to pick her up." He grinned at Lister. "One problem down, one more to go."

"Let's hope so," Lister said.

Luca jumped into the Jeep. Newark. Not a long drive. And the timing could not be better. Tying this up would free him up to devote all his energies to Romy Cadman, and settling with her once and for all.

20

NEWARK, NJ

Meerm lonely. Not hungry. Nibble food save from last night. Watch out window. See peoples walk sidewalk. Not far down. One floor. Meerm listen. Sometime hear what passing peoples say. Sometime happy. Sometime mad. Meerm like happy better.

Meerm watch street. Many car but no sim bus. Wait sim bus. Hope come soon. Then friend Beece come. Belly pain hurt less when Beece near. Beece talk Meerm, help Meerm.

Meerm see car come fast. Stop outside. Four sunglass mans come. Look round, look sim building. Meerm quick step back. Who mans? Why here? Why look at sim building?

Meerm fraid mans come in. Peek so mans not see. No mans come in. All stand by car. One talk little phone. Why here?

Then Meerm see new car. Also fast. Stop next first car. One man come. New man talk loud. Point this way and that way. Other mans go. New man voice . . . Meerm hear before. But where?

Now Meerm see new man and other man come sim building. Meerm fraid. Mans come take Meerm away? Back to new needle place?

Meerm hide. Go closet. Push self into dark corner. Make ver small.

Hear yell downstair. Benny mad. Shout loud. New man yell back.

Meerm shake. Know new man voice! Same voice in old home night loud noise and fire. Hear on roof too. New man come get Meerm!

Hear loud feets on stairs. Must not find! Must not find! Meerm climb up in closet. Get on shelf. Curl up. Make small-small. Tiny-tiny-tiny. Push back into high corner and—

Corner move. Meerm turn, feel loose board. Meerm push board, move more. Black space open. Cold in hole. Meerm not care. Too fraid be cold.

Hear new man voice yell, "Damn it, where is she?" Voice close now. In sim sleep room.

Meerm squeeze into black hole. Ooh-ooh-ooh. Too tight. Meerm so fat now. Meerm fraid get stuck, but more fraid new man. Push-push-push, get fat self into hole.

"I tell you," Benny say, "we ain't got no sims here inna day!" Benny sound fraid. "Not till tonight when they all bussed back from the city."

"She's here!" new man say. "And we're going to find her! Look under every bunk! Check every closet!"

Meerm in cold place inside wall. Ver tight. Ver dark. Meerm push on board, push back where belong. More dark now. All dark.

Meerm hear closet door squeak. Some man open. Meerm can't see man but hear thing move. Meerm stay ver, ver still. Not breathe.

"Nothing in here." New man voice ver close. Meerm so fraid. Want go pee. Bite lip stop cry. "Where the fuck *is* she?"

"Maybe she goes out," say other man voice. "You know, walks around."

"Since when did you become a sim expert?"

Other man say, "Hey, I'm just thinking out loud, okay? That sim at the sweatshop described her to a T: she's lost, she's sick, she's blown up. So we know she's staying here. She's just not here now. Probably going stir crazy here alone all day."

"All right. Here's what we'll do. Bring in the others and we'll do a sweep of the building. If we don't find her we'll back off and put the place under twenty-four-hour watch. When she returns, we nab her."

Meerm hear mans go way but still not move. Still fraid. Meerm must stay in sim building. Mans will get Meerm. Hurt Meerm if try leave. Meerm so sad she cry.

21

Luca wanted to skip this—he had far more pressing things to do than listen to Sinclair-1 yammer. But the man had said he was calling this late meeting specifically to address a security issue. In addition to everything else going on, SimGen security was still his responsibility.

But he didn't have to arrive on time. He was punctual by nature, and his years in Special Forces had reinforced that, so it took considerable effort to force himself to walk slowly down the hall, pacing himself to arrive at least three minutes late.

Luca balled his fists. Coming up empty in the sim crib this afternoon still rankled him. Fury and disappointment had mixed into a combustible compound in his bloodstream. His head felt like a ticking bomb. He'd left four men to watch the building—all sides, all day, all night—but he had a gnawing premonition that the missing sim wouldn't be back.

Then, just fifteen minutes ago, Lister calls, supposedly concerned about the well-being of the sim because he hadn't heard any word on her. Luca had had to eat some bitter crow.

As if that wasn't bad enough, Lister then proceeded to twist the knife: "Someone handed you the address where she was staying and she ducked you? If a monkey can outwit you, how can we expect you to find out who's behind the woman and her lawyer?"

Don't worry, Luca thought as he approached the door to Sinclair-1's office. She's next on my list. And I know just how I'm going to handle her. As soon as I finish with these assholes . . .

When he stepped into the office he found only two of the usual crew in attendance: Both Sinclairs were present, but Abel Voss was missing.

"Mr. Portero," Sinclair-1 said as soon as the door closed. "We've been waiting for you."

"The wait is over," Luca replied. He wanted out of here as quickly as possible, so he pushed right to the subject, "You mentioned a security matter?"

"Yes, Mr. Portero. Were you aware that we had an attempted break-in this afternoon?"

"Of course." A group of sim huggers had tried to run the front gate. His men had detained them until the State Police arrived. "They're in jail."

"How gratifying that you know. But my question is, Where were you?"

"Busy with other matters."

"Matters more important than the security of this campus? Security here is your number-one priority. There are murderous bioterrorists running around out there, slaughtering humans and sims, and yet when this group tried to attack us, you were nowhere to be found."

"Harmless nobodies," Luca said, allowing a sneer to work its way onto his face. What an old woman he was.

"Lucky for us. But with you hiding out somewhere, there's no telling what damage we might have suffered if they'd been the SLA."

A flash of anger added heat to the pressure pushing against his eardrums. Hiding? Had this empty suit just accused him of hiding?

"Easy, Mercer," said Sinclair-2, turning his head to look at Luca. This was the first sign of life he'd shown.

With difficulty Luca kept his voice level. "But they weren't the SLA."

"But they could have been!" Sinclair-1 said. He pointed over his shoulder at the darkening hills visible through the oversized picture window behind him. "The SLA could be out there now, in the trees, readying an assault."

"They're not, and they never will be." Luca had had just about enough of playing games with these two. "I guarantee it."

Sinclair-1's eyebrows rose halfway to his forehead. "You guarantee it? How interesting. You're clairvoyant?"

"No," he gritted. "I'm the SLA."

Immediately he wished he hadn't said it.

"This is no time for sick humor," Sinclair-1 said.

Luca knew from the dubious expression on the CEO's face that he still had a chance to take it back, but decided against it. Fuck 'em. He stepped up to Sinclair-1's desk, rested his hands on its cool onyx surface, and leaned forward, literally getting in the other man's face.

"That was not any kind of humor."

"What?" The voice from his right, Sinclair-2, on his feet, his face pale. "You?"

"Ellis, he's joking."

Luca fixed Sinclair-1 with his gaze. "Have you *ever* known me to joke?"

The CEO wavered, then took a step back, his eyes wide.

Movement to Luca's right. "Monster!" Sinclair-2 charging, face distorted with fury. Luca pivoted, drove a fist into his gut, and that was all it took. The man doubled over, then dropped to his knees, gasping.

"Dear, God! Ellis! Are you all right?"

The kneeling man, still clutching his belly with one hand while the other clutched the arm of the sofa for support, shook his head. His voice was a half-strangled whisper. "I'll never be all right."

Sinclair-1 stared at Luca. "Why? In God's name, *why?*"

"To find your million-dollar sim."

"For what?" Sinclair-2 said as he hauled himself back into the couch. He sat hunched over, rubbing his belly. "To harvest her organs along with the rest?"

"No. To give her to you two."

"Why would we be interested?"

"Because she's pregnant."

A pause as the two brothers glanced at each other, then stared at Luca. Sinclair-1 snorted. "Impossible!"

"So I've been told." Luca shrugged. "And maybe that's true in theory. But I deal in facts, and everything I've discovered about this particular sim confirms that she is pregnant."

"How on earth did you find out about her?"

Might as well tell them the whole story, Luca thought. Well, most of it.

"It started with a phone call last month. A woman said she had to speak to Mercer Sinclair right away, said she had information that would affect the entire future of SimGen. That sounded like a security matter to me so I took the call and—"

"And pretended to be me?"

"Of course. The woman, whose name I later learned was Eleanor Bryce, a Ph.D. in microbiology, told me she was in possession of a pregnant sim."

"You accepted that?" Sinclair-2 said. His color was returning along with his voice, but pure hatred gleamed in his eyes. "Just like that?"

Portero returned his stare. You want another try for a piece of me, fancy man? Next time I spread your nose across your face.

"Of course not. In an involved back-and-forth that took almost two weeks she sent enough information to convince our people that she could be telling the truth."

"*Your* people!" Sinclair-1 now. "The ones in our Basic Research facility, I suppose. Why not ours?"

"We were going to bring in your people later, but first we had to secure this sim. The Bryce woman made enough slips during our communications to allow me to pinpoint her location. When she presented her ultimatum I decided it was time to move."

"Ultimatum?" Sinclair-1 said.

That's not what you should be asking me, Luca thought. Why aren't either of you asking the right question?

Because he was dying to lay the answer on them . . . and watch both the Sinclair brothers' hair turn white before his eyes.

Luca said, "She wanted to sell us the sim."

"*Sell* us? Sell us something that already belonged to us? What did you tell her?"

"Since I was pretending to be you, I said exactly that, then I asked her how much she wanted. She told me to bid. And she warned me not to be 'chintzy'—her word—because there'd be another bidder: the Arata-jinruien Corporation."

Sinclair-1 pounded a fist on his desktop. "*Those* bandits? Outrageous!"

"Wait just a minute," Sinclair-2 said, holding up a hand. "Let's take a step back here."

Here it comes, Luca thought. His gut tingled with anticipation.

"Let's just say," Sinclair-2 continued, but he spoke to his brother, as if Luca weren't there, "that this Bryce woman, through hormone treatments or a recombinant patch, did somehow manage to induce a female sim to produce a fertilizable ovum. That will cause SimGen problems because it means people will be able to breed their own sims—and no one on this planet wants that less than I do—but it doesn't invalidate our patent on the sim genome. So—"

Not the question!

"She didn't do anything to the sim," Luca snapped. "She's a microbiologist. Knows nothing about reproductive medicine."

"How can you be sure?" Sinclair-1 said.

"She told me."

Sinclair-1 barked a laugh.

Luca glared at him. "At the time I questioned her she was loaded up with a drug that made her incapable of lying."

"The compound mentioned in the autopsy report," Sinclair-2 said, his tone dripping contempt. "Did you torture them before or after you had your information?"

"That was just window dressing, to muddy the waters while I eliminated everyone with firsthand knowledge about the pregnancy. I didn't know what the sims knew, but I didn't want any loose ends, so they were removed too."

"Dear God, why?" Sinclair-2 said. "A pregnant sim, even if it were possible, opens up a can of worms, but it's not worth the lives of three people and a dozen sims!"

Here's the moment, Luca thought. Time to rock your world.

"It does if the father of the sim's baby is human."

Silence, a moment of glorious, absolute silence in the office as the Sinclair brothers froze. Luca could have been looking at a photograph, or an elaborate sculpture. Then the thump of Sinclair-1 dropping heavily into his chair as if the bones in his legs had suddenly dissolved.

Luca inhaled the mixture of shock and terror filling the air. Moments like this made life worth living.

He's wrong! Mercer Sinclair thought, fighting a vertiginous sense of unreality. Portero's wrong! He has to be!

. . . the father of the sim's baby is human . . .

Those words hung in the air before him, almost visible. He sensed that if he reached out his hand he might touch them.

He looked at his security chief's smug expression and knew that Portero believed it, but that didn't mean it was true. Being a tough guy didn't mean you couldn't be scammed.

Mercer worked his lips, forcing out the words. "A hoax!" he cried, but it sounded more like a bleat.

Portero shook his head. "I have it from all three farmers: They all believed they were in possession of a pregnant sim that was going to make them rich beyond their wildest dreams."

"Then they believed wrong!"

"Wait a second," Ellis said. "They believed. That's important. They may have been morally bankrupt, but they weren't ignorant. A globulin farm requires a fair amount of scientific sophistication. And if they were convinced that one of their sims was pregnant . . ."

Mercer stared at his brother. Ellis seemed to have shaken off the pain and humiliation of Portero's gut punch. But instead of feeling, as Mercer did, that his lips were encased in lead, Ellis seemed almost . . . energized.

And he was thinking the unthinkable.

"Ellis . . . it can't be. Read my lips: Sims. Are. Sterile. Want me to write it out on a piece of paper for you?"

"But a sim gene can mutate," Ellis said. "Sims can't evolve, but they're as prone to mutations as any other organism. Murphy's Law, Merce: Shit happens, especially when it comes to reproduction. Nature abhors a dead-end species nearly as much as a vacuum."

"Don't talk to me of 'Nature' and what it abhors," Mercer said. "*I* abhor teleological concepts. Life is chemicals, pure and simple."

Ellis went on as if Mercer hadn't spoken. "I remember reading years ago about a woman who'd lost her left ovary due to a ruptured cyst and her right fallopian tube due to a tubal pregnancy. She was told she'd never have to worry about birth control, but years later she showed up in her doctor's office with a positive pregnancy test. An ultrasound showed that her left fallopian tube had migrated across her uterus to link up with her right ovary."

"Apocryphal garbage."

Ellis looked at Portero. "This Bryce woman who called, this microbiologist, did she tell you how she found out the sim—what was her name again?"

"Meerm," Portero gritted. The name burned like acid on his tongue.

"Did she tell you how she discovered Meerm was pregnant?"

Portero made a face. "What difference does it make?"

"Humor me."

A sigh, then, "When she first called she told me she'd been working up a sick sim—vomiting, pain. Couldn't find out what was wrong so she sent blood out to a commercial lab and ordered a preset battery of tests for abdominal pain. The battery was designed for humans, and one of those tests was for pregnancy. It came back positive. She repeated it at three different labs, and all came back positive. She rented an ultrasound rig and that removed all doubt. She overnighted me copies of the blood work and the ultrasound. I had our people go over them. They said it could easily be a hoax, but there was enough there to be worried about."

Mercer said, "So you made a preemptive strike before the Japanese could get involved."

Portero inclined his head a few degrees. "Exactly."

Had to hand it to the man: His methods might be loathsome, but he got things done.

"But why invent this SLA group?"

"For cover. I didn't want anyone to guess the real reason for the raid, and a bunch of wacked-out sim huggers seemed perfect. The op would have gone down without a hitch if their security guy hadn't decided to take his job seriously. Four of us went in and the jerk started shooting, so we had to take him out. The shots must've spooked the pregnant sim who was being kept separate from the other cows. When I couldn't find her I figured she was hiding somewhere in the building; since I didn't have time to look for her, I fired the place."

"But no sim remains were found," Ellis said. "Which meant she escaped." He shook his head. "I can see the logic, sick as it is, of killing the humans. But why the sims? Even if they somehow knew about Meerm's pregnancy, who'd believe them?"

Portero's eyes narrowed and his tone skirted with a snarl. "First off, I wasn't about to nursemaid a bunch of monkeys. Second, they could identify us. And third, our people over in Basic Research wanted to look at their gonads, just in case they'd undergone any changes like the pregnant one. I covered that by taking hearts and kidneys and livers too—made it look like a harvest."

Mercer clenched his teeth and stared at Portero. You shit! he thought. Just yesterday you stood right there and played all innocent about organlegging and xenografts.

He wanted to throw something at him but feared Portero might return it with interest. Or worse, shove it down his throat.

"What ice-cold womb did you spring from?" Ellis said, still shaking his head.

Mercer feared Portero might react violently, but the insult seemed to roll off him. And Mercer realized that neither of them could insult Luca Portero, because Portero didn't care what they thought.

We're of a different species, and our opinions are irrelevant.

Mercer watched as his brother closed his eyes a moment, took a breath, then said, "How did the globulin farmers know the father was human?"

"They asked the sim and she fingered Craig Strickland, the farm's security guard—"

"The corpse that was found in the fire?"

"Yeah, him. Seemed he'd been spending some of his guard time diddling the livestock. Before he ate a few bullets."

Mercer slumped back in his chair, rubbing his eyes. This can't be happening.

"You realize what this means, don't you, Merce." His brother's voice.

It wasn't a question. Mercer lowered his hands to find Ellis staring at him. Yes, he knew exactly what this meant: the end of SimGen.

But only if somebody else found the sim first.

"Five million dollars," Mercer blurted. "I'm raising the reward to five million for information leading to the successful 'rescue'—and I want that term emphasized—of the missing sim. We'll say the reason we're willing to pay so much is that she can lead us to the killers of the twelve dead sims, and that nobody slaughters and mutilates our sims and gets away with it."

"What if she's dead?" Portero said. "She can't be 'rescued' then."

Mercer thought about that a moment. "I want her to be worth more alive than dead, so we'll offer to pay just one million for her remains. But I want her alive, get it? Alive, alive, alive!"

Yes. Get their hands on this sim before anyone else. And once she's safely tucked away, find out how she became fertile. Then take steps to make sure it never happens again.

Somewhere, out there, walking around, was living, breathing proof that humans and sims could cross-fertilize . . . Mercer's worst nightmares had never even come close to such an apocalyptic scenario. If news of this ever got out, sims would have to be reclassified closer to human, too close to be property, too close to be leased . . .

Imagine having to announce that at the stockholders' meeting next week. SimGen shares would crash and burn . . . they'd be the Hindenberg of the NASDAQ. He'd lose everything. *Everything!*

And so would SIRG.

"Find her, Portero," Mercer said. "This is as important to your people as it is to me. All that SimGen stock they hold will be toilet paper if someone beats us to her. If you do nothing else in your life, you must find that sim. That is your number one priority."

"Not quite," Portero said softly. "There's another, equally pressing matter that requires my attention."

Looking at the security chief's dark expression, and knowing his ruthlessness, Mercer was glad he was not that other "equally pressing matter." He wondered who might be involved, then decided he'd rather not know.

"But don't worry about your pregnant sim," Portero went on. "I've got a good idea where she is and I'll have men watching the area twenty-four/seven. You'll have your sim."

22

Mans go way. Meerm hide in wall. Too fraid come out. Meerm feel something move inside. Not first time. Meerm feel before but nev so much. Move-move-move inside. What do that? Is why Meerm belly so big?

When sim come back work, Meerm climb out wall. Not leave closet because hear other man come. Yell-yell-yell.

"You, you lousy monkey bastard! You made me look like a jerk!"

Meerm hear Beece say, "Please, sir, Beece not understand."

Meerm peek through crack. See big red-hair man stand over Beece.

"Don't give me that shit! You lied to me!"

"Beece tell truth!"

"You said there was a sick female sim here! Do you see her? Where is she? Show her to me, you lying monkey bastard! Show me!"

Meerm see red-hair man raise fist. Meerm close eye, turn away. Hear hit sounds, hear Beece make hurt sounds.

"Hey-hey-hey!" Benny say. "You kill him, you replace him!"

Meerm hear other hit sound, hear more hurt sound.

"I oughta drop-kick your sim ass right out the window! All right, I'm outta here. If I have to look at another monkey I'm gonna puke!"

Man and Benny leave. Meerm want hide more but must see Beece. Beece friend, Beece hurt. Meerm leave closet. Find all sim in circle round Beece bunk. Beece eye swoll, nose bleed. Hold side. Poor Beece. Hurt-hurt-hurt.

"Beece! Meerm sorry! Ver sorry."

Beece say, "Not Meerm fault. Beece fault. Beece want help Meerm but Meerm right. Bad mans. Ver bad."

"Poor Beece!"

"Beece not tell ever again." Beece look at other sim. "No sim tell mans bout Meerm. If tell mans come hurt Meerm like hurt Beece." Beece close good eye now. "Beece tired. Sleep now."

Meerm stay by Beece. Stroke arm. Poor hurt Beece. Meerm so sad. Keep hand on Beece arm. Stay by Beece all night.

FOUR

ZERO

I

"This is fabulous!" Patrick shouted, venting his glee. "Ab-so-lute-ly faaaaa-bulous!"

He shuffled in a circle around the cracked concrete floor, punching the air, wanting to laugh aloud but fearing if he ever let himself get started he might not be able to stop.

Zero had called Romy and him to a meeting here in the garage without hinting at what it might be about. Patrick wished he could have watched Zero's face, especially his eyes, as he'd laid the news on them about a sim made pregnant by a human. He hadn't been able to fathom the mystery man's feelings through the ski mask and shades, but Patrick knew exactly how *he* felt. Suddenly his whole world had burst wide open in a blinding blaze of glory. Lawyers dream about an opportunity like this. Dream, hell, most of them didn't even have the capacity to imagine something like this.

It was a home run.

In the bottom of the ninth.

With the bases loaded.

On Christmas Day.

With a winning lotto ticket waiting in the dugout.

Life was good, life was sooooo good!

Finally he turned back to Romy and Zero. As usual, Zero hung back in the shadows; Romy stood by the panel truck; both were watching him as if he were mad. He glanced up at the square of darkness in the ceiling above the ladder fastened to the rear wall. No eyes peering at him this time. But even if there were, it wouldn't have fazed him. Not today.

"I get a feeling I've made Mr. Sullivan's day," Zero said, ostensibly to Romy.

"I think you made his year," she said, her expression troubled.

Patrick couldn't figure that. She should be beaming.

"Year?" he cried. "This makes my *life!* A baby with a sim mother and a human father! Don't you see what this means?"

"Of course," Zero said. "Undeniable proof that humans and sims can cross-fertilize."

"Right! And that means they have to be upgraded into the same category as humans."

"It's called 'genus,' " Zero said, "not category."

"Oh, right." He'd never found science very interesting. No juice. "Genus and species. We're *Homo sapiens*, right? So what genus are sims?"

"Start with the root: the animal kingdom; from there you move to the Chordata phylum, then to the Mammalia class. The next divisions are known as 'orders.' Humans, apes, monkeys, even tree shrews are all members of the Primate order. But after that we branch into different families. Chimps, gorillas, and orangutans are classified as members of the Pongidae family, while humans are the only existing members of the Hominidae family."

"Pongidae . . . Hominidae," Patrick said, rolling the unfamiliar words over his tongue. He guessed scientists were like lawyers, using dead languages to confuse and confute.

"Even before sims were created," Zero was saying, "there were movements in the scientific community to shift chimps to the Hominidae family, and they might have succeeded if not for SimGen. Once SimGen got into the act, the movement ran out of gas."

Romy said, "I've never understood how one corporation could wield so much influence."

"Money," Zero said.

Her brow furrowed. "I can see that working where legislation is involved, but how can you buy a scientific classification?"

"With grants. The right amount of money to the right universities to see the right man as head of the right department, and suddenly there are more important concerns than to which family *Pan troglodytes* belong. And so chimps stayed Pongidae."

"*Pan troglodytes*," Patrick said. "That's the chimp genus and species, right?"

Zero nodded. "And sims are known as *Pan sinclairis* of the family Pongidae."

"*Pan sinclairis*," Patrick said, shaking his head. "Talk about ego." Then he grinned. "But no amount of grants is going to keep them out of Hominidae once word gets out about this baby. We'll move them up to the *Homo* genus and get them a brand new name: *Homo simiens*. How does that sound?"

"It sounds like the end of SimGen," Zero said.

"Damn right. Move sims to genus Homo, they become humans. And since owning a human hasn't been legal since the Emancipation Proclamation, SimGen loses everything. Tome and I are going to lead the biggest class action lawsuit this world has ever seen. The tobacco settlements will look like chump change. Every sim will have a Caddy and a condo, and the Sinclair brothers, when I'm through with them, will be living on the street."

Patrick waited for a reaction—a laugh, a cheer, encouragement, anything— but Zero remained silent behind his shields, while Romy frowned and seemed to be miles away.

"I won't even take the customary thirty or forty percent," he added. "I'll settle for one point." Plus expenses, of course. He could handle one percent of a zillion—last him the rest of his life and then some.

Still no reaction from either of them. He felt like a singer with a dead mike.

Finally Zero stirred, lacing his gloved fingers and popping the knuckles. "All fine and good, Patrick, but your scenario is missing one crucial element: You need proof."

"Oh. Yeah. Right."

No arguing with that: no pregnant sim, no case.

"And we can't offer five million for a tip."

"No," Patrick said, "but maybe you can intercept that tip."

"How do you propose I do that?"

"Obviously you've got a line into the heart of SimGen."

He noticed Zero stiffen into a wary pose. "Obviously?"

"Sure. How else could you come by all this inside information. I don't know if it's a person or a bug, and I don't want to know. What I'm saying is, if we can intercept the crucial tip, or even get it at the same time SimGen does, maybe we can reach this sim—"

"She's got a name: Meerm."

"See? You even know her name. So if we can use the tip to reach her before SimGen does, we're golden."

Zero shook his head. "I doubt that's possible. All tips will be directed to Luca Portero, and he's not the type to share information, even with the Sinclairs."

"Well . . . ," Patrick said slowly, discarding a new idea immediately, but voicing it just to get a rise out of Romy. "He does have the hots for Romy . . ."

"Don't even think about it," she snapped.

"Joke, Romy." At least she'd been listening. "Are you okay?"

She shook her head. "Not really. Something about this bothers me. How can a sim and a human cross-fertilize? Sims have twenty-two chromosome pairs and humans have twenty-three. Somewhere along the line they're not going to match up, and a pair of chromosomes is going to be left hanging."

"Not necessarily," Zero said. "Look at the mule. Its father is a donkey, which has thirty-one pairs and its mother is a horse, which has thirty-two, though both are members of the genus *Equus*. Mules have been around for ages with no problems from the dangling chromosomes, other than the fact that they're usually sterile."

Romy's frown deepened. "Then this baby, if it's ever born, will probably be sterile too."

"We'll have to see. We're in uncharted territory here."

"So a mule," Patrick said, "is the offspring of a male donkey and a female horse. What if it's the other way around?"

"That's a less common combination, but then you get something called a hinny. They look like mules but tend to be smaller because most donkeys are smaller than horses."

"Where do all these fascinating tidbits of animal husbandry leave us?" Patrick said.

"With the realization that, given a fertile sim, a human-sim hybrid is a very real possibility."

"I keep thinking about that baby," Romy said. "What's going to happen to it? Who'll take care of it? And being neither sim nor human, what place will it have in the world?"

Zero's tone softened. "Until we find Meerm I suggest you put off worrying about the baby. Given your nature, I know that won't be easy, but your own safety should be at the top of your list right now. You won't be able to help that baby if anything happens to you."

Patrick felt the muscles between his shoulder blades tighten. "What do you mean, 'happens'?"

He sighed. "You haven't heard the whole story yet."

"What are you holding back?"

"Nothing. I never had a chance to finish. Your war dance got us off track."

Romy eyed Zero. "There's a poor, frightened sim whore out there pregnant by a human degenerate. Isn't that enough?"

"I never mentioned a whore, sim or otherwise."

"I just assumed . . ."

Zero looked at Romy. "You might want to sit down."

"Oh, no." She stood blinking for a few heartbeats, then retreated two steps and dropped into the chair by the wall. "Do I want to hear this?"

"Probably not, but you need to."

Zero then went on to explain who was behind the SLA and the reasons for its atrocities. Patrick listened, but all the while his eyes were fixed on Romy. He watched her initial disbelief give way to unwilling acceptance of a horrifying truth. Her expression was slack by the time Zero finished. He wanted to step to her side and slip his arms around her, but thought better of it. Jostle her now and she might explode.

Patrick too was shocked. To think that just two weeks ago in front of the burned-out ruins of the Bronx globulin farm, Romy had introduced him to the engineer of all this death and destruction.

"There's got to be some way we can nail Portero for this," Patrick said.

"Don't count on it. He's a pro, a very careful one."

"That doesn't mean we can't manufacture some evidence."

"No," Zero said, shaking his head. "Too dangerous."

Romy finally spoke, her voice barely above a whisper. "I . . . I'd always figured Portero for a snake. But . . . I never dreamed . . . I mean, executing three humans and twelve sims . . . just to cover his tracks."

"And those are just the ones we know about. You two might have been added to list if we hadn't intervened when Patrick's car was knocked off the road."

"That was him?" Patrick said, turning toward Romy. "You mean I was standing two feet away from the guy who tried to kill me and I didn't know it?"

"Not him directly," Zero said. "But he planned it."

"Why didn't anyone tell me?"

He shrugged. "No one said, 'Let's not tell Patrick.' When it happened, we still weren't sure of you. And after you came on board, it simply never came up."

"Just as well, I guess," he said. "If I'd known I might have opened my big yap and given something away."

"Which brings me back to what I was saying before," Zero said. "Watch your backs. You and Romy have put yourselves on the wrong side of Manassas Ventures. Manassas is connected to SimGen and therefore, by extension, to Luca Portero. We've known he was ruthless, we just didn't know until now *how* ruthless. There's nothing this man won't do, so please be careful. I'll do whatever I can to back you up, but the organization can do only so much."

Patrick turned to Romy. "Maybe we should move in together."

She rolled her eyes. "Not that again."

"For mutual protection, of course."

"Of course."

"Not such a bad idea, actually," Zero said. "I know I'd rest easier, but I'll leave that up to you two."

Zero, I think I love you, Patrick thought.

But Romy didn't appear to be buying. "Let's worry about Meerm," she said. "How do we find her first?"

"Why don't we try thinking like a sim?" Patrick said, hating to leave the subject of cohabitation. "If I were a lost and frightened sim, where would I hide?"

"With other sims," Zero said. "The trouble is, if she's hiding from humans she's not exactly going to come out and announce herself."

Patrick had a thought. "How about my roomie? Is there some way Tome can help sniff her out? You know, set a sim to find a sim?"

Zero pointed at him. "Now that's an idea."

"As long as it doesn't put him in any danger," Patrick added. He'd grown fond of that old sim, and the possibility of anything happening to him put a twist in his gut. "I don't want him hurt."

"None of us do," Zero said. "Let's sit down and see where we can take that. Meanwhile, I've appealed to a higher power for help."

"You've been praying?" Romy said.

"No, I meant that in a more literal sense. I was speaking of the Reverend's satellite."

2

"Watch this," Sinclair-1 said the moment Luca stepped into the darkened office. The sun was down but only a corner floor lamp was lit.

Luca glanced around. No one else present. "Watch what?"

"*This*, goddamn it. I just recorded it off the dish."

Sinclair poked his desktop and the plasma TV screen on the wall flickered, then lit with the face of the Reverend Eckert.

"*My dear brothers and sisters. I had an entirely different sermon prepared for this broadcast, but just moments ago I experienced an epiphany, a revelation of such staggering importance that I felt it my duty to you and to my ministry to discard my prepared sermon and immediately address this matter.*

"*Do you know what an 'urban legend' is? I'm sure you do, but in case some of you don't, let me explain. Urban legends are stories that are told and retold so many times that they take on a patina—or should I say, the appearance—of truth. We never get the story firsthand; usually we're told that somebody's uncle or aunt, or that a friend's grandmother knows someone who personally experienced the incident.*

"*You might have been warned against bringing home a large cactus because somebody knows someone whose cactus burst open to let out a torrent of deadly tarantulas.*

"*Or you heard about the burned corpse of a frogman found in the ashes of a forest fire, the story going that he was SCUBA diving when he was scooped up by a firefighting helicopter as it filled its bucket from the lake near the fire.*

"*Or the 'documented facts' that eelskin wallets erase magnetic cards and giant alligators infest New York City sewers, and on and on.*

"*Brothers and sisters, I could spend the whole program cataloguing these tales, but that's not why I'm speaking to you today. I pray you've caught my meaning, because I want you to believe that what I am about to say is not an urban legend.*

"*As I told you earlier, I've had a revelation from On High. But some people, for their own selfish reasons, will want to deny its truth. My words, as they spread,* will be written off by these professional doubters as just the latest in a long line of urban legends. But don't listen to them, friends. I have it on excellent authority, not from a friend of a friend, but from the ultimate Unimpeachable Source that what I am about to tell you is God's Truth.

"That Truth concerns a sim, a female sim, lost, alone, frightened, hiding somewhere in New York City. Yes, I'm talking about the same sim that Satan's own corporation, SinGen, has offered five million dollars for. But have you asked yourselves why SinGen is offering so much for one lowly sim? They'll tell you it's to help bring murderers to justice, but is that really the case? The humans these murderers killed were criminals themselves. And sims are killed every day without SinGen offering so much as a dime to find the culprits.

"So there I was today, sitting alone in my home chapel, spending quiet time in communion with the Lord, wondering what was so special about this particular sim to make the devil's company squander so much of its tainted lucre to find her.

"And then it came to me. In a blaze of inspiration that could only be the result of the touch of the Lord his own self, I knew!

"This lost sim is pregnant!

"Now, now, I know we've all been told that sims can't procreate, but think about who's been telling us that: the devil corporation run by Satan, the Father of Lies. Only God is perfect. Satan makes mistakes—that's why he rules in Hell after all, instead of in Heaven. And Satan made a real whopper of a mistake this time.

"What's that? Yes, I hear you. I hear what you're saying. You're saying, 'A pregnant sim, Reverend Eckert? How can that be? Who is the father?'

"And that, brothers and sisters, is the worst part. This was no immaculate conception. No, this is an abomination. This sim pregnancy is the result of unplumbed wickedness and moral decrepitude. For the father, I say to you, the father of this sim's baby is human!

"Of course, I use the term loosely, for what sort of human would defile himself so by doing such a thing to a helpless animal? But yes, you heard correctly, the father is human!

"Now, I know what you're saying in your hearts, if you're not crying it out loud, 'Why, Reverend Eckert? Why would God allow such an unspeakable thing to occur?' And I must tell you, friends, that I asked myself the same question. I wondered if this could be a sign of the End Times: Could the child of this unholy union be the Antichrist?

"But the Lord his own self was guiding my thoughts because I suddenly realized that this unborn child is just the opposite of the Antichrist. For it will not *be born to establish Satan's rule on earth, but to dislodge his foul foothold, destroy the satanic beachhead we know as SinGen!*

"That is the real reason the company is offering so much to find this poor, mistreated, pregnant sim.

"So I say to you, my brothers and sisters, do not listen when you are told that this can't be true, that it's just another urban legend. It is not! *If you live in the Northeast, live anywhere in or around New York City, I beg you, as soon as I am finished here: Leave your homes and hie into the streets to look for this unfortunate creature.*

"And if you find her, do not call SinGen, no matter how much money it is offering. Do not allow yourselves to be tempted by the devil's offer. Sell this sim and you are selling your soul. Instead, call the number flashing at the bottom of your screen and I will personally see to it that this sim and its child are protected from Satan's forces.

"And when the child is born, I shall bring it to the halls of Congress and display it to the leaders of our nation. And then the scales shall fall from their eyes and they will see that they have allowed an abomination to move into their house; and the shackles shall loosen from their limbs and they will act, casting SinGen into the outer darkness whence it came, where there shall be weeping and gnashing of teeth.

"Go now, my brothers and sisters. Fill the streets. Waste not another moment. Find—"

The screen went blank. Another touch on the desktop and the lights came up.

Luca blinked, momentarily mute with shock. He opened his mouth to speak but Sinclair voiced his thoughts.

"He knows! How the *hell* did he find out?"

"A leak," Luca said. "I've suspected one for some time now."

"You think the room is bugged? By someone other than you, I mean."

Luca was taken aback by the casualness of the remark.

"What?" Sinclair said, a tiny smile twisting his lips. "You think I don't know your people have this office bugged? Probably the whole campus as well, am I right?"

He was. Offices, labs, even rest rooms—all bugged. Luca shrugged it off.

"We sweep this office regularly. No listening devices of any sort." Other than ours.

"*I* found out yesterday," Sinclair said, then pointed to the blank TV screen. "*He* knows today. How else but a bug?"

"A person. I've long suspected your brother. This confirms it."

"It confirms nothing of the sort. Ellis? Ridiculous!"

"Really? Until yesterday, only a select few of our people knew. Even the men I've had combing the city don't know; they think we want this sim because she's got a rare immune globulin in her blood. Weeks of searching without a hint of a leak. But yesterday afternoon I tell you and your brother, and today, just twenty-four hours later, the Reverend Eckert is telling the world. If it's not your brother, then it's you."

Sinclair sat down and drummed his fingers on the desk. "Well, it's not me. And I can't believe it's Ellis, not after the way your people threatened his children."

"I'm not aware of any threat."

"No? Well, I guess it was before your time."

That part was true. But Luca knew perfectly well what the CEO was talking about. A brilliant little op, involving nothing overt, but it had kept Ellis Sinclair in line ever since.

Sinclair looked at him. "Maybe Eckert did have a revelation."

"You don't really expect—"

"I don't mean from God."

"Then—"

"Hear me out. Here's this guy who's got a hard-on for SimGen. He hears we're offering five million to find this lost sim, so he figures out the worst-case scenario for us, and broadcasts it. It's just a coincidence that he happens to hit on the truth."

Luca snorted. "You don't believe that any more than I do."

Sinclair sighed. "No. No, I don't."

"However Eckert came to it, we can count on a lot of his people on the streets looking for that sim, trying to find her first."

"Does that worry you, Mr. Portero? Don't let it. The more the merrier. Eckert's people merely increase our chances. They may believe in God, but when it comes down to five million dollars' worth of cold hard cash, they'll believe in that even more."

"We'll see." Luca wasn't so sure about that, but saw no point in arguing. He had another point to press. "In the meantime, my people will expect you to do something about your brother."

"Very well. From now on, any meetings concerning matters of a sensitive nature will be conducted without him." His eyes narrowed. "But you don't have any hard evidence against Ellis, do you. Otherwise you wouldn't have looked so shocked when I played you that tape. I'd be surprised if you weren't monitoring his calls. Have you been following him as well?"

"No. But we will."

Truth was, he'd set tails on Sinclair-2 a number of times but they always lost him. Looked like he'd have to tail him personally.

I can spread myself only so thin, damn it.

"Starting when? Tonight?"

"No, not tonight. But soon."

He had a more pressing matter to attend to. He and Lister had spent much of the day setting up an op for tonight. The target, Romy Cadman, knew Luca's face so he could not be directly involved, but he'd be on standby, eagerly awaiting the results. By the end of the night he'd have established a solid link of money and information between Cadman and Ellis Sinclair.

And then there'd be no need to follow anyone anywhere.

3

MANHATTAN

"Really," Romy said as their cab climbed the on-ramp to the Brooklyn Bridge, "this is unnecessary. I'm more than capable of finding my own way home."

"You heard what our friend said this afternoon," Patrick replied. " 'Be careful.' And that's what we're doing."

Beside him, in the darkness of the rear seat, he saw her shake her head. "An awfully long trip."

"Not if I'm with you."

Light from a passing car reflected off her smile. "What a nice thing to say. But perhaps I should have phrased it a little differently: This is going to be an awfully long *round* trip."

As the bejeweled towers of Lower Manhattan dwindled behind them, Patrick thought about the day. A good day. Any day with more ups than downs was a good day. After the shock of learning who was behind the SLA and the globulin farm murders had worn off, and Patrick had settled down from his initial elation over the news of the pregnant sim, they'd brainstormed ways to find Meerm. Reverend Eckert's exhortation to his followers to track her down for him instead of for SimGen—a message he'd be hammering into his viewers day after day—would help, but they still hadn't figured out a way to fit Tome into the equation.

As darkness fell they'd called it a day, Zero taking off in the van, and Romy accepting Patrick's invitation to dinner. They'd walked downtown and found a bistro in Chelsea that looked inviting. A pair of Rob Roys before and a shared bottle of pinot noir during a meal of various pastas and sauces had left Patrick in a genial mood. He figured Romy, who'd matched his Rob Roys with Cosmopolitans, had to be feeling mellow herself.

"Am I that bad?"

"No," she said. "Not bad at all." He felt her take his hand, interlace her fingers with his, and give it a little squeeze. "In fact, you're good. Taking Tome in like you did is, well, I don't think I've ever heard of anyone doing that for a sim."

She rested her head on his shoulder. The scent of her hair and the wave of warmth seeping up from where their hands coupled enveloped Patrick, making him feel as if he were riding a cloud.

What is it with this woman? he wondered. We're only holding hands but it feels like we're having sex.

He rode that cloud all the way to Brooklyn, and too soon they were stopped in front of a neat, four-story brick-faced building.

"I'll walk you to your door," he said.

Romy shook her head. "No, you won't."

"We've got to be careful, Romy . . ."

She leaned forward and kissed him lightly on the lips. "You're not walking me to my door. You're coming up."

"For a nightcap?"

"A drink, coffee, anything you want."

Patrick couldn't see Romy's face in the dimness, couldn't read her eyes. His first impulse was to ask her to repeat her last statement, but he feared she might take it as a wisecrack. Some sort of spell had been woven here tonight and he wasn't about to risk breaking it.

"Let's go," he said, and fumbled his wallet out of his pocket to pay the cabby.

The stairway within was too narrow to ascend abreast so he had to follow Romy, which positioned her hips at eye level before him. Their rhythmic sway within her cleathre coat only exacerbated the electric ache in his groin.

They stopped climbing at the third floor. Romy keyed open a door marked 3A. She stepped through, turned, and pulled Patrick inside. Without turning on the lights she slammed the door and slipped her arms around his neck. Patrick responded instinctively, pulling her close. His lips found hers, he felt her left leg sliding up the outside of his thigh as he slipped his right hand along her ribs toward her left breast—

—and then the lights came on.

Romy spun, ending up beside him, hands out, ready to fight.

But the blond-haired guy with one hand on the lamp switch held a silenced automatic in the other. A second man, his dark hair tied back in a neat little ponytail, sat in an easy chair and held an identical silenced pistol. Both wore dark suits and white shirts buttoned to the top.

The seated man smiled as he spoke. "Well, well. Look at this, won't you. A two-for-one special." He had a faint Texas accent.

Amazing how fast lust can fade—Patrick's insides had already turned to ice.

"What do you want?" Romy said.

"You, Ms. Cadman," Ponytail said. "Not for anything carnal, I'm sorry to say, although I'm sure that would prove to be a mutual pleasure. We simply wish to ask you some questions. And as long as your lawyer friend is here, we have questions for him as well."

"Forget about it," she said, turning and reaching for the doorknob.

"Please don't," Ponytail said. "These silencers aren't in place for show. We *will* shoot if necessary. Not a killshot—a knee, a thigh, just to get across the point that we have questions that we intend to have answered. We can do this friendly, where no one gets hurt and you both walk away wound-free, or we can do it messy. I prefer the friendly path, don't you?"

"Friendly sounds good, Romy," Patrick whispered, nudging her with his elbow. "Especially when we're outgunned two to zip."

She didn't look at him. All he heard was a soft, "Shit!"

Patrick raised his hands, hearing the words to that old blues song about being a lover, not a fighter. "Let's do friendly."

"A practical man," said Ponytail. He rose and moved toward two ladder-back chairs sitting side by side on the carpet. "We took the liberty of moving these in from the kitchen." He did a mocking, maitre d'-type flourish. "Both of you remove your coats and be seated, s'il vous plait." It sounded weird with that Texas accent.

Patrick tossed his herringbone overcoat onto the couch and guided Romy to one of the chairs.

"Portero sent you, didn't he?" she said as he helped her out of her coat.

"Portero . . . Portero . . . ," Ponytail said slowly. "No, I don't believe we've met. Is she as pretty as you?"

Blondy guffawed.

That laugh says it all, Patrick thought as he seated Romy, threw her coat on the couch, then dropped into the other chair. He tried to relax but quailed as he felt the muzzle of Ponytail's silencer suddenly press against his temple.

"Ms. Cadman," the man said, "my associate will put down his weapon while he affixes you to the chair. You will allow him to do so without resistance. If you resist you will end up with a very messy carpet and we will be faced with the unfortunate circumstance of having only one person to interrogate."

Patrick's bladder clenched. He wasn't cut out for this. He'd been trained to pose logical arguments based on law and precedent in an arena overseen by a supposedly impartial magistrate. If he won, great; if he lost, at least he could walk away knowing—hopefully—that he'd acquitted himself well in the contest. But this . . . the loser here didn't walk anywhere.

The blond guy laid his pistol on the carpet far from Romy. He produced a roll of aluminum duct tape and began taping her arms and legs to the chair. When he finished he bent over her and cupped one of her breasts in his hand.

"Nice," he said, grinning.

Romy jerked her head forward, ramming it into his face. He staggered back, clutching his nose. When he recovered he bared his teeth, cocked his fist, and started toward her.

"Uh-uh-uh!" said Ponytail in a schoolmarm tone. "Mustn't mar the merchandise. Tape up Mr. Sullivan, please."

Scowling, Blondy taped Patrick to his chair, winding it blood-stoppingly tight. When he finished, he retrieved his weapon from the floor and holstered it inside his jacket.

But he wasn't quite finished. He stepped over to Romy and grabbed the tip of her breast through her sweater. He gave the nipple a vicious twist and said, "*That* won't mar the merchandise."

Romy winced but didn't give him an iota more.

Patrick twisted against his bonds. "You shit!" He didn't kid himself about being a tough guy but the way he felt at that moment left no doubt he could kill the bastard.

"All right now," Ponytail said, holstering his own weapon under his left arm and pulling a leather case from under his right. "Enough fun and games. Let's play *Who Wants To Spill The Beans?*"

He snapped open the case, revealing an inoculator and two vials of amber fluid. He loaded one of the vials into the chamber of the inoculator, then pulled a recorder out of his pocket and set it on the coffee table.

"Now," he said, smiling. "Who wants to be first? Let's see . . . eenie, meenie—"

A soft *thump* sounded from an adjoining room.

"What was that?" Ponytail said.

Blondy shook his head. "Don't know. I checked it out when we got here. It was empty."

"Probably just my cat," Romy said.

Ponytail snarled, "You don't *have* a cat!" He jerked his head toward the doorway and told Blondy, "That could have been the window. Check again."

Blondy pulled his gun and edged into the dark doorway. He poked his head inside, looked around, then reached his free hand inside for the light switch.

And then—Patrick couldn't be sure—it looked like he either tripped and fell into the room or something pulled him in. Whatever the cause, one second Blondy was there, leaning through the doorway, the next he wasn't. A faint sound, something like a strangled grunt came from within, followed by a thump—it didn't sound heavy enough for a falling-body thump; maybe just a dropped-gun thump.

"Duke?" Ponytail said. He placed the inoculator kit on the coffee table next to the recorder and retrieved the pistol from under his suit coat. "Duke, are you okay?"

No answer from the bedroom.

Ponytail edged toward the doorway, pointing his pistol at Romy's head. "I don't know what kind of shit's going down here, but if anything untoward happens, you go first."

The first thought that ran though Patrick's mind was, *Untoward?* Did he really say *untoward?*

Ponytail reached the doorway. He peeked around the molding and suddenly cried out, reeling back as Duke's limp body came flying out of the room to crash against him. He grunted as he tumbled to the floor, his pistol discharging and sending a bullet over Romy's head to punch a fist-size chunk of plaster out of the wall above one of the windows.

He didn't get a chance for a second shot because Duke's body wasn't the only thing flying through the doorway. Something else followed directly behind—a snarling, barrel-chested apparition in a sleeveless black coverall, its furry, black-eyed head split open to reveal yellow teeth and a pair of huge fangs in the upper jaw. But even more frightening was the scarlet coloring that blazed along its upper snout as it flew through the air, long arms outstretched, fingers curved into claws.

Ponytail let out a panicked bleat at the sight of it, and Patrick caught an odd light in the man's eyes; shock and terror, yes, but something else: recognition.

He tried to bring his pistol around but it was knocked from his grasp and sent skittering across the floor.

He wailed, "Kree—!" but whatever he intended to say was choked off as long fingers wrapped around his throat and squeezed.

Patrick was just registering that they might be in worse trouble now than a moment ago, when Romy started talking to the thing.

"Kek! Don't kill him, Kek! We need him alive!"

"You *know* this thing?"

She didn't respond but stayed focused on the creature that continued to throttle Ponytail. The man's mouth worked spasmodically as his eyes bulged and his face purpled.

"Kek! Let go! Let go now!"

Finally her words seemed to get through to the thing. It released its stranglehold and leaped up, but it didn't stay still, didn't seem able to. It wandered back and forth, growling, flailing at the air, as if working off a rage. On the floor, Ponytail coughed and retched, sucking in air, but it was purely reflexive. He was out cold.

As for Duke, he wasn't breathing at all. And the unnatural angle of his head on his shoulders made it clear that he would never breathe again.

Nipple-twisting bastard, Patrick thought. Good riddance.

"Good, Kek," Romy was saying in a soothing voice. "You did good, very good. Zero will be so proud of you."

That seemed to calm the beast. It stopped its agitated pacing and cocked its head as its dark eyes peered at Romy from beneath a prominent brow. The crimson coloring atop its snout was fading. Still staring at Romy it made a chirping sound.

Patrick didn't know what to think. It looked like some bizarre sort of gorilla, but nothing like Patrick had ever seen in any zoo he'd visited. More like a mutant sim who'd overdosed on steroids. The creature seemed to be on their side, but just barely. Patrick had never sensed so much aggression packed into a single being.

"What *is* that thing, Romy?" he whispered.

"Just be calm," she said, nodding and smiling at the creature. "He's been told you're on our side but he doesn't know you, so he's not sure of you. Whatever you do, don't make any sudden moves."

He glanced down at his duct-taped legs and arms. "As if I have a choice."

"I'm about to remedy that." She looked at the creature. "Kek, you've got to cut me free," she said softly, as if talking to a child. "So I can call Zero. Use your knife to cut me free."

Kek unsnapped a safety strap from a scabbard attached to the belt around its waist—Patrick hadn't noticed the belt till now—and whipped out one of those huge, saw-toothed Special Forces knives.

Patrick's gut clenched. "Oh, Christ! Someone gave that thing a knife?"

"Quiet!" Romy hissed. "Kek's a 'he,' and you owe him."

"I know, but—"

"I'm not talking about tonight. Now be quiet and I'll explain later." She turned back to Kek and dipped her head toward the tape around her right arm. "Could you cut that, Kek? I can't call Zero and tell him what a good job you did until you cut that tape."

Kek loped over and Patrick gasped as the creature raised the knife and, in a move so casual in manner yet so blindingly fast in execution, slashed the duct tape with a single thrust. He expected blood to gush from Romy's wrist, but only the tape parted, leaving her without a scratch.

"Good job!" she said as she wriggled that arm free and began the laborious task of unwinding the tape trapping her left wrist.

"Ask him if you can borrow his knife," Patrick said. "To speed things up." Being trapped in this chair was making him claustrophobic.

She gave him a rueful smile. "I wouldn't advise you or anyone else to try to take Kek's knife away from him. Even if you say, 'Pretty please.' "

She freed her left and, then began to work on her legs. As she did, Kek retreated to a corner where he squatted and watched.

When she was finally free she rose and walked away.

"Hey!" Patrick said. "What about me?"

She stepped through an alcove and Patrick heard the rattle of cutlery from within. A moment later she emerged holding a wicked looking carving knife.

"Ginsu," she said. "Cuts through tin cans."

"But will it cut duct tape?"

"We'll see."

It did, of course, and seconds later Patrick was free. He started to rise, then sat back down. He looked at the two men on the floor, one dead, the other halfway there, then at the creature squatting against the wall, watching them, and felt weak, as if someone had pulled a drainage plug from his ankle and all his energy had run out.

"What's going on, Romy? What have we got ourselves into?"

"Life!" she said, turning, bending at the waist, and leaning toward him. "Don't you feel alive, more alive than you've ever felt in your life?" She held the Ginsu blade before her face. "This is it! This is the cutting edge! This is where your vote is counted! This is where you make a difference!"

She's high, he thought. Stoked on adrenaline. And me? A total wreck.

"You're very scary right now," he told her.

"Am I?" She straightened. "Sorry. That was someone else talking."

"What?"

"Never mind." She pointed to the unconscious man. "Can you believe it? We've finally got one of them!"

"One of who?"

"They're from Manassas, or whoever's behind Manassas. And the people behind Manassas are behind SimGen. This blows the lid off, breaks everything wide open. We're finally going to get some answers."

"What if he doesn't want to talk?"

"Oh, he'll talk." She turned and lifted the inoculator from the kit on the coffee table. "Do unto others what they were about to do to you, right?"

Patrick stared at the amber liquid in the vial. They'd been about to inject some of that into Romy and him.

"You think that's the truth drug we heard about? The one they found in the dead globulin farmers?"

She nodded. "Totuus. I'd bet my soul."

"And then what?"

"I don't know." She gestured to the dead man. "Maybe we'd have ended up like him."

"Speaking of him, how do we explain a dead body to the police?"

"We won't."

"We can't very well say he broke his own neck."

"I'm sure Zero will have a way to handle it."

Romy picked up her coat from the floor. "Kek, you did good," she said soothingly to the creature as she rummaged in a pocket.

Patrick noticed that the red coloration had faded completely from its snout, replaced now by a bright blue.

"Can I ask again: What *is* he?"

"Oh, I'm sorry," she said as she pulled a phone from the coat pocket. "I'll introduce you."

"That's okay."

She motioned to the creature. "Come over here, Kek. I want you to meet Mister Sullivan."

"Really," Patrick said out of the corner of his mouth as Kek rose and started toward them. Something about this creature stirred a primal fear in him. And the way its gaze veered to Patrick's left and right, never making eye contact, didn't help. "That's okay."

"Kek," Romy said, "shake hands with our new friend, Patrick Sullivan. And Patrick, meet the fellow who saved your life back in October."

"My life? You mean, when we were knocked off the Saw Mill?"

As Romy nodded Patrick relived the moment in the inky grove as the massive arms of the man named Ricker wrapped around his head and shoulders, felt them tense as he prepared to snap Patrick's neck, and then the sudden release. Moments later, Ricker and his friend were dead.

He considered Kek's muscular arms, sensed the power in the thick shoulders bulging through the sleeveless coverall. Yes, power to spare, more than enough to take out two hardened pros, especially if they didn't see him coming.

"I guess I owe you big time, Kek," Patrick said, thrusting out his hand. He still didn't know what kind of mutant monkey thing stood before him, but he most definitely wanted Kek on his side. "It's a pleasure to meet you. Thank you for saving my life. Thank you very much."

Kek pulled back his shoulders and puffed out his chest. Finally he made eye contact. His hand was warm and dry as his long fingers wrapped around Patrick's. He bared his teeth, revealing those fangs. An attempt at a smile?

"Does he speak?" Patrick said.

"Not more than a few syllables—one of them being 'Kek.' But he understands speech and he signs."

Kek released Patrick's hand and turned to the two men on the floor. Ponytail groaned and stirred. Kek bent, grabbed the man's hair, and slammed his head against the floor.

"Easy, Kek," Romy said. "We don't want to scramble his brains."

"What *do* we want to do?" Patrick said.

Romy said, "Zero," to her PCA, then smiled. "That's what I'm about to find out."

4

Every muscle in Luca's body wound tight as he let himself into the foyer of Romy Cadman's apartment building. Something had gone wrong. He didn't know what, couldn't imagine what, but Palmer and Jackson weren't answering his calls.

They'd been flown in from the Idaho facility especially for this op—both of them experienced men who'd return there immediately after they completed their work. The chance of Cadman or Sullivan ever seeing either of them again was nil. They'd called in when they'd set themselves up in the apartment; they'd responded when the surveillance team in the car outside let them know that both the woman and Sullivan were on their way up.

But that had been over an hour ago. No one had heard from them since. No one had entered or left the building since Cadman and Sullivan's arrival.

He couldn't help remembering the first time he'd run an op against these two: a humiliating failure and two of his men dead.

Not again, he thought, almost a prayer. Please, not again.

But the previous op had been a complicated outdoor job, with innumerable variables; this one was in a small apartment, a limited, controlled field of operation that Palmer and Jackson had secured beforehand. What was wrong? An hour was more than enough for a pair of armed pros to deal with two unarmed civilians, juice them up with Totuus, and record the answers to a few questions. Like, who do you take instructions from, where do you get your money, and so on.

Luca had wanted to be there, and would have been if termination had been in the plan; but since Cadman and Sullivan were going to be released, he couldn't risk showing his face.

He hurried up the stairs. Key in hand, he pressed his ear against the door to 3A and knocked. No sound from within, not a whisper, not a rustle. He knocked again, same result.

Steeling himself for what might lie within—visions of Ricker's and Green's smashed skulls from the last time flashed through his brain—Luca unlocked the door and stepped inside.

Empty silence. Quick dodges in and out of the rooms, another circuit to check out the closets, and then back to the center of the front room, to wander in a slow, baffled circle. Where the hell was everybody? Could he be in the wrong apartment?

And then he spotted white fragments and powder on the carpet in the corner. He stepped closer and recognized it as plaster. A quick look up and he found a deep pock in the wall. Bullet hole. Fresh one. Looked for more but came up empty.

He felt his pulse kick up. Someone had got off a shot, but only one. That confirmed that he was in the right place. But where did everybody go? He stepped to the window and looked down at the small rear courtyard. No way out here—the fire escape was in front. They had to be hiding in another apartment—the only possible answer. He'd keep the building under surveillance. Sooner or later they had to show themselves.

But what if they weren't here? What if they'd got away clean?

He pulled out his PCA and called down to the surveillance car across the street. "Anybody leave since I've been inside?"

"Negative." Snyder's voice. He and Lowery were on watch. "Saw a grayish van pull out of an alley half a block down right after you went in, but that's about it."

A van. Could that be . . . ?

"Did you get the plate number?"

"Yep. You want a read back?"

Luca closed his eyes. Thank God for Snyder. At least someone was on the ball. "No. But don't lose it. It might be important."

And then again, it might not mean a goddamn thing.

Luca Portero dried his sweaty palms on his coat sleeves. Two more men gone, and he knew no more now about who was behind Cadman and Sullivan than he did before.

How the hell was he going to tell Lister?

5

"You know," Patrick told Zero after they'd pulled into the West Side garage and the door had closed behind their van, "I could get used to this. And that worries me."

The cascade of emotions from the threats and the violence had faded now, leaving him oddly exhilarated. But it had been harrowing.

When Romy had called Zero they'd learned that he had an escape route all worked out. Following his instructions, they'd taken the stairs to the roof—Romy in the lead, Patrick bringing up the rear, Kek in the middle carrying their two attackers, one over each shoulder. Romy's was the second of four joined buildings. They'd walked across two neighboring roofs to a ledge where a fire escape led down to an alley. After a short but nerve-wracking wait, Zero's battered Econoline pulled up and they'd all climbed aboard.

Patrick had handled the driving on the way back, with Zero in the passenger seat, and Romy in the middle. That was when his mood had begun to change. They'd done it! They'd faced murderous opposition and—with no little help from Kek—overcome it. They were wheeling away with no one in pursuit, no one even aware that they'd turned the tables.

As soon as they'd reached Manhattan they found a deserted spot under the FDR Drive where they leaned Duke's corpse against a steel support. Throughout the night anyone who saw him would think he was passed out drunk; in the morning light they'd think differently. Patrick then piloted the van across town with Duke's unconscious partner.

Masked as usual, Zero stepped out of the passenger door and regarded Patrick through his dark glasses. "Yes. It's the high of victory. Not a good thing to get too used to. You can't expect to win all the time."

"I know." Patrick opened his door and hopped out. "But after all the bad news, after being pushed around and running into wall after wall, this feels very, very good. It'll feel even better if it turns out that one of these two poisoned my clients.

"And maybe," Romy said, taking the hand he offered to help her out of the van, "he's one of the SLA creeps who butchered the globulin farm sims as well."

"Wouldn't that be sweet."

Zero leaned back inside and spoke toward the darkened rear section. "Kek. Tape the man into the chair by the wall."

They'd brought everything along—the tape, the inoculator kit, the silenced pistols. Neither man had carried any identification.

Poetic justice, Patrick thought as he watched Kek get to work. Bound with his own tape, injected with his own truth drug.

He looked around, noticing how his senses felt heightened. Despite the low light in the garage, he seemed to see everything with day-bright clarity. The tang of gasoline and the heavier odor of DW-40 were sharp in the air;

the ticking of the van's cooling engine was like a ball-peen hammer rapping an anvil.

Zero was away from the van now, moving to the darker shadows of a corner. Why wouldn't he let anyone see his face? What was he afraid of?

Patrick followed him, but not too closely. "What is he and where did you find him?" he said, pointing to Kek.

"In Idaho. Last year."

"Idaho?" Romy said. "You never told me that. I thought you'd found him around SimGen."

Zero shrugged. "Sorry. It never came up. And it didn't seem to matter until you saw that Idaho license plate on the SimGen campus."

"I wondered why you were so psyched about that."

"How do you just happen to 'find' something like him in Idaho?" Patrick asked.

"Don't you remember hearing reports of people claiming they'd spotted Bigfoot in Idaho last winter?"

"Vaguely. I try not to devote too many memory cells to that sort of thing."

"I do . . . if it sounds furry like a sim. I sent a couple of volunteers out there to track down the sightings, and they returned with Kek, suffering from starvation, frostbite, and half dead from exposure. Dr. Cannon and I nursed him back to health and—"

"Who's Dr. Cannon?"

"You met her at Beacon Ridge," Romy said. "She was the woman doctor who tried to save the poisoned sims."

"Right," Patrick said. "I remember her. But what *is* Kek? Where did he come from?"

"I don't know," Zero replied, watching as the creature taped the still unconscious Ponytail into the chair. "But he's obviously the product of a recombinant lab, an advanced one. He looks to be part mandrill and part gorilla, and I'd be very surprised if he didn't have a fair amount of human DNA spliced into his genome as well."

Patrick shook his head in wonder. "He's scary looking."

"I doubt that's by accident. Nor his aggressiveness."

"But why?" Kek had finished his task and now squatted by the prisoner, his eyes fixed on Zero as he awaited further instructions. "Who'd want to create something like that?"

Zero walked back to the cab of the van and reached through the window. "I'll show you." He withdrew one of the silenced pistols and held it up. "A .45 caliber HK SOCOM. Ever seen one before?"

"Never," Patrick said. "What's 'HK' mean? Hong Kong?"

Zero laughed. "Hardly." He swiveled the pistol toward Romy. "Romy? Know it?"

"It's Heckler and Koch, but beyond that . . . sorry, no."

"Heckler and Koch Mk 23 Special Operations Command model. Its barrel comes threaded and suppresser ready." Zero held it out to Kek. "Kek? Would you break this down for me please?"

"Are you nuts?" Patrick whispered as Kek loped forward. "That's a loaded weapon!"

Zero didn't respond. He placed the pistol in Kek's outstretched hand and said, "You can use that workbench over there."

Kek took the pistol and inspected it, turning it over in his hands a few times before he ejected the clip and then worked the slide to remove the chambered round.

"He knows guns!" Patrick said, his voice hushed in awe.

"You ain't seen nuthin yet," Romy told him.

Kek stepped over to the workbench and Patrick watched in amazement as his long, nimble fingers removed the silencer and disassembled the gun with practiced speed, then arranged its innards for inspection, all in less than thirty seconds. When finished he took one step back and stood with his hands behind his back, awaiting approval.

"He's military!" Patrick said.

"Or paramilitary. Or perhaps intended as some sort of semi-human mercenary. Who can say? But he can break down just about any weapon you hand him, and he knows no fear."

"A perfect soldier."

"Maybe not perfect, but damn near."

"What happened to his left hand?" Patrick said as he noticed that Kek's ring and pinkie fingers were missing a joint or two.

"Frostbite," Zero replied.

"So he owes his life to you?"

"And Kek knows it," Romy said. "He's totally devoted to Zero."

"An overstatement, I assure you," Zero said.

Patrick didn't think so. He'd noticed that Kek's eyes had stayed focused on Zero since his arrival. Even now, as he awaited approval of his breakdown of the pistol, his eyes never left Zero.

"I believe he's waiting for your okay," Patrick said.

"Oh, sorry," Zero replied. He saluted Kek and said, "Excellent job, my friend. Please reassemble it."

Patrick had no way to gauge this creature's emotions, but he sensed a burst of pride and pleasure in response to Zero's approval. Oh, yes, Kek might be hell on wheels when it came to confronting an enemy, but he was Zero's kitty cat.

"Who made him?" Patrick said as Kek's flying fingers clicked the pieces back into place. "SimGen?"

"The most likely suspect," Zero said.

"But if so, how did he get from New Jersey to Idaho?"

"Our guess is he was put aboard a truck from the SimGen basic research facility; the truck was driven aboard a plane at the SimGen airstrip and flown to Idaho."

"Why Idaho?"

"Because it's largely empty. Because you can buy big parcels of land that allow you to operate in near absolute privacy."

"But who?" Patrick said. "Who wants to operate in secrecy? Who wants to stockpile a bunch of Keks?"

"Kek might be just one of many new species quartered in the hinterlands."

The possibilities made Patrick more than a little queasy. "There's a thought to take to bed with you."

Just then Ponytail stirred, groaned, and lifted his head.

Zero glanced his way and said, "A font of information on these very subjects is about to become available to us. I hope."

"I don't think you have to hope," Patrick said. "I'd swear he recognized Kek when he jumped him. He even tried to say something. It sounded like, 'Kree—' but he never got to finish it."

Ponytail's eyes were glazed and it was obvious to Patrick he had no idea where he was or why he was tied up or what was going on. Tell him he's at an S & M beerfest in Sydney and he'd buy it. After ten seconds or so his chin dropped back onto his chest.

"We'll have to ask him about that," Zero said. "He should be ready to talk soon." He turned to Kek. "Take your position upstairs at the window now."

Kek turned and scrambled up a metal ladder affixed to the rear wall.

"The garage comes with a loft," Zero said. "The window up there affords an excellent view of the street. It also serves as Kek's home."

"So it was him I saw peeking down on us that day," Patrick said.

Zero nodded. "Kek has a curious nature." He turned to Romy. "Where did we put that inoculator kit?"

"Right here," Romy said, and handed it to him.

"The moment of truth, as it were," Zero said, opening the kit as he approached the captive. "Now we find out if Luca Portero is as involved as we think he is."

"How safe is that stuff?" said Patrick, eyeing the amber fluid in the inoculator's chamber.

"I've never used it," Zero said. "But they were willing to dose you up with it. Any objections to returning the favor?"

"None at all," Patrick said.

"I didn't think so." He handed the inoculator to Romy. "Would you do the honors?"

"My pleasure," she said.

She tilted Ponytail's head to the side, exposing his neck.

"You know what you're doing?" Patrick said.

She nodded. "Used to work research. Injected a lot of animals before I decided I'd rather work the other side of the street."

She placed the business end of the inoculator gun against the side of Ponytail's neck. She look as if she were about to execute him.

"What about the dose?" Patrick said. "How do you know how much to give?"

"Haven't the faintest. But this is the dose he was planning to put into us, so that's what goes into him."

"And if it's too much?"

She shrugged. "That'll be his problem, won't it."

Patrick realized he was seeing another side of Romy, a new persona, cold, efficient, almost ruthless in simmering fury. Was this the "someone else" she'd mentioned before? Not that he could blame her: This man had invaded her home, bound her, watched as his partner had mistreated her, and had been about to invade the very core of her privacy—her mind. Add to all that the possibility that he might have had a hand in the deaths of dozens of sims and the guy was lucky she wasn't jabbing the inoculator into his eye.

Patrick felt his shoulders bunch as the Romy pressed the trigger and injected the liquid through the skin of Ponytail's neck with a soft *pop*.

The man flinched, his eyes fluttered open. He raised his head and looked around, dazed. Patrick saw the purpling welts on his throat, mementos of Kek's fingers. He blinked. Patrick watched a look of utter horror flow through his features when he saw the inoculator in Romy's hand.

"No!" he rasped, his voice barely audible through his bruised larynx. "You didn't! Please tell me you didn't!"

Romy bounced the inoculator in her hand. "Shoot you up with your own junk? You bet we did."

"Not Totuus!"

"If that's what's in your vial, then, yes, Totuus."

And then Ponytail did something that took Patrick completely by surprise: His face screwed up and he began to sob. Romy took a step back and regarded him with mute shock.

"You didn't have to do that!" he squeaked in his laryngitis voice. "I would have told you! I would have told you anything you wanted to know!"

"Sure, you would have," Romy said. "And we would have been able to take every word to the bank, right?"

"What's wrong with him?" Patrick said, turning to Zero. The man's genuine terror was getting to him. "What don't we know about this drug?"

Zero's expression was unreadable behind his ski mask, but his tone was puzzled. "I researched it after hearing that it had been found in the globulin farmers' bodies. Its main side effect is a headache for about a day afterwards."

Romy seemed unfazed by the man's abject terror. She pressed the red RECORD button on his own recorder and held it before his face.

"What's your name?" she said.

Ponytail squeezed his eyes shut and gritted his teeth, fighting the drug and the question.

"Come on," Romy cooed. "This is a simple one. Your name . . . what is your name?"

The man's face reddened with effort, then the words broke free in a hoarse rush: "David Daniel Palmer!"

"Excellent. Now, Mr. David Daniel Palmer, who sent you?"

He began to blubber again. "Please don't ask me that! Please!"

"And if I'd begged you not to shoot me up with this stuff an hour ago, you would have spared me, right?"

"*Please!*"

Romy's voice hardened. "Stop stalling! Tell me now: Who do you work for?"

Parker screwed up his face, chewed on his lips, then blurted through a sob, "SIRG—"

But as soon as the word escaped him, his eyes rolled back in his head. He stiffened, bared his teeth, and began to shake, violently enough to start his chair walking across the floor.

"Ohmigod!" Romy cried. "What's happening?"

Zero leaped forward. "He's having some sort of seizure! If he swallows his tongue he'll choke to death!"

Patrick watched in horror as Zero's gloved hands worked past Palmer's foam-flecked lips, trying to pry open his jaws.

And then as suddenly as the attack had started, it stopped. Palmer drooped in his chair, breathing raggedly, his eyes glazed.

"Daniel Palmer," Zero said, leaning close, all but shouting. "Are you all right?"

Palmer mumbled something.

Zero shook his shoulder. "I said, are you all right?"

Palmer stared at him as if he were speaking a foreign language, then said, "Crash want rag lay hedge knock two."

"What?" Zero said.

"Numb bag five sense peel drawer another stop see."

"He's lost his mind!" Romy said, her hand over her mouth. The cold bitch goddess with the inoculator and the tape recorder was gone, and she was back to the Romy Patrick knew . . . or thought he did. "Did I do this? Is this my fault?"

"I don't know," Zero said. "I've never seen or heard of anything like it." He glanced at Romy and Patrick. "There's also the possibility he's faking."

"He gets an Oscar if he is," Patrick said.

Zero leaned close again: "What's your name?"

"Realize game attached."

"Oh, God!" Romy whispered.

Zero pulled out a phone. "I think we need help."

"Who are you calling?" Patrick asked.

"A doctor."

6

"Duke Jackson is dead," said Lister's voice through the receiver.

Luca Portero tightened his grip on the encrypted phone and kept kicking at the leaves. He'd been out in the woods surrounding his cabin, taking some fresh morning air, taking precautions . . . the way things were going, precautions might come in handy. The news didn't surprise him.

"How?"

"Broken neck. His body was found around 5:00 A.M. A red flag went up at our end when NYPD tried to run his prints this morning. They've got him listed as a John Doe and he'll remain that way."

"What about Palmer?"

"Not a peep. And that worries me more. I'd almost prefer to have his corpse surface."

Luca knew what Lister meant. An experienced operative caught in the act while carrying a supply of Totuus was a recipe for disaster. But Luca had taken precautions for just this eventuality.

"We're protected," Luca said. "I had him and Jackson down a dose of MTW before they went out."

"Thank God for that. How did you ever convince them to take it?"

"I told them they had no choice, that it was a direct order from the Old Man himself."

"Lucky they believed you. Still . . . MTW is still pretty new. Not much field experience with it. Better pray it worked. Because if it didn't . . ."

Lister didn't finish the sentence. Didn't have to. If the MTW had failed, Palmer would have spilled everything by now.

The MTW *did* work, Luca thought. It *had* to.

"But even if it works perfectly," Lister went on, "you're not off the hook for muffing another operation. And neither am I."

"We didn't muff a *thing*!" Luca said as a cold lump formed in his belly. "The Idaho hotshots blew it."

"The people upstairs don't see it that way. They're out four skilled operatives in two months with nothing to show for it. And they keep asking me, 'Where's the pregnant sim? All our resources at your disposal, a five-million-dollar reward for information leading to her, and what have you come up with?' Do you hear what they're saying, Luca? It used to be, 'When's Portero coming up with something?' Now it's, 'When are *you* coming up with something?' Me. Like we're Siamese twins."

Luca thought he heard a tremor in Lister's voice. He'd never known Darryl Lister to be scared. When they'd been pinned down by Taliban mortars outside Gardez, he'd been the picture of cool. But now . . .

"Shit. I'm sorry, man."

"Hey, we're not dead yet. We've gotten out of tighter places. But they want results by the end of the year."

The end of the year—two weeks!

Luca said, "What about the plate number Snyder spotted on that van last night?"

"Nothing. He must have got it wrong. The number's not in use. Tell Snyder he needs glasses."

Luca didn't think so. More likely the plates were phony, and Palmer and Jackson had been in that van along with Cadman, Sullivan, and who knew who else.

"All right then," Luca said. "What's the status of Cadman and Sullivan now? Do we keep after them?"

"The decision's been made to back off for the time being. They'll be on guard now and—"

"Obviously they were *already* on guard."

"Yes, well, be that as it may, they'll be on full alert now, and we can't risk losing any more men. The legal people can put the stall on any discovery motions Sullivan files; we'll find out who's behind them later. Right now concentrate on finding that sim."

"It's possible she's dead," Luca said, hoping it was true. "That cold snap after she escaped was pretty mean. She could have crawled into a pipe somewhere and froze to death."

"Then find her body. Since that fool Eckert started blathering about her being pregnant and the baby's father being human, SimGen stock price has slid six points. Most people think he's crazy, but he's making a lot of investors nervous. And that makes everyone upstairs nervous. You know what SimGen stock means."

Luca nodded. It meant independence for SIRG. No strings, no brakes.

"We've got to find her, Luca. I don't have to tell you what will happen if Eckert or Cadman and Sullivan get to her first."

Luca closed his eyes. That would finish SimGen, finish SIRG, and leave him running for his life.

"They won't."

And to make sure they wouldn't, he had to nail Ellis Sinclair as their informant and serve up his head on a silver platter.

7

MANHATTAN

Patrick checked the cars on Henry Street outside his office building before stepping out. All looked empty, no plumes of idling exhaust. After the other night, he was spooked, and not ashamed to admit it. You weren't paranoid when they really were out to get you.

He stepped out onto the sidewalk and cried out as he collided with someone. He jumped back, ready to run back inside, when he noticed it was an older woman. He grabbed her arm to keep her from falling.

"I'm sorry," he said. "I wasn't looking."

"Did I frighten you, Mr. Sullivan?" she said.

He looked at her face. Uh-oh. Alice Fredericks. The Mother of All Sims.

"Hello, Miss Fredericks. Nice to see you again. No, you didn't frighten me. I just didn't expect anyone there." He made a show of glancing at his watch. "I'm just heading off to a meeting and—"

"You didn't call me, Mr. Sullivan." Her look was reproachful. "You said you would and I've been waiting every day but you haven't called."

"I told you," he said, backing away, "I'll call when my schedule lightens up. It's just that there's been so much going on."

No lie there.

"You're not afraid, are you?"

Maybe he should tell her he was very afraid, that he was terrified. Then she'd look for someone else. But he couldn't make himself say it.

"Not of space aliens." True enough. Too many other truly frightening things going on in his life right now to worry about space aliens. "Not a bit."

"Very well," she said. "I'll be waiting."

He turned and hurried toward Catherine Street to find a taxi.

After a ride during which Patrick spent more time looking out the rear window than the front, the cabby dropped him off at Penn Station. He wandered around Seventh Avenue, going in and out of stores to make sure he wasn't being followed, then headed further west.

Finally he arrived at Zero's garage just behind a middle-aged woman. Despite the parka-like hood cinched tight around her head against the cold, he recognized her.

"Dr. Cannon," he said, extending his hand. "I'm Patrick Sullivan. I don't know if you remember me, but I was—"

"You were helping at the Beacon Ridge atrocity," she said with a smile as she pushed back her hood. He noticed that her long graying mane had been shorn to an almost boyish length. "Yes, of course I remember. And call me Betsy, please."

The door opened and Romy was there, smiling. "A two-fer! Come in, Betsy. So good of you to come."

"No problem. It's easier for me to come to Zero than him to come to me."

"And you cut your hair. I love it!"

Patrick stepped inside and closed the door behind him, remembering Zero's hurried phone conversation with Dr. Cannon last night. She was on staff at Nassau County Community Hospital and, following her instructions to Zero, Patrick and Romy had driven David Palmer out to the hospital and left him in the parking lot for her to "find."

Now, as the three of them trooped toward the rear of the garage, Kek suddenly came bounding down the ladder from his domain in the loft and charged them. Patrick tensed, waiting for Zero or Romy to call him off, but they said nothing. Then Betsy Cannon opened her arms and embraced the beast.

"How is my friend Kek doing?" she said.

Kek signed something to her and Betsy laughed. They had a brief conversation—Betsy speaking, Kek signing, then Kek scrambled back up the ladder to his observation post.

"You nursed him back to health, I'm told," Patrick said as Kek vanished into the ceiling.

"Not really. Zero did most of the nursing. I tried to save his frostbitten fingers but was only eighty-percent successful. As an OB-GYN I have surgical training, but—"

"OB?" Patrick glanced past her at Zero who nodded. "Then if we find this pregnant sim—?"

"You'll bring her to me, of course. I've lots of experience delivering sims."

"You have?"

"Certainly. I spent six years as medical director of SimGen's natal center. When it finally seeped through to me that I was delivering a race of slaves into the world, I quit. And not long after that I received a call from Zero."

The idea of birthing sims thrust Alice Fredericks's crazy, tortured face into Patrick's mind. "Let me pop you a question out of far left field: Do you know if SimGen ever used human women to bear sims?"

"What?" Romy said. "That's not out of left field, that's from the bleachers!"

"Not while I was there, I assure you," Betsy said. "Why do you ask?"

Patrick told them about Alice Fredericks and her story.

"She certainly sounds delusional," Betsy said.

"I'm ready to believe that SimGen's connected to almost anything bad," Zero said, "but I draw the line at space aliens. Let's get back to reality, shall we?" He turned to Betsy Cannon. "Any idea yet as to what's wrong with the patient we sent you last night?"

"The more we learn about his condition," she said, shaking her head, "the more mysterious it becomes. He has a form of aphasia that's both expressive and receptive."

"Sorry?" Patrick said.

"He can't understand what's said to him, or even written out for him, and can only jabber word salad when he wants to speak."

Patrick shivered inside. "Sounds like an inner circle of lawyer hell."

"Syndromes like it can occur with strokes or sometimes with tumors that affect the Broca speech area of the brain, but an MR scan showed a perfectly normal brain. We shipped him out to NYU Medical Center this morning where they did a PET scan—that's positron emission tomography. It gives us a functional as opposed to structural view of the brain, and Mr. Palmer's Broca area has been damaged."

"Damaged how?" Romy said.

Betsy shrugged. "Neurology is not my field but I've been asking a lot of questions under the guise of being interested because I found him in the parking lot. The experts' best guess is a toxin."

"Totuus?" Romy said. "You mean I did that to him?"

"No. Totuus was found in his system, but the NYU neurologists believe he had another compound in his bloodstream that combined with the Totuus to form a neurotoxin specific to the Broca area."

"Pretty damn sophisticated," Zero said.

Betsy nodded. "Amazingly sophisticated, according to the experts. All just theory, of course, one they have no way of testing at the moment, but it goes a long way toward explaining his syndrome."

"And it fits with his behavior last night," Romy said. "Remember how he broke down and cried when he found out we'd injected him with the Totuus? He must have known he had the other compound floating through his bloodstream, and knew what was coming."

Zero said, "A failsafe to prevent anyone from using Palmer's own Totuus against him."

"Is it permanent?" Romy asked.

Betsy shrugged. "Who can say? No one I've spoken to has ever dealt with anything like this."

"My guess is it's temporary," Zero said. "I can't see anyone willingly taking something that could cause irreversible brain damage. But temporary can be a long time."

"Talk about covering your tracks," Romy said, shaking her head. "How are we ever going to nail these monsters?"

Betsy smiled and tightened her scarf around her neck. "That I will leave to you. As for me, as long as I'm in the city I believe I'll do some Christmas shopping. Good luck. And you know I'm available anytime day or night if you find that pregnant sim."

Patrick showed her out, then returned to where Zero and Romy were standing.

"I've been thinking," he said. "What if it wasn't just the mixture of the two drugs in his bloodstream? What if saying a vital word was what triggered the—what was it?"

"Aphasia," Zero said, then shook his head. "That sounds even more far-fetched."

"Maybe. But what was he saying at the very instant something tripped the circuit breaker in his brain?"

"I don't remember," Romy said, "but it's easy enough to find out."

She went to a shelf on the wall and retrieved the recorder. She reversed it for a second, then hit PLAY. Romy's voice burst from the tiny speaker.

"—*op stalling! Tell me now: Who do you work for?*" was followed by Parker's hoarse rasp: *"SIRG—"* and then strangled noises and cries of alarm.

Romy switched off the player. She looked pale. "Want to hear it again?"

"That's okay. You heard the word: 'Surge,' right?"

Zero shrugged. "I doubt he was talking about a fabric or an electric current. I believe he got out the first syllable of the answer—'s-u-r' or 's-e-r' or 'c-e-r' or maybe even 'c-i-r' for circle—and then the seizure hit and the rest of the word or words were crushed into a guttural mess."

"But this was in direct response to 'Who do you work for?' so it's got to have some relevance, don't you think? I mean, at least it's a start. Question is, how to find out if it means anything?"

"Why don't we simply ask?" Romy said.

"Oh, sure. I'll just call up Mercer Sinclair and say, 'What does the word "surge" mean to you?' That'll work."

A smile played about Romy's lips, the first since last night. "Why call when you can ask in person?"

8

NEWARK, NJ

Meerm feel ver bad today. So fat belly. Legs swoll. Hard move. Many move inside, like thing kicking. Kick-kick-kick. And dizz. Ver dizz.

Oop. Meerm trip, fall against bunk. Make noise. Loud. Must hide. Benny come.

Climb top closet. So hard climb. More hard squeeze into hole. But Meerm push hard. Push back board and wait in dark. Soon Benny come. Talk self. Always talk self.

"Who's up here? Goddamn it, I heard you. I been hearing you all week! Now come out!"

Benny come closet. Pull door. Meerm not breathe. Hear Benny voice through wall. Shout-shout-shout.

"Where are you, dammit! You gotta be somewhere! Or maybe I just gone loco! No! I know what I heard, dammit!"

Benny leave closet. Many loud noise in room—dresser move, bunk move, door slam-slam-slam. Then noise stop.

"All right so maybe I am hearing things. Next I'll be seeing things. That's it. I'm losing it. I been babysitting these monkeys so long I'm going bugfuck nuts! But I coulda sworn . . ."

Benny go way but Meerm stay. Too tired. Too scare to move. And hurt. Kick and hurt all time. Poor Meerm. When hurt stop?

9

MANHATTAN

DECEMBER 19

Romy was late for the meeting. On purpose.

For the past few years she'd made a point of keeping a few shares of SimGen stock in her 401(k) for the sole purpose of being invited to shareholders' meetings. She'd been to a number of these and knew how they went—blather and hype from beginning to end. The only interesting part was the finale when Mercer Sinclair took questions from the audience.

By the time she reached the upper floors of the Waldorf Astoria she already knew from the ecstatic talk in the lobby that SimGen—or "simgee," as the stockholders liked to call it, phoneticizing its SIMG stock symbol—had come in with earnings of $1.37 per share, beating not only the analysts' predictions of $1.26, but the whisper number of $1.31 as well.

She walked into the magnificent four-story Art Deco grand ballroom just in time to fill out an index card with her question for the CEO. Instead of passing her card down to the center aisle, she walked it to the rear of the ballroom and personally handed it to the elderly gent who would be reading them.

"I'd really like to know the answer to this," she whispered, laying a hand on his arm and flashing her warmest smile.

He looked at her over the top of his reading glasses and smiled. "I'll see what I can do, miss."

Then she found an empty seat along the side and waited. Mercer Sinclair, dark-haired, dark-eyed, and impeccable in a charcoal gray silk Armani suit, stood behind a podium on the dais and breezed through the usual run of inane questions from the audience about future earnings projections and new product outlooks—all of which were explained in detail in the annual report—and deftly fielded inquiries about the Reverend Eckert's assertions that the lost sim was pregnant, laughing them off as a crude and transparent ratings ploy.

And then the reader-man got to Romy's question.

"Mr. Sinclair, a stockholder wants to know, 'How big a part does surge play in your day-to-day operations?' "

Romy leaned forward, studying Mercer Sinclair's face as it floated in the glow from the podium. She saw him stiffen as if touched by a cattle prod, watched his eyes widen, then narrow. Even if she were blind she'd have detected his shock from his stammering reply.

"Wh-what? I-I don't understand the question. What does it mean? Could the person who asked it please identify himself and clarify the question?"

Romy didn't move.

"Please," Sinclair said. "I . . . I'm quite willing to answer any question, but I have to understand it first. Who asked it? If you'll be kind enough to clarify . . ."

Romy sat and watched him stumble and fumble, peering into the great dark lake of faces before him.

Finally he fluttered a hand at the reader and said, "Very well . . . I guess he left . . . next question."

He went on responding but Romy could tell his heart was no longer in it. His answers were terse, his manner distracted, as if he couldn't wait to be done with this.

Before the lights came up, Romy wandered back to where the elderly question reader was winding up the Q and A session, and grabbed the discard pile of cards he'd already read. No sense in leaving any unnecessary traces behind.

She had a bad moment when two men in suits followed her into the elevator down to the lobby, but they spent the ride talking about hockey and got off on the twenty-second floor. She used a side exit and stepped out onto East Forty-ninth. She waited to see if anyone followed, then hurried downhill to sunny Lexington Avenue where Patrick waited. His face was too well known to SimGen stockholders to risk his presence at the meeting, but he hadn't been able to stay completely away.

"Well?" he said as he took her arm and began walking her uptown. The cold snap had broken and the day was clear and mild. "Did he react?"

"Did he ever," Romy said. "He just about lost it. Looked as if he'd just been stripped naked and hosed with ice water."

Patrick grinned and jabbed the air with a fist. "Knew it!"

She had to hand it to Patrick. He had an acute ear for nuances and he'd heard something in that one syllable from David Palmer. He'd been sure it was significant, and he'd been right.

He threw an arm around her shoulders. "Damn, I wish I could have been there." He waved his free hand in the air. "But forget about that. The question now is, how do we capitalize on this?"

"For one thing," Romy said, "we know the word itself has meaning. It's not just part of another word or a phrase."

"If I'd known that last night I could have saved myself a lot of trouble. I went through an online dictionary and plugged in every spelling of 'surge' I could think of to see if it might be the first syllable of another word. Got nowhere. Didn't do any better when I tried every possible homonym. 'Surge' is not a common syllable."

"For which we should be thankful, I guess. Imagine if he'd said 'con'?"

"Then we'd be cooked. But 'surge' itself doesn't appear to mean any-thing."

"It might if it's an acronym."

He stopped walking as if he'd hit an invisible wall. His arm dropped from her shoulder and she missed it.

"An acronym! Of course! And acronyms usually mean government." He pressed the heel of his palm against his forehead. "Do you know how many Washington agencies, departments, subdepartments, and bureaus are desig-nated by acronyms? It's staggering."

She looked away, glancing around to see if anyone was watching them. "What makes you so sure you'll find it in Washington? You've already traced the chain of subsidiaries leading to Manassas Ventures offshore. Who knows how far offshore the chain goes? Maybe it ends in Moscow. Or Beijing."

"You wouldn't be trying to discourage me, would you?"

"Not at all, but we're still a long way from home."

"At least we've got the Internet."

"Right." He glanced around. "I think I'll head downtown for a little point-and-click session on my office computer. Want to come along?"

"I've got to get back to OPRR, but we can share a cab."

He looked into her eyes. "What almost happened the other night at your place?"

"We almost got dosed with Totuus."

"No. I mean, what was in the cards before we opened the door and found the two uninvited guests?"

Romy held his gaze. She'd grown to like Patrick, even admire him in some ways, but she didn't love him. She enjoyed his company and, even though she knew injecting sex into their relationship might complicate matters, she'd wanted him that night. But that wasn't the same as wanting him every night.

"We'll never know, will we," she said, giving him a warm smile. "It was a moment, one that might come again."

"Or might not." His expression soured, leaving him looking needy.

Well, I have needs too, she thought. Sometimes sex is front and center, but lots of times something else pushes it down the line.

She knew all too well how she'd let the war on SimGen take over her life, but the time to press the fight was now. Every day of delay meant another day of slavery for the sims. Plenty of time later to play catch up.

"It's the Masked Marvel, isn't it," he said.

"Who?"

"Zero. You've got a thing for him."

"Don't be silly. I've never even seen his face."

"That doesn't mean you haven't imagined it, or that you can't be infatuated with him."

She tensed. Patrick had hit a bit too close to home. Yes, she had times when she fantasized about Zero. His inner strength and resolve spoke to her, reaching out through his layers of protective insulation to touch her like no one else she had ever known. And his air of remove that proclaimed him beyond her reach only heightened the attraction.

Fearing her expression might give something away, she stepped off the curb and waved at an approaching taxi.

"You're talking crazy."

10

You've got to love modern technology, Luca Portero thought, smiling as he spotted Ellis Sinclair's silver Lexus SUV half a dozen car lengths ahead on the George Washington Bridge.

Luca had equipped the Lexus with a transponder that let him know its location no matter where it went. He glanced at the locator screen, glowing in the dark on the passenger seat. Luca's car was a fixed dot in the center of the green LCD monitor; the Lexus was a blip floating directly above it. A GPS program laid out a map of the city around them, showing both cars crossing the Hudson River toward the city.

All was well.

Well? he thought. Who am I kidding?

He shook his head. He'd almost forgotten what *well* meant. Nothing was anywhere near *well*.

Darryl Lister had become a raw, twitching nerve after he learned of the fateful question at the stockholders' meeting, a nonstop question box: *Who asked it? How could he know?*

Well, Luca had soon found out that it wasn't a 'he' at all. The meeting had been recorded—a matter of routine—and who did he spot while reviewing the video files: Cadman. Romy fucking Cadman.

Initially Lister had been sure that Palmer had talked under his own Totuus, but then they'd tracked the operative to some Long Island hospital where he was spending his days sitting around babbling gibberish. Obviously the MTW had worked.

Luca shuddered at the thought of such a fate, even if the effect only lasted for ninety days. Ninety days of hell. If you weren't loony before, you damn sure might be after.

But the success of the MTW had sent Luca back to the leak problem.

He already knew it was Ellis Sinclair. But who was he was leaking to? That was what mattered. Tonight Luca would find out. Once he learned Sinclair's contact, the rest would fall into place. Then he'd make his move. And take no prisoners.

He followed Sinclair down the West Side Highway to Fifty-fourth Street, crawled across Midtown—traffic in the city would be murder until after Christmas—to a parking garage across the street from the Warwick Hotel. Shit! He couldn't very well pull in right behind him. He should have brought backup.

He left the car double-parked and running while he trotted to the ramp that led down to the parking area. Crouching, he spotted Sinclair accepting a ticket from the attendant. But instead of walking back this way, he started up the ramp on the other side.

Fuck! He was heading out to Fifty-third!

Luca ducked back into his car. He folded up the locator unit and grabbed the keys. As he slammed and locked the door he heard a voice behind him.

"Can't leave that here."

He turned to see an NYPD uniform. Black, big face, big gut stretching his blue shirt, big black belt laden with police paraphernalia.

"Officer, this is an emergency."

"I don't care if your hair is on fire, you can't leave that car here. There's a garage right there. Pull it in and—"

"I don't have time. I'll be right back."

"You leave that car there, I promise you, it'll be long gone and far away when you come back."

"Fine," Luca said, moving off. He tossed the keys to the cop. "Take it. Merry Christmas."

The cop opened his mouth, then closed it. Luca doubted he'd ever had anyone tell him to go ahead and tow his car.

Luca dashed straight through the garage—down, across, and up onto Fifty-third. He stopped when he reached the sidewalk, frantically peering east and west through the lights, the shadows, the people hurrying to escape the chill.

Which way, damn it?

He glanced longingly at the locator unit, dangling from his hand like a small valise. If only there had been some way to affix a transponder to Sinclair himself.

Never mind the wishing. What now?

He couldn't see Sinclair on Fifty-third. Maybe he'd headed downtown on Sixth Avenue. Luca's instincts urged him in that direction. He started off at a run but the crowds on the avenue slowed him to a crawl. The Radio City Music Hall Christmas Show was in full swing, jamming the Sixth Avenue sidewalks with parents and their screaming kiddies. But that meant Sinclair couldn't move fast either.

Luca bullied and bulled his way through the throng as fast as he could, earning angry looks and comments. Yeah, merry Christmas to you too, fuckers. He kept rising on tiptoes to check the other side of the street—he saw oversized Venus de Milos framing the Credit Lyonnaise Building, and a line of fifteen-foot nutcrackers standing guard against the columns of the Paine-Webber, but no Ellis Sinclair.

An Art Deco marquee directly ahead now, *Radio City* blazing in red neon, and the damned charter busses vomiting tourists onto the sidewalk blocked his view of the opposite side. No sign of Sinclair here, so he stepped between two buses to check the other side—just in time to spot Sinclair starting down a subway entrance by the Time & Life Building.

Luca congratulated his instincts. And his luck. But it occurred to him that Sinclair was moving pretty quick for a guy who was supposedly dosed to the eyeballs on antidepressants.

No time to wonder about that now.

He sprang forward to follow but a horn blared him back. The light was against him and traffic was moving just fast enough to make crossing impossible. Cursing, he edged to the corner. As soon as the light changed Luca lunged forward, damn near knocking down a few slow movers on his way to the subway. He flew down the steps and raced along the longest, fanciest goddamn subway ramp he'd ever seen—marble tile, brass trim, all part of the Rockefeller Center complex.

When he reached the token booth, Sinclair was nowhere in sight.

Uptown or down?

He saw the ALL TRAINS sign and ducked under the turnstile—no time for a token—and followed the sound of a train pulling in. He reached the platform just in time to see the doors of an F train pincer closed behind Sinclair.

Luca pelted after the train as it began to move, intending to grab a handle and jump onto the landing between the cars, but it picked up speed too quickly and he was left standing on the platform.

The lighted sign on the rear car said its last stop was 179th Street in Jamaica. That meant Sinclair could be going across town or to the far side of Queens, or anywhere between.

He let out a roar and kicked the nearest tiled pillar.

"Hey, don't worry, buddy," said a shabby guy a few feet away. "There'll be another along soon."

Luca wanted to kill him.

11

Zero stepped into the small, two-story farmhouse in the middle of a fallow potato field, one of many that dotted eastern Long Island.

Good to be home, even if he had no one to share the place.

He unwrapped the scarf from his lower face and removed the hat with the pulled-down brim. Masking his features was relatively easy in the colder weather, especially at night. Summer was a problem, forcing him into a wig, a fake beard and nose, oversized sunglasses, and a floppy boonie cap.

He shrugged out of his coat and turned on the three computers arranged around the sparsely furnished living room. A couch, a recliner, a TV, three folding chairs before the card tables holding the computers. Not exactly the lap of luxury, but it served his purposes.

As the computers booted up he stepped to the mantle of the cold fireplace where an eight-by-ten black-and-white photo of Romy Cadman leaned against the wall. He loved this close-up, taken with a telefoto lens shortly after a letter to the editor of the *Times* had brought her to his attention. He felt a familiar ache as he stared at her face.

Romy . . . were there other women in the world like her? If so, he'd never met one. But then, really, how many women had he met? Nowhere near enough for a fair comparison.

He ran a fingertip along her cheek, wishing he could do so in the flesh.

And what did others matter, anyway? Romy was Romy, his Romy. He knew he shouldn't think of her as his, for she never would be, never could be. That would require removing his mask for her, letting her see his face. And then she'd reject him, turn away in loathing.

Well . . . he didn't actually *know* that, but he couldn't risk it. Better this way. At least he could see her often, be near her, talk to her, hear her voice. But once she rejected him, all that would be lost. And even if by some miracle

she, superior woman though she might be, didn't reject him, the whole relationship would change, and not for the better.

Tonight's Romy ritual ended with a knock on the front door. Even though
he was expecting it, Zero jumped at the sound. A visitor here was an occasion.
Only one person knew where he lived, and his visits were rare.

He laid the photo face down on the mantle and went to the door. When
he opened it he embraced his oldest and dearest friend, the man who was
like a father to him.

"How are you?"

"Good, Ellis. Very good. How are you?"

"Getting better every day, thanks to what you and your group have been
doing."

Ellis Sinclair did look better. Maybe a little grayer, but less gaunt. Perhaps
he was eating better.

"Come in," Zero said, shutting the door and taking Ellis's coat.

He felt a little awkward. He was unpracticed at being a host.

Ellis did a slow turn, taking in the small living room. "Are you comfortable here?"

"Yes, thanks to you."

He pulled a bottle of Scotch from the cabinet under the TV. He'd never
developed a taste for liquor himself, but he knew his guest was something of
a hard drinker. But Ellis surprised him by waving it off.

"Thanks, but I'm taking a breather from the booze."

Zero almost said, Glad to hear it, but reconsidered. Wouldn't be appro-
priate.

"Coffee, then?"

Ellis shook his head. "I can't stay long. As I told you, the reason I'm here
is because I didn't want to discuss this over the phone. May I sit?"

"Of course."

How strange to acquiesce to a request for a seat from the owner of the
house. Since the purchase of real estate would be—to put it mildly—awkward
for Zero, Ellis Sinclair had bought the place for him years ago.

"I gather this is fairly important then," Zero said as they seated themselves, Ellis on the couch, and Zero in the recliner.

A vague anxiety had been nibbling at him since Ellis's call late this afternoon. What was too sensitive to discuss over an encrypted phone?

"More than fairly. In fact I was followed tonight—by Portero himself, I
believe."

"But you lost him." It was a statement. He knew Ellis would have aborted his visit if he thought he was being followed.

"Yes. Took a subway to Forest Hills and rented a car there." He shifted in his chair. "But let me cut to the chase here: Someone asked a very disturbing question at the stockholders' meeting today."

Zero nodded. "You mean about 'surge'?"

"Exactly. One of your people, I presume?"

"Yes. Ms. Cadman. It was her idea. We heard the word from a man who tried to assault her, and she thought that would be a way to see if it meant anything."

"Just the word?" Ellis said, his eyebrows lifting. "That's all you have?"

Too much had been happening lately to allow Zero time to give Ellis one of his irregular briefings, so he filled him in now on the invasion of Romy's apartment, the Totuus, and Palmer's resultant aphasia.

"So you have no idea what this Palmer fellow was referring to," Ellis said.

"Not yet. But we know it means something. And I figure you're the man who can tell us just what."

Ellis tapped his fingers on the armrest of the recliner. This went on for an agonizing minute. Then, "No, I'm not."

"What?" Zero couldn't hide his shock. "You're a founder of SimGen! This goes back to Manassas Ventures. They gave you start-up capital. You've *got* to know!"

"I do know," Ellis said. "But I can't tell you."

"*Another* thing you can't tell me?" He could feel his blood rising. "When I found Kek you said you couldn't tell me anything about him or about what was going on in Idaho. 'Too sensitive,' you said. Now two men attempt a chemical rape on the minds of Romy Cadman and Patrick Sullivan; we ask one of them who sent him and he tells us 'surge.' You know who that is and won't tell me? Why on earth not? 'Too sensitive' again?"

"No," Ellis said, his gaze boring into Zero. "Too dangerous."

"It's already dangerous."

"But you've sampled only a taste of what's waiting for you if you push this further."

"You're telling me to back off?"

"I'm *begging* you to back off."

Zero couldn't believe what he was hearing. But the emotion in Ellis's voice—fear, desperation—were real.

"Isn't this what you set me up to do?"

"No, it's not. Your goal—our goal—is to turn the public against SimGen and the idea of sims as laborers. *Stop further cloning of sims*—that was the goal, remember?"

"Of course. And how better to turn the public against SimGen than to find its dirty laundry and wave it in the air for all to see?"

"You have no idea what you're getting into, the forces you'll be setting in motion . . . they'll crush you."

"They have to find us first."

"Zero, leave it alone, I beg you. You're making progress on so many other fronts. You don't need—"

"Progress? What progress? SimGen is opening more natal centers all the time!"

"We may soon have to rethink that with the tide of public opinion turning. Manufacturers, one or two of them major, are starting to advertise their products, their clothes, toys, appliances, and so on, as 'sim-free.' Mutual funds specializing in sim-free companies are springing up. The Beacon Ridge poisoning—it's awful to look at it as anything but an atrocity, but something good did come out of it because it's accelerated the process." Ellis leaned forward, his expression intense, alive with hope. "We're *winning*, Zero. Leave Manassas Ventures and the rest alone."

We're *not* winning, damn it, Zero thought, his frustration a fire in his gut.

"What we've been doing until now is like trying to tame a killer carnivore by removing its food supply. Can't be done. Or if it can, it'll take a lifetime. But that was all we had, the only way we knew to deal with it. Until now. Now we may have found a weapon, one that can strike at the heart of the beast. And that changes everything."

"But you're forgetting that there's a pregnant sim somewhere out there. Find her and prove that the father of her child is human and our war is won!"

"*If* we find her. That's a very, very big 'if,' Ellis. And if we don't, and if we neglect this 'surge' lead while we hunt for her, then we may miss a crucial opportunity."

"I know you're chafing to end this crusade, but you have no idea what you're getting into."

"They've already tried to kill Romy and Patrick. What can be worse?"

"They can *succeed*. And they will. Keep pushing this and some of your people will die."

The words jolted Zero. He'd realized that when Romy and Patrick had been run off the highway, but hearing it said aloud . . .

Ellis leaned back and closed his eyes. "You want to strike at the beast. I understand that. But I've been living in the belly of that beast for decades and believe me, Zero, it's dark in there. It's full of things that should never see the light of day."

"What sort of things?"

"Painful things. Things that will hurt me personally, and devastate other, more innocent, parties. Things that no one will want to hear. And don't think you'll come through unscathed, either."

Zero swallowed. "What do you mean?" He couldn't suppress a mocking tone. "Or is it 'too sensitive' again?"

Ellis looked away and shook his head. "Some of it is sensitive. And some of it is . . . unspeakable."

The last word lingered in the air between them. Zero's mouth felt dry, his tongue like old leather. He couldn't bear the thought of one of the most decent, moral men he had ever known connected to something unspeakable. What had Ellis got himself into?

"So," Ellis said finally. "Do we understand each other? Will you concentrate on finding Meerm and back away from Manassas?"

Shaking his head was the hardest thing Zero had ever done in his life. How could he turn down this man who'd been so good to him? But he didn't see any other choice.

"I can't do that. Even if I wanted to, I doubt I could call off Romy and Patrick."

"Of course you can. You're they're leader."

"Causes take on a life of their own. Romy and Patrick are off and running like hounds who've caught a scent. There's no whistling them back."

Ellis rubbed a hand across his eyes, then dragged it down his face. He looked ten years older than when he'd arrived.

Zero said, "But I will do this. I will push the search for Meerm as best as I can. If that pans out, then Manassas and 'surge' will be moot."

"I pray so."

Looking exhausted, Ellis rose slowly from the recliner and shrugged into his coat.

"Is there nothing I can say to make you change your mind?"

"I wish there were, Ellis. You don't know how much it hurts me to go against you."

"Hurt? You don't know hurt, Zero. Keep on this road, and it will come to a very bad end. A terrible end. And you . . . you may end up the sorriest of all."

Without another word, Ellis Sinclair opened the door, stepped outside, and walked to his car, leaving Zero wondering if he'd just made the worst mistake of his life.

12

NEWARK, NJ

DECEMBER 20

Benny come and go. Meerm can't stay hide. Too many kick inside when Meerm squeeze into wall. And must go wee. Meerm go wee so ver much these day. Leave closet now.

Feel stuff on floor. Look see white powder. Meerm touch taste. Mmmm. Sugar. Why sugar on floor?

Meerm not know. Must go wee now. Meerm hurry to bathroom. Do wee. When Meerm finish she flush.

No-no-no! Meerm forget! Must not flush! Nev flush in day when no sim round! Benny hear!

Benny come now! Meerm hurry to closet. Climb to shelf. So hard, so ver hard climb. Squeeze into hole. Squeeze-squeeze-squeeze.

"I heard that! Goddamn it I might imagine a creak or a thump, but I know I ain't imaginin no toilet flush!"

Meerm squeeze into hole, push board back. Wait and listen.

"Ay! Lookit that! Tracks through my sugar! So I ain't loco! Someone's up here, an I know just where you are, man!"

Meerm hear bang-bang-bang on closet door. Jump with every bang.

"I don't know where you was hidin before, but Benny gotcha now! Ain't no monkey gonna outsmart Benny. Benny outsmart *you*! So come on out where I can see you!"

Meerm not come out. Meerm too scare. Meerm stay. Benny nev find Meerm here behind board.

Bang-bang-bang again. "Hey! You hear me? No sense draggin this out. It's over! You tagged!" Meerm hear closet door open. "You—what the fuck?" Hear hangers move. "Hey! What's goin on here?"

Now Benny start bang closet wall—bang-bang-bang! Ver loud to Meerm behind board. Meerm hold breath and hold ear. Now Benny bang Meerm board. No-no-no! Board move. Meerm see light.

"Ay, lookit this shit! Damn me, there's a space back there! Ay, that where you are? That where you been hidin on Benny? Say somethin, will ya? Awright, dammit. That the way you wanna be . . ."

Meerm hear Benny go but Meerm stay. Not move. Then hear Benny come back. Hear chair drag across floor. Benny push board and big light shine in Meerm eye.

"There you are, you lazy monkey. Playin hooky from the job, huh? Wait'll I tell the boss. Ay, you're a plump one, aintcha. Whatcha been doin? Eatin all day? You—wait a minute. Wait a fuckin minute. You that sim they lookin for! The pregnant one! The five-million-dollar sim! Holy Christ! Holy Christ! You her! An I gotcha! I gotcha!"

Light go way, Benny go way, then closet door close. Meerm hear bumps against closet door.

What Benny say? Meerm pregnant sim. What pregnant? Meerm five-million-dollar sim. What five million? Meerm not understand. Meerm try understand later. Now Meerm must run. Benny find Meerm. Benny will call mans who hurt.

Meerm climb out on closet shelf and drop to floor. Push on closet door but door not move. Meerm push so ver hard. Push-push-push, but door not move. Door locked. No-no-no!

Meerm trapped. Meerm ver fraid and ver scare. Meerm shake inside and out, almost hard as kick-kick-kick. Meerm cry. Poor, poor Meerm.

13

"Mr. Portero," Nowicki's voice said through Luca's office intercom, "I think you'd better take this call."

"Who is it?"

"Calls himself Benny Morales and says he knows you. Says he's got the pregnant sim."

"Sure. Him and half a million others."

Luca shook his head. How many times had he heard that since the five-megabuck reward hit the news? People were crawling out of the woodwork with crazy stories, some wishful thinking, others outright lies. Meerm, or an equally pregnant sim, had been sighted in Chicago, San Francisco, Buenos Aires, London, Hong Kong. The world was suddenly full of pregnant sims.

"This Morales says he met you at the Newark crib when you came looking for the pregnant sim; says she's been hiding there right under his nose all along."

Luca remembered Morales now, a quick, jittery little ferret of a man. Remembered that damn crib too. After a weeklong fruitless vigil, he'd yanked surveillance from the place, figuring if the pregnant sim hadn't returned by then, she wasn't coming back at all.

But if she'd never left the building in the first place . . .

"Put him though."

Luca's hand darted toward the phone and hovered over the receiver. He let it ring twice before picking up.

A few minutes later, after listening to Morales's story, Luca hung up and jabbed the intercom button. "Nowicki. Get Grimes and Alessi. Meet me in the garage. We're rolling!"

This was it. Morales's story hung together too well to be anything but the real thing.

We've found her!

Luca felt as if a magnum of Dom Perignom had popped open inside his chest.

14

The rain clouds that had been threatening all day opened up just in time to snarl traffic throughout the metropolitan area. So it was well after dark when Luca and his men arrived at the crib. Benny Morales met them at the front door.

"Upstairs!" he said, leading them up a narrow stairway. "I got her trapped, locked up tight inna closet an I been keepin an eye on it alla time 'cept for when I was watchin for you at the window so I know she still in there."

Morales had reminded Luca of a ferret last visit; now he was a ferret on speed. Luca could understand that. The little man was going to be a multi-millionaire. But Luca was going to recapture his pride and his credibility, and maybe even his future, and that was worth more.

"There it is," Morales said, as he led them into a bunk-filled space on the second floor.

"Where are the rest of your sims?"

"Not back yet." He glanced at his watch. "Maybe half hour. But look here." He stepped farther into the room and pointed to a door on the right. "She in there." He held up an old-fashioned skeleton key. "I got her locked and blocked. She ain't goin nowhere nohow."

Luca smiled. Morales wasn't kidding. He'd wedged a chair under the doorknob. Hiding his excitement, he held out his hand and Morales dropped the key into his palm. He stepped to the door, removed the chair, and poised the key before the lock.

"Meerm?" he said though the door. "My name is Luca Portero. I am from SimGen."

He spoke softly, maintaining a calm, soothing tone. He wanted to take this sim with the least possible fuss and muss. Everyone—from the Sinclairs all the way to the top of SIRG—wanted her and her unborn baby alive and well. The better the condition he delivered her in, the better for him. But if she was going to make this difficult he'd come prepared. One way or another,

Luca intended to leave here tonight with the world's only pregnant sim.

"The company has sent me here to protect you, Meerm. We know you're not feeling good and we're here to take you back to where you can rest and get well. I'm going to open the door now."

Luca slipped the key into the lock and turned it. As he gripped the knob . . .

"Don't worry if you don't see her right away," Morales said from a few feet behind him. "Like I told you, there's this loose piece of wallboard and—"

Without looking back, Luca waved for him to shut the hell up. He turned the knob and pulled the door open—slowly, so as not to appear the least bit aggressive.

As Morales had said, the closet looked empty. Some old shoes, some hanging clothes, a hat or two on the shelf.

"Upper right," Morales said in a stage whisper. "Above the shelf. See the loose board?"

Luca nodded. The remodeling had been done on the cheap, probably not even up to code. Or maybe the codes had been relaxed because the floor wasn't designated for human habitation. Whatever the reason, the framing studs looked to be about two feet apart and the wallboard carelessly nailed. As a result the whole upper corner of the inner wall had popped loose, allowing easy access to a dead space beyond.

Luca held back a hand, palm up. "Flashlight," he said, and one was slapped into it.

He dragged the chair into the closet and stepped up on it for a better look. He pushed back the board and shone the light into the opening. But instead of the expected pair of frightened brown sim eyes staring back at him, he found an empty space. Cold sweat started in his armpits as he quickly angled the beam around, revealing knotty studs, the unfinished reverse sides of wallboard, lots of crumbling brick, but no sim.

No goddamned sim!

"She's not here!" he rasped through his sand-dry throat. "You said she was here! Where is she?"

"Whatchoo you mean, she not there?" Morales cried, a panicky edge to his voice. "She gotta be there! I lock her in myself! She can't be nowheres else!"

Luca poked his head through the opening. The dead space was deeper than he'd have thought. It angled back around the rear of the closet, beyond his field of vision.

"Meerm?" he called, still keeping his voice soft. "Meerm, are you there? We're here to help you."

No reply. Not a rustle of movement, not even a breath.

Okay, he thought. She wants to play it that way, then the gloves have to come off.

He swiveled and hopped off the chair. Morales was waiting for him right outside the closet door.

"Lemme see that light! I find her for you! I know she there!"

Luca studied him a moment. He hadn't been lying about seeing a sim in there. He was too upset. Probably he'd had the five million already half spent in his head and now he saw it slipping away.

Luca shoved him aside. "Go find yourself a corner and stay out of the way, little man. We're going to do it our way." He looked at his three men and jerked a thumb over his shoulder, toward the street below. "She's hiding in the wall. Get the tools."

They were back in two minutes with crowbars, axes, and sledgehammers.

"Hey, whatchoo think you doin?" Morales cried, running over.

Luca held up a crowbar and glared at him. "You want to be alive to collect your reward, right? Then stay the hell out of our way."

With that he turned and smashed the curved end of the bar through the wallboard, gave it a half twist, and yanked back, dislodging one side of the board from its stud. His men did the same, attacking the closet and the walls around it with gusto. In five or six minutes they'd stripped this end of the room back to the underlying brick.

But still no sim. Luca wanted to scream. Where could she be? Had Morales lied to him? But there seemed no point to that.

Then he heard Alessi's voice from his left, near the corner of the room. "Aw, shit, boss. Take a look at this."

Luca hurried over and saw a large hole in the bricks. He grabbed the flashlight and shined the beam through. More bricks inside. He stuck his head inside and looked up and down. Cool musty air wafted against his face from below.

"Looks like an old airshaft." His voice echoed off the walls. He pulled back and found Morales standing a few feet away, his hands rubbing over each other in a nervous, washing motion. "Where's it go?"

Morales shrugged. "I didn't even know it was there. Nobody tell me nothin."

Okay. The sim had crawled from the dead space behind the closet into the air shaft. Once in there she had two directions to choose from: up or down. Considering she was frightened and pregnant, she'd have taken the easiest and fastest route.

"Check out the first floor," he told his men. "Tear out the wall and see if there's an opening down there." To Morales: "You got a basement here?"

"Sure."

"Show me."

He followed the little man down two levels. When Morales turned on the basement lights, Luca saw a piece of plywood and its exposed nails dangling from the ceiling, smears of blood on the floor, on the wall, and on the sill of the open window, and he knew in one spirit-crushing instant what had happened.

The sim had eased herself down the shaft and landed on the plywood that had closed the opening. Her weight knocked the crudely fixed board free and she'd fallen to the floor, cutting herself on the nails in the process. She'd limped to the window, opened it, and squeezed through.

Gone!

Without warning—Luca was barely aware of what he was doing—he grabbed Morales and flung him against the wall. The ferret-man slammed against the concrete and slumped to the floor, wincing and clutching his shoulder.

"Aw, man!" he moaned. "Whatchoo do that for?"

Because it felt *good!* Luca wanted to scream. Instead he said, "Because you had her and you let her slip away!"

"I did everythin I could!"

"Not enough!" Luca sensed his rage peaking toward critical mass. He forced himself to step back, knowing if he let himself get any closer to the whining little bastard he'd break his neck. "You had her! You had her and you let her get away!"

At least that was the way it seemed. Luca glanced around. But what if she just wanted him to think that was what happened? What if—?

Wait. What was he thinking? He was dealing with a sim. They didn't have the brains for misdirection. Still . . . this one had made a fool of him once already . . .

Just to be sure, Luca did a quick search of the basement. Not much down here; no closets or crawl spaces to hide in, just cinderblock walls and solid concrete floor. Satisfied that she was gone, he closed and locked the open window and headed for the stairs, leaving Morales behind on the floor.

He called his three men together and faced them in the front hallway.

"All right," he said, forcing a calm demeanor, "here's the situation: She's gone. Escaped through the basement window."

"Shit!" Grimes muttered. He was wiry and redheaded, and his Adam's apple wobbled in his long neck when he spoke. "We'll never find her out there in the dark!"

Luca wheeled and got in his face. "She's hurt, she's bleeding, she's on foot, she's pregnant, and she's a sim! If you can't track something like that, you should be working for somebody else!"

Grimes backed up. "Okay, okay. Sorry."

Luca turned away. He needed more men. He reached for his phone to call Lister, have him find back-up. They'd comb this area until—

The sound of squeaking brakes just outside the front door made him turn. A battered old school bus had pulled to a stop at the curb. As he watched through the cracked glass, the bus doors folded back and a line of sims began stepping down to the sidewalk.

"Hold everything," Luca said as he headed for the door. "I think reinforcements just arrived."

He hadn't wanted to call for help Now he wouldn't have to. He stationed himself at the top of the front steps and held up his hands.

"Nobody goes inside yet," he told the sims.

He made them wait in the fine drizzle until the bus had emptied out. They looked to number about forty or so.

"Hey!" the grizzled old driver said. He'd come to the bus door and stood staring at Luca. "Who are you?"

"Someone who's commandeering these sims."

"They ain't yours to commandeer! Where do you get off thinkin—"

Luca glared at him. "Move on, old man. This isn't your concern."

The driver looked as if he were about to say something, then changed his mind. As the bus wheezed away, Luca turned back to the sims.

"We've come for Meerm," he told them, raising his voice. "We know you've been hiding her. But that's all right. We're here to help her and—"

"No!" said a sim, pointing at Grimes. "No help sim! Hurt sim!"

Luca looked more closely at the sim who'd spoken and noticed that his left eye sported the yellowing remains of a shiner. He turned to Grimes.

"What'd you do, Grimes?" he said, keeping it low and through his teeth. "Beat him up?"

Grimes blinked and swallowed. "I thought he'd lied to us, so I just—"

"So you just scared the shit out of them, guaranteeing they'd never tell us a thing. This could have been over a week ago, you fucking stupid—" He turned away before he ripped out the man's bobbing Adam's apple and made him eat it. "I'll deal with you later."

Fighting for calm, he faced the sims again. He'd hoped to enlist their voluntary support, make them *want* to find Meerm for him. But Grimes had blown that, so he'd have to take a direct approach.

"I know it's cold out and you're all probably tired and hungry. There's nothing you'd like better now than to get inside and eat and relax, right? Well, guess what? That's not going to happen until Meerm is found. We're going to start searching now, and we're going to keep searching till we find her, even if it takes all night, understand?"

Luca could see from the resignation in their eyes that they understood, all right. They understood just fine. And this would work. He had forty-plus searchers instead of the maximum dozen humans he'd be able to muster on such short notice. And these were better than humans. Who better to sniff out a sim than another sim?

Yeah, this will work. Damn well better. But what if it didn't? What if they came up empty tonight and all this commotion caught the attention of some of Eckert's followers? Or Morales opened his yap to the wrong people? Eckert could wind up with the pregnant sim.

He turned and found Morales standing in the front hallway.

"Listen up," he told the little man. "If I find the sim, you get the five million. Anyone else finds her, you're out in the cold. So keep your mouth shut about this."

Morales stared at him, rubbing his shoulder. "First you push me around, then you do this. You loco, man?"

Not loco, Luca thought, turning away. But if anyone's going to bring in this sim, it's going to be *me*.

15

Patrick closed his eyes and leaned back in his swivel chair.

"My eyes are going to burn out the back of my skull if I stare at this computer screen another minute."

"Here," Romy said, tapping him on the shoulder. "Let me spell you. We've only got a few more to go."

It seemed like they'd been at this all day. Romy had arrived at his office late this afternoon and together they'd cooked up a list of acronyms, using every possible combination of letters that might conceivably be pronounced "surge"—from CERGE, CERJE, CIRJ, and so on, to SIURJ, ZIRJE, ZOORGE and beyond. Then he'd begun plugging them into one Internet search engine after another.

So far the hits had been few and none had panned out.

"Only a few more, you say?" He stretched. "I'll keep at it then. What's next?"

Romy consulted her list. "S-I-R-G."

Patrick typed it into the entry box on the searcher and hit ENTER. Half a second later a string of varicolored type cascaded down the screen. The engine reported 1,753 hits.

"We've got something," he said.

SIRG turned out to be the acronym for a raft of organizations, ranging from the Summit Implementation Review Group to the Spatial Information Research Group to the Student Internet Research Group.

"These sound exciting," Romy said dryly, reading over his shoulder. She'd been nibbling on a sweet roll and her breath carried a hint of cinnamon. He was sure her lips would taste even better. "Hope you didn't get your hopes up."

Patrick shook his head, trying to forget how close she was and focus on the screen. "I've learned better by now."

He clicked his way through one link after another; all the groups seemed pretty straightforward. Then he came to something called the Social Impact Research Group.

"Social impact of what?" he said.

"And on what?" Romy added.

The article was an old one, quoting from another even older article. SIRG received only passing mention in reference to some unspecified appropriations bill.

"Wait," Romy said. "Appropriations means government. Hit a few more links."

He did but found only scattered mentions of the group; nothing of substance, no hint as to its purpose.

"Let me try," Romy said.

They switched seats. Patrick watched her access a directory of US Federal Government agencies and enter a string of asterisks into a password box.

"Don't forget," she said, as if reading his mind, "I work for a government agency myself. I've picked up a few passwords and access codes along the way."

He watched a while longer, then got up and moved away. Romy was far more facile than he at the keyboard. She worked too fast for him—he'd no sooner focus on a screen than she'd be clicking to another. He stepped to the window and stared out at the night.

This block of Henry Street was reasonably well lit. He studied the parked cars for signs of life. None. The only pedestrian was a drab-looking woman making her way along the sidewalk directly below.

This constant vigilance rawed his nerves. When would it end? When could he relax again, if ever?

He wandered over to where Tome was busily filing papers.

"Getting tired, Tome?"

"No, Mist Sulliman," the old sim said, grinning up at him in the narrow confines of the file room. "This fun."

Whatever turns you on, he thought. He patted the sim's bony back.

"Great, my friend. Have a ball."

Patrick was turning to go when he spotted something blinking on a little table in the corner. Tome followed his gaze. He snatched up the rectangular object and hid it behind his back.

"What's that?"

Tome looked down. "Picture, Mist Sulliman."

"A picture? Can I see it?"

"Mist Sulliman be mad," he said, eyes still on his shoes.

"Nonsense. Just let me see."

With obvious reluctance, Tome placed the framed picture, upside down, into Patrick's outstretched hand.

He turned it over and stared in shock. The Virgin Mary . . . Our Lady of Guadalupe, to be exact, but not like Patrick had ever seen her. The traditional gold-leaf glory radiating around her had been enhanced with flashing red rays. Patrick flipped it over and spotted the battery case that powered the diodes.

"This is . . . amazing," Patrick said. "Where did you get it?"

"Buy on street. Mist Sulliman not mad?"

"Why on earth would I be mad?"

"Lady on street yell Tome. Say Mother Mary not for sim."

Bitch. Although he could see how true believers would object to sims taking up their religion, worshipping *their* god. It diminished them, made them feel less special.

"But why, Tome? Why'd you buy it?"

"Tome pray for Mist Sulliman and Miss Romy. Ask Lady to protect."

Patrick was touched, didn't know quite what to say. He stepped past Tome and replaced the blinking icon on the table.

"Thank you, Tome. I . . . we have something called freedom of religion in this country. That means you can pray to any god you want. And . . . thanks."

He wandered back toward Romy, ready to tell her about Tome's prayers, when she called out to him.

"Look at this," she said, her expression troubled. "This particular SIRG— the Social Impact Research Group—had millions and millions of government dollars poured into it through most of the nineties and into the oughts, and then the money stopped."

"Money from where?"

"That's the weird part. I can't find out who picked up the tab."

"Somebody had to. Some department or agency had to be debited before SIRG could be credited."

"I know. There's a whole string of agencies and departments and groups that seem to be intermediaries but I keep running into dead ends or getting lost in the maze whenever I try to track the money back to its source."

Patrick shook his head. "Almost like . . ."

Romy looked up at him. "Manassas Ventures."

"Do you think . . . ?"

She held up a hand. "Before you go getting excited, let me tell you that I think SIRG might be dead. As in defunct. Can't find a mention or a penny of appropriations from any source whatsoever for years."

"Damn! For a moment I thought we were on to something. But then again, how much pay dirt could we expect from something with a name like the Social Impact Research Group?"

"Don't let a title put you off," she said. "Ever hear of SOG?"

"Son of Godzilla?"

Romy smiled up at him. "Close. Try the 'Studies and Observations Group.' It was started in the Nam era. That innocent title covered a joint Special Operations unit that included members from the Air Force, Navy SEALs, and Special Forces. They were sent into Laos to wage a secret war."

"So you think someone who thought SOG was a clever cover might have come up with SIRG?"

"Just a thought." Romy looked back at the screen and rubbed her neck.

"Stiff?"

"Yeah. Been a long day."

He gripped both her shoulders and began kneading the back of her neck with his thumbs. He could feel the warmth of her skin through the light weave of her sweater.

She groaned. "That feels *good*."

You're telling me, he thought.

"SIRG appears to be defunct," she said as he continued to knead. "But it could be operating under a different name. Either way, just to be sure we've turned over every rock before we move on, I think we should know where its money came from, don't you?"

"But how?"

Patrick stretched his fingers forward, working his massage down to her collar bones.

"My . . . office." Romy groaned again. "You're making it hard to concentrate."

"Just soothing those tight muscles. Relax." Patrick himself was anything but as a rapturous pressure built within.

She cleared her throat. "What was I saying?"

"Something about your office." He slipped his fingers over her collar bones onto the upper edges of her pectorals.

"Oh, right. OPRR's computers are linked to the government. And my boss, Milton Ware, is an absolute master at weaving through bureaucratese.

I need to find a way to put Uncle Miltie onto the scent without knowing why. Maybe if I—"

"Excuse me?"

They both jumped and turned at the sound of a woman's voice. Relief flooded Patrick as he recognized the figure standing in the doorway.

"Miss Fredericks! How did you get in here?" He could have sworn he'd locked the door.

Alice Fredericks smiled. "I'm sorry if I startled you, Mr. Sullivan. But I was walking by and just happened to look up and see the lights, so I thought I'd stop in and inquire as to why you haven't called me."

Walking by? Patrick thought. Probably watching the place with a telescope.

He leaned closer to Romy and whispered, "She's the one I told you about." Romy gave him a puzzled look, but before he could elaborate—

"Oh, no!" Alice cried, pointing to Tome who had stepped out of the filing room. "It's one of them! One of my long lost great-grandchildren! Please take him away! The sight of him tears at my heart!"

"Now I remember," Romy whispered. "Dramatic, isn't she."

"Just a bit."

He motioned the baffled Tome back into the file room where he'd be out of sight, then turned to Alice. Though he was still rattled by the way she'd strolled in here off the street, he didn't want to take it out on her. But it was time to put a stop to these intrusions.

"Miss Fredericks, I'm sorry, but I don't think I'll be able to spare the time to take your case. And even if I did, in the long run it will come down to your word against SimGen's, and I don't think—"

"Even if I have proof?"

"What sort of proof can you have?"

"A check made out to me from Mercer Sinclair."

Yeah, right, he thought. "How would you happen to have that? Once you cash a check it goes back to the one who issued it."

"But I didn't cash it," Alice said, eyes wide. "It was the last payment for letting them use my body to incubate the alien child. I didn't know they'd steal him from me. How could I take money from the man who stole my child?" Her eye filled with tears. "That would be like . . . like selling my baby!"

"So why didn't you burn it or tear it up?"

"I kept it as a reminder to stay the course, and because I knew someday I'd have a chance to confront Mercer Sinclair again, and when I did I wanted to be able to throw it back in his face!"

"We'd love to see that check," Romy said. When Patrick gave her an are-you-nuts? look she nudged him with her elbow and whispered, "No stone unturned, right?" Then she raised her voice: "Can you bring it here?"

"Oh no," Alice said. "I never take it out of my room. But if you want to come visit me, I'll be very happy to show it to you."

Patrick regarded Alice Fredericks. Was she completely bonkers and dreaming all this up? Just a lonely lady who'd say anything to have company? Or could there be a kernel of truth at the heart of her crazy story?

Patrick sighed. "Leave me your address and I'll see if I can get over tomorrow."

"He *will* get over tomorrow," Romy said, giving him a wry smile. "Even if I have to drag him."

16

NEWARK, NJ

Meerm shiver in dark. Ver wet and cold. Ver scare. And hurt. Hand bleed, foot bleed, leg bleed. Not bleed lot but still bleed. Blood wash off in rain but come more blood.

Meerm inside now. Clothes all wet and drip. But where? Meerm not know. Meerm run-run-run from sim home. Slip in water. Fall down, get up, fall down. Many fall. Meerm so dizzy and weak. No run no more. See old metal door in brick wall. Pull-pull-pull on handle. Door open loud and Meerm go in. Close door behind.

Not warm here. Ver dark. Meerm feel big metal wire. Go up-up-up. Ver bad oil smell.

Meerm shiver more. Meerm cry. So cold-wet. So lonely. Sim friend gone forever. Meerm no go back. Bad mans wait for Meerm. Want hurt her. Poor Meerm. Nev see Beece friend again.

What sound? Outside. Some call Meerm name. Meerm listen hard. Yes. Some call, "Meerm! Meerm, where you?" Not man voice. Sound like sim. Sound like Beece!

Beece-Beece-Beece! Meerm so happy to hear Beece. Want see. Meerm push door open little. Ver ver little. Just enough see.

Yes! There! There Beece! Meerm go open wider—

No-no-no! Beece bring mans! Bad mans who hurt!

17

Beece walk down dark alley with other sim. Beece cold and hungry-tired, not know where is. Too many turn. Beece pretend search Meerm but not want find. Beece not like these mans. Ver mean mans. But meanest is red-hair city man who hurt Beece. Other mans call him Grimes. Grimes ver bad man. All these mans bad. Want hurt Meerm. Why? Meerm not bad. Meerm just sick. Get big-big belly.

Beece hear run-steps. Crouch down fraid when see red-hair city man run up. But not hit Beece. Stop and talk other man.

"Hey, Alessi! Somebody called the cops. Lowery heard it on the scanner."

"Shit!"

"Yeah, well, had to expect it. Somebody sees a bunch of men and monkeys poking through their neighborhood, they want to know what's going on."

"Don't suppose we've got any suck with these locals."

"Naw. Who'd ever figure we'd have to operate in Newark? Anyway, Portero doesn't want anyone to know why we're here. That's why I'm moving the car around to the main drag out there. I'll be in the McDonald's lot. When the boys in blue arrive, we fade."

"I'll bet he's royally pissed."

"Count on it."

"All right. See you at McDonald's. Hey, while you're there, get some burgers and fries for the trip home. I missed dinner."

"You got it."

Grimes go. Other man look Beece. "Keep looking, monkey. We're not through yet. You go over there." Point other sim. "You come over here with me. Find her, damn it!"

Beece go where told. Lots trash here. Big puddle. Shoe all wet. Beece lost. See top Mickey-D sign between building. Golden arches. Yum. Beece love Mickey-D. Yes-yes. Sometime—

What sound? Beece hear squeak-squeak. Turn see black metal door in brick wall. Look hard see red letter.

ELEVATOR SHAFT
DANGER!
AUTHORIZED PERSONNEL
ONLY!

Beece no read but Beece see blood on door. See eye look out from door crack.

Meerm! Meerm here!

Beece look round quick. Mans not near. Man not look. Beece fraid talk. Wave Meerm to make stay. No speak, no move! Beece bend, get water in hand. Wash blood off door. Get more. Blood all gone now.

Man yell, say, "Find anything over there?"

"No, sir. Many puddle. No see Meerm."

"All right then, keep moving! Time's a-wasting!"

Beece bend and whisper to door, "Beece not tell. Not tell no one."

18

SUFFOLK COUNTY, NY

So . . . Meerm is in Newark.

Zero couldn't be absolutely sure, but it was evident that Portero believed so. Zero had hired a private detective to keep an eye on him. Often the man reported back that Portero had given him the shake, but tonight he'd called and said that Portero and three others had made a beeline from the SimGen campus to a battered neighborhood in Newark.

Zero had driven his van from the West Side garage, through the Holland

Tunnel, into Newark. Although only a few miles, the trip had taken nearly an hour. But well worth it. Arriving, he'd been treated to the spectacle of Luca Portero and his men herding dozens of sims through the streets, all calling "Meerm! Meerm!"

His heart had sunk. The swine had found her—or damn near. Only a matter of time before all those men and sims tracked Meerm down.

And then . . . a reprieve. He'd pounded his steering wheel with glee as he watched Portero and company make a slapdash retreat just before the Newark Police arrived with their lights flashing. They'd left empty-handed, which meant that Meerm—if she were here at all—was still somewhere in the vicinity. It also meant that Portero and his men would be back.

Zero had been tempted to wait until the cops were gone and then try to find Meerm on his own. But as much as his heart went out to that poor, frightened creature hiding somewhere in the dark, searching alone seemed like courting disaster.

All this gave Zero much to think about on the long ride back to Long Island.

By the time he arrived home he had a semblance of a plan, one that had been inspired by Portero himself when he'd conscripted Meerm's fellow sims to find her. The murdering bastard was clever, no getting around that.

But Zero could play that game too, and play it better.

He removed his knit watch cap and tinted lenses, then unwrapped the scarf from his lower face. The air felt good against his skin.

His answering machine carried a message from Patrick saying they still hadn't nailed down "surge" but had a lead or two they'd follow up tomorrow.

Ellis's warnings about digging into "surge" still haunted him, especially his comment that Zero would not come through "unscathed" if he persisted. And his description of some of the secrets behind SimGen as "unspeakable" . . . a word he found deeply disturbing.

But there was no turning back now. Events were gathering momentum, and he had to find a way to control them, or at least steer them in the right direction.

One thing he knew he must control was Meerm. For her own sake, and the sake of all sims, he had to keep her out of SimGen's hands. And to that end, Zero knew of a very bright sim named Tome who would be more than willing to help. If he could find a way to sneak Tome into the Newark crib, the sims there might trust him enough to let him know where Meerm was hiding.

If they knew.

But assuming they did, Zero and Tome could then seek her out and bring her to safety.

Another if: *If* she'd come along.

Meerm probably had been so terrified by Portero and his thugs that she wouldn't trust any human now. Another instance where Tome again might come in handy.

But Zero had reservations about the old sim's powers of persuasion. And that was why Zero had to accompany him. Because if Tome couldn't coax Meerm out of hiding, Zero would have to step in.

He moved to the dusty mirror over the sofa and looked at himself. He did that often. Too often, perhaps, he thought. But that's what you do when you wished you looked like someone else, like some*thing* else.

He looked at his forehead and wished for less of a slope and a less prominent brow ridge; he wished his nose were longer, and his lips thinner.

This was not a face Romy could love, but it might be a face Zero would have to let her see. Because Meerm was that important. He'd risk anything to keep her away from SimGen, even if it meant revealing what he was.

For when Zero took off his mask, Meerm would have to trust him. Because she would know she was talking to another sim.

FIVE

THY BROTHER'S KEEPER

I

"You're sure we've got the right address?" Patrick said.

He and Romy stood before a dilapidated five-story Alphabet City tenement that leaned on its neighbor like a drunk against a lamppost; a rusty fire
escape laced its sooty bricks and sootier windows.

He'd figured Alice Fredericks was poor, but not this poor.

"Let's see." Romy checked the number on the door atop the crumbling
front stoop against the paper in her hand. "Yes. This is what she wrote down.
She's in apartment 2D. I hope she's in."

Patrick had called Alice's number three times this morning to make sure
she was home before they made the trip. Whoever had answered the hall
phone told him—with growing annoyance because he said he was waiting for
another call—that "the crazy bitch ain't answerin her door."

Patrick rubbed his cold hands together and envied Romy's cleathre coat.
The weather wasn't going to let anyone forget that today was the first day of
winter. Near noon now but the sun hung low as a cold wind knifed down the
nearly empty street.

Cold as the knot of tension in his chest. He looked around. Parked cars lined the curb; if anyone was lurking in one of them, watching, readying to spring, he couldn't tell. Only an occasional driver passing on the street glanced their way—Romy tended to draw looks—but no one seemed unduly interested. He'd kept watch during the cab ride over and hadn't noticed anyone following.

"This is all a waste of time, you know," he told her. "She may have had a child at one time, and she may even have sold it, but—"

"Not just a child, according to her," Romy corrected him. "A sim."

"Oh, right. How did I leave that out? A baby sim she says was the result of fertilization by aliens." He shook his head. "Who's crazier—her, or us for coming here?"

"We've come this far, let's finish it."

"Whatever she gave birth to, we know she didn't sell it to Mercer Sinclair, and we know she doesn't have a SimGen check signed by him."

"That's just it: We *don't* know. We assume, but we don't *know*."

"I do. Why are you so gung ho to call her bluff?"

"Because it will nag at me if I don't check it out. That's why I'm here on my lunch hour. I don't want to keep wondering if maybe she's only ninety percent crazy and ten percent of what she's telling us is true. And what if that ten percent puts us on a path to 'surge'? The Idaho license plate on that truck led to Manassas, didn't it?"

"Point taken." But Patrick doubted very much they'd score anything useful here. "Okay, let's get this over with."

He took the front steps two at a time, pushed on the front door, but it was locked. She'd said she was in 2D; he found the 2D bell button, but it was unlabeled. He pressed it anyway. No buzzer sounded to unlock the door. Tried again, but still no response.

He turned to Romy. "Are you getting a bad feeling about this?"

"She may not be in."

"Or she may not be well. Or worse."

"You mean that we might not be her first visitors since she left last night?"

"Yeah."

Just then the door swung open and an anemic-looking splicer goth, twentysomething and all in black, stepped out. She hissed at him, revealing a pair of long, sharp vampire fangs—the real thing, he was sure—then flowed down the steps, trailing black lace.

Patrick caught the door before it latched closed again, and held it for Romy. "After you."

"In this case," Romy said, "gentlemen first."

Feeling his neck muscles bunch, Patrick took one last look at the street, then led the way up the worn stairs to the second floor where they found a narrow hallway lit by low-watt bulbs in steel cages and smelling vaguely of urine.

"Wait here," he told Romy.

She shook her head. "You might need me."

He noticed that she had her hand inside her bag. "What've you got in there?"

"Something I hope I don't have to use."

Listening for a click, a creak, anything that might herald an opening door, he led her to the right, past the hall phone framed by scribbled names and numbers. Finally they reached 2D. Patrick took a breath and knocked on the peeling surface. No answer. He tried again, louder.

"Alice? It's Patrick Sullivan."

He pressed his ear to the door and thought he heard a rustling sound within, but couldn't be sure. Tried to look through the peephole but couldn't see a thing, not even light.

"I don't like this," Romy whispered. "I told her we'd be here today. What if . . ." Her voice trailed off as she frowned.

Patrick knew what she was thinking. He'd been thinking it too. "You mean, what if she's been talking too much about this check and someone finally decided to shut her up for good?"

"Which would mean she wasn't crazy after all."

"We've got to get in there." He lowered his voice further. "What if it's all a set up?"

Romy chewed her upper lip. "Maybe we should call the cops. Report her as a missing—"

The door suddenly swung inward, a hand darted out, grabbed the lapel of Patrick's overcoat, and pulled him inward. He stifled a terrified cry when he recognized Alice Fredericks.

"Come in!" she hissed. "Quick!"

Patrick stepped through, Romy right behind him. Alice slammed the door as soon as they were inside, plunging them into darkness. He could make out glints of light from what seemed to be a window, but she must have left her shades down.

"Alice," he said as his pounding heart slowed. "What's going on? Can we have some light?"

Rustling clothing, shuffling feet accompanied by a strange crinkling noise, and then a lamp came to life. Patrick barely recognized Alice. Her gray hair was in wild disarray, her feet bare, her frayed housecoat haphazardly buttoned. And her eyes—red, swollen, wet . . .

"Alice," he said. "You've been crying. What—?"

The words dried up as his brain began to register his surroundings.

"Oh, my," Romy said softly at his side. She'd seen it too.

Patrick did a slow turn, his feet crinkling on the aluminum foil that lined the floor. And the walls. And the ceiling. And the two windows on the outer wall, which was why the one-room apartment was so dark. In some areas, the ceiling especially, the foil looked as if it had been collected from trash cans—minutely crinkled, in odd-sized squares, some with fast-food logos showing; other areas were covered in long smooth strips, obviously tacked up right off the roll.

"Alice?" he said. "What is all this?"

"What? Oh, you mean the foil. That's for protection."

"From . . . ?"

"From having my mind read. The aliens working for Mercer Sinclair can read thoughts, you know. This protects me from them. At least . . ." Her voice faltered as her face twisted into a mask of grief. She sobbed. "At least I thought it did!"

Romy stepped closer and slipped an arm around the woman's quaking shoulders. "What's the matter, Alice? What happened?"

"The check!" Alice wailed. "They stole it!"

Knew it! Patrick thought. Complete waste of time.

"You mean," Romy said, "someone broke in here and took it?"

"Yes! They knew my secret hiding place and they switched it with another check, a worthless one!"

Romy glanced up at Patrick and shrugged.

"Let's go," Patrick said. He wanted to be angry at this flaky lady for wasting his time, but she was too genuinely distressed. Her bizarro apartment, though, was giving him a grand case of the creeps.

"We can't leave her like this. She's terrified." Romy turned back to Alice. "When did you last see the check?"

"Oh, I haven't taken it out for years. But after talking to you last night, I pulled it out of my secret hiding place, to have it ready for Mr. Sullivan, and it had changed!" Another sob, louder this time. "The date's the same and the money's the same, but it's not a SimGen check anymore and someone else's signature is there instead of Mercer Sinclair's!" She fumbled in her housecoat pocket. "Here. I'll show you."

"Romy . . . ," Patrick began but her quick sharp look cut him off.

"Let me calm her down a little," she said, "then we can be on our way."

Alice produced a slip of paper and shoved it into Romy's hand. "There. See for yourself!"

Patrick saw Romy glance at the check, then take a closer look.

"What?" Patrick said.

Romy angled the paper back and forth in the dim light. "Well, it's for five thousand dollars and it's made out to Alice Fredericks. And she's right about the signature: I don't know whose it is, but it's not Mercer Sinclair's."

"I'll bet she's also right about it not being from SimGen too."

Romy nodded, still staring at the check. "Uh-huh. It was drawn on the First Federal Bank of Arlington, Virginia." She looked up at him, her eyes so bright they fairly glowed. "From the account of something called Manassas Ventures."

2

"I don't get it," Patrick said. His stomach lurched as one of the Federal Plaza elevators lifted them toward OPRR's offices.

They'd held off talking about Alice during the ride over from Alphabet City. The odds that one of New York's current crop of cabbies would know enough English to follow their discussion were astronomical, but still they hadn't wanted to risk it. Now they had an elevator car to themselves.

"I think I do," Romy said. "I think she did perform some service for SimGen in its early years, maybe even before it started calling itself SimGen. And it may well have had something to do with a baby."

"What about the space alien angle? You're not buying into—"

"Of course not. I'm no psychologist, but I can see how she may have felt very guilty about what she did. Combine that with not being too tightly wrapped in the first place, and you can understand someone unraveling. She structured a fantastic scenario that blended fact and fiction."

"But Mercer Sinclair?"

"More mixing of fact and fiction," Romy said. "Alice must have had some direct contact with him because he keeps reappearing in her story—taking the sim baby, signing her check."

"Right. The check. Why did she think it had changed?"

"You heard her. She hadn't looked at it for years, and during that time it did change—in her mind. Maybe Mercer Sinclair had given it to her himself. She remembered that and so over the years her loosely hinged mind substituted his signature for whoever really signed it. And since Mercer Sinclair is synonymous with SimGen, she began to remember it as a SimGen check."

"Poor lady. I'd give anything to know the truth about her."

"I don't think even she knows anymore."

He slipped an arm over Romy's shoulders and pulled her closer. "You were good with her."

"I felt sorry for the poor thing."

It had taken Romy a while, but finally she'd managed to calm Alice Fredericks, telling her she was safe now: The aliens had what they wanted and so they wouldn't be bothering her again. She could take down the foil, let some fresh air into the room, and stop worrying. Alice seemed to buy it. She hadn't seemed quite ready yet to peel the foil from the walls, but she'd been in better spirits, and even gave them the check to take with them. After all, it wasn't the real thing, so it was no use to her.

"How old do you think she is?" Patrick said.

"She said she was forty-seven."

"Yeah, but is that reliable? She looks sixty."

"Poverty and madness can age you pretty fast."

"Yeah, well . . ." He sighed. "I guess there's no way to find out what really went on between her and SimGen—or rather, the proto-SimGen being directly financed by Manassas. Which leaves us no closer finding out who's behind Manassas."

"But we've got a Manassas Ventures check, and it's signed. That's *somebody's* signature."

"Right." With his free hand Patrick pulled the old check from his pocket and held it up. "A C-like letter connected to a squiggle, and then an L-like thing connected to another squiggle, on a check drawn on a Virginia bank that was no doubt gobbled up by another bank that merged with yet another bank which was taken over by still another bank."

"But the check's dated back when all that appropriation money was being funneled into SIRG. If we can connect SIRG to that Arlington Federal account . . ."

"Fat chance."

"Don't be so sure. I've got Uncle Miltie working on SIRG."

Patrick had to laugh. "How do you get your superior to do your scut work?"

She lifted her chin defiantly. "I'll have you know I'm superior to Milton Ware in every way."

"Except in seniority, position, and salary, right?"

"Mere details. Besides, he's crazy about me."

"Aren't we all?"

"And he's an expert at tracking down funding. Nobody better. Knows a ton of passwords and can sniff out an unclaimed research dollar at a thousand paces. That's how I sicced him on SIRG. I told him this group got zillions in funding without ever revealing what it was doing. Maybe if OPRR learned its secret . . ."

"And he bought it?"

"Why not? It's true, isn't it?"

"Did you tell him it hasn't received a dime in years?"

"Of course. But I suggested that if he could find where all that funding came from, maybe some of it might still be around for OPRR to tap into."

"And he bit?"

"Like a dog on a bone. And Milton Ware is the kind of dog who'll work a bone until there's nothing left."

They reached the OPRR offices, a nondescript suite on the eighteenth floor. Romy led Patrick to a windowed office where a peppy, white-haired little man sat hunched before a computer. The plaque on his desk read MIL-TON WARE.

"Any luck?" she said.

The man looked up and regarded them with bright blue eyes. "Yes and no."

After Romy made introductions, Ware took off his glasses and pointed to the inch-high stack of printouts on his desk.

"The good news is that I know where Social Impact Research Group's money came from. The bad news is that OPRR won't be able to get any of it."

"Why not?" Romy said.

"Because its ultimate source was the Department of Defense."

"Knew it!" Romy said, clapping her hands once. "Just like SOG—military bucks laundered through an innocent-sounding subagency. Any indication where the money went after it was cleared through SIRG?"

"Hell," Patrick said, "we know damn well—" But a quick look from Romy shut him up.

Right. They both suspected that the money had marched through a parade of holding companies until it reached Manassas Ventures, which used it to fund the nascent SimGen. But Milton Ware knew nothing of this.

"We know it wasn't anything legit," Romy said, jumping in to cover for him. "Otherwise they would have been more open about the funding."

"I don't see why it matters," Ware said. "It doesn't exist anymore. No trace of it in anyone's budget anymore."

Patrick leaned back and thought a moment. They knew SIRG was still active—Daniel Palmer had said the name before his speech center blew a fuse. But where was it getting its funding now? The path to the answer might not lie with government agencies but with people. He'd seen it happen time and again during his labor relations practice: certain shady characters, on both the labor and management sides, would be found out and sent packing, only to pop up in another company or union local the following year.

"SIRG might be operating under a different name," he said, "but I bet the personnel are the same. Any idea who headed SIRG?"

Ware leaned forward and put on his glasses. "Yes. I remember coming across that somewhere . . ." He began shuffling through his printouts. "Here it is: the director was a Lieutenant Colonel Conrad Landon."

"And where is he now?"

"Easy enough to find out." Ware turned to his computer. After a number of flamenco bursts on his keyboard, he leaned closer to the screen and said, "Conrad Landon retired as a full bird colonel."

"Damn. When?"

Ware stared at the monitor. "The same year the funding died."

"What a surprise," Romy murmured.

Patrick leaned across the desk for a peek at Ware's screen. "Any hint at where he might—?"

The picture of Landon startled him. Something familiar about the man in the grainy, black-and-white personnel-file photo.

"What's up?" Romy said.

"Nothing. I just—" And then he knew. Add a few decades, enough to whiten the hair and deeply line the face, and Patrick recognized him. "Nothing." Repressing a shout of triumph, he rose and extended his hand across the desk. Had to get out of here, had to talk to Romy alone before he exploded. "Nice meeting you, Mr. Ware. I've got to run. Romy, could you show me out?"

He fairly pulled her out of her seat and propelled her ahead of him down the hall.

"What is it?" she said.

"Where can we talk?"

"My office is—"

"Might be bugged." He saw the elevators ahead. "Back to our mobile conversation pit."

He pressed both the UP and DOWN buttons. The upward bound car arrived first, carrying four people. He let it go. The downward was empty. Perfect. He dragged Romy inside, jabbed the button for the lobby. As soon as the doors closed . . .

"Remember when we had our little face-to-face in my office with the Manassas Ventures lawyers?" he said, his tongue all but tripping over the words in his rush to get them out before someone else entered the car. "And remember how I followed them downstairs to their limo, hoping to find someone like Mercer Sinclair sitting in the back?"

She frowned. "Vaguely."

"But it turned out to be someone I'd never seen before. Well, I've just seen him again. The man in the back seat was Conrad Landon, former Army colonel, and former director of SIRG. Maybe not so former. I'll bet SIRG never went away and he's still calling the shots. Find this Conrad Landon and we'll find SIRG."

3

NEWARK, NJ

Something's not right, Zero thought with a pang of unease. We're missing something.

He sat next to Tome in the rear seat of the van as it bounced over the rough pavement of Newark's dark back streets toward the sim quarters Portero had led him to last night. Not quite 6:00 P.M. yet but the sun was long gone and icy night had taken command.

Tome was dressed like the worker sims, but he'd been equipped with a PCA. The plan was to drop him off where he could sneak into the building and mix with the other sims. Zero was confident that Tome's gentle nature and above-average intelligence would gain him the respect and confidence of the other sims, enough so that one of them would trust him with Meerm's whereabouts. When he found out, he'd press the preset speed-dial number and they'd pick him up.

Zero sighed. Not a perfect plan. It hinged entirely on the assumption that the sim laborers knew where Meerm was hiding.

His face itched under the ski mask; he'd traded tinted glasses for the ultra darks he usually wore, but they still impaired his vision. He wished he could pull everything off and ride along like a normal human being. But then, he wasn't a normal human being.

Just ahead of him, Patrick and Romy were a pair of silhouettes in the front seat.

"You two have done wonderful work," Zero said. "You make a great team."

"We do, don't we," Patrick said from behind the wheel.

Zero watched them glance at each other and smile. He could sense the growing bond between him. And as much as it made him ache to see Romy with Patrick, he knew it was for the best. Despite their surface differences, Zero sensed that they complemented each other on the deeper levels where it really counted.

He steered his thoughts away from Romy and toward what she and Patrick had uncovered today.

"We now have an ironclad chain of evidence. It doesn't take a handwriting expert to decipher the signature on Alice Fredericks's Manassas Ventures check as 'Conrad Landon.' That draws a direct line from the Department of Defense to SimGen."

"It's not something that will hold up in a court of law," Patrick said. "Off the top of my head I can think of half a dozen grounds for preventing it from being admitted as evidence. But in the court of public opinion, it's a hydrogen bomb."

"Assuming the public gives a damn," Romy said.

Patrick nodded. "Oh, they'll care all right. We lay it out clear and simple for them. We show how SimGen's early financing was public money: from Manassas Ventures which got it from SIRG which got it from the Department of Defense. The obvious question then is: Why? What did the D-o-D get in return? So we'll explain how Manassas leases trucks in Idaho that show up on the SimGen campus, transporting cargo back and forth, cargo that no one's allowed to see. But we've seen it, and that's when we show them Kek. When we reveal that Kek was found in Idaho, they'll be able to connect the last dots themselves: SimGen is producing hybrid simian soldiers for the Department of Defense to use in black ops or guerrilla operations. When the public learns that SimGen has been turning normally harmless creatures into man-killers, they'll care. They'll care like crazy. SimGen's dirty little secret will finally be out in the open for all to see, and that will be the beginning of the end of SimGen."

Zero had been listening to Patrick, but someone else's words had been echoing through his brain at the same time.

You have no idea what you're getting into, the forces you'll be setting in motion . . . they'll crush you.

"No comment back there?" Patrick said.

"As I told you: wonderful work."

But still that uneasy feeling plagued Zero. Was this the danger Ellis had warned him about? He could see now why the people behind SimGen were so ruthless when it came to protecting the company.

So he added, "Now we know why SIRG's funding was cut off: it didn't need any more. With all the SimGen stock it holds in Manassas Ventures, SIRG is a financially independent organization. Which means we've got to be more careful than ever."

"Right," Patrick said. "More than careers and reputations hang in the balance should their little operation be exposed. Billions of bucks are at stake."

Romy half turned in her seat. "Which raises a scary question: If SIRG has its own billions to finance its operations, who does it answer to?"

"No one with a conscience, that's for sure. Maybe someone high up in the Pentagon, maybe only Conrad Landon himself."

"I think we can count on SIRG to do whatever it deems necessary to protect its investment," Zero told them. "That's why, if we're going to bring SimGen down, I'd prefer to find a way that keeps you two out of the spotlight."

"Which is why we're heading to Newark, I assume."

"Exactly. I think it will be safer for all concerned if we let Meerm and her baby bring down SimGen."

"But that puts the child in jeopardy," Romy said.

"No more so than now. Meerm's baby is just as much a threat to SimGen dead as it is alive. Its half-human, half-sim DNA will tell the whole story, a story that, unlike the money trail you've discovered, can't be denied or stone-walled or spun into something with no resemblance to the truth. That baby is a slam dunk."

"Then it's all on our buddy Tome."

"Yes, Mist Sulliman," Tome said from his seat beside Zero. "Tome ready help."

"I know you are," Zero said softly.

Now Romy looked back at him from the front seat. "Zero, I've been around you long enough to know when you're holding something back. What aren't you telling us?"

So many things . . . but right now Ellis Sinclair's words continued to haunt him, especially his warning about the fallout from what they might uncover.

Things that will hurt me personally, and devastate other, more innocent, parties. Things that no one will want to hear. And don't think you'll come through unscathed, either.

That last part had been particularly unsettling, but not as jarring as his final warning about what they might find.

Some of it is sensitive. And some of it is . . . unspeakable.

Zero couldn't allow Romy and Patrick even a hint of his connection to Ellis, but perhaps he could hint at the man's warnings.

"It's not so much holding back as a feeling that there's something more behind all this, something we're missing."

"Like what?" Patrick said. "SIRG is the bastard child SimGen's been hiding in its basement. That's enough, don't you think?"

"I suppose so."

But he remained dissatisfied and uneasy. What had they missed?

Zero shook off the worries as he spotted a street sign.

"We're getting close."

"Another scenic neighborhood," Patrick said. "The Bronx, East New York, Alphabet City, and now Newark. Where next? Beirut?"

Zero had to admit that Patrick had a point. Low-rent businesses, abandoned, graffito-crusted buildings, stripped skeletons of cars lining the street . . . but just the kind of low-rent neighborhood someone would pick to house sim laborers.

"It's to the right up ahead," he told Patrick, "but don't make the turn. Cruise through the intersection and everyone keep an eye out for surveillance teams."

"You think Portero's watching the place?" Romy said.

"Count on it."

They made a couple of passes through the immediate area, and along the way spotted four occupied sedans. The first, with a pair of men slouched in the front seat, was parked across the street from the front door of the building; a single occupant in each of the other three; two of those were situated on the streets that flanked the sim building, the last sitting opposite a narrow alley that appeared to lead toward the rear of the building.

Patrick pulled into the curb two blocks away and stopped under a dead streetlight. Ahead and to the right, the light over the front door of the sim crib glowed like a star in the darkness.

"This looks too risky, Zero," he said. "Tome's not going in."

"Tome can go," said the sim.

"Uh-uh," Patrick said, shaking his head, and Zero could sense his resolve turning to stone. "I won't allow it."

Zero sighed. "I agree."

He couldn't see any way of slipping Tome past Portero's surveillance.

"Damn." Zero made a fist. "I anticipated two teams, not four."

"Might be five—one roving. I swear we passed the same green Taurus twice."

Just then a school bus rumbled past and pulled to a stop before the sim building. As Zero watched it disgorge its crew of sim laborers, he had an idea.

"All right," he said. "Let's head back."

Romy said, "We're not giving up already, are we?"

"Not a chance. Just changing tactics. And I promise you, by this time tomorrow night Tome will be safely inside that building, and no one will be the wiser."

"Tomorrow's Saturday," Patrick said. "Will the sims be working?"

"Of course. They work *every* day. 'Weekend' has no meaning for a sim."

As they drove back Zero reviewed all they'd learned about SIRG and Manassas. He knew Ellis had been sincere when he'd warned him against digging too deep. Well, they'd dug, and dug deep. They'd discovered a dirty little secret, yes, but nothing "unspeakable."

And that worried Zero.

4

Meerm ver hungry. Drink rainwater some but no food all day. Ver fraid go out. Stay behind metal door till dark. Still fraid go out. Tummy hurt so ver bad. And belly kick-kick-kick all day.

Must go out. Push metal door. Go *skeek* ver loud. But no mans come.

Meerm go out. Smell food, yum-yum food smell. Drool smell. From other side fence.

Meerm creep to fence, peek through. See gold arch. Go under fence, cross street, go sticker bush, come other fence. See Mickey-D! Mickey-D! But can't have. Meerm so sad.

Meerm see boy-mans come out Mickey-D. Hold black bag, throw in big-big metal can. When boy-man go, Meerm squeeze through fence hole and go to can. Top ver high but Meerm climb up and fall inside. Many bag here. Meerm rip one. Yum-yum food smell come out. Meerm reach inside, find much food, half-eat, all mixy-mixy. Meerm not care. Is yum-yum.

Ouch. Hand hurt. Meerm look. See rats. Rat want food too. Bite Meerm. Meerm throw food at rat. Plenty food here. Food for all.

Meerm shove food into mouth fast can. Chew-chew-chew. So good. Meerm not sad now. Still hurt but hunger go. Good. For now.

5

MINEOLA, NY

DECEMBER 22

Romy had called first thing in the morning and told Patrick to pick her up. They had a doctor's appointment, she said.

After she'd settled herself in the car she explained that the appointment was with an obstetrician. That had taken him aback until she explained that it was Dr. Cannon, and they were visiting her to discuss Alice Fredericks.

Betsy Cannon worked out of a small office attached to her home, a modest two-story colonial on a tree-lined street in Mineola. She'd already made her hospital rounds; her office hours didn't start until 1:00 P.M. so they had plenty of time. Looking casual in a loose turtleneck sweater and khaki slacks, she served them coffee and Entenmann's crumb cake in her roomy kitchen.

"Is there a Mr. Dr. Cannon?" Patrick whispered as Betsy stepped out of the room to take a call from the hospital.

Romy shook her head. "No. Never was, and I doubt there ever will be, if you get my drift."

"No kidding?" Patrick said. "Never would have guessed."

Betsy returned then and seated herself on the far side of the kitchen table. "You wanted to ask me about this Fredericks woman?"

"Yes," Romy said. "Her story is such a mishmash of fact and fiction, we were hoping you'd be able to separate the two."

Patrick appreciated the "we." It hadn't even occurred to him to run the story past Dr. Cannon. And considering that she'd spent years as head of sim obstetrics for SimGen, he was disappointed with himself for not thinking of it first.

Betsy smiled. "Well, I'll be glad to try. I can explain parts of her story—especially the ones about being abducted and impregnated by space aliens—with one word: psychosis."

Patrick said, "That's pretty strong, isn't it?"

"She's delusional, she has a persistent break with reality that interferes with her day-to-day functioning. That behavior fits the diagnosis. The sad thing is, she can be easily helped. The right medications could restore her neurochemicals to proper balance and she'd come back to the real world."

"Neurochemicals," Romy murmured. "They'll get you every time."

Patrick shot her a questioning glance but she only shrugged and waved it off.

"Delusional or not," he said, getting back on track, "she gave us the check. And unless I'm delusional too, it looks pretty real."

Betsy smiled. "I'm sure it is. And you'll notice I didn't include the part about her giving birth to a sim as one of her delusions."

"You don't really think . . . ," Romy said, frowning. She glanced at Patrick. "I mean, how . . . ?"

"It's obvious when you think about it," Betsy told her. "Human surrogate mothers were a necessity in the early stages of the sim breeding process."

Romy's face twisted in revulsion. "Why on earth—?"

"Because sims are considerably larger than chimps. A small chimpanzee uterus couldn't carry a sim baby to term, but a human uterus would have no problem."

Patrick was dazed. "So part of what she's saying might be true?"

"Perhaps not about birthing the very first sim, but . . . how old is she?"

"Forty-seven—she says."

Betsy nodded. "Then she's about the right age. Think about the implantation process—flat on her back on a table, bright lights overhead, surrounded by doctors in caps, masks, and goggles as they insert an in-vitro–fertilized ovum into her uterus. You can see how an unbalanced mind might later reinterpret this as an alien abduction."

"But to go through all that for five thousand dollars?"

"I'm sure it was more like fifty thousand: say, five in advance, then five every month until delivery. The process is no different from being a surrogate mother for a human couple."

"Except that at the end you don't deliver a human baby," Romy said.

Betsy nodded. "Right. And perhaps that unbalanced an already fragile mind."

"Which makes her one more casualty left in SimGen's wake," Romy said.

"But she couldn't have been the only one," Patrick said. "How come we haven't heard about this before?"

Betsy shrugged. "I'm sure there were many human surrogate mothers before SimGen developed its breeding stock. I'm also sure they signed non-disclosure agreements with stiff penalties."

"Not exactly the sort of thing I'd want to trumpet from the rooftops anyway," Romy added.

Patrick leaned back, thinking. He had a sense that something important had slipped past him here, something Betsy had said a moment ago.

A small chimpanzee uterus couldn't carry a sim baby to term, but a human uterus would have no problem.

And then he knew.

"Oh, Christ! Meerm is carrying a half-human, half-sim baby. Won't it grow too big—?"

"Too big for her to carry full term?" Betsy said. "Absolutely. Normal sim gestation is eight months, but we don't know when Meerm conceived, so we don't know her due date. That's why you have to find her. If she goes into premature labor while she's in hiding, the baby won't survive. If she's too far along the baby will be too big for a vaginal delivery, which means she'll need a cesarean."

"And if she doesn't get one?" Romy asked, and Patrick could tell from her expression that she didn't want to hear the answer.

"We'll lose both of them."

Romy closed her eyes for a heartbeat or two, then stared at Patrick. "We've *got* to find her."

"Tome is set to go tonight."

Zero had called Patrick this morning to tell him he'd gone back to Newark before dawn and followed the sim bus into Manhattan. He saw where it dropped off the sims at a Harlem sweatshop. Assuming pick-up would be at the same spot, the new plan was to put Tome on line with the workers as they boarded the bus.

"If Tome gets the job done tonight, we could be bringing Meerm here tomorrow morning."

Betsy smiled and raised her coffee cup in a sort of toast. "I'll be waiting."

6

NEWARK, NJ

Meerm hide in cold dark place and hurt. Hurt so ver bad. Tummy go kick-kick-kick. Was food bad? Meerm not think. Not feel sick tummy, just hurt tummy. Hurt-hurt-hurt, then stop. Then hurt-hurt-hurt again, then stop.

Now hurt stop again. Meerm close eyes and breathe. So good when hurt stop.

What this? Leg feel wet. Meerm touch. Yes, wet and warm. Put wet from leg near light from steel door crack. Red wet. Blood? Where blood come? From inside? How come from inside?

Now Meerm cry. Don't want bleed. Don't want die. What wrong Meerm?

7

MANHATTAN

Tome keep head down and walk far back in bus like Mist Sulliman say do. Sit seat and wait. Other sim come, say, "My seat, my seat."

Tome stand wait for bus move, then find other seat.

"Who you?" say she-sim next Tome. "You not shop sim."

Tome remember what Mist Sulliman tell him say. "Yes, not shop sim. Just old sim looking for friend."

"Who friend?"

"Meerm."

Tome know not true, but Mist Sulliman tell say this.

She-sim say loud, "Beece! Beece! Come see old sim!"

Tome look and see he-sim come down aisle. This Beece big. Look down Tome.

"Why here old sim?"

"I am Tome. Look for Meerm. She friend."

Beece get mad face. "You lie! Bad mans send! You want hurt Meerm!"

"No! Good mans send. Friend all sim. Best friend sim have. Try to make sim union. Try—"

"What yooyun?"

Tome try tell but Beece not understand. So Tome tell Beece bout how Mist Sulliman hurt by bad mans, house burned by bad mans who hate sim.

Beece eyes ver wide. "House burn? Because help sims?"

All other sim who hear turn round, look Tome.

Tome say, "Yes! Good man! Best man. Now want help Meerm. Save her from bad mans. Also Meerm ver sick."

All sim nod. Yes, some say. Meerm ver sick.

"Good man help make better. Where Tome find Meerm?"

Beece not speak.

She-sim next Tome say, "Beece not know. No sim know."

No sim speak long time. Tome ver sad. Want help Mist Sulliman but fail. Touch phone in pocket. Must call and tell.

Then Beece say, "Beece know. Not know exact, but can help." Beece look hard Tome. "Must tell true. Must help Meerm."

"Tome help Meerm." So ver happy now. "Tome help good."

8

"Get ready," Zero murmured from the darkness behind her as the school bus pulled to a stop before the sim crib.

Romy raised her binoculars and focused on the front door. Patrick had parked the van in the same spot as last night. He sat beside her behind the wheel, training his own set of glasses on the door, and she knew Zero had his pair aimed between them. They had to know whether or not Tome got off the bus, and all agreed that three sets of eyes were better than one.

Romy licked her lips. Her fingers felt slick against the black matte finish of the binocular barrels. This was the night when it all could come together, when all her years of effort, when everything she'd worked for would come to fruition . . .

Or go up in smoke.

She took a breath. No smoke. This was going to work.

No movement yet. She noticed Patrick lowering his glasses.

He let out a long, slow breath, as if he'd been holding it. "What if somebody spots him and gets suspicious?" he said.

"No reason they should," Zero said. "Tome's dressed just like the other sims. And besides, the surveillance teams are looking for a pregnant female."

"But what about their warden or whatever you call the guy inside—what if he counts one extra and turns him over to the guys outside. I saw how they cut up those other sims."

Romy stared at Patrick. Was that a catch in his voice? He was really worried—not about blowing their chance to find Meerm, but about Tome being hurt. Same as last night when he'd refused to let Tome near the building.

She felt a burst of warmth for him. What a change from the hard case she'd met just a few months ago. She laid a gentle hand on his arm.

"We won't let anything happen to Tome. You know that."

"Better not," he said, staring straight ahead. "He's my roomie, you know."

"I know. And I—"

"There they are," Zero said and the three of them trained their glasses on the small patch of sidewalk between the bus and the front door.

Romy wished there were more light as the sims trooped out in ones and pairs. She fine-tuned the focus on her binocs, training her gaze on their faces. Since they all were dressed in identical coveralls, only the faces would tell. She watched one after another swim through her field of vision in a seemingly endless stream, and then suddenly the parade was over.

"I didn't see him," Romy said.

Neither had Zero or Patrick.

"Do you think this means what it's supposed to mean?" Patrick whispered.

Romy felt her heart rate kick up. The plan was for Tome to enter the sim dorm if he hadn't learned Meerm's whereabouts by the time the bus arrived. If he'd been successful, he was to hide on the bus until the driver parked it down the street, then sneak out and call for pick-up.

"I hope so," she said.

Patrick reached for the ignition but Zero stopped him.

"Wait till we hear from him. We're much less conspicuous sitting still."

And so they waited. And waited.

"Why doesn't he call?" Patrick said, tapping the steering wheel none too gently. "Something's wrong."

Romy prayed not.

Tome lost.

Turn round and round in dark but not know where is.

Tome bad sim. Old fool sim. Not listen Mist Sulliman. Not do what told. Mist Sulliman say call but Tome not. Fool Tome wait driver go, then open bus window. Climb through, drop ground. Tome not call like Mist Sulliman say. Fool Tome go find Meerm self. Show Mist Sulliman can find. Bring back Meerm. Make Mist Sulliman proud.

Tome do bad thing. Wait by bus. See no car. Run cross street. Hide shadow. Try remember what Beece say. Wish Beece knew better where Meerm hide. Only know, "Left side home building. Many, many turn go see Mickey-D gold arch light over fence. Look black metal door. Red writing door. Meerm inside."

Tome go, make many many turn. No see Mickey-D. No see black metal door. Now Tome lost in ver dark place.

Tome keep walk. Hear car noise. Many car. See light. Go to and find big street. Many light and car. And there Mickey-D. Tome find! Tome not bad sim! Not fool!

But where steel door? Tome look-look but no see door, no red writing. Tome fail. Ver sad again. Pull out phone, remember what Mist Sulliman say: First press red button, wait for beep, then press 9 button, then press green button.

Tome hope Mist Sulliman not mad and say no more friend with Tome. That make Tome ver sad.

"Yes!" Patrick cried as his PCA chirped.

Romy watched him jab the SEND button and crush the phone against his ear. He'd been sitting there with it clutched in his hand, thumb poised over the buttons like a mad bomber with a detonator.

"Tome!" he cried. "You're all right?" He turned and nodded to Romy and Zero.

Romy let out a sigh of relief. The last twenty-five minutes had been hell.

"No-no," Patrick was saying. "That's all right. As long as you're okay, it doesn't matter. Listen, you stay there but keep out of sight. We'll come by and get you." He closed the PCA and started the van.

"What happened?" Zero said.

"He thought he could find Meerm himself."

"Oh, God!" Romy said.

"I know, I know, it was foolish. But it's okay. We're picking him up at the McDonald's we passed back there on Springfield Avenue. Now nobody get on his case, okay? He was just trying—"

"But this means he found out where Meerm is."

Patrick nodded, with no little pride in his grin. "That he did. And if we can decipher the directions he got, we'll have Meerm on her way to Dr. Cannon before you know it."

Romy smiled, sharing his infectious optimism, allowing herself to hope.

Lister's voice grated through the encrypted phone line. "Still no sign of that damned monkey?"

Damned monkey was right. Double-damned monkey. Luca leaned back in his sofa, put his feet up on the old coffee table, and scratched his throat. His shaver had been a little dull this morning and it had irritated his skin, but not as much as the events of the past few days were irritating his gut. How many places could a pregnant sim hide?

"Not a trace."

Behind him, in the kitchen, he could hear Maria humming as she cooked up their Saturday night feast. A spicy aroma wafted around him, making his mouth water.

"Shit," Lister said. "I'm getting lots of questions about all the men we're tying up. Let me get this straight: You've got five cars and twelve men involved in this surveillance?"

"Correct: four cars stationary, one on patrol, with rotating twelve-hour shifts of six men each."

Suddenly Maria's face hovered above him, grinning as she dangled a glistening sliver of chicken over his lips. He opened his mouth and she dropped it in. Delicious. He blew her a kiss and she swayed back to the kitchen.

Damn, he was going to miss her.

"And you think that's the way to go?"

Luca chewed and swallowed quickly. "That's what all our sim experts advise. They say she's got to eat, so that means if we don't catch her wandering around or trying to sneak back into the sim crib, we'll find another sim sneaking out to bring her food."

"Makes sense to me, but upstairs is complaining about the manpower commitment."

"It's not as if these guys have anything better to keep them busy."

"Oh, but very soon they will. Guillotine is a go."

Luca stiffened. "When?"

"Can't say more now. Maybe in person."

Luca understood. Even a hard-encrypted phone wasn't secure enough for a conversation about Operation Guillotine. Because Guillotine was what SIRG was all about, and the neck scheduled to be placed under that blade was Aazim Saad's.

Al Qaeda was gone, but its goals and methods lived on in various smaller offshoots. The most active was the Malaysian Mujahideen led by Aazim Saad.

One of his men had ratted out the Omani terrorist kingpin, and his headquarters had been traced to a rubber plantation in Borneo. Operation Guillotine would drop three commando teams of specially trained mandrilla sims into the surrounding jungle and have them raid the compound, killing any-

thing that moved. All their gear—weapons, clothing, communications—
would be foreign-made to obscure their point of origin. Even if one were
captured alive, it couldn't give anything away, because it wouldn't know anything, and couldn't tell if it did. The Malaysian Mujahideen would be wiped
out, and no one would know by whom.

This had been the Old Man's dream: an anonymous strike force that
could operate with greater efficiency and ferocity than any human equivalent.
All SIRG had needed was clearance from the Pentagon to proceed. Now they
had it. And if Guillotine was a success, Conrad Landon would be the toast
of a very small, very elite inner circle in the Department of Defense.

Luca had seen the mandrillas in training. Their ferocity awed him. They
knew no fear, and gave no quarter. Their downside was the difficulty con-
trolling them, and stopping them once they got started. Heaven help any
innocent bystanders near the Saad compound.

"All I can say," Lister said, "is that some of those surveillance men are
going to be needed back in Idaho for the launch."

"I don't think I'll need much more time. It's been only forty-eight hours.
She can't go—"

His PCA rang. "Just a sec. That's from the surveillance team." He put
Lister on hold, snatched up the phone, and recognized Snyder's voice.

"Guess what just happened?"

"What?" Please, Luca thought. Nothing bad. Don't tell me anyone's dead.

But Snyder sounded pleased with himself; almost happy.

"I'm pulling up to the drive-thru window of this McDonald's near the
crib to get coffees for the guys when I see this beat-up old van with New
York tags pull into the lot. And I'm thinking, you know, there's a lot of dirty
old white vans with New York plates, but maybe this is the one I spotted in
Brooklyn, you know, when Palmer and Jackson disappeared from that op.
And I was wishing I had the tag number handy when—"

"Get to the goddamn point!"

"Okay, okay. So I'm watching the van and I see the rear door swing open.
No big deal, but then this sim hops out of the bushes and jumps inside."

The PCA's seams let out a faint squeak as Luca's grip tightened. "Was it
her?"

"Nah. This was a skinny male, but you could tell from his coveralls he's
from the crib."

"He's leading them to her! Where are they now?"

"About twenty-five yards ahead of me, heading back toward the crib."

"Don't lose them. You hear me, Snyder? Do . . . not . . . lose them. And don't let them spot you either. You spook them, they'll take off."

"Maybe I should contact the others so we can tag team them on the tail."

"Good idea. No, wait."

Luca's mind raced over the possibilities. These people had fooled him before. Was it sheer luck that Snyder spotted the sim jumping into the van, or was he *supposed* to see it? The expected response was to mobilize the entire surveillance team, which would leave the sim crib unguarded. Could that be their real purpose?

"Do it this way. Lowery and Stritch have the front door. While Lowery takes the car to back you up, tell Stritch to go inside and find out from that jerk Morales which of his sims is missing. If the sim from the van somehow makes it back to the crib, I want to know which one it is."

"Got it," Snyder said.

"I'm on my way over now. I can't emphasize how important this is, Snyder. Don't blow it."

He returned to Lister. "Gotta go. Tell the folks upstairs our 'big manpower commitment' just paid off."

He ended the call without waiting for a response. He told Maria not to wait up as he rushed for the door.

"You did a good job, Tome," Romy said, feeling for the agitated old sim.

Tome sat hunched on a rear seat of the van, distraught that he'd failed to find Meerm. Romy had moved out of the front. She and Zero flanked him.

"Yes," Zero added. "An excellent job. But now tell us again what Beece said. Try to remember exactly."

Romy listened closely to Tome's recitation of Beece's fractured directions to Meerm's hiding place, trying to fathom a way to put them to practical use.

And then from the front seat Patrick said, "I think we've got trouble."

Zero leaned forward. "What's wrong?"

"A green Taurus has been following us since McDonald's."

Romy tensed. "You're sure?"

"He's hanging back, but I just made a couple of turns and he's still with us."

"Let's leave the neighborhood, then," Zero said. "Head for one of the highways—22, 78, doesn't matter, just so long as it takes us to the airport."

"Newark Airport?"

"It's a maze, and a traffic nightmare. If we can't lose them there, we never will."

"But what about Meerm?" Romy said.

Zero shook his head. "Too risky to look for her now. We'd lead them right to her."

Romy hung on as they bounced along. She saw a red, white, and blue TO 78 sign flash by and cried out, "There!"

"Damn!" Patrick said. "Missed it! Look for another."

Romy peered through the windshield. "Where are we?"

"Haven't a clue." Patrick shook his head. "Don't know a thing about Newark."

The buildings had fallen away behind them and now they were moving through a no-man's-land of junkyards and railroad tracks, bouncing along a rutted gravel path.

"The Taurus isn't pretending anymore," Patrick said, and Romy thought she detected a tremor in his voice. "He's getting closer. And there's another car behind him."

"He knows we've spotted him," Zero said. He moved to the rear doors and crouched among the overnight bags he'd told Romy and Patrick to bring. If they found Meerm, they wouldn't be going home. She watched him peer through a small, unpainted area of one of the windows. "Looks like he brought back-up along. I was afraid of this."

"He's getting closer!" Patrick called from the front.

Romy moved back beside Zero. "What do you think they'll do?"

"Try to stop us, find out who we are, maybe kill us. Except for Tome. They'll want to interrogate him."

Romy sensed a cold wave slip over her, just as it had last week when it had come time to dose the man called David Palmer with his own truth drug. As she felt her emotions crystallizing, falling one by one into deep-freeze hibernation, she reached into her shoulder bag and pulled out a .45 caliber HK semiautomatic. She worked the slide to chamber a shell.

"I don't think so," she said.

Zero's head swiveled to the pistol, then to her. "Where'd you get that?"

"From one of the two creeps who invaded my home."

"How long have you been carrying it?"

"Ever since two creeps invaded my home."

"He's riding my tail!" Patrick cried from the front.

Romy gestured with her HK toward the rear door. "Hold that open and we'll stop this right now."

Zero shook his head. "It may come to that, but let's try my way first." He opened a heavy-duty plastic cooler and reached inside.

"You were ready for something like this?"

"I try to be prepared for everything."

Despite the situation, she had to smile. "You must have been a great Boy Scout."

He looked at her again. "No. Never had the chance." His voice sounded sad. "But I think I would have loved it."

He came up with a red, softball-size object that jiggled in his gloved hand.

Romy stared at it. "A water balloon?"

"Not quite. Put your pistol away and get ready to open the door for me."

Romy didn't know what Zero was up to, but she'd learned to trust his judgment. And his preternatural calm bolstered her confidence. She stowed the pistol and unlatched the door.

Zero called toward the front: "Do we have any curves coming up, Patrick?"

"About thirty yards."

Zero turned to Romy. "Get ready. Five-four-three-two-one-open!"

Romy gave the door a shove. As soon as it swung open, revealing the green Taurus no more than half a dozen feet from their rear bumper, Zero launched the balloon with a gentle underhand toss.

Romy watched it wobble through the air and land on their pursuer's windshield—which then disappeared in a splatter of dark green paint.

The car swerved as the windshield wipers came on.

"Those won't help," Zero said. "Oil-based."

And then the van leaned to the right as it rounded a curve, but the Taurus kept going straight, bounding off the gravel roadway and ramming nose first into a deep ditch. It hung there, trunk skyward, steam boiling from under its crumpled hood.

She heard Patrick laugh. "What the hell?"

"Not in the clear yet," Zero said, staring out the rear door at the second car. He had another paint balloon in his hand. "Come on," he whispered. "Just a little closer."

But the second car, a dark blue Jeep, hung back. Obviously they'd seen what happened to the Taurus.

"Have to try something else," Zero said. He rummaged in the chest and came up with a plastic container. "Here. Toss these out."

Romy lifted the lid to find a couple of dozen steel objects that looked like jacks. But these were much bigger, and instead of six tips, these had only four, each ending in a sharp barbed point.

"What are—?"

"Road stars. Just toss them out. They're configured so that they always land with a point up."

Romy emptied the container, watched the Jeep roll over them, and waited for its tires to go flat.

"Hmmm," Zero said. "Must have self-sealing tires. The stars will chew them up eventually but we don't have time for that. They're probably calling for more back-up now."

He pulled two lengths of chain from the chest, each with a dozen or so road stars attached, and dropped them out the back.

Again Romy watched the Jeep run over them, but nothing happened.

"They didn't work."

"Just give them a few seconds longer. The chains will wrap themselves around an axle, and drag the stars through the rubber—"

Romy saw a puff of dust as the front left tire blew out.

"—tearing the tire to shreds."

The Jeep swerved on the gravel and then another tire blew. The van left it behind in the dark, eating dust.

"Back to that 78 sign, Patrick," Zero called, "and please don't miss it this time."

Romy gazed at Zero and tried to sort through the strange mix of emotions scattering through her at that moment. They were warm—no, they were hot—and if this wasn't love, it should be.

⌇⌇⌇

Luca thumbed the SEND button on his ringing PCA. It was Stritch.

"I'm in the crib now," he said. "Our buddy Benny here is in charge of forty-two sims, and that's how many I count."

"Count again. You made a mistake."

"I've counted three times already. There's forty-two sims here; not forty-three, not forty-one. Forty-two."

"Then he's lying about the number."

"That's what I thought so I made him show me his records. Sure enough: forty-two."

Portero growled and hung up. All sims accounted for? Then where did the sim in the van come from?

The PCA rang again. Snyder this time. His voice sounded strange . . . nasal.

"Give me some good news."

"We lost them."

Luca's car swerved when he heard the words and he didn't trust himself to drive. He pulled over and listened to Snyder's long-winded, jumbled, broken-nosed, ass-covering version of whatever really happened, blaming it on a guy in a ski mask or some such shit. When it was over Luca broke the connection and sat with his forehead resting on the steering wheel. For the first time in his adult life, Luca Portero wanted to cry.

9

NEWARK, NJ

DECEMBER 23

"All right," Zero said, peering through the pre-dawn light at the McDonald's four blocks ahead. "Let's stop here."

He sat with Tome and Kek in the rear of the van. Patrick had the wheel as usual, Romy at his side.

Zero yawned. Tired. They all were tired. And they should be. A long night that he, Romy, and Patrick had spent spray-painting the van. He'd had no way of finding a new one on such short notice, so now the old one sported a glossy black coat and New Jersey tags he'd picked from a pile of old plates he'd found in a Staten Island junkyard.

He glanced at his watch: 6:45 A.M. and still no sun. Not due to rise for another half hour. Newark hadn't risen yet either, most of it still asleep on this cold Sunday morning. He'd wrestled all night with the timing of his approach to Meerm. Assuming he could find her, it would be safer for all concerned to make contact under cover of darkness. But he was sure Meerm would be frightened of anyone she couldn't see. That necessitated a daylight approach, multiplying the risks of being spotted.

He stared at the McDonald's, Beece's key landmark. He'd told Tome he'd been able to see its golden arches over a fence near Meerm's hiding place. Beece had made no mention of crossing the avenue, which meant Meerm was hiding someplace behind the McDonald's.

A detailed aerial reconnaissance photo would have told him all he needed to know, but since he didn't have one of those, he'd have to proceed by trial and error.

"Okay," he told Patrick. "Let's make this first right up here and see if you can position us a couple of blocks behind the McDonald's. We'll work our way back toward it from there."

"Gotcha," Patrick said, and put the van in gear.

"Everyone keep an eye out for Portero's people."

"If you see a green Taurus," Romy said, grinning at Zero over her shoulder, "it won't be them."

Patrick laughed. "Right! I'll bet it'll be next week before anyone can see through that windshield again."

Zero grinned beneath his ski mask. Fortunately no shots had been traded. Romy's pistol last night had unsettled him. Their pursuers undoubtedly had seen Tome get into the van—why else would they have followed?—and so Zero guessed they'd want the sim alive as a lead to Meerm. He'd figured— hoped was more like it—that they wouldn't fire unless fired upon. He was glad he'd brought along some alternative weaponry.

However, if they ran into any of Portero's men today, they'd be edgy, might shoot first and worry later about who they hit. That was why he'd brought Kek along. He glanced back at the gorilla-mandrill hybrid crouched by the rear door. He wore black coveralls cinched with the belt that held his Special Forces knife. His snout was a cool blue and he seemed relaxed, but Zero knew if provoked he could explode into violence in the blink of an eye.

As Zero turned forward again, he caught Romy staring at him, her eyes almost luminous in the dimness. She'd been doing that a lot since their time together in the rear of the van last night. He sensed it was more than combat bonding, feared it might be infatuation. That sort of look from Romy should have made him giddy, but instead it weighed on Zero. A look was the limit, the most he could ever hope for.

After zigzagging through the narrow streets, Patrick stopped the van by

the mouth of an alley running between a rundown tenement and an abandoned brick building that might have been a factory once. Pigeons clustered
in its broken window frames, cooing and watching.

"Unless my sense of direction is completely out of whack," Patrick said,
pointing down the alley, "the McDonald's is two blocks that-a-way."

"All right then, Tome," Zero said. "It's up to you and me now. Let's go
find Meerm."

The old sim looked at Patrick and Zero could sense the bond between
them. Patrick nodded. "Go ahead, Tome. You can do it."

"Yes, Mist Sulliman. Tome try best."

Patrick rolled down his window and checked the street. "All clear."

Zero pushed open a rear door and hopped down. As soon as Tome was
out he started to push it closed and found Romy staring at him again.

"Be careful," she said.

Zero could only nod.

He hurried Tome off the sidewalk and into the narrow alley. As they
moved through the litter and the rubble, their breath steaming in the frigid
air, Zero glanced up and was surprised to see a number of clotheslines stretching above them; one sported a bra and a very large set of white panties.
Apparently the tenement wasn't as deserted as it looked.

"If you were Meerm," Zero said to Tome, keeping his voice low, "and you
were in here and frightened, and looking for a place to hide, which way would
you go?"

"Tome not Meerm."

"Yes, but imagine you were."

"What is 'magine?"

How to explain that? Maybe Tome wasn't capable of imagining. But he'd
imagined starting a sim union, hadn't he. Imagining a solution to a problem,
though, wasn't the same as pretending to be someone else.

But if I can do it, why can't Tome?

"We can talk about imagining later," Zero told him. "Right now we need
to find a spot where we can see the golden arches over a fence, isn't that
what Beece said?"

"Yes. Say Meerm in metal door with red write."

A metal door with red writing . . . that was their best clue. If they had a
big search party, and unlimited time, and could comb the area openly without
fear of being attacked, Zero had no doubt they'd find Meerm before the
morning was out. But with just him and Tome . . .

They arrived in a small quadrangular courtyard that once must have served as a dump for the surrounding buildings. No fence, no McDonald's arches, no metal door with red writing.

They moved on into another alley, misaligned with the one they'd just left. They were halfway to the next street when Zero noticed a low passage, five feet high at most, cutting away through the wall of the building to their left. He stooped and saw daylight at the far end.

"Did Beece mention anything about a tunnel?"

Tome shook his head. "No, Mist Zero."

"Okay, then." He was about to turn away when it occurred to him to check it out. They were here. Foolish not to take a look.

"Tome, we should see what's on the other end of that tunnel. Since you're smaller, you're elected. Hurry though and take a quick look. If you see anything that might be what we're looking for, I'll follow you."

The old sim nodded and ducked into the tunnel. Zero watched his silhouette dwindle toward the far end until he stepped into the light. He moved away from the opening, leaving Zero staring at an empty square of light, and then suddenly he was there again, hurrying back.

"Mist Zero!" Tome cried, his voice squeaking with excitement. "Is here! Metal door and fence and red write!"

Zero didn't wait to hear if the McDonald's arches were visible.

"Let's go!"

Bent in a deep crouch, he splashed through the wet tunnel in Tome's wake and emerged into a small vacant lot. A fenced vacant lot, with the McDonald's arches visible between the buildings across the street. And directly across the lot, an abandoned brick warehouse with a rusty metal door embedded in its flank, a door labeled with a warning in faded red letters. At the rear of the lot was the open end of an alley, probably how Beece had arrived.

They'd found it. Now they had to hope she hadn't moved to a new hiding place. Please, let her still be there.

"All right, Tome. Remember: We have to be calm, we have to speak softly. You'll do the talking as we planned, okay?"

Tome nodded. "Tome talk good."

Zero approached the door with measured steps, making enough noise so that anyone on the other side would hear their approach and not be taken completely by surprise when the door opened. He stopped outside it, waited a heartbeat or two, then gripped the door's upper corner and pulled.

The hinges squealed horribly as it swung open. Inside lay a pool of night, untouched by the dawn. Zero listened but heard no movement within.

As rehearsed, Tome leaned inside and said, "Meerm? This Tome. Friend sim. Friend Beece. Tome bring friend help Meerm."

Silence.

She's gone, Zero thought.

And then, echoing from within, a soft whimper.

"Do you think they're all right?" Romy said as she sat in the passenger seat and stared down the alley.

"They've only been gone a few minutes," Patrick replied.

Romy knew that, but couldn't quell her dark sense of foreboding.

"I should have gone with them."

"No, you shouldn't have. And you know why."

Romy glanced at Patrick. He seemed testy this morning. Lack of sleep, maybe. But she knew what he meant: They'd all agreed that a group of humans would spook Meerm.

"Well, then, I should have gone with Tome instead of Zero. I'm female. If Tome can't talk her out, I think a female human would be a lot less threatening than a male."

Patrick looked at her. "You could be right. In fact, that makes sense—a hell of a lot more sense than sending a guy in a ski mask. I must be overtired. I should have thought of that myself. Hell, why didn't you bring this up before?"

"I did. But Zero was dead set on going himself. Wouldn't consider anyone else."

"Doesn't make sense. You've known him longer than I have, but he doesn't strike me as the my-way-or-the-highway sort."

"He's not. He'll go with the best idea, no matter who comes up with it. But he wasn't budging on this."

"Must have his reasons."

"I'm sure he does. And after last night, I'm more than willing to defer to his judgment." She caught Patrick rolling his eyes. "What?"

"Nothing."

"No, tell me."

"I thought you were going to start gushing again."

"Gush?" She felt a sting of embarrassment, knew what he was talking about, but couldn't bring herself to admit it. "About what? I don't gush about anything."

"You do about Zero. You haven't been able to stop yakking about last night."

Was it that obvious? She'd been so taken by Zero's aplomb in handling their pursuers—was still impressed, couldn't stop thinking about it. He could have got those two cars off their tail by pulling out a bazooka and blowing them both to smithereens. Effective but . . . lacking something. Instead he'd operated like a skilled surgeon, not cutting too deep or too long, inflicting no more damage than necessary to get the job done. And she loved that.

Now more than ever she felt she had to know who Zero was. She needed to see the face, look into the eyes of this man who did what he did, not just last night, but every day of his life. That was the man for her.

She looked at Patrick. Another good man, who managed to surprise her time and again. But he wasn't Zero. There was no one else in the world like Zero.

"Sorry if I've been boring you," she said. "But if you could have seen—"

A growl from Kek, squatting in the darkness behind them. Patrick held up his hand for silence and cocked his head toward the van's oversized side view mirror.

"Oh, shit. We've got trouble!"

Romy tensed and reached into her bag for her pistol. "Like what?"

"Like a late model Impala coming this way, looking like it's got no particular place to go."

She looked down the alley. No sign of Zero and Tome returning yet. Good.

"Duck down. Maybe they'll just drive by if it looks empty."

"Too late. I'm sure they spotted me in my side mirror."

"All right then," she said, her thoughts accelerating. "Let's pretend we're having a fight." She raised her voice and gestured angrily. "You worthless lump of protoplasm! What good are you? Tell me that! What good are you?"

"Protoplasm?" Patrick said.

"The window's closed," she told him. "Doesn't matter what we say; they won't be able to make out the words anyway, but we've got to *look* like we're going at it."

"Yeah?" Patrick cried, getting into it. "Is that what you think of me? *Protoplasm?* Hey, you're nothing but a . . . a . . . ." He lowered his voice. "What's lower than protoplasm?"

"I don't know," she whispered as she shrugged. "Try mitochondria."

"Right!" he shouted, shaking his fist in the air between them. "That's what you are! A mitochondria! Just a lousy, no-good, two-bit mitochondria!"

The Impala slowed as it passed, and Romy saw the passenger's pale face turned their way, his flat gray eyes staring into the van's cab, past Patrick's turned back, at her face. She hoped she looked angry enough.

Romy slammed the dashboard with her fist. "Isn't that typical! You don't even know the word! The singular is mitochondr*ion*, you moron!"

The Chevy pulled ahead and looked like it was moving on, but then it stopped.

Kek let out another growl. Romy glanced back and noticed the mandrilla's snout had turned a bright red.

"Easy, Kek," Romy cooed. "Just stay put."

But as the Impala's passenger door swung open, so did one of the van's rear doors.

"Stay, Kek!" Patrick said. "I can talk us out of—" The rear door closed softly. "What's he going to do?"

"Nothing!" Romy shouted, motioning to him to keep up the faux fight. "Not unless he has to! And if we play this right, he won't have to!"

Patrick matched her volume. "How, goddamnit?"

The passenger, a fortyish redhead wearing a wrinkled green sport coat and a wary expression, was almost to Patrick's door.

Romy cried, "When he comes to the window—which will be in about two seconds—act pissed. We're having a private argument here and he's butting in. Can you get into that?"

"Yeah!" Patrick gritted his teeth and leaned closer. "I can get into that! I can get into it better'n you, you worthless mito—" He jumped at the tap on the driver window, turned, and rolled it down an inch. "Who the hell are you?"

The man's lips turned up at the corners in a poor imitation of a friendly smile. "Hi, we're a neighborhood patrol, just keeping an eye out for trouble and—"

"Yeah, well so what?" Romy said, leaning over Patrick's shoulder and projecting Raging Romy-scale belligerence. "Who needs you? Go patrol some other neighborhood. This one's fine!"

She noticed how the man's eyes were fixed on Patrick, barely flicking her way during her outburst.

"Yeah!" Patrick said. "This one's fine!"

Suddenly the guy's hand darted into his coat and came out with a big pistol, a cousin to the HK in Romy's bag, which she didn't dare reach for now.

"Hold it!" he said, grinning at Patrick. His Adam's apple was bobbing wildly. "I know you. You're that sim lawyer. We've been looking for you. Turn off the engine."

His expression tight, grave, Patrick glanced at Romy and obeyed.

"Hold *real* still now." Without turning his head the man called to the Impala. "Yo, Snyder! Come see what we hooked!"

The Chevy's driver door opened and a taller, beefier man stepped out. He had a small white bandage taped across his swollen nose.

"Well, well," he said as he reached the van and looked inside. "If it isn't Sullivan and Cadman."

Romy knew she shouldn't be surprised that he knew her name, but the way he said it, the sound of it on his lips, jolted her.

"What's in the back there, folks?" Snyder said, grinning. "A ski mask, maybe? And a supply of paint balloons? Mind if we take a—"

What happened next was a blur: Two furry hands appeared, one to the left of Snyder's head, one to the right of the redhead's, and then those heads slammed together with a sickening *crunch!* Both men's mouths dropped into shocked ovals as their eyes rolled up under their lids.

"Jesus!" Patrick said.

Then the furry hands smashed the heads together again, and this time the sound was wetter, softer. Blood spurted from the redhead's nose, splattering Patrick's window.

"Christ, Romy! Make him stop! He's going to kill them!"

"Too late for that," she said, feeling the cold touch of Raging Romy's secret delight. "Kek! Put them back in the car. Quick!"

"I know that sound," Patrick said dully. "I heard it the night we were run off the Saw Mill. I—"

She grabbed Patrick's arm. "We've got to move! They may have a call-in schedule, and if they miss it—"

"Yeah, yeah," he said, looking dazed and maybe a little sick. "Got to move, but . . . Jesus."

She noticed Kek dragging the two bodies back to the car and tossing them through the open driver door like sacks of wheat. She rolled down her window and leaned out.

"Kek! No, sit them up! Sit them *up!*"

The mandrilla looked at her, then nodded and followed her instructions.

She turned back to Patrick. "We've got to find Zero and get out of here!"

"Don't forget Tome." Patrick seemed to be recovering from his shock. "And what about Meerm?"

"I don't know about Meerm. She might not even be in Newark any longer. But I know what these people will do to Zero if they find him."

Patrick nodded. "Right."

Romy heard the van's rear door slam, looked around and saw Kek returning to his standby squat. She glanced at the Chevy and saw two upright silhouettes in its front seat.

"Stay here, Kek," she said. "I'll be right back."

The mandrilla made no sign that he'd heard, but she knew he had.

"*We'll* be right back," Patrick said. He cut her off as she opened her mouth to tell him she'd go alone. "We do this together."

Romy sensed arguing wasn't going to work so she nodded and motioned him to follow her. She moved off at a trot, heard his sloshing footsteps close behind.

Down the alley . . . nothing. Into the courtyard . . . nothing. Down a second alley . . . noth—

Wait. Voices to her left. Where? From that opening. Tome's voice. Without hesitation she ducked and entered in a crouch. She heard Patrick puffing behind her. Ahead she could see that the tunnel opened into a vacant lot. And there, across the lot, Zero and Tome crouched before an open metal door, talking to no one, or at least no one she could see.

"Wait," Patrick whispered. "Don't go out there. Looks like they found her. Two more humans will only spook her."

"She'll be spooked a lot worse if more of Portero's goons show up. They'd better talk her out of there soon or all this will be for nothing. We'll give them a couple more minutes, then we've got to get out of here."

"Might take more than a couple of minutes," Patrick sighed. "I mean, would you trust a stranger in a ski mask?"

"Damn," Romy said, feeling as if the tunnel walls were closing in on her. "She doesn't come out in two minutes, I'll go in there myself and drag her out."

"Shhh!" Patrick hissed. "I'll be damned! I think Zero's going to take off his mask!"

Romy looked and—dear God, Patrick was right. Remaining statue-still, she held her breath and watched.

This is going nowhere, Zero thought. And it's because of me. Or because of this ski mask.

No question about it: Meerm was in that elevator shaft, hiding in the dark, but she wasn't budging. Tome was doing his best, but he wasn't cut out for persuasion. Zero could try going in after her, and that would work if the space beyond the door was limited to just the shaft. But what if it opened into the rest of the warehouse? They'd never find her.

All right. He couldn't blow this chance. It might never come again. Time to put it all on the line.

Zero pulled off his dark glasses, slipped his thumbs under the edge of his ski mask, and ripped it off.

"Look, Meerm," he said, leaning through the open door. "Look at me. I'm not a man. I'm a sim. Not a sim exactly like you, but a sim just the same. And I promise you, Meerm, I swear to you that I am not here to harm you. Just the opposite. I am here to help you and protect you from being harmed by the bad men."

Zero waited, hoping he'd said enough, praying he hadn't said too much. He glanced at Tome who was staring at him with wide eyes. He nodded to the old sim, to let him know, yes, this is true. Maybe . . . maybe if only Tome and Meerm knew, he could still keep his secret. The two sims would talk, of course, but Zero could tell Romy and Patrick that he'd used makeup to look like a sim so he could coax Meerm out. They'd buy it. It was much more plausible than the truth.

Zero refocused on the black hole of the elevator shaft. He heard a rustle within, and then a hoarse, fragile voice . . .

"Is true? You not man?"

"No, Meerm." Zero fought back a sob. It had worked. He could feel Meerm tipping his way. "I'm a sim too. But if I am to help you, we must hurry from here. Now."

"Meerm want go." And now a face, a swollen, care-ravaged sim face, floated into the light. "Meerm not like here. But . . ."

"We must go now, Meerm. The bad men are looking for you. If they come before—"

Meerm stepped out into the light. Zero gasped at the sight of her—her belly so big and her ankles so swollen she could barely move. She took a step forward, but caught her foot and started to fall. Zero grabbed her, then lifted her into his arms. She was heavy for a sim, but nothing he couldn't handle.

"Don't be afraid, Meerm," he said in a soothing voice as she started to struggle. "You're okay, now. I'll make you safe and keep you that way. No one will hurt you ever again."

As he turned toward the tunnel he saw two figures emerging from its entrance. Romy and Patrick, faces ashen, mouths agape, eyes fixed on his nonhuman face. They couldn't miss its yellow eyes and simian cast—his brow ridge was not so pronounced as Meerm and Tome's, he knew, his nose not quite as flat, but he was unmistakably simlike.

Oh, no, he thought as dismay softened his knees and he almost stumbled. Oh, God, what have I done?

Just when they were so close to success, he'd ruined everything. Now the whole organization would fall apart because . . . because who'd want to follow a sim?

Even worse was the uncomprehending look of betrayal he saw in Romy's eyes.

But he had to press on. She looked away as he approached, so he addressed Patrick.

"Help me get her through the tunnel. We haven't got much time."

Patrick blinked, hesitated a heartbeat, then nodded. "Less than you think."

As they eased Meerm into the opening, Zero prayed Romy would follow.

10

Silence ruled the van. Zero leaned forward as Patrick piloted them toward the freeway.

"Follow the signs toward the Goethals Bridge," he told him.

He glanced at Romy, huddled against the passenger door at the far end of the front seat, staring dead ahead without blinking, looking as if she were in a trance.

I've really done it now, Zero thought. I've lost her. She'll never trust me again.

Meerm whimpered at his side. She was curled next to him on the rear seat. He laid a reassuring hand on her shoulder. Tome and Kek hunched behind them in the open rear section.

"Goethals," Patrick said. "Got it. But I think . . . I think we . . ." He seemed to run out of words.

"You think you deserve an explanation," Zero said. "Of course you do."

"I mean," Patrick said, "I feel as if the world just tipped ninety degrees."

Zero glanced again at Romy who still hadn't moved. She'd known him so much longer than Patrick. Her world must feel even further out of kilter.

"You're not human?" Patrick said.

"No."

"I heard you tell Meerm that you're a sim."

"I am."

"But how come you don't . . . ?"

". . . look like the average sim? I'm one of the earliest, so early that you'll find no UPC tattoo on the nape of my neck. Plus I'm a mutant—bigger and paler than my brother sims—too big and too human-looking for the work-force. So they kept me separate. I was raised in SimGen's basic research facility and after a while I became a mascot of sorts. My only contacts growing up were the Sinclair brothers and their most trusted techs. Later, when Harry Carstairs arrived to take over sim training, he took a special interest in me."

Harry . . . how he'd loved Harry Carstairs. The man's daily visits had been the high point of his adolescence.

"He was impressed by my linguistic skills so he tested my intelligence; when he found it to be not only far above sim average but above human average as well, he and—"

He cut himself off. Better not mention Ellis.

"He got permission to see how far they could take me. I learned to read, and built up my own library; I was never allowed out of basic research, but television gave me a window onto the rest of the world. Harry and I . . . I guess you might say we bonded. He taught me to play chess and we spent hours hovering over the board."

He missed Harry, especially their chess games. Every so often Zero would give in to a compulsion to see the man. He'd sneak by Harry's house at night and watch him as he sat and played chess against his computer; he'd longed to knock on the window and challenge him to a game. But Harry believed him dead, and had to go on believing that.

Patrick said, "But how did you graduate from SimGen mascot to Zero, SimGen nemesis?"

"I've always been called Zero. I imagine it's derived from part of my serial number when I was an embryo. As for my 'graduation' . . . I believe I became inconvenient. Here I was, this man-size sim who was an evolutionary and commercial dead end. Somewhere along the line, a corporate decision was made to terminate me."

"Jesus," Patrick whispered. "Just like that?"

"Just like that."

"What were they going to do—shoot you?"

"An injection. They drew blood from me at regular intervals. This time they were going to put something in instead of take something out."

Zero saw Romy glance quickly over her shoulder, then return to her thousand mile stare.

"Scumbags," Patrick muttered, shaking his head.

Only one, Zero thought. Mercer Sinclair had made the unilateral decision.

He looked down at Meerm who'd closed her eyes and seemed to be dozing. Termination would have been her fate if Portero had found her first.

Patrick asked, "How'd you manage to escape?"

"I found I had a highly placed ally in the company who arranged to fake my death."

Ellis again. He'd told his brother that he didn't want a stranger terminating Zero, that he'd do it himself. But he injected Zero with a sedative instead of poison, cremated another dead sim in his place, and spirited him out of SimGen. He told Zero everything, and set him up with a steady flow of cash and data aimed toward one purpose: to stop SimGen and free his brother sims.

"This ally is the source of all your inside information, I take it," Patrick said.

"Yes."

Patrick shook his head again. "A high-up inside SimGen working against it. Is he nuts or does he have a personal beef with the Sinclairs?"

"Both, I think. But it's also a moral issue with him."

All true. But Zero had always sensed something else driving Ellis Sinclair, almost as if he felt he had to atone for something. Something "unspeakable," perhaps?

Patrick laughed. "Put a sim in charge of bringing down the makers of sims. I've got to say, it has a nice symmetry to it. And now that we've got Meerm, it looks like your job is just about over. Congratulations, Zero. They chose the right man. I mean sim. I mean—hell, I don't know what I mean. All I can say is I never had an inkling you weren't human."

And now we come to the crucial junction, Zero thought.

"Does it bother you that I'm not?" He directed the question at Patrick but he was watching Romy. He thought he saw her flinch.

"I don't know. You're not like Tome or any other sim I've met. In fact, you're more human than some humans I know. Smarter too. What a world!

But you haven't steered me wrong yet. So I guess the answer is no. To tell the truth, every day I'm getting less and less sure about what exactly 'human' means."

Bless you, Patrick, he thought, then looked at Romy. He couldn't bear her silence any longer. This had to be dragged out in the open now.

"And you, Romy?" he said. "You haven't said a word."

For a few seconds, she didn't move, then she twisted swiftly in her seat and faced him. Angry tears streaked her cheeks.

"You lied to me!"

"I never told you I was human."

"You pretended to be!"

"I never pretended to be anything other than who I am. I didn't even change my name."

"You hid yourself—that was a lie!"

"No, I had to. Would you have joined me if you'd known I was a sim? A mutant sim?"

Her angry expression faltered, then she turned away again.

"Think, Romy. When was I ever untrue to you? Were the goals of our activities against SimGen ever other than what I said they were? Have I ever misled you into doing something that you didn't want to do, or worked you toward an end that wasn't your own as well?"

She replied in a tiny voice. "No."

"Then can I ask you why you're so angry at me?"

"Who says I'm angry at you?" she said in that same small voice. "Maybe I'm angry at me."

Baffled, he replied, "I don't—"

She held up a hand. "Can we just leave it be? I've got some adjusting to do and I need some time. Okay?"

"I understand, but I need to know: Are you still with us?"

She nodded without speaking, without looking around.

Zero leaned back and closed his eyes to hold back the tears.

After a while Patrick said, "Goethals Bridge dead ahead. Why do we want that?"

"Because it's the quickest route out of Jersey."

"But where are we going?"

"Dr. Cannon's." He took one of Meerm's hands in his. "We're bringing her the most important patient of her career."

11

Two more men dead!

"Shit-shit-SHIT!" Luca Portero screamed as he smashed a glass paper-weight against his office wall. He didn't have to worry about anyone hearing; security staff was minimal on Sundays.

Luca hadn't seen the bodies yet, but Lowery, who'd found them, had told them that both their skulls had been cracked like eggs. That sounded eerily similar to the way Ricker and Green had bought it off the Saw Mill. But this was in broad daylight, damn it!

Could things get any fucking worse?

As if in answer to his question, the secure phone rang. He hesitated—because, yes, things could get a lot worse—then answered it. He repressed a sigh of relief when he heard Lowery's hello.

"What?"

"I've been checking around the area and found some squatters in this broke down old apartment house on the same block."

"Did they see anything?"

"Not what happened to Snyder and Grimes, but they did see this black van parked on the street—"

"They're sure it was black?"

"Double-checked that. They swear it was black. But here's the meat: the one looking out the window says she saw a very swollen looking female sim being led into the black van."

Oh, no! No! They've found her! Snatched her right out from under our noses! How the fuck could this happen?

"She's absolutely sure?"

"No question."

"Who was doing the leading?"

"Two men—one 'very strange looking,' according to her, but she was kinda vague about that—along with a woman, and another sim, an old male."

Luca dropped into his desk chair and cradled his head in his free hand. Cadman and Sullivan. Had to be. Plus that old sim Sullivan kept around, and someone else working with them.

And they had the pregnant sim.

"All right," Luca said, straightening. This wasn't FUBAR yet. It still could be salvageable. "We abandon Newark. Divide the remaining men into four teams: one on Sullivan's apartment, one on his office, one on Cadman's apartment, one on her office. You see them, grab them."

"But—"

"I don't care what you have to do to nab them, just get it done. If there's any flack we'll straighten it out later. I want one of those shits and I want them brought to me!"

He'd interrogate them personally and they'd lead him to this pregnant sim. No need to worry about being recognized because whoever he dealt with would not be leaving vertically.

But what if they'd all gone to ground?

12

MINEOLA, NY

"She's not going to last much longer," Betsy Cannon said as she angled the doppler wand this way and that against Meerm's swollen, gel-coated belly.

Romy, Zero, Betsy, and Meerm were crowded into the tiny, white-walled, windowless procedure room in Betsy's home office. Meerm lay on the table, Betsy working over her, Romy and Zero watching from the other side.

"What do you mean?" Romy said, watching in rapt fascination as the 3-D shape of the fetus within Meerm's belly formed on the monitor screen.

"Her uterus has taken just about all it can. It's too small for this baby. And yet . . . the baby could use more gestation time."

At least Zero had his ski mask back on. They'd all agreed on the way here that no one else needed to know Zero's history. When it was all over—and with Meerm's baby, that could be very soon—he promised to go public.

The mask made it easier now for Romy, but she wished Zero had waited outside with Patrick and Tome; she was still uncomfortable with him, especially standing next to him like this. And she didn't want to feel uncomfortable, hated herself for it.

But . . . how else *could* she feel? She was fighting her way through an emotional maelstrom and still hadn't regained her bearings. She'd admired Zero so; he'd become a hero in her eyes and in her heart, and that was fine, but she'd also been sexually attracted to him, had fantasized about him, and now . . . now to learn that he's not human.

So what? said the ghost of Raging Romy, ever ready to shout *Up yours!* to the world. It's not as if he's a squid or a plant—he's a fellow primate.

That was true and real and forward thinking, but another more primitive part of her was repulsed and kept damning her, whispering that in another time, or in a SimGen-less world, Zero would have been born a chimpanzee, destined to spend his days sitting in a jungle sucking ants off a stick.

Sicko evil girl! Wanting to make love with a monkey! Sick! Sick! Sick!

Romy did her best to shut out that voice, but it wouldn't go away, couldn't because it was part of her, and that was what so dismayed her. She'd always thought she was better than that.

"How much longer?" Zero asked.

Betsy Cannon brushed back strands of graying hair from her face. "Hard to say. If this were a sim baby I'd say she's almost due. If human I'd say premature. But this baby . . . I don't know. And there's another problem: Meerm's uterus is small, smaller even than a breeder sim's. That baby is packed tight in there, so tight I can't determine its sex."

"We could lose the baby?" Romy said.

"It's a real possibility."

Romy stared at the color image on the monitor, watched the rapid filling and emptying of the chambers of its little heart, saw the baby move, squirming for comfort in the confines of the too-small womb.

We can't lose you, she told it. You *must* live. We're so close now and . . . the salvation of an entire species rests on you.

"We could lose the mother as well," Betsy added. "The baby is going to be premature, and I can tell you right now that a vaginal delivery is out of the question. This baby is coming out by section."

"Cesarean?" Romy said, looking at Meerm's distended belly. "How . . . where . . . ?"

"I don't know." Betsy's expression was grim. "Not here, that's for certain. It's major surgery and I'm not equipped for that, not unless we intend to sacrifice the mother."

Romy's gaze darted to Meerm's face. The poor sim didn't have a clue as to who or what they were talking about.

"That's not an option," Zero said. The finality in his tone stabbed Romy with a reminder of why she'd been so attracted to him. "Tell me what you need and I'll arrange it."

"A sterile operating room and a skilled surgical team," Betsy said. "Can you manage that?"

"Tall order," Zero said. His voice had lost some of its confidence.

And then another voice spoke.

"Why Meerm sick?"

They all stared at her a moment, then Betsy spoke.

"You're not sick, Meerm. You're going to have a baby."

Her sloping brow furrowed. "Baby? What is baby?"

"You know babies," Betsy said. "You must have seen many babies on television."

The brow furrows deepened. "Baby?"

"Only this won't be like the human babies you've seen. This will be a *sim* baby." She gave a little shrug as she glanced at Zero and Romy, signifying that she was simplifying the situation as best she could for Meerm.

"Where baby?"

Betsy tapped the sim's abdomen. "Right in here. And the baby will come out soon."

"Baby here?" Meerm said, a slow smile of wonder spreading across her face as she gently rubbed her hands across her belly. "Baby inside? Baby kick-kick-kick?"

"Oh, yes!" Betsy laughed. "I'll bet that baby's been kick-kick-kicking like crazy!"

As they all watched Meerm gaze at her belly, a question occurred to Romy.

"Will she be able to care for a baby?" she said softly.

"She won't have to worry a bit," Betsy said. "That baby will get *great* care. As a one-of-a-kind species, it will belong to the world."

"No, it will belong to Meerm. It will be *her* baby. We're not going to forget that, are we?"

"Ah, Romy," Zero said through a sigh. "That's why we need you: to ask the tough questions."

Something in his voice struck her . . . did Zero . . . could Zero feel about her the way she . . . ?

No. Out of the question. He couldn't. He simply couldn't.

13

"Let's get this started," said Sinclair-1, spinning his chair away from the winter-browned hills beyond his office window to face Luca and Abel Voss. "I've still got a lot to do today."

Luca thought the CEO looked particularly irritable this afternoon. That was going to get worse when he heard Luca's news. Normally he'd relish the prospect of upsetting him, but not now. All the blame rested squarely on him.

"We're waiting for your brother."

Voss shifted his bulk in his chair to face Luca. "I thought he wasn't comin.'"

"I called and told him this was too important to miss," Luca replied.

Sinclair-1 gave him a questioning stare. Luca only nodded. Yes, they'd agreed that Ellis would be excluded from tactical meetings, but Luca had a reason. He was sure Sinclair-2 already knew that Meerm had been snatched from under SIRG's nose, and damn well knew who had done it; he was going to use Sinclair-2 to bait a trap for the people he'd been supplying with information.

They included Cadman and Sullivan, Luca knew, and at least two or three others. Whoever they were, they'd all vanished. He'd hoped to nab either Cadman or Sullivan and wring the pregnant sim's whereabouts out of them, but since he couldn't find them, he was looking for a way to make them come to him.

Because he *needed* that sim. Lister had thrown a shit fit this morning when he'd heard about losing Grimes and, of all people, Snyder. Grimes had been something of a jerk, but Snyder had been their most dependable man. Luca had stashed the bodies in the woodshed behind his cabin—he hoped the cold weather held—and Lister was keeping the news from the higher-ups for now, but couldn't cover it up indefinitely. If Luca could produce the pregnant sim, however—say, today or tomorrow—the deaths wouldn't matter.

The office door opened and Sinclair-2 entered. The older brother looked strange today. And then Luca realized what it was: His usual down and dour demeanor was gone and he looked almost . . . happy.

You son of a bitch.

He fought the urge to grab him by his scrawny neck and twist it till he spilled everything he knew. Every last thing.

But that was not an option. Even though Mercer Sinclair was considered the true untouchable—his was the public face of SimGen, so closely identified with the company that if he went down, so would the stock that made SIRG an entity unto itself—Ellis Sinclair was also considered off-limits. No move could be made against him without direct authority from the Old Man himself.

What Luca couldn't understand about Ellis Sinclair was *why*. Why would anyone in his right mind want to kill this golden goose called SimGen? So that had to be the answer: The older Sinclair was out of his mind.

Which didn't make Luca want to kill him any less.

He swallowed his bile and said, "I won't waste anyone's time here: We have it on good authority that the pregnant sim is in the hands of Patrick Sullivan and Romy Cadman."

"Oh, Christ," Sinclair-1 groaned, closing his eyes.

"That tears it," said Abel Voss.

Sinclair-2 leaned back in a sofa and said nothing.

"When?" the CEO said, recovering quickly. "Where are they now?"

"This morning. And if I knew where, we wouldn't be having this meeting."

"Damn!" Sinclair-1 glared at Luca. "You've got to get her back!"

"We're working on it."

Sinclair-2 finally spoke. "Give it up, Merce. Can't you see it's gone too far? It's past the point of no return now."

"Not yet! Not until they produce that baby!"

"And even if they do," said Voss, "we can call it a hoax, can't we? Some cheap publicity stunt, a twenty-first century version of the Piltdown man or Barnum's Cardiff Giant. We get our PR boys to crank up their bullshit machines and start poundin away at every news outlet they know: A hoax, that's all it is. Just a hoax. Those boys are so good, before you know it, we'll be believin it ourselfs."

Sinclair-1 was shaking his head. "That won't fly in this case. They have a real live sim mother. They can identify the human father—what was his name?"

"Craig Strickland," Luca said. "The security guard at the globulin farm."

"Who's dead, right? But that doesn't preclude fingerprinting his DNA. Plus they can put the sim mother and human father together for months in the same building in the Bronx. And most important, they'll have the baby. With all that, it's a simple everyday process to establish paternity."

Luca could have cheered. He'd been looking for an opening to bait his trap, and this was it.

"I've taken care of that," he said. "Because of his connection to a crime, Strickland's body has been in cold storage in the New York City Morgue since it was pulled out of the ashes in the Bronx. A real crispy critter."

"So?" Voss said.

"So yesterday it was released. Since Strickland's got no family—at least none that's come forward—I had one of my men present himself as Strickland's cousin and claim his body. We're going to have it cremated as soon as possible."

He hadn't done any of this yet. The idea had occurred to him less than an hour ago, and he had to clear it with Lister first. But Sinclair-2 didn't know that.

"That still doesn't help us," Sinclair-1 said. "If indeed his corpse was, as you so elegantly put it, a 'crispy critter,' the NYPD would have had to look into his DNA in the course of identifying the body. Even after he's reduced to ash, his RFLP profile will remain in the department's database."

Voss frowned. "What's R-F—"

"Restriction fragment length polymorphisms," Sinclair-1 said. "A way of testing for the differences in the banding pattern of DNA fragments from different individuals. DNA fingerprinting, in other words."

"We know all about his RFLP in the database," Luca said. "Ever hear of hacking a computer? Hardly anyone's better at it than my people. We'll have someone else's RFLP—yours, if you want it—in that computer before sunrise."

"I get it," Voss said, nodding. "I'm not hearin a word of this talk of illegalities, of course. Matter of fact, I ain't even in this here room right now. But if I were, even a genetics cretin like myself can see what'll happen: They'll hold up this Strickland boy as the father for all the world to see, but when it comes time for matchin up the DNA, there'll come a cropper. They'll go to the NYPD computer and—Lordy, Lordy, will you look at that—no match. And when they look to exhume the body—"

"—they'll be nowhere," Luca interrupted. "Because Craig Strickland will be nothing but a pile of dust. A pile I will personally scatter over the Hudson River."

"And without DNA backup," Voss cried, slapping his thighs, "the hoax angle from our flacks will start lookin mighty acceptable to the Great Unwashed. I like it! I like it very much!"

Luca had been watching Sinclair-2. His sunny disposition appeared to be fading. Rapidly. Good. He'd taken the bait.

"So," Luca said, clapping his hands. "That leaves one more matter to discuss: Who's delivering the sim's baby?"

"Deliverin?" Voss said. "Deliverin how?"

"This sim, this Meerm or whatever she's called, is going to be giving birth. Who's going to handle that?"

Sinclair-1 slapped his palm on the table. "Excellent point." He jumped to his feet. "If, as you say, this OPRR woman and that lawyer Sullivan have the sim, they're not going to handle the delivery on their own. The baby is too important. They're going to seek out expert help."

"You mean some sort of obstetrician?" Voss said.

"Not just any OB. They'll want one experienced with sim births. And if I was looking for a sim OB, there's only one place on earth with a staff that fits the qualifications."

"The Natal Center!" Luca said. Damn it! He should have thought of that himself. "They could be approaching someone on the staff right now."

Sinclair-1 pointed to Luca. "Send a notice to the entire Natal Center staff—MDs and assistants alike—warning them that they might be approached, and to report any feelers that might come their way."

Voss said, "And you might want to remind those folks that they're eligible for the five-million reward."

"Excellent point," Sinclair-1 said.

"We'll check out any Natal employees who're out sick or taking an unplanned vacation," Luca added.

But all this was going to require more manpower. He'd have to go to Lister for it. But that was okay. Canvassing the Natal Center was a good tactical move, and Luca would present it as his own idea.

Sinclair-2 suddenly shot from his seat and began pacing. He looked jittery. I do believe we've hit a nerve, Luca thought.

The CEO stared at his brother. "What is it, Ellis? You have something to add?"

Sinclair-2 stopped at the window and stared out at the hills. "I just thought of something. Something terrible."

"Oh?" Sinclair-1 smiled. "Finally realized what that baby will do to our stock?"

"I'm not worried about the stock," he said. "I'm far more worried about what this baby will do to *us*, Merce—you and me. Personally, not financially."

"I'm not following."

"What if Meerm's baby is a girl?"

The CEO looked puzzled. "Girl, boy, what difference does it make? Its very existence is the threat."

"Competition, Merce." Sinclair-2 turned from the window and stared at his brother. His eyes looked haunted. "Inter- and intragenomic competition. Think about it."

It's finally happened, Luca thought. Sinclair-2 has completely lost it. Even his brother can't figure out what he's talking about.

He glanced at the CEO then and was struck by the change in his expression. His King-of-the-World look was fading—the perpetually raised eyebrows had sagged, the condescending half smile had fallen into a frown. But his eyes . . . his eyes told the whole story, narrowing and then widening into what Luca could only describe as abject horror. His mouth opened, his jaw worked, he took a step backward, almost lost his balance, and fell into his chair where he sat staring at his brother. His gray complexion made him look more dead than alive.

"What's wrong?" Voss said, upset as well, but only by his boss's reaction. He seemed as much in the dark as Luca. "What did he say? What's wrong with it being a girl?"

The CEO was incapable of speech. Sinclair-2 answered for him.

"Not your concern, Abel. This is a personal matter between us."

"It *is* his concern!" Sinclair-1 blurted, getting some of his color back. "It's *all* our concern!" He turned to his brother. "Ellis, for the love of God, if you're involved in any way with the people who have the sim, do something! Stop them!"

Sinclair-2 shook his head. "I can't stop anything. I don't know Meerm's whereabouts. It's beyond you, it's beyond me. It's up to Zero now."

Sinclair-1's brow furrowed. "Zero? What's zero?"

"Not what. Who."

"You don't mean . . . ?" Sinclair-1 blinked. "*That* Zero? But he's dead."

Sinclair-2 stared at his younger brother. "Not quite."

The two words seemed to hang in the air between them. Portero caught Voss's eye and the big man shrugged, obviously as confused as he.

"You liar!" Sinclair-1 blurted, his face purpling. "You traitor!"

Sinclair-2's voice remained flat. "You're amazing, you know that? But the fact remains, Zero's in charge, not me, and I'm afraid events have built to a point of inevitability now where no one can stop them."

"*Nothing* is inevitable!" Sinclair-1 screamed. Now he seemed to be the one losing it. "Not until I say so! There's still a fifty-fifty chance it's a male! But no matter what it is, I want it born *here!*" He pointed with both hands, jabbing his index fingers toward Luca and Voss. "So get out there and find that sim, goddamnit!"

Normally Luca wouldn't have allowed the twit to speak to him that way, but now he was clearly off his head, so Luca turned and led Voss into the hall. As soon as the door closed behind them, Voss grabbed his arm.

"You have any idea what that ruckus was all about?"

Luca shook his head. He was as baffled as the fat man.

"I been with this company since the git-go," Voss said, sweating, eyes darting about like caged birds, "and I ain't never, ever seen Mercer Sinclair lose his cool like that." He shook his head. "Boy baby, girl baby—what the hell does it mean?"

"Haven't a clue," Luca said, turning and moving away.

He had things to do. The first was to pry more manpower out of Lister for his trap; another was to find out what had so unnerved the Sinclairs. Something about inter- and intragenomic competition. Sounded like heavy shit, not the kind of stuff they'd taught him in Special Forces. But it might turn out to be important. It might be *way* important. And right now he needed all the help he could get.

14

MINEOLA, NY

One hell of a day.

Patrick lay awake in the dark in the smaller of Betsy Cannon's two extra bedrooms, and thought about the changes Meerm's baby would bring. He had no doubt that the child's pedigree, despite all the challenges and smoke-screens SimGen would throw up, eventually would elevate sims to the status of "persons." That one change in designation would tumble SimGen and send the world's labor and financial markets into chaos. The simple realization that he'd occupy a pivotal position in the eye of that oncoming storm would have made sleep difficult; knowing that a cadre of ruthless men were on the prowl, looking for him and Romy and Meerm to prevent that from happening made it impossible.

Zero had departed late this afternoon after a protracted debate as to whether or not Kek should stay here for security. They finally decided against that. Zero was the only one who could control him. What if Kek decided he wanted to go outside? Who was going to stop him? If he were spotted, that would blow their cover. Better to keep all nonhumans away from Betsy's.

After a light dinner, they'd all turned in early. Romy was in the next bedroom down the hall, Meerm was on a cot in Betsy's bedroom, Tome and Kek were with Zero at his home, wherever that was, God was in His heaven, and not one damn thing seemed right with the world.

He jumped as he heard the bedroom door open.

"It's only me." He recognized Romy's whisper. "Didn't mean to frighten you."

"Just startled me," he said. Then she startled him even further him by slipping under the covers and huddling against him. "Hold me, Patrick."

"Gladly."

He wound his arms around her. She was wearing some sort of long T-shirt. He didn't know what she had on under it, if anything.

"No, I mean, just hold me," she said. "Nothing more. I don't want to be alone tonight, Patrick. I need a friend."

"That's me," he sighed. He was about to add, Friend to the friendless, but bit it back. She was trembling, as if chilled. So he said, "Tough day, huh."

"Believe it."

"Want to talk about it?"

"No."

"Okay."

And then she said, "I feel lost, Patrick. I used to have some pretty hard and fast ideas about right and wrong, up and down, latitude and longitude, but now everything's been twisted out of shape. Like one of those computer programs that let you distort a photo or a famous painting, you know, push it and pull it this way and that until it bears only a passing resemblance to the original. That's how my world feels. That's how my life feels. That's how *I* feel. Like I don't even know myself anymore." A harsh little laugh. "Not that I ever did."

"You loved him, didn't you."

He heard a soft sob and felt her head nod against his shoulder.

"Do you still?"

"I don't know," she whispered. "I think I was in love with an image I'd concocted. But now that the mask is off . . ."

"Let me ask you something," Patrick said. "If he'd taken off the mask and revealed a face horribly disfigured by birth defects or an accident, how would that have changed things?"

He marveled at the way his thoughts were running. He should have been searching for the best angle to wedge himself between Romy and Zero; instead he was looking for a way to ease her pain. As much as he wanted her—and right now, with her bare legs warm against his, that was very, very much—comforting her seemed even more important.

"Not at all. It wasn't a physical attraction. I see where you're going, but it's not the same. A disfigured man would still be a man. Zero isn't . . ."

"A man? What's your definition of a man, Romy?"

"A male *Homo sapiens*."

Patrick sensed himself clicking into attorney mode, felt the well-oiled teeth of his rhetoric and advocacy gears meshing. He'd always prided himself on an ability to mount a convincing argument for either side of an issue, even one he didn't particularly care for. Like this one.

"But before today, when you thought of both Zero and me as male *Homo saps*, you gravitated more toward him than me. Why?"

"I didn't know you, Patrick. And I didn't trust you. At least not at first. But you've got to admit you've changed."

"How?"

"Well . . . ," she said, drawing out the word, "you've gone from a man with no commitments to one who believes in something and is willing to put himself on the line for it."

"Romy, Zero has been committed since day one, from the roots of his hair down to his toenails, and that was what you responded to. But it went beyond commitment, didn't it. He demonstrated high intelligence, integrity, decency, courage, dignity, a reverence for life that matches, maybe even exceeds, your own. Those are traits you admire in humans. They're what make you value a human, and until this morning you'd thought you could find them only in a human. But this is a new world, Romy, where the definition of 'human' is being revised—and let me tell you, when we take Meerm's baby public, it's going to undergo a total rewrite."

Listen to me, Patrick thought. I'm making his case and killing my own.

But he was on a roll, high on his rhetorical momentum, and couldn't stop himself.

"As for Zero, he says he's a mutated sim. Well, it looks to me like he mutated in the *Homo sapiens* direction, big time. He's more human than a lot of *Homo saps* I know, and we both know *Homo saps* who look more apelike than he does. Meerm's baby is going to upgrade the sims from 'product' to 'person,' from the Pongidae family to Hominidae, but as far as I can see, Zero is already there. A new species of Hominidae—*Homo zero*. So what else do you want from the guy? What else does he have to do to deserve you?"

He felt her stiffen. "It's not about deserving me. I'd never—"

"Then decide what makes a guy worthy of your love—his genome or his values."

A long silence. Patrick had run out of steam, and Romy . . . he wished he knew what she was thinking.

Then she snuggled closer. "Thank you, Patrick. That doesn't settle things, but it helps. Helps a lot. You're a good friend."

Good friend . . . he wished he were much more, but for now he'd settle for that. Didn't have much choice. And who knew? Maybe things wouldn't work out between Zero and her. They'd barely spoken today. Maybe Zero had other plans. But even if they both agreed on trying a relationship, they had a hell of a lot stacked against them.

He'd wait, because he knew of no other woman in the world like Romy Cadman. He'd hang around so he could be close by to catch her if she fell.

15

SHORT HILLS, NJ

The late-night wind cut at Luca Portero as he strode across the crowded mall parking lot toward Lister's Mercedes. A perfect meeting place. The mall was staying open late for last-minute Christmas shoppers. Luca had taken advantage of that, arriving early and picking up a bracelet for Maria. He'd wait until after the holidays to dump her—no sense in spending New Year's Eve alone.

16

Romy watched Betsy adjust the IV running into Meerm's arm. The air seemed close in the spare, windowless little procedure room. Patrick had walked out—the sim's distress had been too much for him—leaving Romy alone with Betsy and Meerm.

Betsy looked up at her. "The contractions have subsided."

"How long can this go on?" Romy asked, relieved the sim's pain had finally eased.

Betsy shook her head. "Not too much longer. I was right in the middle of an ultrasound when she started having contractions. I'd love to give the baby another week but Meerm's uterus won't last that long."

"Why baby hurt Meerm?" the sim said.

"As I told you, Meerm," Betsy said softly, "the baby's not trying to hurt you. It's just that you're too small and the baby's too large." She turned to Romy and lowered her voice. "I tried to give her an anatomy lesson earlier. I don't know how much of it took."

"On the new ultrasound," Romy said, "did you see what sex it was?"

Betsy smiled. "Meerm wanted to know too. Isn't that something? I didn't think sims differentiated that much between sexes, but she was very curious. She wants a girl."

"And?"

"Can't say. The baby's packed in too tight. If I had one of the higher resolution imagers I could tell, but not with this model. I'll do another one tomorrow. Maybe we'll get lucky."

"Yes. It would be nice to be able to call the baby 'he' or 'she' instead of 'it.'"

"Indeed it would. Oh, by the way, Zero called to see how the night went."

"When will he be here?"

"He won't. He thinks it's safer for all concerned if I'm the only one seen coming and going from here."

Romy hoped her disappointment didn't show. She needed to talk to Zero—not on the phone, but face to face. Her emotions were still in wild turmoil, but she needed to know how *he* felt, and what *he* wanted. Once she knew that, she could begin to sort out her own feelings, make some decisions. She didn't know what the future held, but she was keeping all options open for now.

Then Patrick stuck his head into the little room. "I think the house is being watched."

Romy felt her shoulders tighten. "You're sure?"

"I haven't seen men with binoculars trained on us, but someone's sitting in a car parked up the street facing this way, and he's been there for a while."

"Show me."

He led her to the picture window in the living room. It was midday but the low gray sky shed little light into the room. Romy reached for a lamp, then thought better of it.

"Damn," Patrick said. "It's gone. But I tell you, it was sitting right over there for a good half hour."

Romy scanned the street and saw a blue sedan parked against the curb at the other end.

"Was that there before?" she asked, pointing.

"No," Patrick said. "I'm sure it wasn't. And this one's got—doesn't that look like two men inside?"

"Yes, it does," Betsy said, coming up behind them. "I'm calling the police."

"Is that such a good idea?" Patrick said.

Romy smiled. "I think it's a great idea. If they *knew* something, they'd have *done* something. Betsy left SimGen with a roar, so it's no surprise they're watching her. Probably watching a number of ex-Natal-Center people. But why should we let them have an easy time of it? Let's make them explain to the local constabulary what they're doing out there."

17

"Here's what we've got on her," Lowery said, unfolding his notes behind the wheel of the surveillance car.

Luca stared at Dr. Cannon's two-story colonial from the passenger seat. He'd wanted a personal look at the lay of the land, and he didn't like it one bit.

"Elizabeth Cannon, age forty-eight, never married, no kids, lives alone. In solo obstetrics-gynecology practice. Works out of a home office, on the staff of Nassau County Community Hospital."

"Home office?" Luca said.

"Yeah. That extension on the left side there."

"Where are her patients?"

"I called about that. Her answering service said she'd canceled her office hours from today through next week but would still be seeing her hospital patients and doing her deliveries."

"Odd, don't you think?"

Lowery shrugged. "Hey, it's Christmas Eve. And she took Christmas week off. Do the same if I could."

"We don't find that sim," he told Lowery, "you'll have the longest Christmas vacation of your life."

The scanner squawked—Lowery was tuned into the local cop frequency. Something about a fender bender on Maple Street.

"So far she's been a good little girl. Made her hospital rounds this morning, then went grocery shopping."

"Buy a lot?" Luca asked.

"Come to think of it, yeah. Watched her load six bags in the back of her wagon—a blue Volvo, by the way."

Luca straightened in his seat. Interesting. "Six bags for one woman living alone?"

"Like I said, it's Christmas. Maybe she's planning a big family dinner."

"Read your own notes—she's *got* no family."

The more Luca thought about Dr. Elizabeth Cannon, the more he liked her as a real possibility. A loner with tons of experience delivering sims, she'd probably jump at the chance to shut down a place she thought of as a "slave factory." Now here she was, stocking up on groceries—enough to feed a sim and the missing Cadman and Sullivan perhaps? Plus she had a home office, the perfect place to deliver a sim. Was that why she'd canceled her office hours? Wouldn't do to have one of her patients spot a pregnant sim, would it.

He felt some of his fatigue lifting.

"All right," Lowery said, "let's just say this sim is in there. How—?"

"She *is* in there," Luca said. "I feel it in my gut."

"Okay. I'll go with that, because my gut's giving me the same message, but does your gut have any idea how we get her the fuck out of there? Look at this neighborhood, will you? It's *Leave It To Beaver*-ville. There's no room to operate."

Luca had already noticed that. Neat, middle-size houses, most sporting Christmas decorations, nestled side by side and back to back on quarter-acre lots, with wide streets that nobody parked on. Sitting here like this, their car looked as alien as a flying saucer. Only a matter of time before—

Another squawk on the scanner, this one about a suspicious car parked on Cavendish Drive.

"Shit!" Lowery said. "That's us."

Luca slapped the dashboard. "Move. I don't want any local heat seeing our faces."

"So what do we do?" Lowery said as he put the car in gear.

"A raid. Oh-four-hundred tomorrow morning."

"Are you kidding? On Christmas?"

"Can you think of a time it'll be less expected? Six of us hit the place front and back wearing FBI jackets and full assault gear. If we find the sim we secure her, terminate everyone else, and take off. If we don't find her, we apologize for raiding the wrong address, and disappear."

"FBI?"

"Hey, it's not like they never raid private homes and it's not like they've never fucked up before either. Everybody still remembers Waco. It'll take days, maybe weeks, before the feds convince the public they weren't involved."

Lowery grinned. "And by then we'll be long gone. I like it."

"It's win-win," Luca said. "If I'm right, we'll have the sim. If I'm wrong, no more wasting time watching Cannon."

But I'm *not* wrong, he told himself. That sim's in there. I can smell her.

18

"Even though it's only Christmas Eve, we'll call this our Christmas dinner," Zero said as he opened the lids of the pizza boxes on his dining room table. "Because who knows where we'll be tomorrow? No turkey for our sim Christmas, I'm afraid. Just two large pies—a plain and a sausage." He glanced at his two guests. "Do either of you know what Christmas means, by the way?"

Kek didn't even look up; he'd been lured away from one of the computers where he'd been engrossed in *Mortal Kombat XX*, and now he grabbed a slice of the sausage pie and started wolfing it down.

But Tome smiled and said, "Lights and trees and presents."

"Yes, that's a big part of it. A time of peace on earth and good will toward men, I'm told. But what about sims? Does that include good will toward sims?"

Zero had made the mistake of allowing himself a glass of holiday cheer: one Scotch and water. Terrible tasting stuff, didn't know how Ellis Sinclair had drunk so much of it all those years, but he'd forced it down—the season to be jolly and all that. Now he wished he hadn't. Not used to alcohol, and though he wasn't feeling much in the way of physical effects, it seemed to have untethered his thoughts, leaving them to wander. Now they were wandering into terra incognita.

"Tome not know, Mist Zero."

Not know what? Oh, yes . . . about good will toward sims.

"Of course you don't, Tome. Christmas has become a secular holiday for the most part, but it's still a religious occasion for those who celebrate the arrival of their god to save mankind. But what of us sims? Are we included in that salvation? Or are we damned?" He toasted with a piece of plain pie. "Joy to the world."

But he felt no trace of joy, felt instead as if he were standing on the brink of a precipice, gazing into the unknown. The world as he'd always known it was about to change. Radically. And with it his relationship to that world and all the people he knew in it. Nothing would ever be the same.

He tried to imagine what it would be like to come out of hiding, to wander about with his face exposed to the world, to be a *person*. He could not.

He surprised himself by starting to sing: "We three sims of chimpanzee blood, wondering how we'll ride out the flood . . ." He noticed Tome and Kek staring at him. "Come on, sing! You know the words!"

But then he couldn't go on, not with his throat constricting around a sob.

What have I done? My race, my brother sims—what will happen to them when Meerm's baby is shoved in the face of the world? By saving them will I doom them to extinction?

19

SUSSEX COUNTY, NJ

DECEMBER 25

"We leave at oh-three-hundred," Luca told Lowery. The two of them had the SimGen security offices virtually to themselves. He checked his watch. "That gives you ten minutes to get the other four assembled by the cars and ready to go."

"Got it," Lowery said and trotted off.

Luca turned back to the printouts on his desk. This genetics stuff was so complicated. He'd done search after search before tracking down intergenomic and intragenomic competition, and then more searching before finding articles he could understand. Weren't many of those, but he'd managed to glean some idea of what it all meant. He still didn't see what was so frightening about it.

Intergenomic competition . . . a theory that arose back in the nineties about the maternal and paternal halves of the fetal genome competing for dominance during development. Luca understood it best when he translated it into combat terms. In a male embryo, the Y chromosome from the father directs the struggle against the maternal half of the genome. But in a female, with no Y to marshal the forces of the paternal genome, the maternal X has an easier time against the paternal X; it can then push more characteristics from its own underlying genome toward the front, thus showing more of its maternal DNA to the world.

*Intra*genomic competition was a newer and more controversial theory. While *inter*genomic competition applied to all species, *intra*genomic competition applied only to recombinant transgenic species of higher mammals, and it was a double war. While the usual intergenomic competition was being waged, there was also a civil war going on within the recombinant genome. As Luca understood it, the recombinant half would try to express the genes from its original underlying genome at the expense of the foreign genes that had been spliced into it.

Yeah? So what?

If all this held true, a human father meant the pregnant sim's baby would look more like a human if it was a boy and more like a chimp if it was a girl.

Again: So what?

I must be missing something, Luca thought, because the only scary thing here is how boring this is.

He checked his watch again. Time to go. An 0300 departure would get them to Mineola in plenty of time to gear up for the raid.

And they had plenty of gear. Like the others, Luca was wearing a black cotton BDU; but before they went in they'd add body armor and Kevlar helmets with visors; each would carry tactical forearm 15,000 candlepower flashlights and an HK submachine gun equipped with double 30-round translucent magazines.

He hoped to use that weapon. He wanted that sim, yes, but wanted Cadman and Sullivan there too. Especially Romy Cadman. He wanted one last look at that pretty face before he put a bullet into it.

20

MINEOLA, NY

The racket—footsteps in the upstairs hallway, a fist pounding on a door, Betsy's voice shouting—startled Romy awake. She found herself up and moving without knowing how or why.

"Wake up! Patrick! Romy! It's time! We've got to go!"

Go? Where? She pulled open her door and caught Betsy as she hurried by. "What's wrong?"

"Meerm's in hard labor. We can't hold off any longer. Got to get her to the hospital right now!"

Romy saw Patrick stick his head out of his room and called to him. "Did you hear?"

He nodded blearily. "What time is it?"

"Three-twenty!" Betsy cried, moving away. "Get dressed. We've got to move!"

Romy jumped into her clothes and was down the stairs in seconds, Patrick right behind her. They dashed to Betsy's bedroom where they found a very confused and frightened Meerm lying on a cot and wrapped in blankets.

"Patrick, you carry her," Betsy said as she yanked the spread and blankets off her own bed. "We'll fix up the car."

Romy followed her to the garage where they flattened the rear seats in the Volvo and spread out the bedclothes. Patrick appeared a moment later carrying the moaning Meerm. They nestled her in the rear section.

"Patrick, you drive," Betsy said. "Do you know the way to the hospital?"

"No."

"I'll direct you, then. Romy, you stay here in the back with me."

And then they were on their way, Betsy and Romy kneeling on either side of Meerm in the back as Patrick pulled out of the driveway. Romy opened her PCA and left a beeper message for Zero: "It's happening. We're on our way to the hospital."

As she hung up she heard Betsy on her own PCA.

". . . know it's Christmas, Joanna, but this is more than just an emergency section, it's an historical event . . . I wish I could say more than that, but I can't. Have I ever lied to you? Well then, believe me, Joanna, you *want* to be part of this. Okay, good. I'll see you there."

As Betsy hung up and punched in another speed-dial code, she glanced at Romy and smiled. "My surgical team. A dedicated bunch, but it *is* Christmas Day. My nurse anesthetist is Hindu, so she'll be no problem; but both my scrub nurses have small children." She shrugged. "One's coming. I hope I can persuade the other. If not . . . do you faint at the sight of blood, Romy?"

"Me?" Romy said, caught off guard. "No, I'm okay with blood. But if you're talking about assisting on a surgery . . . I don't think . . ."

"Let's hope you won't have to, but be prepared. I may need you."

Slice open Meerm's belly? Romy didn't know if she could help with that.

21

"Second floor—clear!"

"Office—clear!"

"Garage—empty!"

Luca stood in the center of Dr. Cannon's living room listening to the reports through his headset, and felt ridiculous.

The op had started out perfectly. With the six team members divided between two Jeeps and a rented van, they'd arrived in town with time to spare. They'd left the Jeeps in the lot of an autobody shop and headed for Cannon's house in the van. The plan was to ditch the van at the shop lot after the op and make it back to SimGen in the Jeeps. But now . . .

Shit, the house was empty.

Luca had had his first premonition the moment they'd pulled up in front: the lights were on. Upstairs and down. At four in the morning?

They'd crept up to the windows—no one moving about inside. They'd slammed through the rear door—no alarm.

Footsteps pounded down the stairs behind him. Luca turned and saw a helmeted figure approaching, recognized him as Lowery when he lifted his visor.

"Three bedrooms upstairs. The reports on her say she lives alone, but all three have slept-in beds. They're not warm, but I'd guess they haven't been cold too long. Looks like they left in a big hurry."

Luca felt as if he were turning to ice. "You're saying they might have been tipped?"

Lowery shrugged. "Who'd tip them? You and me were the only ones who knew where we were going. Maybe they got spooked. Maybe they spotted us watching the place and decided to take off."

Luca turned away and ground his teeth. He should have kept someone here until the raid, but without Snyder and Grimes he was short-handed. What did he do now?

"All right," he said into his helmet mike. "Everybody back to the van. We're outta here."

They'd return to the other cars, but not to SimGen. Not yet. He was staying in this area. Maybe he'd split up the team and send them looking for Cannon's Volvo. Slim chance there, but better than doing nothing.

Needed time to think. No question now that Cannon and the sim were together. Find the doc and he'd have the sim, and Cadman and Sullivan too, no doubt.

But *where?*

22

Zero watched the surreal scene below with a by-now-familiar mix of antici-pation and dread. The faint aftereffects of the Scotch had evaporated when he received Romy's message. He'd arrived at the hospital shortly after Betsy and the others, and left Tome and Kek parked in the van while Patrick ad-mitted him through the doctor's entrance. Like every other department in the hospital, security was a skeleton crew because of the holiday; so Zero, wearing a hat pulled low, dark glasses, and a scarf around his lower face, made it to the OR suite without being stopped.

Betsy had commandeered the amphitheater OR, and now Zero gazed down at a brightly lit operating table fifteen feet below, where a nurse was scrubbing and shaving Meerm's distended belly. The sim lay tense and trem-bling with IVs running into both arms. The hovering dark-skinned anesthetist, who Betsy referred to as Madhuri, was ready to put her under.

The scrub nurse looked up and said, "Hey! Who's the guy in the mask?"

Zero leaned back out of sight. He'd replaced the hat and scarf with his usual ski mask.

"A trusted friend," Betsy said. "Don't worry about him, Joanna. Just get our patient prepped."

Betsy had told him she'd chosen the amphitheater for its audio-visual system, and Zero thought that an inspired idea. They could still lose this war; maybe an A-V record would provide some insurance. The problem was how to get the system up and running.

"There," Patrick said, close at his side as he sighted along the top of the mounted camera. "That's pointing in the general direction."

Zero turned and seated himself at the computer console. "Good. Now let's see if we can get a picture."

"You know how to work this sort of rig?" Patrick said, leaning over his shoulder.

"Not really, but it seems to be a dedicated system, and if the menu's at all intuitive . . ."

The menu formed on the screen and Zero groaned. It looked like a crossword puzzle with numbered feeds and rows of *input from* and *output to* and acronyms he didn't understand. Suddenly the air in the balcony seemed too thin. He ripped off the mask and took a deep breath. He looked down at his trembling fingers poised over the keyboard. It wasn't just the computer program, it was everything . . . the huge responsibility that he'd taken on over the past couple of years . . . he felt as if it were all crashing down on him at once. Everything he'd been living for hinged on what he and these good humans did here tonight.

He took another breath and focused on the screen. He could handle this.

A little trial and error, a lot of intuition . . . he could do it. He had to do it.

Meerm so ver fraid. Not fraid needle. Fraid this place. And fraid hurt. Hurt so bad.

"Okay now, Meerm," say mask lady. Nice lady. "I'm going to make the hurt go away."

Meerm feel warm, feel hurt go. This ver nice lady.

"I'm going to put you to sleep now, Meerm," lady say. "And when you wake up, you'll have a baby. Won't that be nice?"

Yes. Baby. Meerm baby. So nice. Meerm want hold, want kiss. Make baby safe. Hold-hold-hold and nev let go.

Sleepy now, but not stop think baby . . . Meerm baby . . . Meerm ver own baby . . . happy Meerm . . .

23

"Stop!" Luca shouted. "Pull over right now!"

Lowery slammed on the brakes. As the Jeep screeched to an unexpected halt, the two following vehicles skidded past and swerved to stops ahead.

"Where's the blower?" Luca shouted. "Give me the fucking blower!"

"Here," Lowery said, slapping the PCA into his palm. "What's the matter?"

"I am so stupid," Luca said, punching in 4-1-1. "So fucking stupid!"

"Are you going to tell me—?"

"Cannon's answering service! They'll know where she is!"

He got the number from information, punched it in, and asked for Dr. Cannon.

"Dr. Cannon's not available," a woman's voice told him. "Dr. Moss is covering."

Shit! "I really need to speak to Elizabeth personally. This is her brother and we've got a family emergency that needs her immediate attention."

"Oh, I'm so sorry to hear that. I'll try her house and—"

"I've already called and she doesn't answer."

"Maybe she's at the hospital. I can page her if you wish."

"Would you? That would be wonderful."

Luca waited on hold, feeling the time drag by, and then the operator was back on.

"I just spoke to the hospital. Dr. Cannon is in surgery. I can leave a message for her as soon as she gets out."

Surgery? Could it be . . . ?

"Which hospital?"

"Nassau Community. Do you want me to—?"

He cut her off and turned to Lowery. "Nassau Community Hospital. You know where it is?"

"Not a clue. Give me the address and the GPU will—"

"Right."

Luca punched 4-1-1 again. He'd call the switchboard and ask for the address.

"Why didn't I see it?" he shouted. "The sim's in labor! That's why Cannon's house was empty. Everyone's at the hospital. She's having her baby."

Lowery grinned. "And we didn't bring any cigars."

"Yes, we did," Luca said, patting his HK. "The exploding kind."

24

Romy, capped, masked, and garbed in surgical green, stood between Betsy and Joanna at the stainless steel sink and learned how to scrub. Betsy's other scrub nurse had begged off, refusing to leave her five-year-old son to open his Christmas presents without her. That left Romy to fill in.

"Work the lather into the skin," Betsy was saying, her voice slightly muffled by her surgical mask, "especially between the fingers and around the nails."

"I don't know if I can do this," Romy said. She was shaking inside. "It's not the blood or the cutting, it's just that I've never even seen—"

"You'll be fine," said Joanna to her right. "I'll handle the technical stuff. The most you'll have to do is hang on to a retractor while—"

"She's crashing!" cried an accented voice from the operating room. "Something's happened!"

"Oh, God, her uterus!" Betsy said. "It's ruptured!" She grabbed three packets of sterile gloves and handed them out. "Just put them on! Forget about gowns and sterile procedure. We'll worry about sepsis later. Right now we've got to move or we'll lose her!"

The next ten minutes were a crimson-tinged blur through which Romy watched Betsy and Joanna work like a single four-armed organism. Their communication seemed almost telepathic as Joanna would slap an instrument into Betsy's palm as soon as she thrust out her hand. Romy repressed a cry of

anguish as Betsy cut quickly through Meerm's abdominal wall, releasing a
torrent of blood that gushed down her flanks and soaked the table. Joanna
said something about a uterine artery and Betsy was calling for suction but
Romy's eyes were locked on the glistening bloody dome of Meerm's uterus
floating in that sea of red. And the surreal aspect of being able to glance up
at the TV monitor suspended in a corner and view the scene from a different
angle. And then Betsy was cutting into that muscular sack, reaching through
the slit and pulling out a limp, bloody, silent baby. She held it up by its feet,
slapped it once, then again, and with that the little arms jerked outward and
the baby emitted a piercing cry. And then Betsy was clamping and cutting
the cord as she called for Zero or Patrick, she didn't care who, to get down
here and take charge of this baby because she needed everyone here to help
her stop Meerm's hemorrhaging before she died.

Seconds later, Patrick, looking even more frightened than he had after
they'd been run off the Saw Mill, stumbled through the doors into the OR.

"What do I *do*?" Patrick said as Joanna deposited the squirming, squalling,
scrawny, blood-slippery bundle of baby into his arms. It terrified him. God,
what if he dropped it? "I don't know a thing about babies! I've never—"

"No Butterfly McQueens allowed," the nurse told him. "Madhuri will talk
you through it." Then she turned back to the furious activity on the operating
table.

Patrick turned to the anesthetist. "Madhuri?"

"Take it to the table over there," she replied in a voice that was at once
lilting and rapid fire. "There's a basin of warm water. Rinse it off, wipe it
down, and then wrap it tightly in one of the blankets."

"But—"

"Hurry! Get it wrapped up! You don't want hypothermia! I'd help you
but I can't leave—" She glanced at a monitor and called out, "Heart rate up
to one-sixty!"

Gingerly cradling the slippery baby in his arms, Patrick stepped to the
cleaning table and placed it on a towel. And now, as it screamed and thrust
out its skinny limbs, he could see that it was a girl. He dipped a towel in the
basin of warm water and began wiping away the blood and clinging membranes. This caused an escalation in the wails. She was so small, so fragile

looking. He hoped he didn't rub too hard and break something, but he kept it up, working as quickly as he could. As soon as she was reasonably clean, he found a soft blanket at the rear of the table and wrapped it around her.

He looked over to Madhuri to ask, Now what? but she was busy hanging a new IV bag, a small, red one, on an IV pole so loaded with infusion bags it looked like a Christmas tree. The baby was still crying so he lifted her into his arms—he felt a little more confident now that she was dry and blanket wrapped—and held her tight against him.

Amazingly, her wails tapered off. And now that he had a chance to look at her, he marveled at how human she looked. He'd never seen a real live newborn. He'd seen photos, of course; whenever the associates at his old firm had entered fatherhood, they always brought in pictures taken right after birth showing these homely, scrunched-up elfin faces that everyone pronounced beautiful. But this baby *was* beautiful. Maybe because she hadn't been extruded through a birth canal. A nice symmetrical face, a tiny nose, little bow lips, a light down of hair on her head but none on her body. Damn, she looked human. More so than some of those associates' kids.

He turned to look at the operating table and met Romy's dark eyes, the only part of her face visible between the cap and the mask.

"How's Meerm doing?" he asked.

Betsy stood next to Romy, and answered without looking up. "I clamped the big bleeder but she's not out of the woods yet. She damn near bled out. We've got packed red cells and volume expanders running full blast, and that should bring her pressure back."

"Patrick," said Zero's voice over the loudspeaker, "hold up the baby so we can get a good view."

Patrick turned, loosened the blanket, and lifted her toward the camera lens pointed his way from the balcony. Zero had got the video system working in time; now he seemed to have mastered it. Patrick glanced at the monitor and saw himself, viewed from above, holding the baby.

"Boy or girl?" Romy asked as Patrick turned back their way.

"Girl. A beauty."

Betsy's head snapped up. "A *beautiful* girl?"

"A real doll."

Patrick saw the confusion in Betsy's eyes and was framing a question about it when Madhuri began shouting.

"V-fib! She's in V-fib!"

Oh, no! Zero felt a pang as he saw the sudden frenzied activity around the operating table on the computer screen. *You can't lose her. She just became a mother.*

He watched with growing dismay as Betsy performed CPR on Meerm's chest, then applied the defibrillator paddles, shocking her heart again and again. His eyes drifted from the painful scene to the thumbnail feeds he'd accessed from the hospital's security cameras—an easy task once he'd got the hang of the program. Almost five in the morning and all quiet at Nassau County Community Hos—

Zero stiffened as he saw two Jeeps and a van pull up at the emergency room entrance. No audio, but the way the vehicles rocked on their springs meant they'd been moving fast.

Most likely nothing, he told himself, but he kept watching, and his gut began a quick crawl when he saw six men in full SWAT gear pile out onto the pavement. He couldn't see their faces through their lowered visors but he spotted "FBI" on the back of one of them. He didn't believe that for an instant. This was SIRG through and through, and maybe Portero himself.

He glanced at the OR feed—Betsy was still laboring over Meerm's inert, supine form—then at his upload indicator for the digital movie of the birth. Almost complete. But now he had to slow the invaders, mislead them, divert them.

As Zero slipped the ski mask back over his head, he had an idea . . .

25

Luca's mind raced as he led his men from the emergency area to the lobby. First thing, he had to seal the building and cut off any escape. But for that he needed to know where the exits were, and the place to find out was Information.

As they stormed into the dimly lit, high-ceilinged lobby he found the reception desk empty; the entire population was two gray-haired ladies and an aging security guard clustered before a TV monitor fixed on a wall. He hurried over to grab the guard but stopped dead when he saw what they were watching.

Four humans operating on a pregnant sim.

The guard turned, saw them, and stumbled backward, reaching for his two-way.

Luca reached out and grabbed his arm. "FBI!" He shouted and pointed to the monitor. "Take us to that operating room!"

"W-wait," the guard said. "You can't just come in here and—"

Luca squeezed his arm. Hard. *"Now!"* He shoved him toward a hallway. *"Move!"*

As the cowed guard led them toward a bank of elevators, Luca turned to Stritch and pointed toward the old ladies. "You stay here. Keep them away from the phones."

Behind his visor Luca repressed a sigh of relief. No need to worry about covering the exits. The baby hadn't been born yet. No one would be going anywhere until that happened.

26

"She is gone," Madhuri said, her voice an octave lower than usual.

"No!" Betsy cried. To Romy's horror, she'd had to watch while Betsy cracked open Meerm's chest and manually compressed her heart. She was still at it, working like a madwoman. "We've still got a chance!"

"Betsy, she is dead."

Romy looked at the anesthetist's black eyes and noticed they were rimmed with tears. Joanna's too. Romy knew they mirrored her own. They all knew that Meerm wasn't coming back.

She reached across and gently gripped Betsy's forearms. "She's right, Betsy. Meerm's gone. You did your best but—"

"I should have brought her in sooner!" Betsy wailed. She leaned forward over Meerm's inert heart, and sobbed. "But I was worried about the baby! Damn it, damn it, damn it!"

"You did all you could," Romy said, touching the back of her sweat-soaked scrubs. "But she—"

Zero burst through the OR doors. "We have to go! SIRG just stormed into the lobby, armed to the teeth!"

"Who's SIRG?" Joanna said, gaping at Zero's mask. "And who the hell are you?"

"A friend," Betsy said, ripping off her bloody gloves. She'd regained some of her composure but seemed exhausted.

"And SIRG," Romy added, feeling her gut clench, "is a group that wants to kill that baby."

"Like hell they will!" Joanna cried.

"Let's go!" Betsy said. "We've got a minute, maybe two at the most before they're here!"

"But what about Meerm?" Romy said.

"We'll have to leave her."

"No—"

"Romy," Zero said softly, "I grieve for her as much as you—more than you—but they won't be interested in Meerm now; they'll want her baby, and we can't let them have her."

"We'll take her," Joanna said. "Madhuri, Betsy, and me. We'll put her in an isolette and hide her in a motel or something."

"What's an isolette?" Patrick asked. He was still holding the baby and seemed very protective.

"It's an incubator of sorts," Madhuri said. "A special enclosed container we use for preemies. Keeps them safe and warm."

"Good idea," Betsy said. "Since they probably know my car, we'll leave it here and take one of yours."

Joanna said, "We'll rustle up a portable isolette and meet you at the doctor's entrance."

She and Madhuri bustled off while Betsy and Romy pulled a green sheet over Meerm's body. As the rest of them hurried out into the hall with the baby, Romy hung back. She rested a hand on the lifeless form beneath the sheet.

"You never had a chance, did you," she whispered. "But things are going to change. And whenever people talk about the change, they'll mention your name."

Small goddamn consolation, she thought as she hurried away to catch up to the others.

27

Five men in full gear, plus the guard, made for a claustrophobic ride as the elevator crept to the fourth floor. When the doors opened, Luca and his team piled out and followed the guard to the operating suite.

The old man pointed to a pair of double doors. "The amphitheater's through there."

"That's where they're transmitting from?"

The guard nodded. "But the cameras are upstairs—through that door."

"Any other way out?"

He shook his head.

Luca ripped the guard's two-way off his belt and flung it against the tiles of the nearest wall. "Stand over there and don't get in the way." He signaled to Lowery. "You and Majesky take the stairs. The rest of you—with me."

He depressed the bolt catch release lever on his HK to chamber the first round and stepped toward the doors. He didn't expect resistance, but it never hurt to be prepared. And besides, he knew of no better attention getter than a three-round burst into the ceiling.

He kicked open the doors and stepped through. "All right—!"

Empty. The place looked like a cyclone had ripped through it, but not a soul in sight.

"What the—?"

He turned, ready to go out and bang that guard's head against the wall for sending them to the wrong room when he noticed the shape under the bloody sheet on the table. Three quick steps took him to it. He hesitated, then reached out and pulled it off.

A dead sim, bloody, carved open from chest to groin. Looked like Jack the Ripper had been at her. He saw the gaping belly, the empty uterus.

The pregnant sim . . . this had to be her . . . but where—?

Oh, no . . . oh, no . . .

His knees felt gelatinous, his arms weak, the HK a hundred-pound weight in his hands as he turned and saw the TV monitor—where the operation was still in progress . . . at this table . . . on this sim . . . right in this room.

They'd fooled him . . . played him for a grade-A-prime sucker . . .

He looked up toward the spinning ceiling, saw a camera pointed his way from the balcony.

"Lowery?" he whispered into his comm mike. "Lowery, what's going on?"

A helmeted head popped into view next to the camera. "They're running a movie of the operation."

"Stop it, Lowery," he said, softly at first but with his voice rising. "Stop it right now!"

"I don't know how!"

"Yes, you do, goddamn you!" He was screaming now. "Yes, you fucking well do! *Now do it!*"

"Okay, okay!"

Luca heard the clinking release of the bolt on Lowery's submachine gun, followed by one three-round burst, then another. The monitor went blank . . .

. . . but its final image had been Patrick Sullivan holding up a very human-looking baby girl . . . and Luca remembered how the Sinclairs had feared the birth of a girl . . . and he also remembered all that crap he'd read about inter- and intragenomic competition . . .

I took him a moment to piece it all together, but then suddenly he knew what had terrified them.

You slimy bastards! After what you did, you had the nerve to look down your noses at *me?*

Now more than ever he wanted that baby.

28

Racing along the hallway, Romy hung on Patrick's arm and stared at the baby. She couldn't take her eyes off that pink, perfect little face.

"You weren't exaggerating, Patrick," Romy told him. "She is truly beautiful."

Behind her, she heard Betsy say, "Skip the elevators and take that stairway at the far end of the hall." Then in a lower voice to Zero: "I need to talk to you about that baby."

The two of them fell behind as Romy and Patrick entered the stairwell and started down. On the ground floor they exited and found themselves at the doctor's entrance. Joanna and Madhuri were already there with what looked like an oversized clear-topped bread box on wheels.

"We took the elevator," Joanna said, eyes wide, "and we saw a SWAT guy in the lobby. He had 'FBI' on his back," Joanna said. "Are we in trouble?"

"They're not FBI," Romy told them, trying to keep the dread out of her voice. They must *not* get this baby. "They're dressed-up thugs."

Patrick passed the baby to Madhuri who kept her wrapped in her arms as they made the frigid pre-dawn dash across the near empty parking lot to Joanna's minivan. Patrick loaded the isolette into the rear while Romy helped Madhuri and the baby into the front seat.

As Joanna started the engine, Romy spotted Betsy hurrying their way. Behind her she saw Zero leaning against the brick wall outside the doctor's entrance. Her heart twisted. His posture was strange, as if he was sick.

"Is something wrong with Zero?" she asked Betsy as she arrived.

"He's a little upset. I don't have time to explain now. He can tell you. If you need us we'll be at—"

Romy raised a hand. "Don't say it. Better if we don't know. That way they can't make us tell."

Betsy's face blanched. She nodded, then hugged Romy. "Get the hell out of here before they find you."

The three women and the baby roared off.

Romy watched for a few heartbeats, praying for the baby's survival, then Patrick was tugging on the sleeve of her scrubs.

"Romy. Let's move."

Zero reached the van a few seconds before they did. He pulled off his ski mask as he climbed into the rear seat, moving like an arthritic old man.

"Will you drive, Patrick?" he said in a voice barely above a whisper.

As they got moving, Romy turned in the passenger seat and looked back. Kek was in the far rear; Tome sat next to Zero who was staring at the floor in silence.

"What's wrong, Zero?"

"What?" he said, blinking and looking up at her. "What's wrong? Everything's wrong."

"Meaning?"

"Please don't ask me about it." The lost look in his yellow eyes constricted Romy's throat. "Not yet."

"Where are we going?" Patrick said as they shot out of the parking lot.

"To pay a visit to someone who has answers I need."

"Who?"

"Ellis Sinclair."

29

"Fan out!" Luca shouted. "They could still be in the building!"

He doubted it, but that might be just what they wanted him to do: figure they'd taken off and go on a wild search through the streets, leaving them safe right here, laughing at him. That was what they'd expect him to do, only this time he wouldn't.

"Everyone take a floor, take a hall, go from room to room. Look for a baby, a newborn baby girl."

Luca kicked back through the operating room doors and grabbed the old guard by his collar. "The nursery! Where's the nursery?"

"Th-third floor," the old man cried, cringing.

"Take me there!"

A few minutes later he was standing before a plate-glass window, staring at the rows of bassinets, only half a dozen of them occupied. To his right a frightened new mother cried out and asked him what was wrong. He ignored her.

These babies, all so human looking. But that didn't mean the sim baby couldn't be among them. No way to tell. The safest thing would be to kill all the girls, but he didn't know if he could do such a thing.

Movement on the screen of the monitor over the nurse's station at the rear of the nursery caught his eye. The sim operation film . . . the one Lowery had supposedly shot up . . . it was still playing. Suddenly the film cut off and a man appeared. Luca knew that face . . . the Reverend Eckert! Somehow he'd got hold of the film. Eckert was broadcasting it all over the world!

Luca turned and began a stumbling trot back toward the elevators. Only one thing to do now.

Run.

30

It's over, Mercer Sinclair thought as he turned away from his plasma screen TV and staggered to his living room window. He stared out over the oddly silent Fifth Avenue at the pale, dawn-lit shadows of Central Park. We're done.

He hadn't been able to sleep so he'd turned on the TV and begun channel surfing. He'd paused when he recognized Reverend Eckert's face—that damn fool seemed to be on some channel somewhere every hour of the day and night—and stayed when he heard him rant about a sim giving birth to a half-human baby. And then he'd *shown* the birth.

Portero and SIRG had failed. Miserably. And worse, the sim baby was a girl, an all too human-looking girl.

What do I do now? he wondered, his gaze wandering to the squatting granite mass of the Metropolitan Museum a few blocks uptown. The markets were closed today in the US and most of Europe, and the trading day had already ended in Asia. But when the Pacific Rim markets reopened later to-night, SimGen stock would go into freefall.

Money wasn't the issue; even without SimGen he was worth more than he could spend in a dozen lifetimes. No, it was the company itself that mattered. He'd devoted his life to building SimGen. It was his child, his only family, and now the wild dogs he'd kept at bay for so long would leap upon her and tear her to pieces.

Mercer thought of the .38 caliber revolver he kept in the drawer by the bed. Maybe that would be the best way, the easiest way. Better that than—

He stopped.

What am I thinking? It's *not* over! I'll fight this! Stonewall any questions, deny any and all allegations. Sims are *my* property, and it will take years—decades!—before someone can say otherwise. And that someone will be the Supreme Court of the United States, because that's how far I'll take it. And I'll win that fight.

Oh, no. This is not over.

31

Ellis stared at the screen, fascinated, shouting, "They've done it! They've *done* it!"

He didn't know whether to laugh or to cry. He didn't know what tomorrow would bring, or even what the rest of today would hold, but everything in his life was going to be different from now on. If nothing else, today promised a brighter future for the sims of the world.

His phone rang. "Ellis," said a deep voice he immediately recognized.

"Zero! Congratulations! I just saw the film of the birth. Tragic about poor Meerm, but uploading the film to Eckert was a brilliant move. Where are you?"

"At the front gate."

That startled Ellis. And something about Zero's voice wasn't right. "I'll open it right away. Have you got the baby with you?"

"No. But I have questions. A *lot* of questions."

Ellis's stomach plunged: He'd been dreading this moment, dreading it for decades. "Yes, I suppose you do. I'll open the gate."

He pressed a button on a wall unit that operated the gate mechanism, then went to a front window to watch a black van climb the long winding driveway to the house. The cook and the maid had the day off; he'd planned to visit Robbie and Julie later, but he might have to delay that.

Ellis stepped outside as the van pulled to a stop before the front door. Zero alighted immediately and Ellis was surprised to see that he'd removed his mask, his simian features naked to the world. He walked past Ellis without a word, without a handshake, without even eye contact, and stepped into the foyer. A man and a woman emerged—Romy Cadman and Patrick Sullivan, looking perplexed. Ellis introduced himself and welcomed them. The last to debark were Kek and an aging sim, but they did not approach.

"You two are welcome inside," he said.

"No, sir," said the sim. "We stay. Good air."

"As you wish."

As Tome and the mandrilla wandered out onto the frosty lawn, Ellis stepped back inside and faced his guests.

"Can I offer anyone some—"

"You've seen the film," Zero said, his voice thick. "Meerm's baby is a girl, a very human-looking girl. Dr. Cannon told me she should look more like a sim and she told me why. She also gave me a possible explanation for why the baby looks so human. She didn't want to believe it and neither do I. Do you know what I'm talking about?"

"Yes, I believe I do."

"Then tell me it's not true!"

"I only wish I could."

Zero lunged toward him, teeth bared, hands clawing forward. Ellis braced himself for the impact.

"Zero, no!" Romy cried.

Her voice seemed to pull him back. He turned away and leaned a hand against the wall.

"Monster!" The word came out half growl, half sob. "How could you?"

"I didn't. At least not knowingly."

"Can someone tell me what this is all about?" Romy said.

"Yes," Ellis replied. "I suppose it's time I told someone. Let's all sit down and I'll try to explain."

He led them to the two-story cherrywood library that housed the book collection that had once been a pride, but had long ago stopped meaning anything. Romy and Patrick took a couch. Zero dropped into a wingback leather chair and stared at the floor; the pale morning light through the tall windows washed out what little color was left in his face. Ellis remained standing. This was going to be too painful to tell sitting down. He needed to be up, moving about to release the tension coiled like an overwound spring in his chest.

He wished Zero were alone, but Zero might wind up telling Romy and Patrick anyway, so it was better they all heard it firsthand.

"I've lied to you, Zero. Lied to you from the day you were old enough to understand. You're not a mutant sim. You're the very first viable sim. We designated you 'Sim Zero.' Your cells provided the source material that was modified and remodified into the creatures we now call sims. All sims are your descendants, Zero. You are the sim Adam."

Ellis heard Romy gasp, heard Patrick mutter, "Oh, man!" But he was watching Zero.

Zero looked up, fixed him a moment with his yellow irises, then looked away again. "And who is *my* Adam?"

"That's a longer, more complicated story. But *I* was lied to long before you were, Zero. To see the whole picture, we have to go back to the early days when my brother and I were plowing all our capital and everything we could borrow into germline engineering a commercially useful chimp-human hybrid. We weren't looking to create a labor force then. We had other uses in mind—antibodies and xenografts were high on our list. We could see success down the road but we needed more funding. To get it, we made a deal with the Devil.

"Mercer approached the Pentagon with a plan to co-develop an aggressive warrior-type simian-human hybrid along with the more docile strain we wanted to market for commercial use. The World Trade Towers were still standing then, but everyone in the military accepted that sooner or later we'd be at war again in the Middle East. So the generals jumped at the plan. But they realized the outrage that would arise when the public learned that the army was creating gonzo animal warriors and training them to kill humans—what if they got loose?—so they cloaked their involvement under layers of security and bureaucracy.

"A wing of Army Intelligence was created to develop and train these hybrids as warriors; it was given the innocuous name of Social Impact Studies Group. SIRG in turn created Manassas Ventures as a conduit for the funds funneled to our new company, SimGen. To make this look like a real venture capital deal, the head of SIRG, a colonel named Conrad Landon, demanded that Manassas get a piece of SimGen in return for the investment. We agreed, not knowing at the time that we'd be mortgaging our souls.

"But even with all these millions in funding, the transgenic road to a sim-human hybrid was fraught with obstacles, and at times seemed impassable. Somatic cell nuclear transfer, embryo splitting, and germline modifications are routine procedures now, but not then. We found we were able to increase the intelligence of apes, mandrills, and baboons by only small degrees, which did not make the Pentagon happy. And we were also running into walls trying to 'upgrade' the chimp genome closer to human. We were swapping genes from our own cells into chimp germlines and making a hideous mess of it. With a string of failures and the Pentagon breathing down our necks, I was cracking under the pressure."

Ellis sighed, remembering and regretting his decision to take a sabbatical at that time. Merce had been enraged, screaming that he was jeopardizing both their futures, but Ellis had made up his mind. He'd recently wed Judy and already their marriage was in trouble because he was never home. So for his own sanity and the sake of his marriage, he'd left his brother to work alone while they flew to France and rented a little house in Provence. It had temporarily saved his marriage, but it ruined the rest of his life.

"So I took a breather to rest and recoup. I intended to stay a month but that stretched into two, then three, then longer. I shouldn't have gone at all. I've done many foolish things in my life, but the most foolish was trusting my brother to work alone."

32

SUSSEX COUNTY, NJ

Darryl Lister had been waiting twenty minutes in Portero's undersized back-woods shack. How did he stand this crummy, uncomfortable furniture? The guy lived like a refugee.

But not for too much longer.

He heard a car pull up outside and gestured to Venisi, one of the two men he'd brought with him, to check the window. He looked out and nodded.

Okay. Portero was here. Darryl took a deep breath. He'd been steeling himself for this moment since the word had come down a few hours ago. Now that it was here he wanted to get it over with. They'd been through a lot, Portero and he, but the time had come to put the past aside and deal with the present.

Darryl pointed to either side of the front door; Venisi and Markham nod-ded, drew their pistols, and moved into position.

He's seen my car, he thought. He'll be expecting me, but not them.

A few seconds later Portero stepped through, dressed in black BDU shirt and pants, his face tight, obviously ready for a confrontation. He immediately spotted his two extra guests and his hand darted toward his sidearm, but stopped halfway.

"Let's not do anything precipitous, Portero," Darryl said.

Portero glanced around the room. "Maria?"

"She's in the bedroom. She didn't feel a thing."

Portero squeezed his eyes shut. "You didn't have to—"

"Yes, I did." Markham had held her down while Venisi put a bullet through her brain. She'd looked very peaceful when Darryl had looked in on her. "And it's your fault. If you'd dumped her when I told you, she'd still be alive now, but you're bigger than the rules, aren't you, Portero. Now hold still while these two gentlemen search you."

Darryl had warned his two men about Portero. He'd seen the guy in action—tough, fast, vicious—and didn't want any slipups. Venisi covered him while Markham removed Portero's pistol from his holster and did the pat down.

"What's this all about?"

"Clean-up time. The time when you tie up the loose ends, mop up the floor, close the door, and walk away."

When Markham was done, he nodded.

"You're telling me I'm a loose end?"

"Eminently so."

Portero looked at the ceiling. "I see."

Darryl had to admire his composure. No breakdown, no begging. But he'd expected no less. If he kept this up, the next five minutes would be bearable.

"The Old Man found out about Snyder and Grimes," Darryl told him. "I had to say you hid their deaths from me as well."

That had been one hairy meeting. The Old Man had just received word that the DoD had reversed its approval for Operation Guillotine—soon as the Pentagon heard about the sim's baby, it decided it wanted nothing to do with monkey commandos—and he was in a frothing rage. For a few bladder-clenching moments there Darryl had thought he might be scheduled for a one-way ride into the woods, but he'd managed to shift all the blame to Portero.

"Snyder and Grimes brought your loss total to six men—five KIA and one Section Eight. But that's only part of the reason I'm here." He gestured toward the door. "Let's step outside."

Portero led the way, followed by Venisi and Markham. Darryl brought up the rear.

"It's all falling apart," he said as he ejected the clip from the pistol that had been used on Maria. "The sweetest arrangement ever—*ever*—is tumbling down around us. All because you didn't do your job. So now we have to fall back. Covering our tracks isn't going to be enough. We have to erase them."

One by one he began removing the .45 caliber rounds from the clip.

"For instance, as we speak, there's an inferno raging in the middle of an Idaho nowhere, roasting a lot of monkey meat. When the arson squad, or whoever eventually gets the job, starts to sift through the ashes, they're going to have a lot of questions, but no answers."

When he got down to the last round, he left it in the clip and pocketed the others.

"Since no clean-up can be guaranteed perfect, another aspect of the process is to provide plausible deniability for the high-ups should the dogs come sniffing their way. That means removing the weak or the too-visible links in the chain. You, unfortunately, fall into both those categories."

"I thought we were friends."

"We were. But this goes beyond friendship. It's not like I have a choice, so don't make this harder than it already is. You botched a number of crucial ops and, worse, made a spectacle of yourself at that hospital this morning."

Darryl watched him bristle at this, but Portero said nothing. Couldn't blame him. Why talk? Nothing he said would change anything.

"And because I brought you in, it falls to me to usher you out."

Darryl checked the pistol to make sure the chamber was empty, then wiped it and the clip clean with a handkerchief. He handed both to Portero.

"So . . . it's time. After all we've been through, I feel it's only fair to offer you a chance to do the right thing."

Portero took a deep breath, then nodded and accepted the weapon.

"I'd like to do it alone."

"I think we'd all prefer that." Darryl gestured to the trees. "Do it in the woods." That was where Darryl had planned to leave the body anyway. It might be months before anyone found it, if ever. "But don't try anything cute, Portero. Stay in sight. I'm giving you the option to go out like a man. Try to run and we'll hunt you down like a dog."

Another nod from Portero as he stared at the pistol and the clip in his hands, then he turned and walked into the trees.

"Spread out," Darryl told Venisi and Markham in a low voice. "Triangulate on him. Keep him in sight. He starts to run, take him down."

But Portero acted the good soldier. He walked about a hundred feet along a path into the trees, stopped beside a big oak. He faced them and raised the pistol to the side of his head.

Jesus, he's looking right at us.

Darryl's instinct was to turn away, but he forced himself to watch.

The shot *cracked* through the chill air, Portero's head jerked to the left, and his body collapsed into the brush.

Darryl let out a breath. Done. Clean and neat.

He gestured to Venisi and Markham. "Check him out. If he's still breathing, finish him."

He'd heard of people surviving some outrageous head wounds. And with the way things had been going for Portero lately, who knew? He might have botched this too.

33

FAR HILLS, NJ

"When I returned after six months away in France," Ellis told his audience of three, "refreshed, renewed, ready to work, I discovered that Mercer had made a staggering leap in our research. He presented me with six surrogate mothers, all recently implanted with human-chimp hybrid embryos. We hired obstetricians to watch them carefully through their pregnancies, but to our dismay, one after another miscarried until only one was left. But her fetus was a tough cookie. It held on, and in her thirty-eighth week she delivered a living hybrid infant: Sim Zero."

Patrick said, "By any chance was her name Alice Fredericks?"

"Why, yes," Ellis said, startled to hear that name after so many years. "I believe it was. How on earth—?"

"We've met." He turned to Zero. "We've spoken to your mother, Zero."

"She's not my mother," he snapped without looking up. "I don't *have* a mother."

"He's right, Patrick," Ellis said. "Zero was grown by cloning techniques from a recombinantly hybridized nucleus. But when Mercer saw Zero he said that he'd overdone it: He'd swapped in too much human genetic material.

"He explained to me how, among many other changes, he'd deleted the two chimp chromosomes that millions of years ago fused to form human chromosome 2, and replaced them with a human chromosome 2. He'd also 'cleaned up' the hybrid genome by removing loads of junk DNA—deleting AT-rich regions, shortening CpG islands—along with codons and minisatellites; he even managed to remove an entire chromosome that may have performed some useful function in the past but was now just taking up space.

"So Zero wound up with a largely junk-free twenty-two-pair genome—one shorter than human, two shorter than the chimp's. Mercer told me he did it to make the splicing easier, but I later learned he had a more sinister reason.

"However we both agreed that Zero was too human. The public would never accept the merchandising of something that looked so much like themselves. To make a commercially viable laborer, we'd have to swap back some of the chimp genes he'd removed."

He noticed Romy's hate-filled look. "I fully deserve your opprobrium, Ms. Cadman. But please understand, I was a different person then: young, drunk with the egomaniacal power to shape and create, never looking beyond the next splice. That was why I went blindly along with Mercer's solution to work backward from Zero: Use his cells as a starting point and swap back some of the chimp genes he'd removed. I was ablaze with excitement at the possibilities opening before me. And because I trusted my younger brother, I didn't ask the questions I should have.

"So we worked back from Zero with great success. Seeing that success, and realizing that its own future was tied to SimGen's, SIRG started gathering information on any public official who might have a say in the legalization of sims. When we introduced the species, SIRG contacted those who voiced opposition. When blackmail wasn't an option, SIRG's field operatives went to work using intimidation and violence. It was SIRG's behind-the-scenes manipulations that resulted in the classification of sims as neither humans nor animals but property—SimGen's property.

"And I confess that I knew all this—not all the details, but the general plan—and I approved, thinking, Why should we allow these small minds to block the road to the future? Mercer and I were like gods, leading the way to a new world. To hell with anyone who dared stand in our way."

Ellis stopped, took a breath. "I believe I was crazy then, suffering from some sort of monomaniacal mental derangement. But eventually I sobered. When all the legal hurdles had been cleared and the labor markets across the globe were clamoring for sims, sims, and more sims, when my personal net worth exceeded that of some small nations, when I finally had time to look back and reflect on how I arrived at my position, I became suspicious.

"Something was gnawing at my subconscious and wouldn't let up. So I went back to the source, to Zero, who was still alive; the basic research center's only permanent resident. I took an oral scraping of his cells and started checking his DNA. Mercer's 'cleaning up' of Zero's genome may have made the splicing easier, but I realized then that it also removed links back to the source DNA. After exhaustive efforts, working in secret, I eventually traced Zero's DNA back to its origin."

Ellis looked around at the three faces fixed on his. Yes, even Zero had lifted his head for this.

Could he say it? Could he push these words past his lips? He had to. He'd come too far to turn back.

"That source DNA didn't belong to a chimpanzee. It belonged to me."

Romy's voice was barely audible. "Oh . . . dear . . . God!"

Patrick was speechless, staring in slack-jawed shock.

And Zero had closed his eyes.

Ellis spoke past the lump in his throat. "I confronted Mercer and, after strident initial denials, he reluctantly confirmed it: Zero had been fashioned from one of my cells. My brother had lied to me about adding too many human genes to a chimp genome to make Zero; the truth was he'd swapped chimp genes into *my* genome. And from there I unwittingly helped him in further devolving Zero's genome to create the sims."

"You're telling me," Patrick said, sputtering, "telling *us* . . . that . . . that a sim is not a recombinantly evolved chimp . . . it's a recombinantly *de*volved human being? Tome is a human being who's been genetically adulterated and then farmed out as a slave? I . . . I . . ." He raised his hands, then let them drop.

Ellis understood. There were no words for what he and Mercer had done.

Romy was silent, tears streaming down her cheeks as she stared at Zero.

"Then I am—or was—a man?" Zero said, eyes open now, his too human features tortured. "But I'm really *not* a man, am I. I'm a thing. A freak!"

"Zero, don't!" Romy sobbed.

But Zero went on, glaring at Ellis. "What have you *done* to me?"

Ellis could barely hear his own voice. "The unforgivable. The unconscionable. The unspeakable. But I didn't know, Zero."

"That's a little convenient, don't you think?" Romy said, the edge on her voice slashing at him. " 'Fess up: You didn't *want* to know."

"Maybe you're right. But I do know I've been trying to undo this ever since I found out. Until this moment, Mercer and I have been the only two who've known the truth. Not even Colonel Landon of SIRG knows. What astonished me then, and what I still find incomprehensible, is how Mercer could know all along that the sims he was leasing to the world as slaves were his cloned half brothers, and not be bothered a bit."

"But you didn't go public," Patrick said. "You didn't even quit the company."

"I wanted to *dissolve* the company, but Mercer and SIRG controlled too much stock. I couldn't go public with what I knew because I had children by then and I'd been instrumental in creating the sims. If the truth got out I'd be seen as a monster on a par with Mengele, and my children would be seen as offspring of a monster.

"I was trapped, and SIRG knew it, but just in case I had second thoughts, my daughter Julie disappeared for half a day. She wasn't harmed, in fact she had a nice time with the lady who took her to an amusement park, but the message was too clear. To protect myself I hid a number of computer disks revealing everything; they'll be released to all the media in the event of my death. SIRG and I entered a cold-war state of mutually assured destruction, but it was too much for me. Knowing I'd been instrumental in a monumental atrocity made me unfit for human companionship. And since I couldn't tell anyone, not even my wife, my marriage fell apart.

"So I dedicated myself to the only solution I could think of: a Quixotic quest to develop a true chimp-origin sim to replace the human-origin sims in circulation. But I've found it impossible. I don't think it can be done.

"But all the while, Zero had been growing up in the sealed-off section of basic research. Mercer had forgotten about him until Harry Carstairs casually mentioned him. Mercer decided he was a liability, the Missing Link between sims and humans. He ordered Zero destroyed—sacrificed, put down, like any other lab specimen that had outlived its usefulness.

"When I heard I told Mercer I'd take care of it. But I had no intention of allowing Zero to be killed. I was suddenly energized. In Zero I saw a chance to bring SimGen down. Instead of administering a lethal injection, I spirited him off. I financed him, setting him up as the nemesis of SimGen, a fifth column to turn people against the use of sims. I saw him as a way to put the genie back in the bottle, so to speak. And Zero was more than willing to help liberate his brother sims.

"Now Meerm's baby will accomplish that. What I'd hoped for was to put SimGen out of business with all of its secrets intact. That might not be possible now, seeing as the baby is a girl."

"Why is that so important?" Patrick said. "I saw Dr. Cannon react when I told her it was a beautiful girl."

"It's too complicated to delve into here. Just let me say that in an X-dominated hybrid genome with a human father and a sim mother, the mother's non-native genes—that is, the minority derived from another species—would be largely suppressed. Even though they're there in the genotype, they don't show up in the phenotype. In other words, if sims had been truly derived from chimps, Meerm's daughter would have retained significant chimp features. But because the substrate of Meerm's genome was human, the chimp genes didn't have a chance. That's why, in spite of all the added chimp DNA, she gave us a beautiful, pink, human-looking baby."

Romy said, "Then I guess your dirty little secret won't be a secret much longer."

"That will be up to you three, of course. The fact that the baby's a girl will cause people who know genetics to question whether there might be more human DNA in sims than anyone ever imagined, but I doubt they'll be able to prove anything. And their questions will be drowned out in the tidal wave of protests against the cloning of more sims. Thanks to Reverend Eckert the world has watched the birth of a baby born of the union of man and sim. And after seeing that, the movement to have them reclassified as Hominidae will gain unstoppable momentum."

He turned to Zero and felt the lump grow in his throat again.

"And you, Zero, are a man. The finest, most noble man I've ever known. And you can live as a man. Whatever you want of mine is yours, Zero. I don't know whether to call you brother or son, but like it or not, I'm part of you. We're related."

Zero stared at the bookshelves, saying nothing.

Ellis stepped closer to him. "I already have a son, Zero, but for a long time now I haven't had someone I've cared to call brother. There's still a lot to be done; years of struggle ahead before this abominable, tragic mess is straightened out. I helped cause it with one brother; I need another brother to help me rectify it. Can you forgive me enough to be that brother, Zero? Please?"

"I'll help you," Zero said, rising and looking him in the eye. "Because I need to finish what I began. But don't call me brother. And don't ask me to forgive you."

The words struck like hammer blows. Ellis briefly had harbored a hope, a vision of Zero and him tearfully embracing and letting the past be past. But he could see now that wasn't going to be. He ached for absolution, but it wouldn't be coming from Zero or the two people with him. Not yet, at least.

"Fair enough," Ellis said. He resisted an impulse to offer his hand. Even that might be asking too much right now. "As a first step I propose arranging a meeting immediately with my brother. We'll lay out the facts for him and make it perfectly clear that SimGen is dead."

34

Luca Portero waved as he cruised past the guard in the gate kiosk and pointed his Jeep toward the SimGen main campus. He'd wanted to avoid any small talk because he could barely hear his own thoughts, but he'd take ringing in his ear over a hole in his head any day.

When he'd buried an AK-47 and an extra pistol in a waterproof gun case, he'd doubted he'd ever have to use them. It was simply a precautionary measure. But when Lister had told him it was time to "do the right thing," he'd known exactly where he wanted to do it.

Do the right thing . . . was Lister crazy? Like there was some sort of honor in executing yourself instead of making somebody else do it? What century was he living in?

Correction: *used* to live in.

Luca had raised the pistol to his head but pointed at the very rear of his skull. At the last second he'd angled it even further rearward to send the slug past the back of his head. But the report had damn near deafened him. He might never hear out of his right ear again.

He'd dropped right onto the spot where he'd buried the gun case. The two inches of covering dirt scraped off quickly. The pistols Lister's butt boys were carrying were nothing against the Kalashnikov. After they were down, Portero ran back and caught Lister trying to get away in his car. The bastard had squealed for mercy, screaming about friendship—*friendship!* After handing me a pistol so I could off myself!

Luca blew his head off.

Now he had to sky out of the country. No need for panic. No one here knew about Lister. He figured he had hours yet, and wanted to use some of that to deal with his office computer. He'd been scrupulous about avoiding any links to his numbered account in Bermuda, but you couldn't be too careful where SIRG was involved. They had people who could drag all sorts of information from a supposedly destroyed memory chip. So the chip was going with him. The ocean floor dropped to a couple of miles deep off Bermuda; he'd bury the chip at sea.

As expected, the campus was all but deserted. Only a few security personnel about. Perfect.

He'd just sat down before his computer and was preparing to open the box and tear out the memory chip, when he heard his office door open behind him. His fingers closed around the grip of his .45.

"Oh, it's you, Mr. Portero," said a voice he couldn't place. "I didn't expect you in today."

He turned and recognized one of the newer men on the security force— knew the face but not the name. He'd been hired last summer; low on the ladder, which was no doubt how he'd pulled Christmas duty.

"Yeah," Luca said. "Just checking on something before I go home."

"Lots of brass in today."

Luca's ears were singing and the last thing he needed was chitchat with this kid, but his curiosity got the better of him.

"Really? Who?"

"Both Sinclairs. First the big guy copters in. Then Ellis Sinclair arrives in this beat-up van, driving it himself."

"Is that a fact?"

Luca wasn't surprised. If there was any time for a crisis meeting it was now.

"And you'll never believe who was with him: that fox from OPRR—you know, the one who led the inspection a few—"

"Romy Cadman," Luca said, and felt his blood jump a few degrees.

The bitch was back. And with Sinclair-2. So they were no longer hiding their connection. Lister had put the blame on Luca, but that was wrong. This was *their* fault. Especially hers. Things had started downhill the moment she arrived. If not for Romy Cadman he'd still be sitting pretty here, building his retirement account, planning ways to move up the SIRG ladder. Instead he was on the run and would have to keep on running the rest of his life.

Maybe it was fate that had brought him back at this moment. He had scores to settle, scales to balance.

What was the expression—in for a dime, in for a dollar? He'd left a pile of bodies back at his house; no reason why he couldn't leave a few more in Sinclair-1's office.

35

This was a different Mercer Sinclair than the one Romy had seen at the shareholders' meeting. The suave good looks, the debonair poise were gone. This man looked haggard, years older. But he hadn't lost any of his fight.

"As usual, Ellis, you want to give up. You always were a quitter. But I'm *not* giving up. Not by a long shot. We can win, and I can tell you how. But I'm not discussing it before outsiders—certainly not with someone here from OPRR."

"I'm not representing OPRR today," Romy told him, "but I'll leave if—"

"No," Ellis said. "We all stay. We all have a stake in this."

Romy looked around, realizing how true that was. Ellis had led them all to the CEO's office—Romy, Patrick, Zero, and Tome and Kek as well. The last three had the most at stake.

"Then this meeting is over," said Mercer Sinclair. "When you come to your—"

Abruptly the door opened and Luca Portero swaggered in. The pistol in his hand startled Romy, and the wild look in his eyes terrified her.

"Hail, hail, the gang's all here," he said, breaking into a sharklike grin. "And a motley crew if I ever saw one," he said. "Four humans, a sim, a—holy shit! So *that's* how you took down four of my men! Where'd you get the mandrilla? I never would've—" His cold gaze settled on Zero. "And who or what the fuck are you?"

"They were just leaving, Portero," Mercer Sinclair said quickly. "And so are you."

"Am I?"

"Yes. You're fired. As of this minute you are no longer employed at SimGen."

"You talk to me like that?" Portero said. "Where do you get the balls to use that tone of voice with me after what you did?"

"What are you talking about?"

"You stood there time after time and looked down your nose at me and pretended to be horrified at what you called my 'methods,' when all the while you built this company by turning humans into monkeys and telling the world it was the other way around. You can't fire me, you piece of shit. I'm firing *you*!"

And before Romy knew it, Portero's pistol was leveled at Mercer Sinclair's chest. He fired twice, two rapid, booming reports, hitting him in the chest.

Images strobe-flashed through Romy's shocked brain—Sinclair's eyes bulging—his mouth forming an astonished O—his backward tumble with outflung arms—the window behind him cracking as it was splattered with red.

And then Portero was swinging his pistol in her direction. Patrick and Zero stood frozen to her right, Ellis was lunging toward his fallen brother. Portero shifted his pistol toward him, then seemed to change his mind.

"Later," he said softly, then focused on Romy.

Kek growled and started forward.

"Kree-gah!" Portero said and Kek froze.

Portero smiled as he eyed Kek. "Before being assigned here I worked with some of these mandrillas in our Idaho facility. They're conditioned from birth to stop whatever they're doing when they hear that word, then wait for another command—from the person who said it. I'm told the word is ape talk from the Tarzan books." His gaze returned to Romy. "Pretty cool, huh?" He heaved a theatrical sigh. "And now it's your turn, Ms. Romy Cadman. You've messed up my future, so now it's only fair I mess up yours."

Out of the corner of her right eye she saw Zero take a step closer to her, saying, "Leave her alone!"

"Hey, listen!" Portero snarled. "I don't know what kind of a freak you are, but another step and you're a dead freak. Got that?"

Kek growled again and Portero yelled, "Kree-gah" a second time. "Don't make me shoot you, boy," he told Kek. "I've got plans for you."

"What plans can you possibly have for Kek?" Romy said, hoping she could get him talking, maybe long enough for help to arrive, if any was coming.

"I may need a diversion at the airport. I'll just set him to tearing things up in another part of the terminal after I get there." He raised the pistol, centering it on Romy's chest. "But enough idle chatter. Good-bye Romy Cadman."

Romy felt a stunning impact against her right shoulder as, once again, two booming reports split the air. She saw the muzzle flashes as she fell to her left and realized that Zero had hurled himself against her.

No!

She heard Kek's enraged howl as he launched himself through the air, saw Portero try to bring his pistol to bear on the hurtling creature but he wasn't fast enough, heard him shout "Kree-gah! Kree-gah!" but no amount of conditioning was going to keep Kek from anyone who hurt Zero. Portero went down with screams of pain and terror.

Zero!

Romy rolled and was on her feet in a heartbeat, but Zero was down, slumped on his side, his life running out of him front and back into two red puddles.

Romy swims into Zero's vision. Joy bursts within his ruined chest at the sight of her alive and unharmed. Her pale, strained face is framed in scintillating fog as she leans over him and wails for someone to call for help.

Too late. Even though he feels no pain, or perhaps because he feels no pain, Zero knows he's dying. The impact of the bullets tearing though his chest was agonizing, but now . . . now he feels feather light and completely at peace.

He stares at Romy's tear-stained face as she calls his name again and again, begging him to hang on. But he has no strength to hang on. He tries to move his lips but they won't respond. They must! He has to tell her that it's better this way.

If this morning had gone differently . . . if Betsy hadn't confided to him her suspicions about Meerm's baby, and if Ellis hadn't confirmed them, his outlook would have been so different. He could have lived with the belief that he was an intellectual improvement on a nonhuman creature, could have held his head high as the best of his breed that aspired to the next evolutionary step. But the truth changed all that. He is not a step up from anything. He's an adulterated . . . *thing* . . . a freak of science. He doesn't know how long he could have survived knowing that he was cheated of his humanity.

He feels her hand in his. He wills his fingers to move, and they do, they close on hers. She bursts into sobs.

He wants to tell her how he's loved her. And how, thinking he was a sim, he could have been satisfied to go on loving her from afar. But he doesn't know how he could bear seeing her and being with her, and ever dreaming about what, but for the violation of a few genes, might have been.

It's better this way.

The opening in the glittering cloud encircling Romy's face begins to narrow, brightening as she seems to recede.

A sob builds in what's left of his chest. Not yet. Let me look at her a little longer.

But the cloud brightens further as the iris closes. And then she's gone and only the swirling light remains. And Zero wonders if there's a heaven. For Romy's sake he hopes so, because he knows that's where she'll go when her time is up.

But what about him? Did he retain enough of that transcendent spark to allow him to pass on into another life? Will he be welcomed? Or rejected as unfit?

He never fit anywhere during his earthly life. Just once in his existence he'd like to feel he fits somewhere.

Wouldn't that be wonderful.

And now the light suffuses him and he's floating . . .

Dazed, Patrick dropped to his knees beside Romy where she cradled Zero's head on her lap. She was bent over his face, weeping. The sound tore at his heart. One look at Zero's glazed eyes and Patrick knew he was gone. But maybe Romy hadn't realized that yet. He didn't want to be the one to tell her.

"I called the security office, the county sheriff, the state police. Cops and ambulances are on the way."

"Too late!" she sobbed. "He's gone!"

"I know," he said softly. He reached past her arm and closed Zero's eyes.

She leaned over further and kissed his forehead. "I loved him, Patrick."

"And he loved you. You should have heard how he talked about you. And it wasn't just talk. He loved you enough to die for you."

"I want him back."

"I know . . . I know . . ." He put a hand on her shoulder. "I do too."

"Can I . . . ?" she said without looking up. "Do you mind if I just stay here with him alone until . . . until they come?"

"Sure. Of course." Patrick was stung, but he understood.

He rose and became aware of a wet slapping sound. He saw Kek kneeling on Portero's chest. He gripped the man's ears as he repeatedly smashed the back of his head against the floor. That head, wobbly on an obviously broken neck, was bleeding from the eyes, nose, and mouth; the gray carpet was red under his skull.

"He's dead, Kek," Patrick said. "You can't kill him any more."

Kek looked up with tears in his eyes, then, without missing a beat, went back to his work.

Suddenly Patrick remembered Tome. He whirled and found the old sim squatting on the carpet a few feet away, his face buried in the arms folded atop his knees.

"Tome? Are you hurt?"

The sim looked up with tear-filled eyes. "Ver sad, Mist Sulliman. All Tome's fault."

"No way, Tome," he said, feeling a surge of anger. "We *know* whose fault this is, and it's not yours."

With that Patrick turned toward the CEO's desk and saw Ellis rise from behind it. He shot him a question with his eyes, and Ellis shook his head. His expression was grim and sad, but no tears.

Three men dead in less than half a minute. Yes, men. From this day on Patrick swore to remember Zero as a man. Although, considering the two others who'd joined him in death, that might not be a compliment.

As sirens began to wail outside, he wanted to ask Ellis Sinclair where they went from here, but the rhythmic smacking of Portero's head against the wet carpet was turning his stomach.

"Kek! Stop! Please!" But the mandrilla ignored him. "Can't somebody stop him?"

"Let him be," Romy said in a flat tone without looking up. "Let him take as long as he wants."

EPILOGUE

"I still can't believe it," Abel Voss said.

"Neither can I," Ellis replied.

The two of them sat in Mercer's old office. Less than a week now since death had filled this space. Ellis had ordered the carpets cleaned, but the removal of the bloodstains had been only partially successful. He'd expected that, and had declined to order new carpet. Just as he'd declined to repair the cracked picture window. He didn't want to help anyone, especially himself, forget what had happened here.

He'd attended funerals of two brothers since that day. At Mercer's he was part of a huge throng of mourners, none of whom shed a tear. At Zero's he stood among a few select members of the organization—Dr. Cannon and Reverend Eckert among them—all weeping openly. He'd been a central figure at the first; he'd had to invite himself to the second, his presence tolerated only because he claimed a blood relationship.

"Then again," Voss said, "when you think about it, who else was he gonna leave it to?"

Mercer's personal attorney had read his will this morning. He'd left all his stock to Ellis, who was still in shock.

"It was an old will," Ellis said. "If he'd had the slightest inkling he was going to die, I'm sure he would have changed it. But Merce thought he'd go on forever. Or damn near."

"So now that you're the absolute head honcho, what's your first step?"

"I've already taken it," Ellis said, rising and moving to the window. "I'm shutting down the natal centers. No new sim embryos implanted, all unborns aborted."

Killing unborn sims . . . the idea sickened him. But it had to stop now.

Voss grunted. "That leaves us a company without a product. But I guess you're just stayin ahead of the curve, seein as how the government will pretty soon be gettin around to forcin us to do just that."

How true. News networks around the world had picked up the film of Meerm's delivery; repeated broadcasts had raised a firestorm of protest: if sims and humans can interbreed, then sims should be members of the human genus.

If they only knew.

But they never would. Romy and Patrick had struck a deal: they would never reveal what they knew if Ellis never revealed that Romy would be raising Meerm's baby, who she'd named Una. She wanted the child—mother a sim, father a pervert—to grow up out of the limelight without ever knowing her origins.

Fair enough. Una and her mother had already done enough to further the sim cause. Ellis would do the rest.

"Okay," Voss said. "So no new sims. What about all the others out there already?"

"I'm going to start recalling them. I want you to get the ball rolling on building dorms for them on our Arizona land. I want them built as fast as possible. As soon as a block is ready for habitation, I'll cancel enough leases to fill it. That's the way we'll do it: a rolling recall until every living sim is out of the workforce and assured of freedom and comfort for the rest of their lives."

Voss swallowed. "At least they don't live too long, but even so, you're gonna bankrupt the company, son!"

"Most likely." He looked out at the gleaming buildings of the main campus, and the rolling hills beyond. "But we've got lots of hard assets. We'll sell them all."

And when that's not enough, he thought, I'll use my own funds, every last penny if necessary.

Ellis Sinclair figured he was long overdue to become his brothers' keeper.